A TIMELESS WYLL

BY THEO F.W.K. COOKSON

ISBN Softcover POD: 978-0-473-61407-2
ISBN Epub: 978-0-473-61408-9
ISBN Kindle: 978-0-473-61409-6
ISBN PDF: 978-0-473-61410-2

For Paul and Emily.

Acknowledgements

Thanks to my editors: Daisy Coles and Donna Blaber.
Thanks to Charlie Utting for the cover art.
Thanks to my proofreaders. And thank you for reading.

I

THE PROJECTION OF the day's light on the wall shows a waxing crescent. Just a few more hours before nightfall, and the celestial Mother closes Her luminous eye. The light shines through a wire-frame structure, casting a series of line shadows depicting the precise arcs the Mother's eye follows during Her daily blink.

Feilece sits next to the pinhole camera as it collects light and projects it. He watches the shadow slowly shift, counting every second, feeling time move slower and slower.

"Are you still watching that clock? It's been over an hour."

The boy barely responds to the voice of his father.

"Shit, it's not even on the right month." He turns the wire-frame structure on it's disk until all the line shadows become parallel to the current angle of the light. He steps back and strokes his long beard. "There ya go, all better."

The boy appreciates his father's efforts but finds them unnecessary. He can tell the time and date to the minute by looking at the projection alone.

"Anema! Feilece! Give us a hand with this livestock, will ya?" calls a woman's voice from outside.

"Livestock?" his father says, as he steps outside.

The boy, squinting and clenching his jaw, lets his eyes relax as he gazes at the shadow, watching it creep slower and slower. He feels the rhythm of beats lengthen in his heart. For a single second, the shadow appears to come to a complete stop.

He takes an excited breath and the shadow moves again at a regular pace.

"Feilece!" His mother's voice takes on a piercing tone.

Feilece races to the doorstep. He sees his older brother Semnos and his mother wrangling in a flock of sheep.

"And where did you find these beautiful creatures?" Anema asks picking one of the sheep up with a firm but nurturing grip. The sheep goes from uptight to placid in his arms.

"As we were coming back from town, we saw them wandering in the grass. I think they're from the Armen farm. Probably had a bit of trouble with these feisty bastards," says Semnos.

"Guess it's to be expected. Only an idiot tries to teach a Bloomer how to tend to sheep," says Anema.

"And there's my backwards-arse father," quips Semnos.

Anema scowls but keeps his mouth shut.

Feilece stares at the sheep moving and feels time crawl once again. Their wool flows in a slow mesmerising motion.

"You gonna just watch?"

"Sorry, Ma!" he says as he stumbles out of the front door.

"Why didn't you come when I called?"

"He was staring at the clock again," says Anema.

Feilece runs out into the field to herd an escaping sheep, grinning and shouting over his shoulder. "Yeah, it's great. Just watching the eye open and close, I can feel time slowing down. Maybe, if I watch it long enough, I'll be able to control time!"

"Well, if you learn how to go backwards in time and you meet your past self, what will happen to you then?" his mother, Plios, asks with a coy smile.

"Well then there will be two of me."

"Great. Then two of you can help out with the chores. Go back in time four or five more times, I'll never have to work again."

Feilece pouts.

Anema tosses the last of the sheep in the pen with a single hand.

"Alright, Plios, that's the last of them. Feilece, go to the Armens and see if they're missing any sheep."

Semnos chortles. "Yeah, probably best you don't go, Dad …"

"I'm not a fucking racist, you little shit. I have Bloomer friends."

"That's not a good argument."

"They're the racist ones, that Armen arsehole called me a griffit fucker last week."

"That was because you insulted his ancestors."

"Well maybe those fuckin' northerners shouldn't have invaded."

"That was centuries ago, you weren't even alive!"

"Will you two shut up?" Plios puts an end to the debate. "Forget centuries, it feels like we're at war right now."

"Sorry, Ma."

"Sorry." The two men look like the sheep as they speak.

"Also," Feilece chimes in, "do you have to swear so much, Dad?"

"Fuck the Mother. Is my whole damn family against me, right now?" Anema flicks his hands out at the horizon of green grass basking in the Mother's pale yellow light.

Feilece scurries away so he doesn't have to listen to another bad word from his father.

"Wait, Feilece," calls Plios before the boy is out of earshot.

"Yeah, Ma?"

"The Armen's farm is too far away; it'll be dark by the time you get back."

"Does that mean …"

"I dunno."

"Oh let the boy ride him on his own, he's had enough practice."

Feilece smiles at his father; he's trying to make up for all the swearing.

"Alright, fine," Plios says, rolling her eyes.

"Yes!" Feilece bobs up and down.

Feilece runs to the stables. It's a large building without many cabins because Anema opted for space over cabin quantity when building it. Six loose boxes hold a few cattle, a couple of horses and one big ram.

"Djent. Lets go!" Feilece says to the ram as he

bounces up to the gate of the ram's cabin. The ram perks up as Feilece enters. He pushes himself up, standing tall, a giant fluffy creature with big spiral horns. The animal is taller than Feilece, and is stout for a member of the Ovis breed.

Feilece grabs onto the beast's horns and pulls himself up onto his back. He wraps his arms around the ram's head and gives him a hug, remembering back to when they first met.

Feilece was no older than two years, and was innocently waddling around the farm as his father fruitlessly tried to break up a passionate fight between two rams that had found their way onto their property. Anema tried to get to the boy to take him to safety but was knocked onto his back by one of the beast's horns. One of the enraged rams saw Feilece and charged him.

Feilece watched as the beast raced towards him, unable to comprehend his life was about to come to a quick end. But before the ram's horns could reach Feilece, it was butted hard in the face by the fierce charge of the other ram, spewing blood all over Feilece.

Feilece toddled over, looked down at the dead ram with a big dent in its face and said "Djent!" in a bubbly tone. It was his first word. Then he hugged the ram that saved him, saying "Djent! Djent!" over and over again. That night, they ate the dead ram, and adopted Djent as a member of the family.

Feilece rides out of the stable and into the great field of grass separating the Anemelos family farm from their Bloomer neighbours. The two farms are the only inhabitants of this particular land known as Sheep's

Basin. It's only about a day's ride away from the town of Tiris, where Semnos goes to school.

Due to elevated crime in Tiris, Semnos is taking a break from his studies. This makes Feilece happy, usually he only sees his brother on the weekends and he's bored of only spending time with his sisters and the Armen kids.

Sheep's Basin is remote, and all the kids play in the surrounding fields but as Feilece approaches the Armen's house, he's curious as to why no one's outside. The Armen's are a big family, usually there's at least a couple of them outside, even into the night. Why is it so quiet?

He rides up to the entrance to the house and dismounts. Knocking on the door, he hears a faint scramble from inside. There are no voices. How can a house be full of people with no one talking? Something feels off.

When the door finally opens, Feilece is greeted by the Armen's mother. With shuttered eyes belaying the big smile on her face, a tremble underpins her otherwise chirpy voice.

"Hello there, little Feilece. We're a tad busy right now, would you mind if we settled this tomorrow."

Feilece peers inside, and sees two of the Armen girls knelt by the fire before their mother obstructs his vision and pulls the door ajar.

"Uh … we caught some sheep roaming the basin earlier. Are they yours?" he asks.

"Um, yes. We were moving them and they got away on us. We'll sort this out tomorrow, yeah?"

Her tone is bordering on distressed and Feilece is

concerned until he hears another woman's voice.

"Who's at the door?"

The voice is mature but young, quiet but disruptive, curious yet sinister.

The Armen mother adopts a frown as she opens the door wide. Feilece sees most of the family sitting by the fire, all scrunched up together, facing away from Feilece. Feilece doesn't understand, they're shivering as if they're cold. A few members are missing.

Feilece's eyes move over the room until they fall on a woman approaching him wearing revealing attire. Her skin is a light-brown, soft and smooth. Her legs are long and defined. Her stomach is toned and fit. Her presence is alluring and inviting. Gazing into her big eyes, Feilece feels his skin go hot. You don't usually see women like this on a farm.

She kneels down to Feilece's level and pats him on his head.

"So, you're the Anemelos youngest, huh."

Feilece stares at the woman, unable to stop his cheeks from blushing. He feels as if he's in a trance. The curve of her upturned cheeks from her smile, the flow of her hair, the bare skin of her shoulders. Feilece begins to sweat.

"This is my, uh … friend," says the Armen mother as she gestures towards the gorgeous woman. Her voice betrays a particular level of hurt behind the word 'friend'.

The lady runs a finger down Feilece's cheek to his chin, examining his face. Feilece's eyes flutter.

"You're a cute little boy, aren't you? Definitely have your father's blood in you."

Feilece swallows. "You … know my father?"

"Oh, absolutely, he and my father went way back. I haven't seen him since I was a little girl, though. I doubt he would recognise me."

The woman speaks so casually, Feilece feels his nerves calm. "Would you like to come see him? I'm sure he'll love to see you. Are you with your father?"

"No. Sadly, my father died a while back." Her smile doesn't leave her face.

"Oh, I'm so sorry to hear that …" Feilece recalled when they'd put a sheep he liked to sleep last month, and he cried for days. He couldn't possibly imagine having a family member die.

"It's okay, I always keep him in my heart. It's why I'm travelling around to see his old friends. It makes me feel closer to him."

"Shall we go back to mine then?"

"No, no. There's no rush. I'll come by tomorrow. It's getting late, you should head back now."

"Okay … wait, what's your name?"

"Kasi."

"Kasi … that's a pretty name."

"Why, thank you, that's so sweet."

"My name is Feilece!"

"It's very nice to meet you, Feilece. Go on, now. I bet your mother is worried. Oh, and don't tell your father you saw me, we wouldn't want to ruin the surprise."

"Okay, Miss Kasi. I look forward to seeing you again."

As Feilece returns to Djent, he sees someone move in his peripheral vision, stepping behind the house. He turns his head and they are gone. Curious, he takes a few steps closer to get a better look.

"Run along now, Feilece," Kasi says, with a slight bite to her voice.

"Oh, uh, yes. Sorry," Feilece says, taken aback by Kasi's forceful tone. He quickly climbs aboard Djent and rides off home. He can't get Kasi's face out of his mind. He wishes he could stare at it all day like he does his clock. But … why was she at the Armens' house? Why were they all crowded in their lounge? Why have they never spoken about their mum's pretty friend before? His father knew her when she was a child; Anema never speaks about his past and Feilece has never really thought to ask him.

AT HOME, FEILECE quickly turns his attention to the pinhole camera. The arc of the Mother's eye is steep upon the wall. Soon the eye will be completely closed. Anyone looking to do anything nefarious would do best to pick their moment then. The celestial Mother cannot judge what She cannot see.

"Epoooo." Feilece hears the whiny voice of his sister. "Put the book down and play kill-or-die with me."

"Leave me alone, Niria," his older sister Epo says, her eyes fixated on her text. The spine of the book reads, 'The Man Who Gave a Body to Chaos'.

"You're always reading! No one plays with me anymore."

Semnos throws the girl a kindness. "I'll play with

you, Niria. But, after dinner."

A big smile stretches across Niria's face.

Dorean joins the discussion. "Don't encourage her. Her and Epo are teenagers, she shouldn't be acting so childish."

"Ah, but Dorean." Semnos adopts a patronising tone for his closest sibling. "One must endeavour to milk as much out of their childhood as they can, for it is but a fleeting resource of joy."

"Shut up, schoolboy." Dorean prods his stomach.

"Are we jealous, sister?" Semnos prods back.

"Not for long! One more year."

"Eighteen already, huh?" Semnos pretends to forget Dorean's age, an insult that always hits its mark.

She smiles with squinted eyes and smacks the backs of her fingers against her palm.

"Careful now, that gesture might make the committee think twice about enrolling you," says Semnos.

"The committee isn't watching."

"The Mother is though." Semnos points upwards.

Dorean scrunches her face and shakes her fists by her side. It's a shame, she could've gotten away with it if she had waited a little longer.

"Jokes aside," says Semnos. "I wouldn't get your hopes too high, with the way Tiris has been lately."

"It's a whole year away, things will be back to normal by then."

"You sure about that?" Semnos adopts a coy smile.

"Fuck off, stop screwing with me!" Dorean shoves Semnos.

"Ugh, please don't swear, Dorean," Feilece says with a wince.

"Sorry, Feilece."

Niria runs up to Feilece with a big smile on her face. "Hey Feilece! Fuck, fuck, fuck, fuck, fuck!"

"Stop it!"

"Is that you, Feilece?" Plios appears from the kitchen. "Was I right, were they the Armen sheep?" A sizzling sound from the kitchen steals her attention.

"Yep, she said they would come over tomorrow to get them. But it was weird at their house."

"Weird, what do you mean?" She frowns, and then calls to the others. "Dinner's ready!"

Everyone gathers at the dinner table. Epo and Niria are still bickering over how Epo can never take her attention away from her books, and Dorean is glaring at her smart-arse older brother.

"The Armens were all inside and huddled by the fire," Feilece continues.

"Well, you know what they say about Bloomers and fire," says Anema, preparing to laugh.

"Please ... don't," Semnos interjects.

"I'm just fucking with you," Anema says, nudging his son.

"Don't touch me."

"By the Child, that Bloomer girl of yours really has you wound around her finger."

"She's got nothing to do with it. Just drop it, please."

"Fine." Anema directs his attention back towards Feilece. "That is weird; how do they all fit in that house?"

"There was a woman there too, a family friend. She was ... really pretty." Feilece feels his hands go clammy as he recalls her face. Her big hazel eyes, her freckles, her perfect lips.

"Hmm, don't get many pretty girls around these parts …" Anema halts and slowly turns his head to his three daughters and wife who are staring death at him. "Heh, well, of course … I don't mean … fuck."

Dorean turns away from him. "What, was she from town?" she asks.

"I dunno, I haven't seen anyone as pretty as her during our trips. She may be from Koilia," Feilece says excitedly.

A frown creases above Anema's eyes.

Semnos ruffles Feilece's hair. "Aw, the boy's in love."

"She's really nice too; said she knew—" Feilece quickly stops himself, "… never mind."

Anema speaks slowly and with a sense of urgency. "What is her name?"

Feilece presses the back of his tongue against the roof of his mouth, instinctively going to make a 'K' sound, but he stops.

"I, uh, don't know … she didn't tell me."

"Hmm, I think he's lying," Semnos says.

"Yeah, but why would he hide it?" Dorean piles on, playfully.

"It doesn't matter." Anema's voice is uncharacteristically serious. The room grows silent. Even the two younger daughters quit their fighting. Everyone watches Anema as he stares down, frowning at the centre of the table.

Plios brings everyone their food and sits at the foot of the table. "What's going on here?" she asks.

Anema looks up at his wife and smiles. He looks over at Semnos and pats the boy's knee. "It's good to have you here for longer than a weekend, son. The whole family back together."

"Uh, yeah. It's … great." Semnos' voice is understandably awkward.

"You all know I love you more than anything, right? There's nothing in all of Genus that means more to me than the people in this room."

"Why are you crying, Dad?" asks Feilece.

Semnos puts a hand on his shoulder. Anema wipes away the tear and gives a stifled laugh. "I just love you all, is all … let's eat." He begins eating. The room stays silent.

"Okay …" says Semnos, sharing a confused expression with their mother.

"I love you too, Dad!" says Niria with enough chirpiness to extinguish the simmering uneasiness.

Anema looks at Niria. Tears burst from his eyes and he breaks into cackling laughter. Slowly, everyone relaxes. Feilece smiles, but he still feels strange.

He looks at the clock and ponders. Who was that lady? Who is she to his father? Why did Mrs Armen seem so off? Time slows down, the celestial Mother's eyelid creeps as She closes Her sight off to the Child.

THAT NIGHT, FEILECE struggles to fall asleep. He usually struggles when it's a hot night.

He can't get Kasi's face out of his mind. He imagines her walking over the field separating the houses of

Sheep's Basin. She walks slowly, hips swaying side to side, beads of sweat running down her slim but toned arms.

He's never had these types of thoughts before; he figured he was too young. He sees her approach him, looking down at him with half-closed eyes and a sly grin. She bends forward, bringing her face to his. She touches his chest, fingers spread wide over his heart.

He feels himself burning, as if he were kindling and her hand a randy ignition. He feels his skin melt around her hand as she reaches deep into his chest. He feels his ribcage bend around her fingers as they extend towards his heart. It doesn't hurt. It instead makes his whole body tingle.

This doesn't feel right.

She leans down and presses her lips to his.

This is wrong. But he doesn't want to stop the fantasy.

II

⚡

I N THE EARLY morning, the crescent in the sky has started waning. Anema is outside feeding the Armen sheep. He's being cautious with their diet, the Mother only knows what the Armens feed them, or how often. He hears the moans of his own sheep behind him, bleating accusations of favouritism.

"Yeah, yeah, I hear ya, ya pestering cunts. I'll get to you guys soon."

He turns and looks at the chopping block sitting between the pen and the stable, a splitting axe sticks out of the block with a big pile of freshly cut wood next to it.

He feels bad for leaving Plios alone in their bed for the night but there was no way he was sleeping.

He hears footsteps close by. Soft steps, a woman's presence. He ignores it.

"Excuse me."

He hears the woman's voice; a gentle but strong voice. He doesn't look right away, instead he stares frowning at the grass. He takes a deep breath, then looks up at her. She smiles a kind smile and approaches with a springing step. Anema's hand begin to shake.

"Hi there, I'm a friend of Mrs Armen."

Her face is so innocent. Anema thinks to himself that she is certainly as gorgeous as his son made her out to be. "Oh yeah … is she coming to get her sheep any time soon?" He keeps his words cold and stern.

"Yep, and they wanted to thank you with a cart full of hay for your hand in wrangling them up but the cart has a broken wheel. They sent me down to see if you had a spare. And, of course, to introduce myself—"

Before letting her finish, Anema replies.

"They sent you halfway across the basin to get a wheel all by yourself?"

"I'm a fast walker." Her smile doesn't waver.

"Go back and tell them it's fine, they don't need to pay us anything." Anema delivers his words with hearty dismissal.

The woman looks over at the stable. "You've got a wheel right over there that's not being used."

"I said it's fine."

"It's no big deal, I'll get it. You stay right there."

Anema watches as she walks over to the wheel, ignoring his words. He follows after her, pulling the splitting axe from the chopping block. Walking behind her, he holds the axe steady in his hand.

She's oblivious, fixated on the wheel. She reaches the stables and bends over, places her hands on the spokes and pulls the wheel towards her.

"This should do nicely," she says.

Standing behind the girl, Anema stares at her long flowing black hair, axe held firm in his hand. "You shouldn't have sought me out, Kasi." His words feel like spikes moving through his throat.

Without turning her head, Kasi responds. "So ..." she says in a disappointed tone, "you do recognise me after all of these years. Do you intend on treating me the same as you treated my family?"

"I am not to blame for what happened to your family, and I will not carry the baggage of my old family. My current family, though, I will do anything to protect."

Kasi aims her gaze up at the Mother, retaining her refusal to face the man.

"If you stay," Anema continues, "you die. But if you leave and promise me you'll never—"

"No," she interrupts. Her voice is calm. "No, I'm not going anywhere."

"So be it." Anema lifts the axe high above his head. It shakes in the morning light. It's been twenty years since he's killed someone, and now his axe is being forced against this young woman. He'll have to hide this from his family, like he's hidden everything else. Scrub the stable clean, each individual blade of grass. Take the body to the forest and let it go in the river. He'll have to take it deep into the water, so the river carries the body far south. It'll take the whole day to get there, he'll need to explain his absence to his family. He'll think of something. It's a shame, Feilece will never see his crush again. Why did it have to be her? The axe stops shaking. Firm in a resolute hand, the blade of the axe swings forward, aiming to split the pretty girl's neck.

Anema lunges backward, axe-hand swinging to the side. Confused, he looks at his weapon. What was once a long and strong splitting axe is now but a frayed wooden stick. A thud sounds as the axe head comes down and embeds itself in the chopping block.

Next to the stable, stands a woman in battle leathers painted in camouflage dark-green. A leaf-shaped blade in her sword hand, stout and serious faced, long blonde hair tied into a big puffy bun.

"That hair … impossible," Anema says.

The blonde woman looks at Anema, her face barely moving as if she were an automaton. Only, behind her eyes, even Anema can see it … a murderous rage. She lunges forward into a head-on piercing stab.

Anema dodges with a sidestep and grabs the blade at the hilt with both of his hands, trying to disarm her. In return he gets a fast knee to his sternum, a fist to his temple, a headbutt to his nose, a heel to his knee and a roundhouse kick to the back of his neck, all in one speedy combo. Her attacks are quick, and determined.

Anema falls forward, correcting his balance with a hand to the ground. She goes to stab the sword into his back but he dodges and grabs her by the throat. He lifts her from the ground; she's no heavier than one of his sheep. Her jaw clenches and eyes twitch as she kicks and tries to pry herself free. Anema lets out a heavy sigh and hangs his head.

Kasi turns her attention away from the Mother and looks at the two with her untarnished smile. "You alright there, sister?"

Anema squints at her. "Sister?"

The blonde woman slashes Anema's forearm. With his nerves cut, Anema can't hold his grip. She tries stabbing him once again. He knocks the blade away and barges into her with his shoulder. She falls back over a fence and into the paddock of Armen sheep.

The sheep run terrified from the fumbling woman as she fixes her footing. She slowly steps backward as Anema vaults the fence and approaches her. He's done playing.

"Ah, there he is … the executioner, Animia." Kasi whispers to herself as she releases the clasp to the gate, letting the sheep run free.

The blond woman prepares for an attack but before she can execute, Anema leans forward and punches her directly in the face. Her head jolts backward and she rolls through the grass, her hair releasing from its bun. She lies face down in the grass, struggling to push herself to her feet.

That hit would've knocked someone twice her size unconscious but she continues to move. Looking into her eye through a part in her hair, Anema sees a long dead hate reflected in her pupil.

She swipes her sword at his shin but he stomps down on the blade mid-swing, forcing it from her hand.

"Who would've thought there was still one of you alive." Anema bends down, grabs a handful of the blonde hair and lifts the woman's face up to his level. "I was content in the belief I would never see this colour ever again."

The blonde's eyes widen. She spits in his face, knee to the balls, hands clasped around the man's throat, she pulls herself into a fierce headbutt.

He throws her aside. Like an animal, she comes back with more energy. She delivers a flurry of punches to Anema's face, chest and abdomen. Anema wraps his arms around her waist and lifts her high up off of her feet to slam her into the paddock. Once off of the ground, she spins her torso, delivering a sharp elbow strike to Anema's temple. She flips backwards over Anema's head. Her feet stomp into the grass behind the off-balance farmer.

She grabs him by the chin and pulls him onto his back. Pain shoots throughout Anema's body as he hits the ground. She jumps on top of him. Sitting on his chest, she wraps her hands around his throat once again. Her face is still unmoving, expressionless. But her eyes, they're waving and volatile, like flames.

Holding his breath, Anema sits up, grasping her by her thigh with his good hand, keeping her steady as he rises to stand. Once on his feet, he grabs her chest and smashes her into the dirt with enough force to dislocate her shoulder.

She screeches out in pain then tries to crawl away. Her body shakes with every movement.

Anema spies her sword lying in the grass. Slowly, he reaches down and picks it up, breathing in staggered pants. He saunters over to the crawling woman, sword swaying, grip loose between his fingers. He looks over at Kasi as he walks. Kasi doesn't meet his gaze; she looks at the injured blonde, her brow furrowed.

Anema catches up to the crawling assassin and kicks her onto her back. She looks up at him with a scowl.

"You were an impressive fighter," says Anema. "Far greater than the rest of your family." Anema's words aren't intended to be malicious or harsh. He speaks with a tenderness one affords an injured animal before putting them down. "I'm sorry it had to be like this. I'm sorry your family had to die, but it was either them or thousands of others. You wouldn't have known it, but your father was a corrupt man. He would've stopped at nothing to achieve dominance."

She grits and bares her teeth. Her fists clench so hard they start going pale.

Anema sighs deeply. The celestials are cruel. He lifts the blade over her chest; her eyes dart between him and the sword.

"A daughter shouldn't have to pay for the sins of her father … but I can't afford to let the old ties reform and have tyranny once again reign. If you had just stayed away." Anema clenches the sword. "I'm sorry."

"Alright. That's enough." Kasi nonchalantly dismisses Anema's victory and enters the paddock. Anema points the leaf-blade at her as she approaches.

"Do not come between two warriors in battle, Kasi."

"The battle is over, Animia. She wanted her chance at revenge, I gave that to her, she failed. It's a shame, she trained for a long time. I really wanted to see her succeed."

"Look at her, you know we can't let her live."

"I will not let you kill my sister."

"She is not your sister, Kasi!" Anema yells.

A man's voice comes from the doorway to Anema's home. "Family doesn't exactly mean what it once did."

Anema's eyes widen and jaw drops. He looks over at his house and for a split second, he sees a friend. An old friend with red hair down to his shoulders. A friend who died long ago. "Schisma?"

"Not quite," the man says. "Close though."

"Schizo," Anema whispers to himself as he falls to his knees, dropping the sword on the grass.

"It's been a long time, Uncle Ani." Schizo purses his lips as he carves at a piece of wood with his own leaf-blade. Directing his attention into the house, Schizo says "pass her here," to someone inside. Plios is thrust into his arms, struggling. He holds her by the hair and presses the sword to her throat.

"No … Schizo … please, don't." Anema reaches his arms forward, pleading.

Without responding, Schizo pushes Plios into the dirt and tosses the wood carving over the paddock towards Anema. Anema watches as the carving lands in front of him then rolls into view. A roughly crafted head with shoulder-length hair.

"Anema! What's going on? Who are these people?" screams Plios, as she scrambles in the dirt.

"Anema, huh. New family, new name. Tell me … 'Anema', do you still think about us?" Schizo smiles as he speaks.

Anema rises from his knees.

"Please don't involve them. Do what you will with me."

"I'll do what I will, when I will, and how I will. Such is the way of Sickle & Scythe. Your old words, were they not? And what was that will, exactly? To tear apart your family then retreat and to start a new one!" Schizo's words get louder and louder as he speaks. "You treated me like a son, then you left! Leaving me, a little boy, with no more family than that right there!"

Anema looks down at the wooden head.

"The image never left my brain. You were like his brother!" Schizo pulls Plios up by her hair and places his sword back at her throat. "Tell me. How long will it be until you cut this pretty one's head off?"

Anema stares at Schizo, a furrow creasing his eyebrows. He opens his mouth to speak but before he can get any words out, a disturbance comes from inside the house. A disoriented Semnos appears, Feilece huddled behind him.

"No! Semnos, stop!" Anema yells words no one hears.

"Mother!" Semnos dashes at Schizo in a blind rage. Schizo reacts, withdrawing the sword from Plios' throat, spinning into an underhand grip, and stabbing it through Semnos' chest. A splash of Semnos' blood splatters across Feilece's face.

III

〰

F EILECE OPENS HIS eyes to the sound of thuds outside his window. He looks out to see his father chopping wood by the Armen sheep paddock. Feeling his stomach growl, he makes his way to the back of the house to wash his hands under the water pump, then goes back inside to find something to eat. He chews on leftover mutton and stares at the clock. It's still dark so all the projector picks up is a faint circle on the wall.

He watches the clock, feeling time slow down. He tries to reverse the effect, mentally straining to make time speed up. He wants the day to go by quickly so he can meet up with Kasi again. She said she was going to visit today, and she didn't seem like the kind to lie.

Staring at the shadow, Feilece's eyelids begin to droop and he slowly drifts off to sleep. The thuds of his father's wood chopping dissipate into dead air.

Eased awake by footsteps sounding in the house, Feilece opens his groggy eyes to the sight of a man standing in the kitchen. He has shoulder-long dark red hair. The man has his back to Feilece and is signalling to someone outside.

"Hello?" comes crackling out of Feilece's dry

throat. Waking confusion nullifies any feelings of danger he may have felt having discovered a stranger in his house. The man turns with a snap and stares at the boy for a second before adopting a calm easing manner.

"Well, hey there, little boy. I didn't see you when I came in. Shouldn't you be in bed?" The man creeps towards Feilece as he speaks.

"Who … who are you?" Feilece rubs his eyes.

"I'm an old friend of your dad's. I hope you don't mind me letting myself in, I'm hoping to surprise him." The man creeps within arm's reach of Feilece.

"Old friend … like Kasi! Do you know Kasi?" Feilece perks up at the thought of her.

"I should hope to know her, she's my wife."

"What!" Feilece yells, causing the man to promptly cover the boy's mouth with his hand and lift him up into his arms.

"Alright, gonna need you to be quiet now, little boy."

Feilece tosses fruitlessly in the man's arms. He sees each member of his family in a similar position being dragged from their rooms and into the lounge by toughs in warrior garb.

"Anyone of you make a noise loud enough for that murderous fuck outside to hear and I snap the boy's neck, understand?" The man speaks sternly.

The warriors release their grip and everyone crowds by the fireplace. When Feilece sees the parallel between this situation and the Armens', his brain finally clicks onto what's happening.

"Now, little boy, you know if you scream or anything … I'll kill you."

The Anemelos family collectively flinch. Plios quietly whimpers.

"Then I'll have my friends here cut down each member of your family one after another. I'm going to take my hand away from your mouth, are you going to keep quiet?"

Feilece nods, panting through his nose. The man releases the boy's mouth, hand moving to the back of his neck.

"Why are you here?" Feilece speaks in a hushed tone, his voice shaking.

"Don't speak, Feilece," Plios whispers.

"Nah, it's fine. We can talk, only quietly. I don't want Animia knowing I'm here yet."

"Animia?" Semnos asks.

"Your father … tell me, what does he go by nowadays?"

Semnos keeps his mouth shut, scowling.

"Hah, guess it doesn't matter. I spent years tracking that bastard down. Who would've thought I would just happen upon him, walking through the streets of Tiris. The Mother always corrects her childrens' mistakes."

"My father is a simple farmer," says Semnos. "What could a man like that possibly do to justify invading his home and threatening his family?" His voice rises in volume as he speaks.

"Keep this up, Animia spawn." Feilece feels the man's hand get tighter around his neck.

Semnos swallows and lowers his voice. "Look around … this is a farm. You're in fucking Sheep's

Basin, not Koilia, we don't have fighters around here. You have the wrong man."

"If you're so sure, why doesn't your mother agree with you?"

Plios looks up and meets her eldest son's gaze. Her eyes look guilty.

"What are you hiding, Mum? Did you know this was coming."

"He told me I had nothing to worry about … that those looking to find him were already dead." Plios' words are soft.

"And you didn't think to ask him why they were dead?" The red-haired man speaks plainly.

She shakes her head. "I didn't want to know about his past. I only wanted to make a family."

"Well, you got what you wanted."

"Who are you?" Semnos' words are slow and low in tone.

The red-haired man's voice takes on a sympathetic tone. "If it weren't for your father, you and I would be cousins."

Semnos' eyes squint. "What?"

Feilece perks up at the sound of Kasi's voice outside.

"It looks like it's commencing, Schizo," says a particularly gruff warrior with a bald head and long scraggly beard. "Maybe Seemo will finally be happy."

"Oh Popoki, when will you admit you have feelings for her?" the red-haired man asks playfully. "It would be sad if you lost your chance."

"You don't think she will win?"

"I do not. That bastard was one of the best Sickle

& Scythe had to offer. Even after twenty years, he'll still be a force to reckon with."

As the two men talk, Feilece is released. He rushes into the arms of his mother. It seems the man doesn't care about alerting Anema anymore, but the Anemelos family keeps quiet anyway. It wouldn't be a good idea to start making a ruckus with so many warriors around.

Niria is whimpering; she cuddles next to Epo who is holding her close. Dorean is sharing glances with Semnos, silently plotting something. Plios is looking guilty, hugging Feilece tight. Feilece is concentrating on one thing over the rest, the pleasant tone of Kasi's voice coming from outside. It's the only thing keeping his mind.

Before long, a fight starts outside. Plios raises her head, her breathing is quick. Epo holds Niria as the girl sobs. It sounds like when Anema wrangles the sheep but instead of their dad sounding playful and happy, he sounds pained and angry. Semnos and Dorean stay strong. Feilece distracts himself by looking at the clock.

As he watches the shadow of the Mother's eye, he somehow feels above everything, as if what's happening around him isn't real. There are no invaders in his home. There is no tension on his shoulder from the squeezing hand of his mother. There is no battle outside. There is only him and the shifting yellow light of the celestial Mother.

Without asking, the red-haired man takes a wooden fruit bowl from the dining room table and begins carving into it with his leaf-blade. A screeching wail is heard from outside, the sound of a woman in great pain. It's loud enough to break Feilece out of his trance.

"Told you," the red-haired man says to his henchman.

Popoki stares with wide unmoving eyes out of the window, hands shaking.

"Bring the mother," says the red-haired man as he walks to the doorway.

Feilece feels his mother's heart begin to race.

Popoki doesn't respond, he continues to stare blankly.

"Popoki?"

"Huh, what?"

"Bring the wife."

"Right."

"It's unlike you to be loose with your attention, Popoki."

The red-haired man takes a deep breath then adopts a smug expression and walks outside.

The gruff man turns towards Plios.

"No!" blurts Plios as Popoki drags her from her family. Semnos pulls Feilece close to him.

Feilece takes a tally of the home invaders. There's the red-haired man, the bearded man, a stocky woman, two long-haired slender men—one with white hair and the other with black—and an intelligent looking older man whose attention is fixed on Epo and Niria. Feilece looks at his brother. Semnos' eyes are scanning, darting between the invaders. Whatever Semnos does, Feilece decides he will follow.

The red-haired man leans inside and says, "pass her here."

Wearing a concerned frown, Popoki pushes Plios into the red-haired man's arms and she is pulled from the house with a sword at her throat. Popoki stays standing at the door.

Feilece watches as Dorean and Semnos share a few glances coupled with head nods to indicate directions. Feilece has no idea what they're planning but he can tell by the stocky female captor's shrewd smile that she's following along. Feilece sees Semnos ready himself and his heart starts beating faster. It's the opposite feeling to when he's watching the clock; time isn't slowing, it's speeding up.

The stocky woman watches, smile growing larger.

"Now!" Semnos rushes at Popoki pressing him against the wall as Dorean takes the leaf-blade from his belt and turns it towards the other invaders. Feilece quickly jumps in behind Semnos, keeping close but making sure not to get in the way.

The invaders collectively begin to laugh, except for the old man who is still staring at the girls.

"You don't want to be doing this, little man." Popoki's voice is dark and serious.

"Shut up or I'll have my sister stab you with your own sword." Semnos tries to put on a tough voice but even Feilece can hear his fear.

"She's not going to do anything," says the stocky woman as she unsheathes her own sword and approaches with a sinister gait.

"Don't tempt me, lady," says Dorean. "My father's had me put down sheep before, sheep I grew to love. If I can put them down, I can sure as fuck take down some bitch." Dorean does a better job than her brother at putting up a tough front.

The stocky woman smiles. "I like you. Come on

then, show this bitch what you've got."

The old man takes his attention away from the girls to watch the fight.

Dorean, sword grip shaking in her hands, steps forward with a lunge, stabbing her sword towards the woman's chest. The woman knocks the blade away effortlessly and it's flung onto the floor. The two huddled sisters get a fright as the sword clangs on the ground in front of them.

Dorean stares at the woman with a face stricken by fear. The woman stares back with a domineering smile.

"Bravo," the old man says with a tired sigh.

"You shut the fuck up, old man!" the stocky woman says. They glare at each other.

"Get off me, then." Popoki spins on his heel and delivers a harsh elbow to the side of Semnos' head, sending him crashing into an adjacent wall.

Semnos slides down the wall, blinking profusely. Feilece grabs at his legs trying to get his brother's attention but he's in a daze.

"Semnos! Are you okay?"

"Feilece? What's happening?"

Feilece watches as Semnos' eyes struggle to focus, then fixate on something outside.

"Mother!" Semnos scrambles to his feet and runs out of the door.

Blood spatters across Feilece's face. Looking around everything feels so fast and tense until his eyes meet Kasi's. Enamoured by her hazel eyes, time slows to a halt.

Anema is moving in slow motion as he vaults over the paddock fence. Plios takes a whole minute to fall to her knees, face contorting into a wail. The red-haired man takes his time pulling the sword from Semnos' chest. Blood gushes from the wound, flowing slowly, cascading across the grass. Semnos' legs give out and he creeps through the air as he falls to his side.

Feilece, eyes locked with Kasi's, feels above it all, like it's not really happening. Kasi gives the boy a kind smile. Her kindness pierces through all other emotions and Feilece, face covered in his brother's freshly spilled blood, smiles back.

IV

ANEMA HUDDLES WITH his family, arms wrapped around them. They're sitting in the barn, cuddling in a pile of hay. Plios is shivering, Dorean is quiet and sombre, Epo and Niria weep and whine. Feilece stares blankly into nothingness, face still partially stained with Semnos' blood.

Anema sits quietly, staring at Popoki who has been put in charge of watching over them. Popoki stares back, mimicking Anema's expression. Anema wants to launch from his spot and force the man's eyes into his skull with his thumbs, but he knows he needs to comfort his family. His mind is going berserk. He feels the erosion of a hatred from a time long passed, a degradation he thought he would never have to feel again.

He was stupid thinking he could fix his world with blood. He was stupid thinking he could maintain a life of harmony. He was exceedingly stupid. Genus is a land supposedly creeping towards its fourth century of peace, yet hatred, brutality and death seem to forever reign.

Schizo walks into the barn and meets Anema's

deathly gaze. Hours have passed since he killed his first born; it's about time he showed his face. Anema draws his family closer, covering their eyes so they don't have to see the murderer.

"Sorry for the wait. I was thinking of the best way to approach this situation. When I couldn't think of anything, I figured I might as well just wing it." Schizo's demeanour is aggravatingly casual.

"You're a coward and a disgrace. Your father would be ashamed of the callous monster you've become," says Anema.

"Why? Because I instinctively retaliated against an incoming threat?" Schizo's composure doesn't sway.

"Because you would kill an unarmed boy without a thought passing through your psychotic brain."

Plios moves swiftly, standing and punching the man in the face before he can reply, sending him lunging backwards.

"Plios! Don't!" Anema springs to his feet.

"I'll let you have that one," Schizo says, rubbing his face.

"I'll fucking kill you!" Plios lays into him, throwing punch after punch. Schizo pushes her back then delivers a hook to the side of Plios' head. Plios falls unconscious to the barn floor.

"Mum!" Dorean rushes over to Plios' side followed by Epo and Niria. Feilece continues his trance. Anema stares at Schizo, eyes glossy with rage.

"Alright … I agree, Dad would probably be a little ashamed of me for punching a mourning mother, especially after killing her son." Schizo speaks out the side of his mouth. "But, he would be infinitely more proud of me for what's outside. Come, look."

Schizo beckons Anema outside where he's greeted by the view of hundreds of individuals wearing battle attire walking around the Anemelos farm.

Over the past few hours, Anema had heard them arriving in wagons and conversing among themselves, talking about how much they like this place, the space, the privacy, the utilities. Their clothing bears the embroidery of Anema's old brand, a sickle crossed with a scythe. Only, it's been changed. In-between the blades are two dark-red predator eyes. Anema is taken aback by how many warriors there are.

"And these are only the spectators, there are more on their way … many more," Schizo says, grinning.

"You reformed Sickle & Scythe … but I severed the kinship, how?" Anema doesn't want to believe it. He killed his best friend and brother-in-arms for nothing.

"It wasn't easy. After you killed my father, all of the old members went off on their own. Without my father's noble cause, they had no choice but to turn wayward. You didn't just kill one man that day, you destroyed a future and a family."

"Your father was insane, drunk on power. His cause was no more noble than that of the Demons."

"You don't get to say that name," says Kasi.

Anema's nostrils flare to the sound of Kasi's voice.

She enters the conversation with sinister tonality. "My father once told me you were one of the good ones. That you were merciful and always talking about peace. Well, congratulations executioner, while it was rather indirect, you still achieved your goal." She leans over and shares a gratuitous kiss with Schizo.

The gears turn in Anema's head as he watches the progeny of his past friend and enemy showing off their intimacy. It's a crude and distressing sight. "You travelled all the way here to take over my farm, for what? Revenge?" Anema's aggravation grows.

"There's enough revenge here to fill all our cups of hate; most here are hurting in some way from your actions. But alas, no. My father taught me not to waste the efforts of those that follow you." Schizo paces as he speaks. "We were getting too large, the Koilian authorities caught wind of our expansion. They would've crushed us out of fear alone. We were forced to escape and look for better lodgings, preferably somewhere far away from the Grothia. What better place than Tiris, where they hold their own sovereignty. By only the luck of the Mother, I was delivered you, you who owe a great inheritance to your former family. This lovely farm is to become our base of operations."

Anema watches him like a beast being taunted by his prey.

He continues. "No one from Koilia would come this far north to look for us. Here we can expand, prepare for our great battle. You put a stop to war, now I'm going to use your farm to spark the war back up and fulfil my father's cause. We will fight the Grothia and we will be the first in history to win."

"You won't fight the Grothia; they wouldn't even glance your way. All you will be fighting is the innocent people of Koilia."

"We will force their glance, then their sword, then take their castle and liberate our country."

"Liberate," Anema says, tilting his head back and closing his eyes. "You're just like your father, you don't want liberation, you want the power for yourself."

"You don't know anything, Uncle. My father would've done it … he would've saved this world if you hadn't cut him down."

Anema sees red. He grabs Schizo by the throat and screams at him. "Your father wouldn't have invaded a humble farm. He wouldn't have attacked an innocent family. He wouldn't have killed my son!"

Schizo's people spring to his aid but stop when Schizo raises his hand. Schizo grabs Anema's wrists and pulls the man's hands from his throat, overpowering him. Then he thrusts a knee into Anema's stomach, causing a spasm in his diaphragm and sending him to the ground. Schizo squats down to speak into Anema's ear. "You are right … my father wouldn't approve of this, so in his name, I will be merciful. Like I said earlier, they're only spectators."

Anema's eyes meet with Schizo's and they both rise to their full height.

"One final fight," says Schizo. "We'll let the Child decide. If you win, by my father's honour, my soldiers will withdraw from your home and never return. If I win, this will become the new base of operations for our new family, the Reapers."

"Reapers?" says Anema, eyes squinting.

"All the benefits of Demons and Sickle & Scythe combined," says Kasi. "A family capable of matching the Grothia themselves."

"So you took an honoured kinship and poisoned its title with the mentality of brutes and psychopaths."

Anema feels a deep pain in his heart. An old part of him is still attached to his old position.

"Says the man who killed that 'honoured kinship'."

"I killed corruption!" Anema yells involuntarily. "I tore out my own soul and ripped it to shreds to stop this wanton barbarism, and you just brought it all back. You're putting this country back onto a path of ensured destruction!"

"And how powerful that must have felt, saving the world like that," Kasi says with words dripping in contempt. "You should be thanking us, now you get a chance to do it again."

"How can you expect me to trust the word of a Demon?"

"The old honour system of Sickle & Scythe remains intact," Schizo says. "If I die, they will leave."

"You swear upon your father?"

Anema knows he can't trust his word, but no man would sully their father's name, especially if he has the blood of his old friend in him.

"I swear upon my father: we will let you live in peace with what remains of your family."

Although rage continues to flare in Anema's heart, boiling and bubbling his will, he keeps himself calm and walks over to a nearby weapons cache set up by the Reapers. He looks the guard in the eyes. He recognises him, only last time he saw him, his eyes were wide and full of tears as he lay paralysed on a battlefield. The scared teenager he spared that day is now looking at him with a bloodthirsty smugness.

Anema sighs, then he reaches out and grabs the worn handle of a rugged double-bladed battleaxe.

V

———◆◆◆———

D OREAN HOLDS HER unconscious mother in her arms. She'd been staring into Popoki's eyes while eavesdropping on the conversation between Schizo and her dad, looking for weakness. She's noticed his attention has jumped to Schizo a few times.

"Don't you want to see what they're talking about?" she asks.

"You're trying to get me to leave so you can escape with your family. Do you really think that's possible?"

"Can't blame me for trying, right?"

"I've been tasked with watching you so watching is what I shall do."

"Your leader, what does he plan to do with my father?"

"He plans to fight your father."

"And what if my father wins?"

"We will leave."

"It's that easy, is it?"

"I assure you, it won't be easy."

"So … what, my father wins and you'll all pack up and leave? Forgive me if that sounds like horseshit."

"You have my word, girl."

"Well, once my father wins, what do you think he will do as soon as he's finished chopping your leader into pieces?" Dorean's eyes squint as she speaks. "You know he'll come right back in here to his family, are you sure you want to be here when that happens?"

"In the state he'll be in after the fight, I'm sure I'll be able to take him."

"Your girlfriend couldn't."

The two exchange dark looks. Popoki doesn't say a word as a wet glaze comes over the man's eyes. Dorean expects the man to hurt her and she doesn't care if he does. It's because of this man that her brother is dead. She's too angry to be scared.

Anema shouts from outside. "Your father wouldn't invade a humble farm!" Popoki diverts his gaze.

Hearing her father's aggression, a surge of energy rises in Dorean.

"You hear that?"

Popoki looks back at Dorean.

"That's the man that beat up your girl. Next, he's going to kill your leader, then kill you, so you better get the fuck out of here."

Popoki stands up and approaches Dorean. Dorean instinctively pulls away. Popoki looks down at her with sombre eyes. "Do what you want," he says, then leaves the barn.

"Finally." Dorean whispers to her family, "okay, we're going to get out of here. Make for the forest, if we can get to the river, we can take Dad's boat down south. They said something about Koilia being dangerous for them. If they have enemies there, maybe they'll help us."

Plios is unconscious, Feilece is still in a trance and Niria is so distraught she's detached herself from the situation to cry over her mother's unresponsive body. Epo is the only one listening.

"What about Mum and Dad?" she asks, keeping her tears from escaping her eyes.

"We'll take Mum with us, Dad …" A frown creases above her eyes.

Dorean doesn't believe they'll leave the farm if Schizo loses, and she knows Anema will want them to take this opportunity to escape.

"He can't join us, can he?" says Epo.

"Let's just go, Epo. Here, help me with Mum. Niria, help Feilece."

Epo heaves, picking up Plios' legs as Niria holds Feilece's shoulders and directs him.

There's only one entrance to the barn; if they try to leave, they'll be spotted. The two sisters carry Plios to the back of the barn, trying to move as quietly as possible so they don't draw attention from anyone outside. Even the chooks keep quiet. Behind the barn is a small hill leading down to the woods. If they can make it to the trees, Dorean is sure they can escape into the lush forest. They just need a way out of the barn.

Dorean rests her mother's body on the floor and searches the back wall looking for a weak or loose panel. She'd assumed there was a broken panel somewhere because chickens had been randomly escaping, and she'd been meaning to come fix it. Frustratingly, she finds nothing. Maybe they were escaping another way, or perhaps her father or Semnos had already fixed it.

A vision of Semnos smiling flashes in her mind and she butts her head against a wood panel, tears streaming down her face.

"Uh, Dorean?"

Dorean looks over at Epo who is pushing back a loose panel next to one of the coops. She wipes her face and kisses Epo's forehead. "Thank you, sister."

Dorean pulls the neighbouring panels away to make a hole big enough to squeeze through. She crawls halfway out and checks for any invaders. There's no one around. They must be watching her father's fight. She crawls out then pulls Plios through. Epo follows with Niria dragging Feilece behind her.

"Okay, hurry. Into the woods," Dorean whispers urgently, scurrying down the hill with Epo, carrying their mother.

"For fuck's sake, Feilece!" cries Niria.

Dorean snaps her head back to Niria who is trying to pull an unresponsive Feilece from the barn wall.

"Shh, Niria!' Dorean's tone is harsh enough to make Niria start crying. Leaving Plios with Epo, she rushes over to Niria's side. "Hey, hey, it's okay. I'm sorry for getting angry, but we must be quiet, Niria. Please be strong."

Niria sniffs and struggles to control her sobs.

"Look, go and help Epo with Mum. Hey, would you look at that! Epo's willing to play, you wanted to play kill-or-die, right?"

Epo waves at her from the bottom of the hill.

"What about Feilece?" Niria asks, sniffling.

"I'll bring him, don't worry. Run along now,

Niria." Dorean watches Niria run over to Epo then feels a wave of worry wash over her as she turns back to Feilece. She kneels down and looks up at him with a big kind smile. "Hey, Feilece … I know this is difficult but please, come with me now."

Feilece stares into nothing, barely moving.

"Hey." Dorean tries shaking him to get his attention but it doesn't work. Touching his wrist, Dorean notices his pulse is intense. She puts a hand to his chest, his heart is beating incredibly fast. She grabs his face and makes him look directly into her eyes. She speaks at him, trying over and over to get his attention. Eventually, his eyes adjust and meet Dorean's.

"Dorean?"

"Oh, thank you, Child!" Dorean says, hugging him. "Okay, come on, we have to leave now. We've lingered for too long." She tries to pull him with her but he doesn't follow.

"Wait, what about Semnos?"

Dorean frowns at him.

"I just saw something terrible happen to him," he says. "Where is he? How did we get here?"

"Oh, Feilece … that happened hours ago."

"What!" Feilece stumbles back against the barn wall.

"Are you okay?" Dorean puts a hand on Feilece's shoulder.

"But it just happened, only a moment ago."

"Look, we can't waste time here, okay? We have to go." Dorean stands and takes Feilece by the hand.

"Wait, what about Kasi? Is she okay?"

"What? Fuck it! Enough questions, let's go!"

Dorean speaks harshly, pulling on Feilece's arm and dragging him down the hill. Feilece doesn't fight back. They pass a few trees and catch up to the girls. Plios is on the ground behind a tree next to Niria, and Epo is surveying the canopy.

"What's going on? Why have you stopped?" Dorean whispers to Niria.

"Epo stopped and told me to wait, she says they're watching."

"Shit." Dorean creeps up to Epo. "What's wrong?"

"I don't know, they're just standing there … watching us."

Dorean looks up in the direction of Epo's gaze. She looks around for anyone or anything dangerous but all she sees are leaves, branches and a few birds.

"What are you talking about Epo? Who's there?"

"Can't you see them? Long black and white hair."

"I see nothing, Epo. Look, we can't linger. We have to keep going."

The hairs on the back of Dorean's neck stand on end at the sound of the stocky woman's voice behind her.

"Keep going where exactly?"

VI

⚬

ANEMA AND SCHIZO face each other in the middle of the sheep paddock, surrounded by Reapers. Anema's grip on his battleaxe feels weak, the cut Seemo gave him earlier is going to provide issues. Schizo spins his sword around effortlessly, a big gloating smile upon his face. Anema is taller than Schizo, perhaps he can use his height to his advantage. Though he is bigger, he is also older and slower. Anema's height won't count for much if he can't even catch his opponent. He's been spending the last twenty years fighting sheep while Schizo has been training for war.

Schizo's body is just as toned as his own with scars peppering his taut skin, the body of a seasoned warrior. A man in the prime of his twenties, and he's already collected himself quite the fighter's mural. He must have had a hard life after Anema left. This is all his fault.

"I really didn't mean to kill your son. That aggression in his eyes ... he would've made a great addition to my ranks." Schizo speaks with honesty, making his words even more taunting.

Anema steps in, swinging the axe with an underarm vertical arc towards Schizo. Schizo dodges. Anema continues the axe's momentum, looping it around his head and into a diagonal downward slice at Schizo's shoulder. Schizo catches the axe with his sword, close to the hilt.

A small divot chinks into the sword.

Pain shoots through Anema's arm as he pushes down hard on the axe. Schizo keeps it from touching him, taunting Anema with a clearly superior strength. Schizo twists his blade, redirecting the axe away, then he delivers a swift slice to Anema's thigh, drawing blood and sending the farmer into a pained kneel.

A confident smile slices Kasi's face.

"Twenty years of fucking around with sheep has dulled your fighting instincts, Uncle." Schizo continues to taunt as he saunters around Anema.

If this were war, the match would already be over. It appears to Anema that his opponent wants to spread his revenge out. He could use this to his advantage.

Anema pushes himself to his feet with the axe then swings it at Schizo in a horizontal arc. Schizo ducks under the swing and goes to slice at Anema's torso but his face is met with Anema's knee.

Blood pours out of Schizo's nose as his head juts back. Anema punishes with another swing but Schizo rolls away and the axe digs into the grass.

Schizo looks at the axe and whistles. "Now that was close. Looks like you still have some fighting spirit left in you from the old days."

"Animia is dead. I killed him along with your old man. Who you fight now is a man who will stop at nothing to protect his family!" Anema walks as he talks. The pain in his arm dulls.

Spinning the axe around above his head like a baton, Anema builds up momentum then twirls the axe into a barrage of relentless swings upon Schizo. Anema proves he can still wield an axe like a professional killer.

Schizo dodges and deflects every swing with systematic precision, one would think it was a performance where he'd memorised every step ahead of time. Anema can't believe the man's speed of cognition. If Anema was still of the mind he had twenty years ago, he reckons he would be proud of the boy. Schisma would be.

Schizo switches from reactive to proactive, and he gets in close to Anema, slicing at his heel.

Anema trips to the ground. He swings the battleaxe up at Schizo but the nimble man dodges and cuts at the axe's haft, severing the head from the handle. The axe head, reduced to a blade with a frayed stick sticking out of it, falls to the grass.

Armed with only a piece of wood, Anema goes on the defensive. Schizo encroaches, delivering a succession of swift and accurate attacks. Anema is able to block a few strikes but then he loses track. Schizo slices at the farmer's arm, cutting out a large chunk of muscle and covering him in blood. Anema reacts, trying to dash away but is stopped by a stab through his thigh, forcing him back to the ground.

Schizo kicks him onto his back. Anema tries propping himself up on his good arm but Schizo kicks it out.

Anema is a beaten and bloody mess, while Schizo stands strong with nothing but a busted nose.

Schizo directs his voice outward, casting his words into the ears of his followers. "As you can see. Even the great Animia, relic of Sickle & Scythe history, the great executioner, even he falls, as all of our enemies will fall!"

Cheering breaks out among the Reapers.

Schizo projects his words like a politician, cheers following every statement. "We will take back the PanoApo estate. We will demand the respect of the Koilia houses. We will carve the name Reaper into Abdominals' history. Then we will turn our gaze towards those blue-eyed Grothia freaks and finally put an end to their tyranny!"

The final statement earns louder applause than the rest combined.

"Heh …"

Slowly, Schizo turns his head towards Anema.

"Heh, heh. Hah! Hah! Hah!" Anema's voice crackles like a fire as he cackles.

The Reapers go silent as the gruff farmer pushes the head of his axe into the grass, rising to his feet. His legs shake but he feels solid. One of his arms hangs uselessly while the other holds a tight grip around the shoulder of his axe. He doesn't feel the weight of the blade, as if the axe has replaced his hand.

A strange glint of purple can be seen around the edges of the farmer's vision. While looking deep into Schizo's eyes, Anema sees the man go weak. Anema begins walking towards Schizo. His legs twitch in pain with every step. He knows the pain is there, but it's stolen away before he can choose to care about it.

Schizo dashes at the man, rearing up his sword for a horizontal slash to Anema's neck. Midway through the slice, Anema lifts his arm, catching the axe against the same divot the blades made during the last round. Cracks spread throughout the sword and burst the leaf-blade into shards. Shrapnel cuts into Schizo's face as he scampers away.

Anema, also hit with shrapnel, continues walking unperturbed. His mind keeps telling him that he is in control, that he is still Anema. But he knows that if he tried to stop right now, it wouldn't work.

Blood leaks into Schizo's eyes, and he frantically rubs at them.

"Schizo!" screams a distressed Kasi.

Anema stares down at Schizo as the man regains his sight. A paralysed fear can be seen in Schizo's eyes. Anema slowly lifts the axe above his head then brings it down in a swift hack. Schizo blocks it with his forearm. The axe tears through his skin and bone. A piercing scream wails from his mouth. A collective wince is shared throughout the Reapers. Anema butts the screaming man onto his back and stands over him, holding his axe and smiling. In this moment, he's enjoying the carnage.

Anema, bereft of thought, feels words escape his mouth, spoken with a slow, demonic rasp. "Hah … hah … hah. Little man. Small, little man. Trying to mount the land. Trying to carve out a name. Your efforts are nothing. Your father was nothing, you will inherit … nothing. Your blood will be added to the grass of my farm and your body will decay into an empty husk of your former wyll."

Schizo stares up, jaw shivering.

Anema has no control over his voice. "You may not be welcome here, but you will always have a place in the black."

Anema lifts his axe into the air for one final strike. The strike that will free his home and his family. The strike that will sever Anema from his history, and finally bring him peace.

A metal leaf extends forth from Anema's chest. Blood trickles down the blade onto Anema's abdomen and runs down the contours of his abdominal muscles.

The purple glint fades from Anema's vision. Anema turns his head to the sight of blond hair behind him. Seemo's eyes are shivering and staring at nothing, crazed. She moved so silently.

"You would interfere in your commander's battle?" Anema wheezes as he speaks. Seemo's mouth remains closed.

Schizo, holding his bloody arm as he steps up to a stand, says, "I am not her commander. None of us are bound to the whims of another, we are free."

Anema coughs up a spurt of blood then falls to his knees, dropping his axe to the ground.

Schizo removes his belt and ties it around his arm to stop the bleeding. "Did you really think we came all the way out here only to turn heel and bolt? I can't die just yet, not before I'm done fixing what you broke."

Reapers leap over the fence into the paddock and approach Anema, weapons held firm in their hands.

"I did tell you there was enough revenge for all of us, did I not?" Schizo walks away to leave the Reapers with their toy.

The Reapers crowd around Anema. Anema's weary eyes take in the familiar faces: old members of Sickle & Scythe; family members of old comrades; members of the old Demon group; victims of his from time long passed.

Another blade is stabbed through his back, another through his chest, another through his stomach. Methodically, the Reapers skewer the old farmer one after another.

"I found some strays," says the stocky woman, dragging Plios and Dorean from the forest. Dorean struggles against the woman's grip fruitlessly while Plios remains unconscious. Two lanky men follow; a white-haired man carries Niria, while a black-haired man carries Epo. Both are unconscious.

Anema's eyes twitch and fill with water as they watch his family be treated like captive animals.

"Where's Popoki? I thought he was watching them?" says Schizo, holding his mangled arm.

"I'm here," Popoki calls from the barn's entrance. "Your arm alright?"

"There is no war without fine lessons learned along the way. How did they escape?"

"I wanted to watch the fight."

"Well, I guess that is your freedom."

Schizo turns back to the stocky woman. "Where's the boy?"

"He's over there, I'll grab him." She throws Dorean to the ground.

Anema meets eyes with Dorean. He watches as all hope drains from his first daughter.

"No need," says Kasi. She walks towards the barn and beckons. Feilece, scared and awkward, runs to Kasi's side.

"Good boy."

Anema sees his youngest in the arms of the daughter of his old nemesis. Such cruelty … tears stream down his face.

"Pass the wife," Schizo says.

The stocky woman tosses a now semi-conscious Plios towards Schizo, who grabs her with his remaining arm. She struggles but he headbutts her and she stops. Schizo drags her into the paddock where Anema remains kneeling, swords sticking out of him in all directions.

Anema stares at the ground. Plios is tossed in front of him and she crawls over, eyes wide and crying. Anema's gaze meets hers. A brief moment of happiness streams through him, like a wave through a desert.

Schizo, taking a sword from the stocky woman's offering hand, strikes at the back of Plios' neck, cleaving off her head.

Dorean's agonised wails drown out all sound in Sheep's Basin.

Anema, gazing down at the unmoving expression on his wife's disembodied head, loses all will to live. He feels the weight of his body lighten and become like air. His skin loses its colour then begins to flake off like ash, followed by the underlying muscle.

VII

F EILECE WATCHES HIS father, his mentor, his guardian, the calm and kind man who raised him thus far, who taught him and cared for him, turn to dust and bone before his uncomprehending eyes. In one day, half of his family is gone. Thoughts try to find their way into his mind but they're faded and in a foreign language. Most of all, he feels a sensation of pure emptiness. All complex machinery working behind Feilece's eyes is stymied. Time moves in short lagging bursts with every second. A piercing monotone rumbles in his ears. Colours are washed out in his vision, and contrasts are dull.

By means uncontrolled by his input, he turns his head and looks at Kasi. She smiles at him, kind and warm. Around her face, reality begins to warp, swirling and blurring.

He blinks. The world goes black and refuses to return. Only the imprinted image of Kasi's face remains.

Over time, Feilece's vision heals to the sight of wooden panels. He's inside one of the cabins of the stables. He tries to move but his movement is quick and erratic. He tries to rub his eyes but accidentally smacks himself in the face because his hand moves too fast.

All he hears is a crackling hum, a combination of all sounds coming at him at once. He huddles at the back of the cabin and tries not to move, worried he'll hurt something.

When he finally looks out, the world is moving incredibly fast. He watches as the day turns to night, night turns to day, over and over.

The Mother is blinking; the clock is leaving him behind.

Someone comes by his cabin to check on him regularly but he can't make out who it is. He concentrates on it, using this person as a focal point. He's able to slow time enough to see her face for a second.

It's Kasi.

Kasi's face calms Feilece's heart. Time slows back to normal.

Kasi disappears out of the stables. The first thing he distinguishes as his hearing comes true, are the sounds of painful screams and grunts from neighbouring cabins. He recognises the screams; it is his sisters, Epo and Niria.

Feilece hugs his knees as he tries to ignore the sounds. Thuds come from Djent's pen, the animal must be trying to escape.

Thud, thud, thud; the screams get louder.

Feilece cups his hands over his ears. The mechanical sounds of his mind operating and his quickened heartbeat take over. He tries letting the hum and beat soothe him but once he begins concentrating on them, they grow louder and quicker. He feels time speed back up. All thoughts of reality diminish. All Feilece hears is the erratic beats of his heart—slowing, speeding up and overlapping. Polyrhythmic sounds of chaos. It's still better than hearing their pain.

Feilece watches out of the window, the flow of time. Day to night to day to night. Before he knows it, a week's worth of cycles have gone by. The metronome of the days passing soothes his heart and the tempo slows down. His mind grows quiet. Feilece dozes off to sleep.

Feilece wakes to a world operating at a normal pace. It's night-time. He's starving. A bowl of meat soup is on the floor by the cabin's entrance. It looks like it's been there for a couple of days. Feilece doesn't care, he pours the cold soup into his mouth and devours the meat. It doesn't taste like beef or mutton. He can't hear Djent's thuds anymore. A disturbing thought enters his head. He throws the bowl down and scurries back, vomiting up the food.

The screams of his sisters have subsided into a single soft wail. It's Epo; he can't hear Niria at all. Could she be dead? Feilece shakes his head, trying to flick the thought from his mind. He tries to look for new thoughts to replace it but when he closes his eyes he sees his father crumbling into dust, his mother's headless body toppling to the floor, his brother's blood splashing against his face.

Tears fill Feilece's eyes and he lets out a wincing, sorrowful, growling, heave of breath.

"I was wondering when you would come back to me."

Feilece reacts to the voice of Kasi by frantically scrambling to the back of his cell.

"Hey, hey, hey. It's okay, I'm not going to hurt you. I heard some commotion and came to see if you were okay."

"Did … did you feed me Djent?" Feilece struggles to get his words out through his shivering.

"What's a Djent?"

As Kasi says the ram's name, Feilece hears a soft thud from Djent's cabin. Feilece's eyes flutter as he lets out a deep sigh.

Kasi opens the gate to his cabin and enters. Feilece keeps his distance, pushing himself against the wall.

"It's okay, Feilece, I'm here for your—"

"What's happening? What are you doing to my sisters?" Feilece interrupts. His voice is stifled and cracking, he hasn't spoken in over a week.

Kasi smiles. "Don't worry about them, they're going to be fine."

"I … I heard them screaming."

"We're helping them adjust. It can be painful at first, but they'll learn to enjoy it."

"Are you going to hurt me?"

"Oh, no, we're not going to hurt you, Feilece. You're special." She sits next to Feilece. She stretches out a hand to place on Feilece's knee but he pulls away.

Feilece can't control his shaking, tears torrent down his face, his mouth's agape.

Concern crosses Kasi's face. She tries placing a hand on Feilece again. This time, he lets her. Her hand is warm. It moves from his knee to his thigh. For a second, it soothes Feilece's rampant fear, and in that second, in his perception, time comes to a halt.

For what he counts as a full hour, he's stuck staring at Kasi, unable to move his eyes as they gaze into hers. In that hour, he can think of nothing other than her.

He memorises her face. Her beautiful hazel eyes, her smooth brown skin, her delicate nose, the cute mini-line of her nasolabial furrow, the curved joy wrinkles on the edges of her smile, her perfectly pointed chin. He could stare at this face until the end of all things, but visions bleed into his mind. His father teaching him how to wield an axe, his brother setting up the pinhole clock, his mother embracing him when he couldn't sleep. He sees his father standing in front of him, illuminated by the Mother's light … then the man starts crumbling. Slowly, his father's protecting presence drifts away in the wind, and on the other side of the ashen man, is the beautiful face of Kasi.

Time turns back to normal and Feilece finally re-acts to Kasi's touch by screaming and running out of his cell. Kasi calls to him but he doesn't stop.

Outside his cell, he trips into a pile of sheep bones. Horrified, he rises to a stand and catches sight of a bunch of Reapers hanging around, drinking and smoking outside his sisters' cabins. Feilece sees a squad of demons all preparing to devour him. He scrambles to his feet and rushes out of the stables.

Meeting the hot air outside, Feilece stops. His shoulders slouch and his knees sweat and shake.

What was once acres of empty farmland is now a town of tents stretching all the way to the forest. Each tent has a brazier on top housing a lit fire, lighting up the night sky with embers.

Sheep's Basin looks like it has been set ablaze.

"Feilece!" Kasi's voice increases Feilece's anxiety and he starts running. Gruff-looking warriors watch as the boy bolts through their ranks. He doesn't slow down, bumping into tents and boozed Reapers. He continues running, aiming for the maize fields his family shared with the Armens. Over his shoulder, he sees Kasi chasing after him, calling out his name. He doesn't stop.

A Reaper tries to grab Feilece but he dodges and stumbles into a homemade adobe furnace. The furnace tumbles into the Reaper, spilling embers everywhere and lighting him on fire. Reapers gather to put it out.

Feilece uses the distraction to escape. He reaches the fields of maize, pushing his way deep into the thicket until the sounds of the Reapers' camp becomes a distant background noise.

Adrenalin wears off and his steps become arduous. Feilece trips on a piece of maize and falls flat on his face. Lifting himself onto his knees, he can't help but contort into a screaming cry. He feels alone and helpless. His body feels ready to burst into flames until Kasi's embrace envelops him. Her calming energy seeps into his heart.

"You don't have to run from us, Feilece. We may look intimidating now, but we are friends. We are family, and you will find your way to us in time."

Feilece doesn't respond, he simply stares blankly into the blackness of the night.

"You are the son of the great executioner. Believe me, I know how daunting it can be. We are the children of fighters and killers … of soldiers."

"There is no war here!" Feilece blurts out his words. He is no soldier and neither was his father. They're simple farmers.

Kasi holds him tighter and lowers her voice into a whisper. "Budding boy, I was once like you. Sitting, wishing, feeling outside of it all. Waiting for things to correct themselves."

Feilece's defences loosen. He relaxes into Kasi's arms.

"Fighting … we're surrounded by it. Our first second in life is as long as our last. That's what my father used to tell me. I ran those words through my head as I watched Animia's axe hit his neck. I had hoped the sight of me made his last second somewhat joyous. But I realised later that it probably just made him worry."

Feilece feels a strange strength overcome him, a bubbling need to rectify something wrong. "Anema … My father's name is Anema. He was no fighter, the only time I saw him kill something was a sheep who had broken her leg."

Kasi hugs Feilece tighter. "Your father killed my father, my mother, my brothers. Your father wasn't only a fighter, he was a killer."

"I don't believe you."

"That's alright; you don't have to."

The two share a quiet moment. Feilece feels Kasi's breath upon his neck. From this alone, he can tell she's hurting. He feels her heartbeat on the back of his chest and his heart instinctively slows to meet the rhythm. He doesn't want to believe her about his father, but he knows she isn't lying.

"Why?" Feilece doesn't bother completing his question.

"Your father wanted to end the fighting. His family against mine. If they were both gone, there would be no one left for the war. But he was wrong. War is what Koilia is built upon. It's what Genus is built upon. In the grand scheme, all he stopped was a small feud. He wanted to stop the fighting the only way he knew how, by fighting. The thinking of a soldier."

"He wasn't a soldier, he was my dad." Feilece's words become hard to speak. "Why … did you have to … kill him. Why did you kill my brother? Mum … why did you cut off—"

Kasi spins him around and presses her lips to his.

Astonished and smitten by the woman's sudden action, Feilece's brain empties of thought. His entire body becomes numb.

She pushes him onto his back, continuing to kiss him. She reaches into his pants. Feilece feels her finger rubbing him. Relaxation flows from his pelvis throughout his body, making every muscle feel slack. He feels ensnared, trapped inside of her grasp.

Feilece is old enough to know that this is wrong, but also old enough to feel how amazing it is. He had only just picked up the habit of doing this to himself within the last year, but it never felt anywhere near as good as this. His back arches and hands grip as every cell in his body sparks.

Kasi leans in. She looks him deep in the eyes and whispers. "I love you, Feilece."

Growing up on a farm, Feilece doesn't have much of a framework for romantic love. He always knew of love, and he knew his parents loved each other differently to the way they loved him.

Before Feilece's mind has the chance to wander, Kasi steals back his attention. "Do you love me?"

The question sinks into the mixing pot of the boy's psyche, disintegrating and dissolving with his emotions and his hormones. He lets out a relaxed and hushed, "yes," and in that moment, Kasi's presence was solidified in Feilece's head, forever associated with feelings of affection, obsession, lust, protection, relaxation, ambition and adoration.

Kasi smiles and lies down next to him, holding him close. He feels her warmth like the heat of the Mother's light on a cold morning. Gazing into Kasi's pretty eyes, Feilece drifts off to sleep.

Kasi's whispers send him off into the black. "You will be a great soldier one day."

VIII

FEILECE'S SQUINTING RHEUM-FILLED eyes open to the sight of Kasi sleeping. His first thought is of how beautiful she looks as she slumbers. Feilece can't help himself, he leans in closer and kisses her on the mouth. A tingling sensation excites Feilece. It feels bitter and cold and it stings his heart, but he savours it nonetheless.

"She taste good, little boy?" a quiet husky voice asks from above.

Feilece jumps back and pushes himself against the maize surrounding them. He recognises the dark-haired man from the day of the invasion. The light-haired man is here too, standing with his back to his blackened counterpart.

The dark-haired man laughs at the sight of Feilece scampering.

"Please don't kill me," Feilece says, waking up Kasi.

"I will not kill you, little boy, for you are not yet worth killing."

"Brothers, a fine morning it is," Kasi says as she sits up, eyes squinting in the Mother's light.

The dark-haired man looks at Feilece then back at Kasi, judging them. "My, my, little sister. Don't you think the boy's a bit young?"

"I like him. I see in his eyes a type of affection I don't see very often." Kasi stands and stretches her arms out wide. Seeing her in the Mother's light, Feilece can't help but stare.

"A type of affection your husband, no doubt, does not provide."

"That, my prying sibling, is none of your business."

"You …" Feilece says, though he feels a pressure to keep his mouth shut. "You two are brother and sister? Like me and my sisters?"

Kasi gives Feilece a kind smile; he relaxes.

"We are brother and sister in every way that matters," she says. "But no, not exactly like you and your sisters. They are though." Kasi gestures towards the two men.

"That's not exactly true either. We are more than just brothers."

Kasi rolls her eyes.

The light-haired man stares intently at the horizon.

"What's he looking at?" Feilece asks.

"Out," the dark-haired man says.

"Huh?"

"He's not looking at anything, he's looking out. He's got that side, I've got this one."

Feilece doesn't understand. "Why hasn't he said anything?"

"Because everything he would want to say, I've either already said or am about to say."

"Will you stop confusing the kid," says Kasi, kneeling beside Feilece and placing a hand on his head. "The dark one is called Diakho, and the light one is Choris. I've known these two since I was born. After your father broke our family, they found me and took care of me. I wouldn't be alive if it weren't for them."

"They raised you?"

"Uh." Kasi looks back at Diakho. "More, I raised them."

Feilece gives up on trying to understand and tries to think of a way to make them leave so he can be alone with Kasi. "Why are they here?"

"That's a good question," Kasi says, standing and crossing her arms.

"Schizo sent us, he wants to know how Animia's youngest is faring."

The sound of Schizo's name makes Feilece want to curl up into a ball and never move again. Was Kasi's husband ... the man who killed half of his family?

"Tell him that Anema's son is in my hands. What he should be concentrating on is amassing more recruits."

Hearing Kasi correct his father's name, Feilece's shoulders relax.

"He said he wants an audience with the boy."

Feilece's shoulders tense again. His heart rate quickens, making everything feel faster.

"I forbid it," Kasi says forcibly.

Feilece's heart slows and his body relaxes. He looks at Kasi, face struck with awe. She's siding with him against her own husband.

"You forbid it ..." says Diakho.

"I forbid it."

"That's a strong word to use against one who relishes his freedom as much as he does."

"And I am not one to choose my words carelessly."

Feilece can't help but be impressed with the way Kasi speaks; she's fearless.

"You know he won't be pleased; he still hasn't gotten over Animia's death."

"Animia …" Feilece says but is too quiet for them to hear.

"He will forgive me," Kasi continues.

"That wyll you have over him, you must teach me the trick to it."

"That day will never come."

"Ani!" Feilece tries to speak loud enough to be heard but is overtaken by a wet cough. His fit demands everyone's attention, even Choris gives him an eye.

"Are you okay, Feilece?" Kasi rubs Feilece's back.

"That's … what you call my father."

Diakho speaks in his sinister voice. "Animia."

Animia's death. A flash of his father's decaying body blinks in Feilece's mind and he can't help but vomit up a dry heave of air.

Quickly, Kasi cradles the boy, pressing his head to her chest. "Oh, poor Feilece. It's okay. Just try to breathe."

Diakho scoffs. "Schizo told us the Animia blood was supposed to be strong."

"Don't be unbecoming, Diakho, show the boy some heart."

"Is that why we came here? Is that why we took turns stabbing swords into his father's back?"

"Stop it, Diakho."

"And as the man succumbed to wyll-death, and every skin and muscle cell crumbled into dust around the man's rib cage, were we showing heart then? I guess, technically, we were."

"Shut up!" Feilece stands and fires a furious look at the dark-haired demon. In this moment, Feilece feels more in control of himself than he's ever felt. His heart rate slows, and time slows with it.

Feilece shares a determined stare with Diakho for what feels like minutes. Reading the man's face, Feilece can almost pinpoint his exact thoughts. First the man acknowledges the boy, then grows a little respect.

In time, Feilece calms down and time returns to normal.

Diakho's voice adopts a tone of sincerity. "I apologise, little boy."

"Feilece."

"Yes ... Feilece."

Feilece looks at Kasi. Her eyes are half closed and a big grin grows on her face. "Ane ... my father ... What happened to him? Why did his body ..."

"Wyll-death," Diakho says.

"Will death ... what is that?"

Kasi stands and looks down at him. "Tell me, Feilece, what do you know of wyll?"

"Will? Isn't that just when someone does something?"

"Ah, will it, and it shall be done. Wyll, though it sounds the same, speaks more specifically to one's will to stay alive. When you lose the will to live ... well, you saw what happened."

"But why? Why did it happen? He was always so

strong ... Then he was just ... dust." Tears form in Feilece's eyes.

"You grew up on a farm," says Diakho, frowning. "I'm surprised you've never seen it before. Sheep wyll-die all the time."

"Not if they're treated right," says Kasi.

She kneels down, puts her hands on Feilece's shoulders and looks him in the eyes. "I don't have all the answers, Feilece. I don't think anyone has the right answers, but it is believed wyll belongs to the Child. That our wyll is the very ground we walk upon, and as we live, the Child lives with us. And when we die, we go back to Genus. I don't know how true it is, but it's possible your parents, and your brother, are where we all belong, back with the Child."

Feilece knows she's trying to cheer him up, but it's not working. Below his feet, all he feels is dirt. Now his family is dirt too.

"I'll go tell Schizo you're still working." The two long-haired brothers turn to leave. "I'll tell him you'll be back when you please."

"Tell him we will be back if and when Feilece chooses."

Feilece looks up at Kasi. "If?"

"Yes, if."

"Aren't I your prisoner?"

"Prisoner? No, that is not us. We are not like the pampered kings of Koilia. Every one of us is free to do as they please."

"So ... I can go?"

"Of course."

"And you'll come with me?" Feilece struggles to

keep the excitement out of his voice.

"Well, no. My place is with my people. In time, I hope you learn it is yours as well."

Feilece doesn't want to leave her side. He may have only known her a short time, but there's already no place he would rather be in Genus than with her. However, he can't give up this opportunity for his family. Though it makes him feel sick, he has to give Kasi up.

"Fine … I'll take my sisters and leave."

"Oh … I'm sorry, Feilece. They can't go with you."

Feilece's heart sinks in his chest. "What?"

Diakho steps in. "Your sisters are entertaining our troops. They're ours now. Consider yourself lucky. There's a lot of Reapers that would prefer you over your sisters. If it weren't for Kasi, you would be in your own cabin next to them."

"But … but you said … freedom." Feilece looks at Kasi.

"Yeah, well, it's difficult. If I let them go, I'm then going against the freedom of my family. If I have to pick one or the other …"

"You're a liar."

"They'll be free eventually, we just need them for a bit longer is all."

"Liar!" Feilece turns his back to Kasi and stares at the ground.

"I'm sorry you feel this way, Feilece," Kasi says, sighing. "I was really hoping you would stay with us. I really do love you. I'm going to miss you."

Feilece hears her footsteps, walking away. He already feels a churning guilt from his outburst. Why did he yell at her? He wishes he knew what to do. She says he's free, but he has no choice. He turns and runs back to Kasi's side.

IX

T HE MOTHER SHINES Her morning crescent light
down upon the land, illuminating the infant
Reaper village. Dorean kneels naked, tied to a stump
in the middle of a tent. Around her are bloodied
weapon caches and torture devices. Her body is
peppered with cuts that bleed and patches of burnt
skin.

Her legs are weak and shaking. Her vision is vacant
and dark, unable to sleep from the pain. Her mind is
almost broken, but her heart continues to beat, her
blood continues to flow, her wyll is intact.

The stocky woman sits on a chain in front of
Dorean, sharpening her leaf-blade with a grindstone.
She leans in close to Dorean's face and speaks in a low,
soft rasp. "Would you like to hear a story?"

Dorean offers no response.

"Once, there was a great house, belonging to a
great family. A prosperous family known as the
PanoApo Family, always distinct by their flowing blond
hair. It was said their hair was the source of their great
wealth, that the Child was attracted to the colour so he
adorned them with riches and long lasting life. They

were truly amazing, and their benefits spread out among those around them."

The stocky woman grabs Dorean by her hair and forces the girl to look at her. "Looking at this face, how old would you guess I am?"

Dorean's tired eyes slowly blink, unable to truly focus.

"Thirty? Forty years maybe? Not even close." She releases Dorean's hair and her head slumps back down. She stands and circles Dorean, running the steel of her blade across her skin.

"I served under them for eighty years, the majority of my life. I lived with them, I ate with them. I even had the honour of sleeping with a few of them. I was valued, like family, and gave my all for them. And they were an old family," she draws out the 'o' sound in old. "Some boasted about being around during war times. Some thought they were invincible, though, that's a pretty outdated concept now. I'll admit that even I believed it." She stops walking and her eyes stare. "Once, I saw an Apo with his limbs torn off, a week later, they'd grown back. But they weren't normal arms and legs that grew back, no, they had changed." Her eyes widen. "Deformed, spiked appendages. Purple and red blood could be seen flowing through the transparent skin. A horror to lay your eyes upon. Doctors said it was the way their wyll reacted to pain. Physical pain caused their mind to rot. They would begin losing their ability for complex thought and slowly devolve into bloodthirsty beasts akin to the demons of the old lore." She looks over at Dorean. "When word of this rare quality spread, it attracted the attention of a particularly vicious group of mercenaries … the group known as Demon."

Dorean screams as the leaf-blade harshly cuts across her cheek, letting loose a dribble of blood. The stocky woman puts her fingers under Dorean's chin and lifts her face up, letting the blood run onto her knuckle.

"They would capture members of the PanoApo Family and do this to them. Cut them, collect their blood." She rubs Dorean's blood across her forehead, painting a jagged frown on her face. "And wear the blood into battle, believing it made them live longer. They would torture the captured Apo until their wyll made them turn into those beasts, then set them loose against their enemies." She scowls. "Collecting my beloved family members like game monsters and battling them. It was sickening."

The woman spits on the floor. She stands over Dorean. "Me and my soldiers … we couldn't protect them by ourselves. We reached out to Demon's biggest rival, a well known group at the time called Sickle & Scythe. They seemed virtuous; always helping out small villages and families from animal attacks and bandits, and especially Demons. They were Koilia's heroes. Plus, they had one of the best warriors in all of the Abdominals, an executioner by trade, a man called Animia …"

Dorean's eyes widen. A memory resurfaces of her mother calling her father by that name. Plios was angry and blurted it out. It sounded like an insult, but it turned out to be far worse. Anema stayed in his room for days afterwards. Plios never called him that name again.

The stocky woman throws her sword at the

ground, embedding the blade in the grass. She grabs Dorean by the cheeks and makes her look into her eyes. "I met him, you know. A few decades ago, he and his fellows traipsed their stink into my home, staining the great PanoApo house in commoner filth. They were stoked, like a hungry fire, to have an esteemed house call on them for help. It meant a lot back then. They swore to provide protection against the Demons, but they were just sick lies. Your father looked me directly in the eyes and lied. The true demons that day were these so-called heroes. I watched your father, along with his fellows, do what they do best: slaughter. My friends, my colleagues, my family."

The woman's grip on Dorean's face gets stronger, digging her nails into her cheeks. "Watching your father's bones topple to the floor was one of the most gratifying sights my eyes have ever had the pleasure of viewing. Now, he gets to watch from below the soil as his daughters get raped, cut, maimed, burnt and broken. He gets to listen through the vibrations of the dirt to his family's screams. As I did mine."

Her grip tightens further. "For days, you wailed, asking why this was happening to you. Now you know."

Before the bones in Dorean's face break, the woman releases her grip. Dorean's head slumps.

"I will make you hurt," the woman continues, "more and more, until your mind fails and you lose all sense of yourself. From there, we will sculpt you anew, and you will be added to our ranks. Your father will then have to watch as his own kin die in the very wars he sacrificed his life to stop."

"Louma!" A voice calls from outside.

"What?" says the stocky woman.

"Popoki's asking for you."

"What does he want?"

"Hold on." A moment passes. "He's saying Schizo asked his generals to track down Kasi, no one has seen her since last night. The brothers have already been told."

"Mother fucker," Louma whispers under her breath, then she gets up and storms out of the tent, leaving Dorean in a daze.

Running the story through her head, Dorean's strength returns.

She thinks about her father; the goofy man she grew up with. She couldn't imagine him slaughtering anyone, the man used to cry when he had to put down a sheep. But then, she thinks back to the night before the invasion. His sad eyes as he told his family he loved them. He knew they were coming; he knew this was going to happen. The stories must be true, Anema was a killer. The man that raised her, and her simple little family, was an executioner who slaughtered people. Daughters, sons, mothers, fathers, families.

Louma was right, he was a demon. But he had changed, he was just a man, a good man. People can be rehabilitated. They didn't kill this Animia person, they killed an innocent man. Dorean can't let these freaks get away with what they've done. But what can she do? Strapped to a piece of wood in the middle of a torture tent in the middle of enemy grounds in the middle of nowhere.

She looks over at the sword Louma threw into the ground earlier. She estimates it's within reach.

X

STANDING OUTSIDE HIS old home, Feilece can't stop his eyes from producing tears. Half of the house is under renovation. The wall that stood behind the kitchen has been completely removed, with tables and chairs set up outside to make a communal eating area. Reapers chat and eat and walk around, as casual as Feilece used to. This is their home now.

"We can go somewhere else if you like, Feilece," says Kasi, her hand rubbing his shoulder.

Feilece doesn't reply, he doesn't know what he would like to do. He turns and casts his eyes over the farm. All the tents look less intimidating now that they're being illuminated by the Mother's light. Still, he can't stop crying.

A woman emerges from a nearby tent. Feilece recognises her; it's the stocky woman Dorean attacked on the night of the invasion.

"Kasi," the woman says as she approaches. "So the brothers found you. Quick bastards. I was given the order to come look for you. Someone better tell Popoki."

"Order?" Kasi asks.

"Right, request," she corrects herself.

"How many years will it take for you to learn you're no longer a slave."

"Habits die harder with age. If it makes you feel better, I wasn't going to take the order."

"Oh?"

"I knew those hunting brothers would be quicker. Plus, I have plans."

"How *is* your project coming along?"

"Nicely, I'm currently in the process of testing her strength."

Feilece can't help but wonder who the 'her' is that she speaks of.

"And yours?" the stocky woman asks, glancing at Feilece.

Feilece looks up at Kasi who gives him a kind smile and says calmly, "nicely."

"Have you seen the brothers?" Kasi asks her. "I sent them ahead of me earlier and I want to know if they've come by here yet."

"Sorry, I've been in the tent. It's been a busy morning. Speaking of which, my test is about to start. Pleasant morning to you, Kasi."

"And you, Louma."

Feilece watches her walk back towards the tent she came from. A curious thought makes him want to follow her but he's scared of what he'll find.

Feilece spots Choris stepping out of the house. The man crosses his arms and stares out at the sky.

"They're probably finished talking to Schizo now," says Kasi.

Feilece feels an uncontrollable jitter come over

him. "He's here? He's inside?"

Kasi rubs the back of Feilece's neck and he calms down. "It's okay, he won't disturb us unless I allow him. We do have to meet with the directors though, so you have to come inside."

Holding Feilece by the hand, Kasi directs Feilece into the house. He stands in the kitchen where he used to eat meals with his family, now he's surrounded by strangers.

Kasi goes up to Diakho. "Did you speak to my husband?"

"Fear not, little sister, Schizo has gone off to Tiris. He decided to do as you wished of him."

"Very good."

Feilece steps into what used to be his lounge. Feilece knows the feeling of the floorboards on his feet but his eyes barely recognise what they see. The place is completely redecorated in Reaper regalia. The rooms are in the process of being renovated; walls are missing and their old belongings are gone. The lounge is bereft of what once made it the Anemelos home. In pride of place is a large table, around which sit Reapers in robes of different colours. Feilece has seen these colours before; every tent outside is painted in one of them.

"This is the youngest?" says one of the reapers.

"His name is Feilece," Kasi says to the room. She then kneels down and looks Feilece in the eyes. "These, Feilece, are the directors. Every Reaper is designated a director and they are then responsible for that Reaper's wellbeing, their training, and pretty much every ..."

Feilece's concentration drifts away from Kasi's

words as his eyes fall upon the burned remains of a book in the fireplace; a blackened book spine with the word 'Chaos' on it. It's the same book Epo and Niria were fighting over the night before they invaded. That was the last night he will ever have with his family. His heart begins to beat quickly and time quickens with it.

Tears stream from Feilece face and he can't stop himself from bursting out crying.

"Hey, hey, it's okay," Kasi says as she wraps him in a hug.

"This is Animia's blood?" one of the directors says, unimpressed.

"Perhaps Schizo was wrong," another adds.

"Are we to start recruiting every crying baby north of Eftheia now?"

"Diakho," Kasi says in a dark tone while keeping her head still. "Cut the next one that speaks."

Diakho puts a hand on the handle of his dagger and the room goes silent.

Kasi takes Feilece's crying face into her hands and looks him in the eyes. "Hey, come with me, I want to show you something."

She takes Feilece's hand and leads him to his old room. His eyelids blink as they enter. It's almost the same as he left it. He instantly feels more comfortable; time slows back to normal.

"I told them to keep the room how it was in case you wanted it back. I've spent a couple of nights in here myself, I like the feel of the room."

She talks words that make the butterflies living in Feilece's stomach flutter. He walks over to her and gives her a hug.

"You may speak now, directors," Kasi calls out loud enough for those in the lounge to hear.

"Great, can we have our meeting now? We have information from our lord to relay to you."

"Come on, Feilece," Kasi says softly as she brings him back out into the lounge.

The directors talk among themselves.

"The siege on PanoApo castle was fierce."

"Apparently, the castle was taken over by berserkers after we were gone. They've turned it into a den of booze and debauchery. Such an insult."

"Fear not, we'll take it back in time."

"That depends on how fruitful this land is. We have amassed what forces we have left. We will see no more Reapers coming from Koilia."

"That can't be right," Kasi says. "There aren't nearly as many here as there should be."

"Not all of us could escape Koilia in time, Kasi."

"What are we looking at?"

"We're just short of a thousand Reapers."

A tear comes to Kasi's eye. "Are you telling me we've lost over two hundred family members?"

Seeing the Mother's light sparkle in Kasi's wet eyes, Feilece knows she is feeling a similar pain to his own.

The directors continue. "We will need at least four thousand strong to take a Koilian castle. Three thousand to meet on the field and the rest to launch assassination procedures. If Nomia hadn't driven us out, we'd probably have the force we need by now."

"How long will it take us to amass our new army?"

"Depends on the source. Where will we find strong individuals all the way up here?"

"Tiris is our best bet; it's close and has a large enough population."

"Tiris has issues." The gruff voice of Popoki interjects as he enters through the kitchen and approaches Diakho. "Thanks for telling me you had already found Kasi." His tone is sarcastic.

Diakho smiles. "Well, we're off. Have a good meeting."

"Where are you two going," says Kasi in a tone suggesting she already knows the answer.

"Hunting."

Feilece notices a concerned frown appear fleetingly on Kasi's face as she watches the brothers leave.

The meeting continues.

"What issues have your investigations yielded, Popoki?" asks one of the directors.

"The pros: Tiris is sovereign so there are no political ties to Koilia. The cons: Tiris was victim to a random attack a few years back. The town now suffers from a bad outbreak of weak wyll."

"The whole town? What kind of attack could spread such weakness?"

"A horrific one." Popoki takes a seat at the table. "Speaking to the residents, it seems some creature came in the night and killed over a thousand people. The morning after, mangled bodies and wyll-dead remains littered the streets."

"What could possibly cause such carnage?"

"I have no idea." Popoki casually pulls out a small sack of nuts and starts munching. "Whatever it was, it was bloodthirsty. There are no eye witness accounts of the perpetrator. What can I say, the Child can be cruel."

Popoki looks over at Feilece with sad empathetic eyes. "One must always be prepared for their entire life to be completely changed within a second."

Feilece looks at the grisly man. They make eye contact for a moment before Popoki looks away.

The directors continue. "With their wyll weak, they'll be easier to convert into Reapers."

"Yeah, but how long can one last if they're stricken with weakness?"

"We will make them strong, that's what we do, right? The weak are made tough by the Reaper label."

Popoki speaks in a sombre tone. "I wonder about that."

The whole room frowns at him.

Popoki puts his container away and stands back up. "In any case, Schizo's going to do what Schizo does; I'm going to go lie down."

"That was a short report."

"Life is better spent resting than it is talking."

Feilece thinks of Tiris. More frightened little boys just like him. The Reapers are going to invade Tiris like they did his home and take their people to war. He shudders as he thinks about it. As Popoki leaves, he shares one final look with Feilece. Feilece watches his eyebrows contort into a sad frown. A strange sincerity emanates from the man, something different from the rest of the invaders, even Kasi.

"Before you rest, may I request a favour of you?" Kasi asks Popoki.

"Request away, my lady."

"Can you check on Seemo for me?"

Popoki's eyes widen. "Must I?"

Kasi smiles. "I think it would be good for you both."

Popoki's eyes go red, as if he's about to cry. "I will do as you ask."

"Take your time, I suspect you will meet some of our friends along the way."

Feilece's eyes gaze as Kasi mentions time. He looks at the wall and sees his beloved clock. How did he not notice it until now? It's the only thing left in the room from his former life. He stares at the clock, letting his mind sync with the slow creep of the projected light.

Time slows. The Reapers talk but their voices are dragging, lagging and impossible to understand. Feilece lets their speech drift through the air without letting the words land on any particular part of his brain. He watches the clock and lets thoughts drift through his mind.

What's going to happen to him now? What will happen to his sisters? Are his sisters still alive?

There's nothing he can do. Should he have left when Kasi let him? Should he have gone into the woods, to his dad's boat, and sailed down river to Koilia? He doesn't know anything about sailing. And what would he do in Koilia? Send people to take his home back? Then they would kill Kasi.

He looks up at her. She's so beautiful, especially when she's moving so slowly. There's no way ... he can't let anything happen to her. He's stuck.

Kasi's face slowly turns angry as she speaks to the directors. Curious about what could be making her angry, Feilece lets time speed back up to normal.

"—will not have it! Feilece is one of us now, I won't put him back!"

"What?" Feilece says, shock slowly sparking in his chest.

Kasi looks down at him. "You're a Reaper, Feilece, these men can't make you do anything."

Flashes of his parents dying play in his head: Semnos' blood on his face, burning braziers, demon eyes, screaming sisters, Anema crumbling.

"No!" Feilece shoves Kasi away. "I am not one of you!"

Feilece's outburst causes the whole room to turn dark.

"Oh Feilece," Kasi says, closing her eyes. "Why did you have to say that?"

Kasi pulls away from him, distancing herself. Without her close to him, Feilece feels incredibly vulnerable, settling into a deep and freezing fear.

One of the directors stands and approaches Feilece. "If you are not one of us, then we will do as Schizo says."

Feilece stares at the intimidating man, shivering.

"You are to go back to the stables. We'll see how you fare without Kasi's protection."

The man puts a hand on Feilece's shoulder and Feilece sees time speed up incredibly as his heart rate spikes to the touch.

Feilece is dragged back to the stables and thrown back into his old cell. To him, the trip lasts less than a second. The Reaper says something but he's talking too fast for Feilece to hear. The man speeds off and Kasi shows up, time slows back down.

"Kasi, help me."

"Don't worry, Feilece, I won't let them hurt you."

"Why does it have to be like this? Can't we go back to my room?" Feilece can't keep the desperation out of his voice.

"Not after what you said, Feilece."

Feilece can't help but curl into a ball. "I'm sorry."

"It's okay, Feilece. Soon, you will see things our way. Then we can be together. Please, don't make me wait too long." She waves then leaves, not taking her eyes off him until she's outside the stable. Feilece is once again left alone, with nothing but the sounds of his distressed sisters to keep him company.

XI

DOREAN SLUMPS HER shoulders to give her hands access to the rope binding her ankles. She fiddles around with the knot, mapping out the orientation of the rope in her head. It seems to be a farmer's loop, a knot Dorean would likely know. Why would they choose this knot? She unties her legs then tries to fiddle with the knot on her wrists but can't reach. She will need the sword … the sword Louma left for her. Dorean throws the thought away, she doesn't have time to dawdle.

She props herself up on one knee and wraps the top of her opposing foot around the handle of the sword. She tries pulling the sword towards her but it's embedded too far in the ground; it doesn't budge.

Her knee is tired, her legs have pins and needles, and her shoulders feel like they're about to dislocate, but she keeps holding strong. She kicks the sword handle hard enough to bruise her ankle. It tilts towards the ground. With her heel, she presses down on the handle of the sword. The sword's hand-guard presses against the floor, leveraging the blade from the dirt.

Dorean closes her eyes and takes a breath, reward for progress.

"THAT'S GOOD." DOREAN hears the voice of Anema as she plays a flashback of him teaching her how to chop wood in her head. "Make sure your grip is tight, you don't want the thing bouncing back and smacking you in the face, trust me."

Dorean's hands shake. "What if I do it wrong?"

"Then try again. It's just wood, it's not gonna hurt you. You have to just make sure not to hurt yourself."

Dorean raises the axe up and brings it down on the stump. The log breaks in two.

"I did it!"

"Very nice, how do your wrists feel?"

"A little bit sore but they're alright."

"Then you can keep going." Anema picks up another log and places it on the stump.

Dorean picks up one of the halves of the wood she cut. "I want to celebrate; I'm a lumberjack now."

"Hah!" Anema takes the wood from her hands. "This is just the start," as he throws the wood in the pile. "Do not rejoice small victories, Dorean, not when there's still work to be done."

DOREAN'S EYES SNAP open. She pulls the sword close to her then bends down to grasp the sword handle in her teeth. She tastes Louma's gross hand sweat, but she keeps her teeth clenched.

She lifts the sword and rests it on her shoulder. It's

harder than she thought it would be, she takes another small breath. Then she hears footsteps on the grass outside.

In a panic, she slides the sword down her back. The blade cuts at her arms, but the pain is something she has grown accustomed to. She holds the blade in her fingers and rubs the rope up and down on the edge.

Louma walks back into the tent, catching Dorean in the act. "Well, look at this. You really do have your father's wyll." Louma approaches Dorean slowly as she speaks.

Dorean cuts a hand free and releases herself from the pole. She quickly aims the sword at Louma. Louma gives a patronising smile.

"You know you can't beat me with that thing, and you're stuck in here with me. You either surrender now, or I take back my sword and make you," Louma says, sternly.

Dorean, thinking faster than she ever has before, quickly turns and slices a hole in the back of the tent.

"Huh, clever," Dorean hears Louma say as she rushes out of the opening.

The sudden light of the Mother blinds Dorean but she doesn't let it stop her. She runs without direction, stumbling into another tent.

"What the fuck!" yells a voice inside.

Hemp fabric wraps around Dorean as she falls, and she struggles through it. When she gets back to her feet, her eyes have adjusted to the light.

She can't believe her eyes. Her precious home has been reduced to a den for these torturous barbarous fucks. Her heartbeat rises, her skin goes hot, her pain lessens, her fists clench and shake. These Reaper shitheads will pay with their lives.

A confused and annoyed man crawls out of the tent Dorean knocked down. Dorean puts her blade to the man's throat while he's still half stuck in the tent.

"Woah," the man says cautiously, looking up at the naked and bloody teenager. "Alright, calm down, lady."

She's never killed anything but chooks before, the thought of taking this man's life makes her queasy. But if she doesn't kill him ... There's no way she's going back.

Dorean looks up and sees Louma step outside the torture tent. The two women, separated by a bunched up heap of hemp, eyeball each other. Whatever happens, Dorean swears that monstrous bitch won't have her plaything back.

Dorean looks back at the man. This arsehole's tent was right across from hers the whole time. He sat, this whole time, listening to her screams and cries ... and he did nothing.

Dorean looks back at Louma. Without taking her eyes off her, Dorean pushes the sword through the man's neck.

Louma gives a sinister grin.

Dorean pulls the blade free and runs away. Reaper tents mask the Basin, nothing looks as it was, but having grown up here, she knows its every elevation and grass type. She knows exactly where she is and where she needs to go. West, to the forest, to the river, the old plan is still in play. She races past series after series of tents, trying to keep herself hidden wherever possible. Realising that her naked body will attract attention, she cuts some hemp from an empty tent and wraps it around herself.

Continuing towards the forest, she notices there aren't many people around considering how many tents there are. This is suspiciously easy.

Closer to the forest, Dorean catches sight of the stable. Her heart pounds. It's Feilece. She sees her brother being dragged by his wrist into the stable. He's in another trance.

Instinctively, Dorean wants to help him but if she's caught now, she'll lose this opportunity.

Tears stream from her eyes. With everything she's been through, she shudders to think what they've been doing to her younger siblings. Something tells her these freaks won't go easy on them just because they're kids. She falls to her knees and drops the sword to the ground. There's nothing she can do for them. She has to hope they can last however long it takes for her to bring help.

"Farmer girl!" Dorean shudders. Louma is coming.

"Where are you, farmer girl!"

Louma is tracking her but she hasn't spotted her yet. Dorean wipes the tears from her eyes, grabs her sword and continues into the forest.

Feeling safe, Dorean takes a quick rest, slumping her aching body down next to a thick tree. She can't stay for long, Louma will still be tracking her. She tries getting up but it's much harder to move her body now that it has felt the soothing feeling of stopping.

Dorean wants to close her eyes, but if she does,

she'll be asleep within seconds. She can't let that happen. She takes the blade and cuts it across her wrist to remind her of the pain of torture. She holds onto the feeling to help force her mind into action. She takes the hemp from her chest and wraps it around her arm to stop the bleeding. Noticing the rope that once bound her hands is still attached to one of her arms, she briefly contemplates cutting it off but figures a rope could come in handy. She wraps a loose thread around a branch and uses it to lift herself to her feet. Her legs are almost non-responsive. It'll be hard but she will continue on, she has too. She carries on towards the river, telling herself she can rest when she's on her father's boat.

The bruise on her ankle gets worse as she staggers through the woods. She can really feel the pain now that her adrenalin isn't as potent. For an hour, she pushes herself from tree to tree, resting for a second or two now and again. There has been no sign of Louma since she reached the forest, but she has been seeing things, and feeling things. A dark presence.

She would see a face for a split second in a dark recess of a tree, or an arm or a leg, but as soon as she tries to focus on it, it's gone. Black. She leans against a tree and wonders if the trauma of what she's been through is messing with her head. She wonders if the things she sees are demons manifesting from her mind. She wonders if she'll ever be normal again.

Dorean stops and looks around. It's quiet, she feels alone. The boat's too far away, she needs to rest. She sits at the base of a nearby tree and, finally feeling safe enough, she closes her eyes. If she's going to remember her father's rowing lessons, she needs to regain energy. She can feel her mind drifting off to sleep but as her ears relax, she hears something that invigorates her. Rushing water.

She's closer to the river than she thought. She pushes herself to a stand. Freedom is right there; she can hear it. Strengthened, she continues.

Her rope hand sways in front of a tree and the loose thread moves in the wind. Dorean hears a dense thud and her arm jerks back. Confused, she looks at her wrist. Following the rope to the tree, she finds an arrow pinning her rope to the trunk.

Dorean starts breathing in short bursts. Her eyes dart in the direction of where the arrow is pointing and land upon a man standing a few hundred meters away. He has long white hair, and a long bow is in his hand. He hit a moving rope from such a distance, his precision is uncanny.

Dorean sees him pull another arrow from his waist quiver and load it onto the string. Quickly, she cuts the rope from her arm and hides behind the tree, hearing another thud upon the bark. Her heart thumps in her chest. She's too afraid to move. An arrow hits the ground next to her foot and she screams. Frantic, she runs deeper into the woods.

Arrows hit the ground and trees close to her as she runs. With the man's aim, she should already be dead. Every time Dorean sees an arrow, she runs in the opposite direction. The white-haired man is herding her.

Dorean moves without thought, too scared to give her brain a second of cognition. Two knives dart into the ground in front of her, causing her to halt. She looks up and standing on a tree branch is the black-haired man.

The man smiles. "Hi."

He's the presence she felt; they've been hunting her the whole time.

An arrow flies past her head and she screams, continuing to flee. She runs until she comes across a small meadow in the middle of the woods. The arrows cease. A massive smooth slab of rock sits in the middle of the meadow. She recognises this monolith.

Her legs give out, and she stumbles into the rock; she struggles to catch her breath. The canopy is less dense, letting the light of the Mother shine through in large rays. Her eyes stay alert, scoping the trees, looking for movement. They find nothing but branches swaying in the wind.

She uses the downtime to let her legs rest. It's not long before she sees a silhouette of something among the trees. It doesn't look human. It has the parts of a person but they're not in the normal positions.

As the creature gets closer, Dorean's heart begins to thump again. She tries to get up but her legs don't want to move. She shifts herself back, laying them out in front of her and hits them, trying to get feeling back.

The creature comes into the light and Dorean freezes. Her body quakes.

Big blonde hair, dishevelled and covered in greenery. A crazed look in its beaming yellow eyes. Its legs are normal, revealing this was once a normal girl's body … but the torso. Large bulbous purple growths have burst through the skin on her chest and back. Her arm's dangle out of place. Blood can be seen flowing through the growths, and it drips from them, staining the grass.

Dorean can't move, she can't speak, she can't think. What her eyes see horrifies her. It's unlike anything she could even imagine.

The beastly looking woman screeches and races towards Dorean, hunger plastered across her face.

Dorean's instincts kick in and she picks up her sword, aiming it at the beast with both hands. The blonde doesn't sway, she throws herself onto the sword trying to get to Dorean. The sword grinds as it pierces through, as if the purple skin has the texture of stone.

Dorean, flat on her back, holds the beast at bay as it tussles above her. The growths restrict her arms, they flail by her sides fruitlessly. The thing bites at the air close to Dorean's face.

Dorean keeps her strength holding the sword up, but the beast drips blood on her. It burns Dorean's skin like embers from a fire. She doesn't know how long she can keep this up. But before her strength gives out, a man wraps his arm around the beast's neck and pulls it away. Dorean lies there, breathing heavily.

"Popoki? Why?" Dorean hears Louma's voice.

It can't be. All this just to get recaptured. She focuses her eyes on the man holding the beast, it's the bald man that attacked her brother.

He talks with a low, grizzled voice. "I won't let you use Seemo for your sick games." His voice is calm, as if he isn't holding a grotesque monster in his arm.

He holds her at arm's length and looks into her manic eyes. "You poor thing."

He pulls the sword from her chest and pushes her to the floor. The beast writhes as the stab wound heals and another plump purple growth grows from it. Then she whimpers and scampers into the forest.

"See what you did? Now she's even worse," Popoki says to Louma as she walks into the meadow. "You were a PanoApo guard, I thought you would show a bit more compassion to your own."

"She is no longer an Apo; she is no longer Seemo. Do yourself a favour and see her for what she is," Louma says.

"What would Kasi think about you getting her beloved sister stabbed?"

"Well, Diakho was supposed to knock the sword out of her hand when she was in the forest. Blame him. Plus, I was kind of hoping we could keep this between us."

"Of course you roped Diakho and Choris into this."

"They wanted to see a real demon in battle."

"I thought you hated Demons."

Popoki turns to Dorean and helps her sit up.

"I'm coming around to them," Louma says, sneering.

Popoki hands Dorean a canteen of water and she sculls it back feverishly.

"Why are you helping her?" says Louma.

"She's been through a lot."

"Yeah, that's the point."

"Why couldn't you stick to the normal forms of torture?"

"It wasn't working. She was too strong. I needed to

get creative."

Dorean stares into Popoki's eyes. It was all a test.

The grizzled man places a warm hand on her shoulder. "It's okay, girl. Soon, the pain will end. I'll be proud to call you comrade."

XII

FEILECE SITS IN his cabin, hugging his knees. The sounds of his sisters being abused fill the stable. He can hear Epo's cries and screams clearly, but Niria, he can barely hear at all.

He rocks back and forth. He wants to see Kasi, he wants to feel her skin and smell her hair and kiss her lips. It's all he can think about.

Some time has passed since he declared he was not a Reaper and chose to come here. A regret that has solidified in his mind like a callus on the knuckle of a broken fist. Gone are the thoughts of his family. He sits and waits, day after day, for Kasi to come back and ask him to become a Reaper. If asked, he would jump at the opportunity and scream yes as loud as he could. Then he could stay in his old room ... with Kasi.

He would do anything, he would go to war, he doesn't care. He wants to be by Kasi's side. He just has to keep waiting.

The Reapers haven't done much to maintain the stable since they invaded. Feilece notices a wooden panel about to come loose in his cabin. He watches it swaying in the slight breeze, it's almost mesmerising.

The panel finally detaches and falls to the ground, giving Feilece a view into the neighbouring cabin. His eyes stress at the sight he sees. Niria is being violated. Feilece recognises the Reaper, he was one of Semnos' school friends.

Why … Why is this happening? Niria is barely responsive. She lays there, splayed out, eyes solemn and vacant. She's only a few years older than Feilece; they've stolen everything from her.

Niria's eyes latch onto Feilece's. He sees them strain; she has no energy to move anything else. It's as if she was in a daze and the sight of Feilece has sparked her back into reality. With a staggered creeping movement, her arm reaches towards Feilece.

Looking into her eyes, he can read her thoughts. She wants to touch her brother: the touch of someone who doesn't mean to harm her. A remembrance of the old life she once had. But Feilece is scared. He wants to reach out and grab her, but he knows that if he does, they'll see him. They'll think he still has love for his old family and won't let him become a Reaper. They'll hurt him like they hurt her. He'll never see Kasi again.

Niria's eyes strain further, silently screaming at him 'please, brother!' but Feilece won't move. He wants to, he tries to, but his arms just shake in place. There's a disconnect between his body and brain; his heart and his mind at odds.

Niria's eyes dim. Her skin starts to flake, dropping like dust to the stable floor. Her face first, then her shoulders, her torso. Her reaching arm is the last to be affected.

"What the fuck!" The Reaper paedophile stumbles

back, as the girl disintegrates in his hands.

"You fucking idiot!" A second, older Reaper enters Niria's cabin and slams him against the wall.

"I don't know what happened, I was just … and then this!" the young man says, panicking.

"Yeah, you moron, you were supposed to be hitting her. Smacking her around, keeping her angry to stave off depression. Your little cock fucked the wyll right out of her."

"It's a shame." A new, calmer voice enters the conversation. "She was so close to breaking."

The angry Reaper turns and kneels for the newcomer. It's the old man who was there when the Reapers first arrived.

"Rago, sir, forgive the lad. The simpletons around these parts don't teach their kids much about wyll. He was bound to be a fuck-up."

Rago speaks in monotone, the calculating voice of a pragmatist. "It is not the young man I blame. The act of indoctrination on the unwilling is a difficult process. One must know the point at which they lose their old life so you may inject a new one … and you gave this task to an amateur recruit with a tenuous grasp on the mechanics of wyll at best." The old man's voice doesn't change with his words but even Feilece can tell he's angry.

"You're correct, Rago. This is my fault."

"Now we are down precisely one viable convert. And she was so young, with so much potential. How do you think Schizo will react when he finds out you lost one of his precious Animia spawn?"

"No … I'll make it up to him!"

"There aren't many of Animia's children left, how will you pay for this misdeed?"

The Reaper man shifts closer to Rago and whispers; Feilece can't hear him. They haven't realised Feilece can see them through the broken panel; he knows they're talking about him. An annoyed expression appears on Rago's face.

"You imbecile."

"Why not? He's just sitting there. I know Kasi said we can't touch him but if I can convert him—"

"He is male."

"So?"

"You know nothing of conversion therapy. The male mind is weaker and more prone to depression. Trying to force out their prior attachments, like what is required for the more emotionally aware sex, will only result in lost wyll. Do you want to go to Schizo with two piles of bones instead of one?"

"If we can't convert him then why is he even here?"

Feilece doesn't want to listen to them anymore. He instead focuses on Niria. His poor, beloved sister. Visions of her playing, her laughing, her smiling, stream through Feilece's head. He looks at her outstretched hand, watching as the decay spreads down her forearm towards her hand.

If he had grabbed her hand, she would still be alive. He just killed his sister. The thought causes his heart to stop. He feels it seize halfway through a beat, and with it, time stops also.

He can't move, not even his eyes. He is stuck in time, staring at his sister's hand. Through his peripheral vision, he can see the two Reaper's have seen him, but they too are stuck in time. Semnos' old friend hugs himself in the corner of their cabin.

Feilece attempts to make time move but cannot. Deep down, he doesn't want it to. Without time, things cannot get worse than they already are. In complete stillness, the only freedom to be had, is the freedom of mind.

He sifts through his thoughts at a slow pace, slogging through regret, anguish, guilt, fear, identity, past, future, loyalty, fealty.

He thinks about who he is as a member of the Anemelos family, who he would be as a Reaper, who he is as an inhabitant of Genus as a whole.

Because he failed to save his sister, is he a monster like Schizo? Is there any way to save the rest of his family, and have a life with Kasi? Is he selfish for wanting to be with Kasi?

He loses track of how long he spends running through the same thoughts over and over again, never falling on a single answer for any of his questions, or solutions to any of his problems.

He wonders what the point of everything is. Are the stories his mother told him real? Does he really live on the torso of a giant child that was abandoned by its mother at the beginning of time? Is that really the eye of the Mother in the northern sky, blinking to the rhythm of day and night as She watches over all of the cosmos? Or is he just on a big piece of dirt? Was he only watching the projection of a candle flickering on his wall when he used to sit by the pinhole camera? Will the Mother never return to claim Her Child, because there is no Mother or Child? No design … no higher field of consciousness. Just Feilece, and a pocket of abstract time where nothing matters.

He's too young, too confused, but at least he knows it. He can't be expected to know the answers to anything, he first needs growth and experience. He forfeits to his naivety, then chooses to journey towards maturity. Think deeply and learn the mechanics of the mind. He is convinced answers can be found in time and without the ability to restart his heart, he has all the time he needs.

He plays old memories in his head, pleasant memories with family, over and over. He switches them around, envisioning scenes from other people's perspectives: weeping through his father's eyes as he's forced to kill sheep; exiting his brother's school doors to the sight of a loving family after a hard week's study; seeing himself through the eyes of Kasi as she kisses him. Of all the memories he plays around with, the one sexual experience he had with Kasi is the only memory that doesn't get boring.

He meticulously analyses everything in the memories, picking out information he didn't notice at the time, experiencing everything with a different light. He feels a familiarity with the celestial Mother, shining his light upon his own world as She shines Her light down upon Genus.

He learns a lot through his efforts but with only a little over a decade of life preceding this moment, he doesn't have much of a memory to draw from.

After a few years of being stuck in this bubble of stillness, his entire past becomes dull.

To stave off boredom, he begins employing his imagination to make the memories more colourful and exciting. Before long, the new memories are nothing like the old. Almost every memory has Kasi in there somewhere, cheering Feilece on and rewarding him.

The sexual memory he held with Kasi grows into something much more extravagant than a simple working of her hand. Through nothing but the stagnation of unmoving time, Feilece's mind teaches itself an ability that's hard to come by on Genus, the gift of fantasy.

As his talents for imagination grow, he conjures up potential futures. Delusions of fiction begin to feel far more important than reality.

XIII

———❧———

STARING DOWN A brute twice his size with a giant scythe in his hands, Feilece, a young adult, twirls his axe in his hand casually. With a bleating roar, the brute swings his scythe in a murderous arc. Feilece smirks, dashes at his opponent, flips over the scythe and embeds his axe in the brute's head.

The thud of the corpse hitting the ground is accentuated by cheers from Feilece's comrades.

"Someone fetch my breastplate." Feilece's voice is low and tough.

"Here, sir. Can I ask, why you didn't wear it in battle?" The cute voice comes from one of the prettier recruits.

"Makes it too easy. A battle is no fun if your life isn't on the line."

The girl's eyes bloat. "Hey, you should come by my tent later. I'm having a few friends over." She follows her words with a coy nibble of her bottom lip.

"If I have time."

Feilece dons his armour then turns to address the army of his fallen opponent. They all look upon the large insignia on his chest: a sickle crossed with a scythe in front of two large demon eyes.

He speaks loud enough for all to hear.

"Your leader rests among the dirt! I ask you: will you follow him? Or will you follow me?"

"What is your name, soldier?" A faint voice comes from the crowd.

"You may call me Animia!"

"It can't be!"

"Animia lives?"

"That's impossible!"

Voices come from the crowd. In awe, they murmur among one another.

Feilece goes to turn away but his eyes stop upon a little naked girl among the crowd. Her skin glows yellow, as if emitting the light of Mother. He decides to ignore her and retreat back to his quarters.

He enters into his tent to the sight of the cute recruit lying naked in his bed with two of her friends. "We couldn't wait, and we know how fixated you are on time."

Feilece smirks, removes his clothes and joins them. He finishes them one after another, over and over, until they extract all the energy the man can muster. Smothered in clouds of bliss, Feilece falls into a deep sleep.

"Well, isn't this erotic."

Feilece wakes to the voice of Kasi at the entrance to his tent. He sits up and smiles at her. "Is that jealousy I detect?"

"No, just disappointed I didn't get an invite."

"If it's any consolation, you were here the whole time." Feilece taps the side of his head.

Feilece gets out of bed, puts his pants on, and meets Kasi with an attempt at a kiss but she leans away.

"Ah, wash your face first. I don't know what lips those lips have been on."

"Fair enough."

They exit together and walk by a series of tents housing the ever-expanding Reaper army.

"I wanted to come and see you after your victory yesterday but I was tied up with Schizo," Kasi says, holding herself close to Feilece. "He says he's very proud of you."

"Pride," Feilece says, annoyed. "It's an insult. He thinks he can replace my father. He doesn't hold a candle to that man, or any Anemelos for that matter. And don't worry about it, it turns out I was rather entertained last night without you."

"Harsh," Kasi says, raising her eyebrows. "But I will say, three girls … you must be getting better."

"The great Animia has a standard he must stick to."

"I wanted to ask about that. Why have you adopted your father's name?"

"It's not his name, his name was Anema," Feilece says. "Though I cannot deny the power his old title has over this land. I want to remind everyone of who he was."

Feilece looks up at the Mother. "Animia is my inheritance. Also, I would be happy to show you how 'good' I've become if you weren't spending so much time with Schizo."

They reach a water reservoir and Feilece fills up a bucket. He sees a yellow light glowing in the flowing liquid.

"You know, he's not as bad as you think he is," Kasi says, while Feilece splashes his face with water.

"No, Kasi, you are wrong. You've been wrong the whole time. Schizo has been using you for your connection to the old Demons. Listen." Feilece holds her close and looks deep into her eyes. "He could never love you like I do."

Kasi doesn't reply, she just stares with infatuated eyes at Feilece.

"He has his castle now," says Feilece. "We helped him get here, now we can be done with him. Soon, I will be making a move … and I hope you are there with me in the end."

"Oh, I don't know, Feilece," Kasi says.

"Look, I know it's hard to have to choose between us, and telling you about this is a gamble for me because of it. But I don't care. I know you'll make the right choice."

Passionately, Feilece presses his lips to Kasi's and they embrace under the shadow of the PanoApo castle.

A GIRL'S SOFT hand, bone extending from the wrist.

FEILECE WALKS INTO the throne room. It's giant and magnificent, with a high ceiling of stained glass. It looks like something out of a children's picture book. Schizo sits upon his extravagant throne. Kasi sits next to him, wearing a frown. The entire castle has been renamed to 'The Towers of Schizo'. The arrogance makes Feilece sick.

"Ah, Feilece, a pleasure to make your acquaintance. Or ... should I be calling you the great Animia now?" Schizo's voice is full of smarm.

"May I approach?" Feilece asks.

"Of course, you're my star soldier, I can't deny *you* entrance."

Feilece approaches. He sees his sisters, Dorean and Epo, on either side behind Schizo. They're fully clad in armour. He made them his personal guard. Feilece's brow furrows at the sight of them, a small leak of the hatred burning within.

He stands before Schizo, a few metres from the man play-acting as a king.

"So, what matter may I help you with today, young Feilece?" Schizo's face holds an egoist's smile; he's loving every moment upon his new throne. The thought of tearing him from that throne causes Feilece to adopt his own smile, one with a sinister twitch.

He stands at the bottom of a set of steps leading to the platform where Schizo sits.

"I'm here for one simple matter," he says, pulling an axe from his waist and aiming it at Schizo. "Your death."

"Is that so? And how do you intend to pull that off?"

"I'm going to walk up these steps and cut off your head like you did my mother. Like I said, it's simple."

"You know, I find it a shame. You were just a small farmer boy, destined to be nothing but a small farmer boy. You would've died in your boring hills like one of your sheep. But I picked you up, and brought you to a world where you could shine and be glorious. Look how far you have come … you would seek to throw it all away, and for what? Revenge? How juvenile."

Feilece ponders his reply, unable to set aside the truth in the man's words.

"Revenge? No. Don't get me wrong, it will be sweet. But that's not why I'm here. You asked if you should call me Animia before … well, tell me, does it suit?"

Schizo frowns. "You're not saying …"

"Yes! I am here to finish what my father couldn't. I'm here to put an end to your bloodthirsty wars. I fought and killed for you, so you could sit upon this throne you wanted so badly. I wanted to give you this feeling so I could have the pleasure of pulling it out from under you."

"Tell me," Schizo says, sighing. "After everything we've been through, did you grow any love for me at all?"

"It's because of everything we've been through … everything you've put me through. All that grew in me was hate."

"Well, luckily for me, I still have some that love me." He looks over at Kasi. "Enough to help me prepare for this exact meeting."

Feilece and Kasi share a wary expression with each other. Schizo steps up from his throne and shouts out, "guards!" Within a few seconds, Feilece is surrounded by spearmen, all pointing their weapons at his neck.

"You should not have trusted Kasi." Schizo slowly

walks down the stairs towards Feilece. "I tasked her to make you into a great warrior and here you are, a product of her good work. Perhaps, she did too good a job."

Feilece keeps his eyes engaged with Kasi's. He doesn't show any anger towards her, or disappointment. He just smiles. A tear escapes Kasi's eye.

"You know she never loved you." Schizo's words cause Feilece's gaze to flicker, and he stares at the Reaper lord.

"If I had asked her to murder you in your sleep, she would've done so without hesitation. And I would have made her do it if I ever thought you were a threat. She's told me all your little secrets; about the times you've wanted to murder me. But I kept you around. You owe me your life, boy."

"You are wrong, Schizo. The only thing I owe you is death. You will die, and I will take Kasi far from here. Mark my words." Feilece talks calmly.

Schizo grimaces. "What do you know! Idiotic little soldier, I made you! I am a king now! What could you know of my death?"

"I know it may come sooner than you expect." Feilece gives the king a coy smile.

"You know what?" Schizo says. "I'm going to have Kasi kill you. You will know the feeling of having someone you thought loved you stab you in the—" Schizo coughs and gargles up blood as the blade of a sword comes bursting through his chest. Kasi stands behind him, holding the sword's grip.

Feilece quickly jumps into action, deflecting the spears away from his face and engaging the guards in vicious combat. Epo and Dorean join the battle, fighting alongside their brother.

Schizo slowly turns to Kasi, face in shock. "Why? You said you'd … chosen me."

"I changed my mind," Kasi says.

With help from his sisters, Feilece dispatches the guards. The two Anemelos sisters approach the dying Reaper king.

First, Dorean says, "Semnos sends his regards," and then she stabs her sword through the man's stomach.

Then Epo says, "as does Niria," and follows her sister's lead, stabbing the king's abdomen.

Feilece feels a warmth inside himself. He looks up and sees a yellow glowing girl on the opposite side of the stained glass in the roof.

Schizo's legs give way and he falls down the steps to Feilece's feet, stealing his attention. Feilece kneels down, grabs Schizo by the throat and squeezes.

"You sealed your fate the day you killed our parents. You spoke of freeing the land through conquest, but you were never anything more than a barbaric murderer, a monster without a heart."

As Feilece speaks, Schizo's skin begins to darken and turn to ash.

"Today, you die a broken man!" Feilece lifts his axe up high and brings it down on Schizo's neck, cleaving his head from his body.

Schizo's body and head crumble away until only his bones remain.

Kasi throws herself into Feilece's arms and the two embrace. "I'm so sorry, Feilece."

"It's okay, I knew you would come around in the end."

"What now, brother?" asks Dorean.

Feilece puffs out his chest. "The Reapers fight for a cause, to liberate the city of Koilia and bring strength to the people. Schizo was never needed for that and a lot of Reapers didn't trust him for the task anyway. But the Reapers do need a leader, someone needs to direct them towards the goal."

"So that was the plan. Steal the throne and carry out father's will to end the wars," says Epo.

"No … the throne will not be mine. I will not ask the Reapers to trust a usurper to be their leader. But luckily, there is someone better suited for the task. Or, rather, two someones."

"Who?" Dorean and Epo ask in unison.

Feilece smiles at them. The two sisters look at each other for a second then back at Feilece.

"You want us to lead the Reapers?"

"Tell the Reapers Schizo died by my hand." Feilece looks deep into Kasi's eyes. "Tell them I kidnapped Kasi. Tell them I've gone far away." A smile forms on Kasi's face.

Feilece turns back to his sisters. "I wasn't the only one to inherit the title of Animia. It rests with you now, my beloved sisters." He rests his hands on their shoulders. "You two will make this world great."

NIRIA'S HAND.

FEILECE TENDS TO his crops. He wipes his brow and looks out at the horizon. With beautiful yellow Abdominal skies overhead and lush grass all around, Feilece breathes in the sweet air of the endless farm-land. Djent runs up to the middle-aged Feilece and nudges him with his horns. The ram is old but still as strong as ever. Feilece pets him tenderly and lets out a sigh. Never before has he ever felt so at peace.

Feilece enters his humble farmhouse to the beauti-ful sight of Kasi reading to their three wonderful daughters. Feilece sits down with the girls and Kasi smiles at him, then continues reading. Feilece stays until the end of the story, letting the girls drift off to sleep in his arms.

They put the girls to bed. Once Feilece's arms are free, Kasi nestles into his embrace. They kiss. They stare into each other's eyes and Feilece knows this is the best world he could ever be in.

A budding teenage boy dashes into the house.

"Dad!"

"Hush, now, the girls nodded of to sleep."

"Oh … sorry."

"It's alright, Anema." Feilece lets go of Kasi to give his son his full attention. "Now, what's the matter? Did you have fun at the neighbours?"

"Yeah, it was great! There was a young woman there, the most beautiful woman I've ever met."

"Wow, besides your mother here, we don't see many beautiful women around these parts."

"Aw." Kasi hugs Feilece's waist.

"I don't think she's from around here, she said she was from Koilia."

Feilece and Kasi share a worried look.

"What if it's one of Schizo's supporters?" Kasi asks, urgently.

"It's okay. I won't let what happened to me, happen to them. I will go and meet this person."

"No. What if it's a trap?"

"It'll be fine. I am not my father. I will not falter and I will not fail. I will keep my family safe."

He kisses Kasi on the forehead and walks out of the house. He goes into their barn and grabs his axe.

Feilece walks across the fields between the neighbour's house and his until he comes across a figure atop a hill, silhouetted in the Mother's light. The figure of a woman.

"Who are you? And why are you here?"

"I am a messenger from your past."

The woman's voice is eerie and otherworldly. It's as if it's not only coming from where she stands, but from all directions simultaneously. Feilece doesn't let himself fall to fear. He holds his axe firmly.

"Are you here to kill me?"

"Do you want me to kill you?"

Feilece's brow furrows.

"Perhaps I'm here to tell you your sisters have succeeded. That Koilia is now liberated from the kings and the people there live in harmony. Perhaps I'm an old member of the Reapers coming to thank you for setting Koilia on its path to peace."

Feilece calms down. "Well, if that's the case—"

"—perhaps I'm here to tell you your sisters are dead. That all the Reapers are dead. That Koilia itself has been eradicated. Perhaps the Mother sent a ball of fire and lit the entire city ablaze. Perhaps Koilia is nothing a giant pile of ash."

"What is this?" Feilece's grip tenses.

"Perhaps I am only here to tell you a story. I know you like stories, you've been telling them to yourself for years now. Which story would you like to hear?"

"I don't want to hear any stories. What I want to know is who you are!"

The ground begins shaking under Feilece's feet; he makes a solid stance to keep himself standing. Looking at the ground, Feilece notices embers shooting out of the tips of every blade of grass.

The Mother disappears from the sky, sending the land into a completely pitch black darkness. A moment passes, then, in an instant, the fields burst into flames.

Feilece stumbles. He feels the heat of the ground burning beneath his feet.

He looks up at the woman. Her face is illuminated by the light emitted from the fire. It's Kasi, but she's younger. She looks the same as she did the first time he saw her at the Armen house.

"Kasi," he whispers to himself. Fearing for the lives of his family in this immense fire, he turns to look at his house but the building isn't there. Nothing is there ... just darkness and fire.

"Kasi!" Feilece runs towards his home. He runs for hours but nothing changes. He grows tired and falls to his hands and knees.

They're gone, and he knows it. He failed. His tears

evaporate in the flames as they fall from his face.

A young girl's feet approach and stand unaffected in the burning grass in front of him. Her skin shines yellow like the day's sky.

Feilece's eyes travel up her body to her face. He hasn't seen this face in decades. It's Niria. She smiles and bends down to hug her shins.

"Niria? How are you here?"

"Oh, little brother, I've always been here."

"What is happening? How can this be real?"

"Are you sure you care about what's real anymore?"

"What do you mean?"

Niria stands and looks down at Feilece, a caring look in her eyes.

"Knowing that they're gone … does it hurt?"

"Yes. More than anything."

"Then stop time," says Niria as simultaneously all the flames halt in space, as if they were only drawings. "Stop time … when time stops, the pain stops," she says.

Feilece ruminates on her words. He could stay in a state of elevated time forever. He would never have to worry again, never have to subject himself to anymore pain.

"If I were younger, I would certainly take that opportunity … but I'm older now. I can't stop the pain. Pain is important; it deserves more respect than that."

"You have matured, little brother."

"I don't want to stop the pain. I want to use the pain. I want to fix things … the real things."

Niria smiles and sighs. She extends her hand to Feilece. Feilece takes a deep breath then clasps a loving hand around hers.

XIV

———❧———

Feilece stares at Niria's hand. It rests in the same place it has for many years now. The Reaper recruit is still shocked in the corner of their cabin. The two older Reapers continue to stare at Feilece. As Feilece lived a lifetime, Genus hasn't moved at all.

To come back to this static reality, Feilece can't help but feel anxious. A feeling of habituation towards the notion of things not moving; a desensitisation to the sight of his dead sister.

With so much time passed, he must reach far back into the depths of his mind to restore his understanding of the world as it was. By forcing his thoughts, memories return from their long untouched recesses.

Anema crumbling into dust, Plios' head falling from her body, Semnos with a sword stabbed through him. The memories hurt, like prodding an old wound, but they motivate him. Eager to rejoin reality, Feilece attempts to restart his heart and release time back onto its natural trajectory … but it doesn't work.

It seems impossible. Not only does he have no idea where to start, he's also compiled years' worth of habits into actively not restarting time. Nevertheless, he cannot stay trapped inside his mind forever.

He practices by concentrating on his heart, imagining it as if it were a clock. He projects an imaginary circle of light over his chest, a recreated image of the Mother's light as seen through a pinhole camera. He imagines the turning of the day and attempts to sync his heart to the movement of the Mother's eyelid, opening and closing.

He feels like he's getting somewhere, that his heart wants to move with the flow, but it remains still. He has a thought: perhaps, the solution isn't simply about moving time itself forward, but instead moving himself through time.

He decides to give his body something to do; something important so his body will want to do it. Before pondering upon what that task might be, he realises the answer is staring directly at him, or rather, he's the one staring.

He attempts to reach out and grab Niria's hand. At first, nothing happens, but after a while, something groundbreaking occurs. His heart finishes its lifetime long beat.

Reality stutters forward; it's working. He syncs his heart to the light on his chest and continues. Slowly, his arm begins to move, nanometre by nanometre.

A month passes, two months, three. His arm is moving at a rate of a millimetre per hour; he's getting better at this. There is no rest, there is no relief, he can only keep going, keep practising, keep progressing.

Through undying perseverance, he gets there. His hand hovers over his sister's, fingers outstretched, ready to grapple.

He observes the Reapers as they slowly comprehend his presence. He knows that once he grabs her hand, time will go back to normal. He will no longer be a chrono-prisoner.

He takes a moment to reflect on how far he's come. His life as a soldier; his wife and children. It's time to make it real.

He clasps his hand around his sister's. Niria's hand detaches from its forearm. Dust trickles through the cracks of Feilece's hand. Time is restored.

"Hey! What are you doing?" The aggressive Reaper reacts while Rago remains inactive, watching Feilece intently.

Feilece opens his palm and looks upon the bones of Niria's dead hand, he can almost feel the last of her wyll electrocute the nerves in his fingers. He frowns an old, long-worn frown.

Rago's head tilts back and he looks down his nose at Feilece.

Feilece stands, expecting his bones to feel brittle and his muscles to ache, but instead he finds himself in the spry body of a teen boy. He feels taller than his little body can reach and stronger than his muscles show.

The aggressive Reaper steps towards him but is stopped by Rago.

Rago addresses Feilece directly. "Who are you, boy?"

Feilece waits before answering, relishing and examining his old/new self.

Rago grows restless. He goes to speak but Feilece interrupts him.

"I am just a young boy … an entire lifetime ahead of him."

"And what is your name?"

"My name is Feilece Anemelos, son to Anema and Plios, brother to Semnos, Niria, Epo and Dorean." Feilece reminds himself of these important facts.

A disappointed look shows on Rago's face until Feilece says something that causes him to reassess. "Lover to Kasi."

"Do you hold Kasi in similar regard to your family, Feilece?" Rago speaks in monotones.

"Kasi is my family."

"That she is," Rago says with a smile. "What of your wyll, boy? Is it strong?" Rago speaks in a clinical tone, as if evaluating the boy like a test subject.

Feilece smiles and looks up through a hole in the ceiling. In the sky, he sees the glowing ring of the dusk Mother. He leaves the question unanswered.

"You alright there, little brother?"

Feilece hears the voice of Niria in his head. He looks down at her bones, they remain unmoving where they rest.

"What a sad fucking sight." Niria's naked body appears next to Feilece, fully fleshed and beaming with the Mother's light. Feilece looks around, no one seems to see her but him.

"Don't be daft, Feilece, only you can see me. I tell ya, it feels nice being bigger than you again." She places her hand on Feilece's head.

Feilece looks back at her bones, knowing there's no way she could be real. This manifestation is a product of his imagination.

"Look, maybe I'm not real," Niria says, "but neither were you for the last … fuckin, how many years was it? Eh, it doesn't matter. Ya know, looking down at these old bones of mine, I can't help but remember how weak I used to be. Thank you, Feilece, for giving me time to do a bit of growing up." She puts her arms around Feilece. "Now, let's go."

Feilece turns to the cowering Reaper recruit in the corner of Niria's cabin: the man who failed to keep his sister engaged.

"Paldi!" He looks at Feilece. "Go get Kasi, I wish to speak with her."

Paldi nods and goes to leave but is stopped by the aggressive Reaper.

"And who are you to start directing my men around? You aren't even a Reaper. What power do you think you have, here?"

Feilece walks out of his cabin and to the adjacent pen, Djent's old resting place. His eyes widen as he finds the hearty ram is still alive, they haven't eaten him yet. Djent's eyes portray excitement but he struggles to move. Feilece smiles at his old friend then turns his back to the ram and faces the men.

"I have no power here," Feilece says. "I only wish to tell Kasi something important."

Niria whispers, "mind if I take control of your hand for a second? Thanks."

Discreetly, Niria moves Feilece's hand to the clasp of the gate holding Djent's cabin closed and half opens it. Feilece hears Djent rustle behind him.

"And what is that?" Rago asks.

"That I wish to become a Reaper."

XV

E PO HEARS FEILECE'S voice from across the stable. It distracts her from the hulking man on top of her, and the pain. It's the first she's heard from her family ever since Niria's cries stopped.

This is the first noise she's heard that hasn't made her shiver in fear since the Reapers invaded. Endorphins flood her brain, making her numb to the torture, giving her time to reflect on everything she's gathered since her imprisonment. Frequently, Rago would walk by her pen, talking about his plan of indoctrinating them. He would speak freely, confident in the fact that once their wyll was broken, he could do as he pleased with their minds.

Epo is wary of the old man. While he doesn't touch the girls himself, he does something much worse, he watches. Often, she'll be locked in a staring contest with the old man while one of his acolytes had his way with her. While the men would do what they wanted with her body, she saw the old man aiming for something much more important, her brain.

The information she has gleaned from the old man is thus: he must break her wyll to make her susceptible to indoctrination; breaking of the wyll is a form of disconnect between a person and their identity; and in order to break one's wyll, they must first be put through significant trauma.

In order to save herself, she has to convince these men they've succeeded, and that she is broken. Then, once she's afforded a bit of freedom, she can find her siblings and find a way out of this disaster.

"I wish to become a Reaper."

Feilece's words hit Epo hard, causing her body to go limp.

They must have already broken him.

Poor little brother, forced into this horrid gang. Have they broken Niria and Dorean also? Is she all alone? The last remaining Anemelos?

She receives a hard slap to the face by her abuser.

"Aye! You paying attention, girl?"

Snapped out of her depression, her thoughts turn positive. Feilece is a smart boy … sometimes. Maybe he's had the same idea she's had and is fooling them into thinking he's one of them. Maybe they can escape together. That must be it. There's no way he would turn against his family and that goes the same for Niria and Dorean.

They're strong; they'll make it through this, then they can go back to being a family.

Epo sees the old man about to walk past. She's been practising for a while, waiting for the best opportunity to implement her act. She figures now is a better time as any.

Looking at her abuser with glossy vacant eyes, she finally responds to his question loud enough for the old man to hear. "Girl? Who is that?"

Rago's ears perk up. Epo watches him in her peripheral vision as he turns his attention towards her cabin.

"Aye?" the abuser says.

"Get off her, get off her now!" Rago enters and pushes the man off of her. He examines the girl. A lost look in her eyes, unable to concentrate, confused expression: Epo estimates these are the signs of a broken girl.

"I'm not done here, old man." The abuser is drunk and unsatiated.

"If I say you're done, you're done. We're not losing both of them in one day," Rago says, sternly.

Epo thinks hard on the old man's words, 'we're not losing both of them'. She wonders if that's what the arguing she heard was about. She worries about Niria. She realises her worry may be showing on her face and quickly abolishes it, returning to her act.

Rago appraises her. "Tell me, what is your name?"

"Name? What is that?" She keeps her voice is floaty and simple, imagining what she would sound like if there was nothing inside her brain.

Rago smiles at her. He looks strangely proud.

"This family just keeps getting better."

"So what? Is she broken, or whatever?" the drunk asks, slurring his words.

"Yes, I believe she is."

"This mean I can't fuck her anymore?"

"That is correct, thank you for paying attention." The sarcastic tone in Rago's voice betrays his irritation.

"Well, what am I gonna do about my nuts?"

"Just *fuck* the older one. Or, as most adults do, find yourself a mate among your peers."

The drunk stands up, his hairy dong swinging close to Rago's face. Rago rolls his eyes then stands and meets the man eye to eye.

"The other one's too old … I like this one."

Epo watches Rago assess the man.

"Revealing tattoo," says Rago, pointing to the artwork on the man's arm: a bleeding circle with layers reaching into the centre making it look three dimensional. Epo has seen this tattoo many times.

"Judging by your physique," Rago continues, "I assume you were an enforcer for the Church of Lixi. Correct me if I'm wrong, but that's the cult that practices pederasty, yes?"

"It's not a cult!"

"Ah, so you maintain a level of affection towards the organisation. Tell me, with the Church of Lixi's level of exclusivity, how is it you are here, so far north, so far away from your constituents?"

The brute doesn't respond.

"Is it perhaps that you did not adhere to the rules? Lixi is strictly about robbing little *boys* of their innocence, girls are nowhere to be found in the scripture. Did your perversion perhaps stretch a little too far; a young labial fixation perhaps?"

A look of shame creeps onto the brute's face.

"You failed your people, your teachings, and you even failed the Child. All because of those nuts of yours."

A tear runs down the brute's cheek. "I don't like

boys. Girls are softer and smell nicer."

"It's okay, you are not with them anymore. There are no Reaper scriptures; we won't judge you here."

"Thank the Mother, for the Reapers."

"Now run along. Be with your new brothers and sisters."

The brute nods, wipes away his tear, then collects his clothes and leaves the stable.

Rago watches him with a sly look in his eye. "Religious idiots, so easily manipulated. Weave a few words their way and you can lead them as if on a string." He turns back to Epo. "You may drop the act, girl."

Epo, retaining her façade, looks around as if in a daze. "Act? What is that?"

"A broken wyll doesn't affect a person's cognition, just their sense of identity. I know you're not broken. You're lying so the torture will stop. A valiant effort."

"I ... I don't understand."

"I think you do." Rago kneels down and looks into her eyes, engaging her in one of their staring contests. "Yeah, you're still in there. It's incredible, after everything you've been through, you still have the faculties to devise a plan of deception. First your brother transforms from a cowering weakling to whatever it was I just saw, and now this. Coming to this farm is proving to be more interesting than I thought."

Epo stares into his eyes. If he didn't believe her wyll was broken, why would he lie to her abuser?

Rago stands and extends a hand out. "Come now, girl. You'll be spending the rest of your time in my tent."

Epo is cautious. She has no idea what to expect. Nevertheless, nothing can be worse than the state she's in already. Plus, she feels a strange allure towards the older man, as if, somehow, he's safe. The only viable safe option in this whole place.

She takes his hand.

XVI

FEILECE IS BROUGHT before the table of directors. He stands opposite the colourfully dressed Reapers with Kasi behind him, smiling proudly.

Feilece stands tall, keeping his body stiff like a soldier. He looks up at the clock on the wall. The pinhole camera and wire-frame calendar feel like distant relics of his past. He feels a strange confidence as he watches the shadow shift.

Though it is nostalgic, something feels different in the clock. There's a new force hidden in the light beams he can't quite explain. It's a feeling. A feeling he both feels like he's drawing from and feeding to at the same time.

"So … you've changed your mind?" a director in yellow clothes says in a tired tone. "How long will it be before it changes once more?"

"Given the reaction I had all those years ago, do you really think this is a matter I would take so lightly as to lie about it?"

The confused faces of the Reapers tell Feilece his response was far too mature sounding for a kid. He has to rein it in a bit, or else he looks suspicious.

"What do you mean, years ago?" Kasi asks.

"Uh, figure of speech. It feels like years."

He's not going great so far. He's here to gain their acceptance and he's already misjudged himself and misspoken. His old mind is having trouble adjusting to his young body.

"Why?" asks the black-clothed director.

"Why what?"

"Why do you want to be a Reaper? Why renounce your family?"

"I want a better life. I still feel for my old family, but there's nothing much I can do for them." Feilece tries to make his voice sound clinical but he fails and finds emotion in his tone.

It's not a lie. His parents and brother are dead, and his sisters have their own hardships to overcome. He can't help them, he's known this for years. These are old wounds but Feilece can't help but feel them more presently than he did when he was trapped in time.

The directors murmur among themselves for a moment. Feilece watches patiently. Whatever becomes of his future, the first step is escaping the stable and to do that, he must first convince these men to make him a Reaper.

"What is your plan, exactly?" Niria's incorporeal body wanders into the room. She sits her bare arse down on the Reaper table. "Become a Reaper, then what? Get an audience with Schizo, kill him, steal his wife and run off in a Mother's wink?"

Feilece continues to look forward, trying not to react to his sister's words.

"Come on, little brother. You're not the big hardened warrior you fantasised, you're a little boy. Why would she want you? Why wouldn't you become her sole enemy once your intentions were made? And why would they want a boy who's never even held a blade in their ranks?"

Feilece frowns and looks back up at the clock. The Mother's shadow moves slower than he remembers.

Niria appears in front of him. She puts a hand on his shoulder and looks into his eyes.

"I'm not trying to discourage or depress you, little brother. I'm just saying, you need a plan. Be strong, show them your value."

"Very well," says the yellow-clothed director. "We will have to test your loyalty. We'll think up a suitable trial, until then, you will stay in your cabin."

Kasi steps forward. "He's here saying he wants to be one of us and you're going to send him back?"

"We have to know where his allegiances lie, if he's holding resentment for the death of his parents—"

Kasi interrupts. "Are you telling me my husband is scared of a boy?"

"He has Animia's blood, who knows what his intentions are."

"We are not in the position to be passing up converts, especially those who hold Animia's blood. We've already lost one of the girls."

"Her name was Niria," says Feilece. He speaks in a calm tone, he doesn't want to make it harder for himself. "I understand. I'll go back to my cell and await my test."

Feilece turns and walks towards the exit of his old home, though the only room he recognises is his own.

It's been kept the same; this must be Kasi's doing. He walks inside and sits on his bed, surrounding himself in childhood memorabilia. Toys his mother would make out of hemp and wool, letters from his brother while he was at school, terrible wood carvings his father made.

He picks up a boy doll, made by his mother.

"Did your mother make that?"

Feilece looks up and sees Kasi standing in the doorway. He nods.

Kasi sits down next to him and wraps an arm around him. "She was talented."

"Was she?" Feilece asks, laughing slightly.

"It's you, right?"

"No, it's one of the Armen boys, our old neighbours."

"I see." Kasi's voice trails off as she speaks.

"What happened to the Armens?" he asks.

Kasi takes a long breath. "Are you sure you want to know?"

"Either they're Reapers, or they're dead. Nothing will surprise me now."

"Schizo … he won't allow Bloomers. We hung them in the forest and burned their bodies."

"What!" Niria screeches and tirades around the room. "Those fucking pricks! They were my friends, my only fucking friends!"

Feilece lets her have her tantrum but his mind doesn't register the same pain as she exhibits. He hasn't thought of the Armens in decades. Hearing of their deaths, he feels more of a distant grieve than a full depression. Then he realises his eyes are crying.

Though his mind doesn't feel much, his body definitely does. Not only is he an old man trapped in a young body, he is also a kid disconnected from an old mind.

"Aw." Kasi hugs Feilece. "I'm sorry. I know what it's like to lose friends."

"Loss is a part of life. If no one ever grieved, that would mean no one was ever truly alive."

Kasi pulls away. "You've changed a lot from the excited little boy I met at the Armens' house."

They both look into each other's eyes.

Kasi smiles. "And I'm liking it."

Feilece chuckles and wipes his eyes. "That's good. And this is only the beginning."

"Alright, it's time to go back to your cell, boy," calls the yellow-clothed director from the hallway.

"Can't he just have a second," says Kasi.

"It's alright." Feilece gets up. He takes one last look at his toy. "Soldiers shouldn't be playing with dolls." Then he throws the toy out of the window.

Kasi looks at him, shocked. "Why?"

"All this stuff isn't mine anymore anyway, it all belonged to a different me."

Feilece walks outside and heads back towards to the stables.

"Wait," calls Kasi as she follows.

Feilece turns to face her.

She frowns at him. "Why do you want to be Reaper?"

"It's not exactly fun sleeping in hay."

"Then leave. My offer still stands, you can go if you like. You are free. You've already admitted you can't help your family, so what's keeping you here?"

Feilece needs time to think.

He takes a deep breath and slows his heart to a crawl. All moving things slow to a creeping pace around them. Reapers hammering pegs into the ground, each hit at least a minute apart. Looking into Kasi's beautiful eyes, all he wants to say is he's here to be with her. He can't imagine a life without her. He spent a lifetime pursuing her, being with her, loving her, growing with her. Now he has to figure out a way to do it all again, only this time, he doesn't have the advantage of fantasy.

He knows she loves him, he can tell by the way she fights for him, but he can't put all of his trust in destiny. They may have had sex once but that's not going to be enough to turn her against her husband.

"But you didn't have sex though," says Niria, her head poking through Kasi's chest and looking up at her face. "She is pretty, I'll agree with you on that, but she doesn't shine like I do."

Feilece doesn't understand his sister. They did have sex; he remembers it clearly.

"No, remember, she just gave your thing a little fiddle with her hand. The sex, and all the other stuff you forced me to watch you do with her," she says in a disgusted tone, "you made all that up."

Feilece is shocked. It's true. He's lost touch of what was real memory, mixing them all with fakes.

Niria gets in close to Feilece. "That's what I'm saying, brother. Find your value, because you're not in one of Epo's books anymore."

It's worse than he thought. He can't rely on love without attraction. First, he has to elevate his presence in Kasi's mind. He knows she's into soldiers—strong fighting men. That is what he will do, he will become the soldier he fantasised about being. It should be easy; he's already done it once before. Reapers make people strong; he has his answer.

Feilece finishes his breath and time goes back to normal.

"I want to be a Reaper so I can become strong. Strong like my father … but better."

"Okay." Kasi nods. "Then you may become a Reaper."

"You have that authority?"

"Those men will do as I say if I use the right words." Kasi ponders to herself. "We'll first get the grey director on our side, and he'll give you your colour."

"I'll go back to the stable until they come up with their test."

"Reapers do not sleep in stables, Feilece."

"I don't want to get on anyone's bad side."

"If you want to be strong, you first have to be able to fight to get what you want."

Feilece shifts nervously then nods.

"Sorry for eavesdropping," says Popoki, leaning against the side of the house. "But I may have a better idea."

"Have you been there the whole time?" asks Kasi.

"I've been watching the boy a lot lately, at Schizo's request. When I was told he wished to become a Reaper, I had to come over."

Popoki kneels down to Feilece's level and looks him over. "Hmm, yep." He returns to standing. "I will be your director, boy."

"You're a general, Popoki, not a director. It's not your job to—"

"Then I'll make it my job."

Kasi sighs. "Very well. You two are free to do as you please."

Looking into Popoki's eyes, Feilece doesn't know what to feel. He hasn't completely figured the man out yet.

Feilece bows. "Thank you, sir."

"Don't think everything is fine just yet. Schizo … he worries about you. You may have to fight a bit to make the Reapers accept you as one of them."

"I'm prepared to do what it takes."

"We'll first work on convincing the directors, that should go a long way."

A scream comes from close by. The sound alerts Kasi. "What's that?"

"Ah." Niria shows back up. "It's about time. Remember, little brother: value." Then she disappears.

Kasi and Popoki rush in the direction of the scream. Feilece follows, walking.

Djent is raging around, tearing down tents and bashing into Reapers. The Reapers attempt to fight back but none are capable of contending with the beast.

"Who let that thing out!" a director in red clothes screams from the other side of the house.

"We don't know! He busted out of his pen!" says one of the nearby Reapers.

"Why didn't we kill it?"

"The thing bit one of us a while back so we decided

to let it starve instead of giving it a quick death."

"Who did it bite?"

"Him …" A Reaper points to a bloody body on the ground, buck marks in his chest and head caved in from hoof stomps.

Djent continues his crazed ravaging. Feilece walks towards the ram, bearing no fear to the carnage.

As Feilece approaches his old friend, he doesn't know if he can calm the ram's rage. He slows his heartbeat, taking the reins of time into his mind. He watches the ram tear around in slow motion. Feilece's own body becomes sluggish.

Djent catches Feilece's eye. Feilece analyses the animal's intentions, slowing time down even further just to be safe. One could drop a rock from their hand and it would take at least an hour to touch the ground. Feilece scans Djent's eyes, looking for any sense of familiarity between them. If Djent doesn't snap out of his fury, Feilece may have to act quickly. Luckily, he has all the time he needs to know when to react. The ram charges. Feilece sends the signal to his body, and in the last split second, he dodges the bucking animal.

He hears Reapers all around him gasp.

"Djent!" Feilece calls out.

Djent looks back at him with scared eyes as his legs shake and body slumps down.

"It's okay, boy. You're okay." Feilece rests his hands on the animal, petting him.

A collective sigh is heaved by everyone in the vicinity; a few Reapers start clapping.

Popoki approaches Feilece. "I'm impressed, boy. Tell me, why did the beast calm itself to your call?"

"This ram and I go back a good while," says Feilece, knowing this memory to be true. "He saved my life once."

"As you saved a lot of Reapers from being killed just now," Popoki says, observing the damage.

"Think that'll convince the directors I'm trustworthy?" Feilece looks up at the man, eyes squinting in the Mother's light.

"Maybe."

"What is this beast still doing alive!" says the red-clothed director entering the paddock.

"It's okay." Popoki stops them. "Feilece got him under control."

"It is not okay, that thing just tore up part of our town and killed our members."

"Yeah, but now he has stopped, thanks to Feilece. They're old friends, if it weren't for him, you may be laying there covered in dents too."

The black-clothed director steps forward and looks down at Feilece with dark eyes.

"Old friends, huh." He smiles. "I have found a suitable test for the boy's loyalty." He pulls a knife from his belt and tosses it at Feilece's feet. "Kill the beast."

Feilece's heart starts to beat quickly, causing the speed of time to rise. He takes control of it before he loses track.

He picks the knife up from the ground.

Popoki speaks up. "You're seriously gonna make the kid kill his own pet? After everything he's been—"

"If that is what it takes." Feilece cuts Popoki off. "I will do what is necessary."

He puts the knife to Djent's throat. The ram

doesn't react. He stares into Feilece's eyes, defeated.

Feilece holds the knife tightly, bringing it closer and closer to Djent's neck until it's brushing up against his fur.

Djent starts to whimper. Feilece tries to be strong. He has to do this … but he can't.

"Stop!" Popoki grabs the knife from Feilece's hand.

"What are you doing?" asks the black-clothed director.

Popoki gestures at the mess Djent made. "Five dead Reapers to this starved, tired, abused old ram. In the state he is in, this friend of Feilece is still worth five of your warriors. How much do think he's worth when he's well fed and full of energy?"

The directors say nothing. The black-clothed director smiles.

Popoki looks back at Feilece. "Reckon you can keep command of that thing?"

"Absolutely," Feilece says without hesitation.

"There you have it. We are not one's to waste good warriors, and we have one addition fit for the Mother Herself right here."

Feilece stands and addresses the directors.

"Djent is worth more to us alive, and I give you my word I will train him. He will be kept under control, and in great fighting shape."

"Are you sure? You are just a child."

"I am no child." Feilece looks over at Kasi. "I am a soldier."

Kasi frowns, eyes looking sad as she looks around at her lost Reapers. Feilece feels a spike of guilt in his chest.

"You know what?" says the black-clothed director. "I know the feeling. I had to grow up pretty fast when I had my innocence ripped from me. In fact, I think I see a lot of me in you. Keep your pet. Make sure it doesn't kill more Reapers. We'll trust you for now, but you will be watched."

Popoki steps forward. "I'll keep watch over him."

The director grins. "You looking to demote yourself, Popoki?"

"What if I am?"

"Fine by me."

Niria rejoices. "Fuck yeah!"

XVII

"TELL LOUMA I'M ready to see the older one," Rago says to one of the Reapers walking past his tent. The Reaper nods and carries on his way.

"In here, girl." He parts the entrance of the tent and leads Epo into his quarters.

It's a spacious tent. There's room for a bed, a work table, a wooden bathtub, a clothing station, but what takes up most of the space is a bookshelf tall enough to touch the ceiling of the tent. Epo is fascinated, there are so many books that piles have built up around the shelves from a lack of space.

Rago watches her admire the books. "I knew I would be held up at this location for a long time. Sadly, the carriage I used to travel could only hold part of my collection. Do you read many books, girl?"

Empty eyed and adopting a distant expression, Epo responds. "Books? What are those?" She of course loves books. Semnos used to lend her books from his school when he was done with them. They would always be about something new, social studies, agriculture, history. Though she favoured fiction, she never really cared what the books were about, she just loved reading. After seeing Semnos die, she worried she would never read a book again.

Rago laughs in intermittent-closed mouth nasal expulsions, as if he'd heard a lame but mildly clever joke. "So you intend to keep up the charade. Very well, do as you will. I advise you to you clean yourself up and put on some clothes. I trust it shall feel refreshing, restoring a little bit of one's decency."

Rago sits down at his work desk and begins writing in a journal.

Epo walks by the bath. A wood base coated in lacquer and filled with warm water. She dips her hand in the water and feels her arm relax. Quickly and without thought, she climbs the steps and dunks her whole body in the water. Month's worth of dirt, dead skin and soiled innocence float away, dissipating in the water. The pain she thought she would be living with for the rest of her life eases slightly.

"I've used a combination of substances imported all the way from the Brain to heighten the water's restorative qualities," says Rago.

Epo has read about the land of the Brain in one of Semnos' books. People living north of the Heart are great thinkers and scientists. Not much information about them is available in the Abdominals since the old wars. Even after centuries of peace, animosity still remains prevalent between the nations.

Epo dunks her head under the water and lets her worries wash away. With her face out of view of the old man, she feels she can drop her act and think seriously about what to do next. The man doesn't believe she's broken; he's too smart. But he still brought her into his tent and treated her to this amazing bath. The tonics used wouldn't have been easy to get, it is as if he's been planning for this.

Is he on her side? Can she drop the act? Will she be safe? No. She can't trust anyone, not yet. He may be acting nice now, but that doesn't discount all the time he spent simply watching.

After feeling sufficiently clean and refreshed, Epo exits the bath and moves over to the clothing station. Clothes have been tailored to her measurements, Reaper insignia branding every article. He means to drape her in their symbol, this must be part of the brainwashing.

Epo slips into the clothing. It's nothing like the clothes she used to wear; it's tauter with less space for her skin to breathe. Gone are the baggy hand-me-downs from Dorean. She feels like one of the princesses from her books.

Epo looks at herself in a nearby mirror, she looks like a Reaper.

"Come to me, girl." Rago puts down his pen. Epo walks over to his desk, making sure to maintain her expression of vacant curiosity.

Rago stares into Epo's eyes, and another staring contest ensues.

"It was Epo, correct?"

Epo flinches, it's the first time she's heard her own name spoken out loud in months. She had almost forgotten the sound of it, perhaps the process of her indoctrination was affecting her after all.

"E...po?" A convincing reply, Epo thinks to herself.

If she can hold out her act, perhaps this old man will start believing her. Rago leans forward, places his elbows on the table and rests his chin on his crossed fingers, his eyes adopting a more serious tone.

"Listen to me, Epo, for I will say this only once. You have nothing to fear with me. I will not be sending you back to the stables, I will not be subjecting you to anymore torture, I will not be trying to convince you that you are anything different than what you are."

Epo continues staring. She wants to believe him but won't let herself. It's a test. Once she falters, he'll throw her right back in her pen and it'll go back to how it was.

"Watching you over the last few months, I have noticed your level of awareness growing with the harshness of your treatment. Instead of opting for depression and degradation, your brain instead chose to heighten your cognition in retaliation to your situation. It is an uncommon survival mechanism, a testament to an incredibly potent wyll. In fact, it's so uncommon that, before today, it only ever existed as one of my hypotheses."

Epo had never felt particularly smart, only ever curious. Now that Rago has pointed it out, she knows she would have never thought of a plan this complex before the Basin was invaded.

She can recall her books down to the sentence, and she picks up on cues much quicker, dissecting intent and predicting outcomes with precise accuracy. The way Rago speaks—his adept level of speech—she would have barely been able to understand him a month ago. Now, it's as easy to grasp as Niria's whining.

"Look, I understand your fear. You do not want to go back to the stables. It's hard to believe anyone would be doing you a kindness, so let me give you a more pragmatic explanation. You are worth much more to me as you are now than if you were broken. I'll prove it to you."

A hand pushes through the fabric of the tent's entrance and in walks the stocky woman, looking proud. Epo remembers her from the day of the invasion.

Rago stands and walks around his desk to stand next to Epo.

"Louma, a pleasure as always," he says.

"There is no pleasure in the sight of your ugly old face, sadistic fucking cunt," she says back at him.

"I always did love how colourful your language was. Now, you said you have a development for me."

Epo identifies Rago won't give her the pleasure of his hurt feelings which she so obviously desperately wants.

"I do." Louma snaps a finger and into the tent walks a staunch-looking woman, dressed in Reaper leathers complete with leaf-blade at her waist.

At first, Epo doesn't recognise her but then it hits her like a mallet to the face.

"Dorean …" Epo whispers under her breath. Her chest tightens and aches. Rago discretely covers her mouth. Epo stares at her sister, horrified. Not an ounce of familiarity can be found in her.

"So, you have succeeded?" Rago speaks to Louma as a teacher speaks to a student.

"I believe I have." Louma steps aside, putting Dorean on full display. "Meet, Killer."

"Killer?" Rago says.

"I wanted to name my first solo convert something punchy. Plus, once I've trained her up, no other title will suit her better. Why?" A scowl appears on Louma's face.

"No, it's nothing. Call her whatever name you want, no matter how tacky."

"Fuck you." Louma slaps the back of her fingers against her palm.

Rago examines the new Reaper.

Louma looks at Epo then back at Rago with a frown. "This is the little sister, right?"

Louma approaches Epo who resumes her broken act.

"Have you broken her yet?"

"Mm? Yes, of course." Rago answers quickly then goes back to analysing Dorean.

Louma smirks, a frown still creased across her eyebrows.

Rago tests Dorean. "Tell me, Ms. Killer. What was the purpose of this land before it became occupied by Reapers?"

"It was a farm, sir."

"Farming what?"

"Wool, wheat and meat."

"And who did the farming?"

"Farmers, sir." Dorean's words are robotic.

"Very good," says Rago. "Next will be a test of her ability to follow orders."

"I have the perfect test." Louma speaks quickly and directly. "Killer, cut this little girl's head off."

"As you wish." Dorean pulls the sword from her waist and turns towards Epo.

Rago's eyes widen. Louma watches Rago, smiling smugly.

Epo trembles as her sister approaches with unmoving eyes. Her heart sinks. Killed by her own sister ... after everything these people have put her family though, how can their levels of cruelty continue to surprise her.

Epo doesn't try to run ... she doesn't move at all. If anyone's going to kill her, it might as well be Dorean. She only hopes that her death will spark something in her sister and snap her out of this insanity.

Dorean lifts the blade up over her shoulder. Epo looks into her eyes and smiles. She wishes for the safety of what remains of her broken family.

Dorean swings at Epo's neck without hesitation.

"Stop!" commands Louma. The blade comes to a halt at it touches Epo's skin. A dribble of blood runs down her neck.

Rago stumbles through his words as he attempts to regain his wit. "Uh, very optimal. Quick response time, zero detectable levels of hesitation, zero familiarity with the subject. I would agree this is an acceptable conversion."

Louma draws close to Rago. He doesn't back down at all, meeting her gaze with his own.

"That little girl is not broken. You are lying."

"I'm trying a new method. It's an experiment, you wouldn't understand."

"Is that all? Then why were you so scared for her when I threatened her life?"

"The importance of this new specimen far exceeds that of any brute we've currently added to the ranks. I see promise in her, scientifically."

"Scientifically." She squints her eyes. "Right. Even through this veneer of academia, you're still a lonely old man. To think you'd stoop to this level of depravity," Louma says with a laugh.

Rago doesn't respond.

"Whatever, do what you want with the little one. We'll see what Schizo has to say about your little experiment."

"Schizo will side with me … as he usually does. Or have you forgotten all the times you've embarrassed yourself while trying to turn him against me?"

Louma smirks and backs away from the old man, keeping her eyes on him. "Soon, Rago, I will have the pleasure of watching you die. And it will be fucking euphoric. Come, Killer."

Dorean puts her sword away and follows Louma to the exit.

Louma turns back to Rago. "Now that it's been demonstrated that converts can be broken without your aid, how much value do you think Schizo will see in you. How long before you're pushed out here with the rest of us 'brutes'?" She leaves without waiting for a reply.

"Stupid woman, assuming I don't know every thought inside of her head." Rago returns to his desk and looks at Epo. "No doubt, that was probably rather traumatic for you. I apologise. But try to look at that occurrence objectively and try to analyse it."

Epo stares out the exit of the tent blankly. Shocked stiff.

"Your sister could still recall where she was and the function of this place, she just couldn't remember *who* she was. That is a broken individual."

Rago rubs his eyes. "If I'm being honest, I'm surprised Louma was able to achieve such a result. In any case, when you first adopted this façade, you acted like you didn't even know what a name was. I understand why you're lying, but I'm telling you, you don't have to."

Epo turns towards Rago but stares at the ground, unable to face the man.

"You saw your sister, moving like an automaton, not a single free thought in her head. Useful, if all you need is someone to swing a sword. But that is pedestrian compared to my ambitions. You will live here, you will read, you will learn, you will be a scholar. We have enough soldiers; we need to start making thinkers."

Epo looks at the book he's writing in. "What … are you writing?"

"I'm writing about you."

Scientific notes, behavioural analyses, observations. Louma may not have believed him when he said she was an experiment but Epo knows he wasn't lying. He means to bring her up as his own, his protégé, his child, his copy. She's another convert, but in a different form. Louma's parting words proved it, he needs more than what he's been providing. Epo knows now she can trust he won't send her back to the stable.

She looks at the library of books at her disposal, there must be something in there about unbreaking people.

She will be his student, for now. She will find a way to bring back her sister, and she will find a way to save her family.

XVIII

—⌇—

"**L**ISTEN TO ME, Killer. Do not grow attached to that old man." Louma throws out orders as she walks through the village, Killer following behind her. "You can't trust a thing he says, the man knows a lot of words and not a single one of them are off limits for his lies." Louma shivers as she speaks.

Killer is paying just enough attention to register the woman's words, but her mind can't help but wander.

"Be prepared to kill that man as soon as I order it, understood?" After receiving no reply to her question, Louma turns to face Killer. "Are you listening to me?"

"Yes, master. I will kill the old man upon your order."

"Where was your mind just now, Killer?"

"My … mind?" Killer says, confused.

"What were you thinking about while I was talking?"

"Um." Killer struggles with her words, her thoughts having to slog through a viscous medium of confusing emotion. "Who was the girl, the one back at the old man's tent?"

A frown appears on Louma's face. "Oh, her. What

do you care? She was only a target."

"Then why did you stop me from killing her?"

"Don't worry, my precious murderer, that time will come." Louma puts her hands on Killer's shoulders. "For now, I'm curious what his plans are for her. I suspect he will use her to fill a void and I want to see how that turns out. Then, be prepared to kill them both."

"Yes, master."

"Master ..." Louma takes her hands off of Killer's shoulders and crosses them. "Master is a rather impersonal title, don't you think?"

Killer stares at her.

"You know." Louma begins playing with the straps on Killer's armour in a playful manner. "I made you. You do know that, right?"

"Of course, master."

"I know I asked you to call me master before, but I've changed my mind, don't call me that from now on."

"Okay ... what shall I call you?"

"Well, what does one call someone who made them? Someone who gave them life?"

"I don't know what you mean."

Louma rolls her eyes. "When a couple gets together and makes a person, what do they then become?"

"Parents."

"Correct! And If I made you, what does that make me?"

"My ... mother."

"Yes!" Louma wraps her arms around Killer. "You will call me Mother from now on."

Killer feels something heavy behind her association with the word 'mother'. A feeling she cannot begin to comprehend. She feels a loving warmth within her through Louma's embrace.

With hesitating hands, Killer lifts her arms and wraps them around Louma. She can't help but hold Louma tightly, and tears form in her eyes. "Mum," comes out of her mouth in a whisper.

"Hey, are you alright?" Louma gently tries to push Killer off her but she won't budge. Louma takes Killer's face in her hand.

"Aw, isn't that nice, you love your new mummy enough to cry. Mum loves you too, now release her." Louma's voice quickly goes from cute to sharp and Killer steps back with haste.

She blinks and wipes the tears from her face. She has no idea what came over her. But as she looks at Louma, she feels a deeper attachment.

"I'm sorry, Mother. I don't know why I started crying."

"It's okay, Child. It's a reaction to this new connection we've made. We're going to be an amazing family, you and I." Louma puts a hand on Killer's shoulder. Her heart quickens to her touch.

"Louma!" Popoki calls out.

"Popoki, I wonder what you want to talk about," she says rhetorically.

"Have you been—"

"To visit Seemo?" Louma interrupts. "Because what else would we ever have to talk about?"

"Well, you're not exactly the best conversationalist."

"Those are my words, arsehole."

"In any case, have you? I haven't had time to see her today."

"The ever-caring Popoki missed a day?" she asks.

Popoki frowns at her.

Louma sighs. "I have not."

"Of course you haven't … as usual," Popoki says.

"Because she's never there anymore."

"And you've never thought it might be because you've given up on her?"

"You're a pathetic man, Popoki. Do you really think she still registers her old friends? Do you think her crazed brain registers anything anymore?"

"A week ago, I heard her. She was behind the big rock that looks like a blade stabbed into the Child."

An image of the rock flashes in Killer's mind and she feels an urge to speak spring to her mouth. "Monolith Meadow …"

The two Reaper generals look over at Killer with quizzical expressions.

"It's called … Monolith … Meadow," Killer says.

"Okay, whatever." Louma turns back to Popoki. "So, what? You heard her?"

"Then I left, I didn't want to disturb her … I wish I hadn't. I fear it was the last time I'll ever be close to her."

"Oh Mother." Louma says, exasperated. "Bestiality doesn't suit you, Popoki."

"She was crying."

Louma is taken aback for a moment but then Killer perceives an anger building inside of her.

"Whatever. There's nothing to be done. Hopefully

she fell in the river and drowned."

"I don't understand you, Louma." Popoki's voice takes on a gruff tone. "You used to love that girl like your own child. You raised her, taught her to fight. She was the last member of your precious PanoApo, how can you throw her away as if she meant nothing? Do you feel anything at all for her?"

"Do not presume to understand my emotions, Scythe," She hisses as she says the word 'Scythe'. "Do you want me to grieve, break down and cry? Oh why," she says in a pleading tone, "did you have to die? Poor, poor Seemo." She throws away her put-on voice. "Please. Only the weak let their minds falter over something as pathetic as loss."

"But she didn't die, she's still out there. She's lost, she's scared, and she's obviously depressed."

"Oh come off of it. You may have been a lad at the time but surely you remember the PanoApo massacre. You know what they become. You know there's no bringing them back. She is dead." Louma's voice is surly. "Just another dead child."

Popoki sighs. "Look, I know, alright. I know there's no saving her. But I … I don't want her to be alone."

"And there's nothing wrong with that, Popoki," says a woman emerging from a nearby tent.

"Kasi." Louma salutes. Her peers frown.

"You getting me back for eavesdropping on you earlier?" Popoki asks Kasi.

"Maybe."

"What happened? You disappeared after the commotion earlier."

"Yeah, I went to visit a convert of mine. Where's

Feilece?"

"He's getting comfortable in my tent, I made a room for him."

'Feilece', the word sparks something in Killer's head but it quickly fades.

"Can I ask you a question, Popoki?" asks Kasi.

"What?"

"Are you in love with Seemo?"

Popoki doesn't answer; he just looks away.

"Your concern for our sister is touching, more so given what she has become. I had no idea you had such strong feelings for her."

"Neither did I, not until she was gone."

"Hmm," Kasi says "The paradox of the heart. I, too, miss our sister very much. I wanted her to be the third leg of the tripod with me and Schizo. Demons, Scythes, and PanoApo, all working together. Just another thing Animia stole from us."

Kasi's eyes stare at Killer. "You are wrong, Louma. Grief from loss is a sign of strength, not weakness. Through our grief, we're all truly alive."

"Excuse the delivery, but do not assume to teach me about grief over loss." Louma speaks through her teeth.

"True, no one's grief is the same as another's. I apologise."

Kasi approaches Killer. Staring in her eyes, Killer sees delight spark in her pupils.

"This is Feilece's sister, correct?" Kasi asks Louma.

A flash of pain flares in Killer's head and she winces. She brings a hand to the side of her head and drills a knuckle into her temple, trying to correct it. It fades and she stares into her palm, wondering what happened.

"Yeah, I converted her myself, first time." The stocky woman speaks with pride.

"Wow, that is impressive, I bet Rago is sweating."

"What's so impressive about it?" Popoki asks out of curiosity. Louma stares daggers at the man but he doesn't pay any heed. "There's converts everywhere."

"Yes, but they're all male," says Kasi. "All a pretty girl like me has to do is throw a smile their way and they'll do whatever I please." Her words are devious but her voice is sullen, as if the fact saddens her.

"Speaking on behalf of my sex, I have to argue we're more complex than that," says Popoki.

"But you aren't speaking on behalf of your sex, you're speaking on behalf of a subset of your sex, one that opts for thinking with their brain instead of their genitalia. The real men. My converts tend to be the young, the dumb, those that still believe love is the answer to all things."

Popoki sighs. "Damn, hearing everything the men say about you, I thought you had an extremely large heart. But if you're just manipulating them to pad out the army, then maybe that chest of yours is empty."

Kasi looks at him with stern eyes but he doesn't back down.

"Can I trust the love you have for Seemo?" he says.

Kasi smiles. "Why do you think I'm so good at converting them?"

"Because ... you're pretty?" he says, repeating her own words.

"No, it's because I too believe love is the answer to

all things. You can't really call what I'm doing manipulative if I actually love them. I love my converts, I love Seemo, I love you two. I love every Reaper in this village, and now, I love this beautiful new recruit right here." She places her hands on Killer's cheeks and they stare deeply into each other's eyes. "As if they were family."

The word 'family' prickles like a thorn in Killer's mind. At first it hurts, but then an incredible sense of belonging follows.

"I will go with you into the woods Popoki, maybe Seemo will come if I'm there."

Kasi turns to Popoki, placing a hand on his chest. The disdain clears from Popoki's face and he nods, anguish in his eyes.

Kasi walks Popoki west towards the forest. Louma watches with trembling eyes.

"Fools. Lover, sister, these connections are thin compared to what we have." Louma turns to Killer and takes her by the hand. "You're all I need, my lovely Killer. The only true family love is between a mother and her child."

The only similarity Killer has to draw upon is that of the celestial Mother and Her Child, Genus. She will do as the Child does; she will orbit her new mother and embrace her warmth. She will do all that is asked of her. She would even follow her mother into death.

XIX

FEILECE, POPOKI AND Kasi trek through the western forest. The skin on Feilece's shoulder is raw from the strap of a heavy two-handed battleaxe resting on his back.

"Ya know, you could've chosen a lighter weapon if you wanted," Popoki says to the boy as he watches Feilece stumble on his feeble legs.

Feilece grunts at him, not wasting energy on a reply. When choosing his weapon, Popoki recommended a sickle and Feilece wishes he'd listened. Feilece pushes the thought out of his head; he made the right decision. If he's going to become the soldier he envisioned, he can't waste time learning to use inferior weaponry.

"He wants to be like his father," Kasi says, smiling at him. "Let him prove himself."

Feilece has a hunch about Popoki so he asks, "did you used to know him? Back when he was Animia?"

Popoki stops walking and looks at Feilece with a frown. Kasi stops too and they share a look. Feilece takes this moment to drop to his knees and take a breath.

Kasi nods at Popoki and he finally responds.

"I did. I was in Sickle & Scythe with him when he was still the great executioner. Pass that here." Popoki extends a hand to Feilece and he passes him the axe.

"What was he like back then?"

"He was very much worthy of the legend that sprung up around him. I was just a young man when I fought beside him against the Demons. Watching him in battle was one of the most amazing things I had ever seen. I once saw him split a man from nuts to chin. The brutality, I lived for it. The way he killed … it was inspiring. I idolised him. Up until …" Popoki's eyes stare at the axe head.

"Brother!" Kasi says, unexpectedly.

Popoki's eyes turn angry as he looks at her in a twitch. "What did you say?"

"It's our brother, Choris," Kasi says walking towards Choris who stands unmoving, bow in hand and arrow at rest on the bowstring. Four dead wildebeest lay next to him.

Popoki hands Feilece his axe back and they follow after her.

Kasi goes to speak to the man but is stopped by a "shh" coming from the branch of a nearby tree, where Diakho sits, balancing a dagger on his finger. "Don't distract him. He hasn't moved in twenty minutes," he whispers.

Choris, using perfect form, sets up a shot and fires an arrow at a dark spot in the woods. The arrow flies for a few seconds before everyone hears the sudden screech of a pig.

"Wow," says Feilece. "I couldn't even see what he was aiming at."

"Neither could he." Diakho jumps down from the tree and speaks to Popoki. "Off to the meadow again, sickle?"

Popoki looks at him, frowning.

"Well, before you ask, we haven't seen her."

Kasi examines the dead wildebeests. "How many will this feed?"

"Not much but we're not even close to done. The greys were on hunting duty this week and they came up short. Thought we'd show them what's expected of them."

"It would work better if you actually brought them out here and showed them how it is done."

"Not our style, sis. Plus, we can't have them getting too good. These woods aren't used to so many people running around killing all the fauna. We don't want to use up our resources before we have our army."

"Yeah … I really need to speed my husband up on that front."

"Also, the quality of fighters he's bringing in leaves much to be desired. It'll take a good while to get them battle-ready."

Choris looks at Diakho and they share an unspoken conversation.

"We gotta go, sis. Good luck with Seemo," says Diakho, as the hunters turn heel and walk off in the direction of the pig Choris killed.

"Good luck." Popoki spits. "I wouldn't be surprised to find they've killed her and strung her body up somewhere as a monument to my misery."

"You need to drop your resentment of the Demons, Popoki."

"It's not me, it's them. You saw how bloodthirsty they looked after killing that pig. Those 'brothers' of yours are the exact reason we were hired to hunt you people."

Kasi looks at Popoki with serious eyes.

Popoki sighs. "I'm sorry, lets carry on."

The three navigate their way to Monolith Meadow. Feilece presses a hand against the giant rock sticking out of the ground. He hasn't seen this rock in so long yet his hand still remembers its smoothness.

"Take out your axe, boy," says Popoki, putting down his gear.

Kasi leans against the monolith and watches.

"We're starting now?" Feilece asks, hoping they could rest for a bit beforehand.

"No point in delaying."

Feilece removes the axe from its strap and struggles to hold it in front of him. With its long handle, it is taller than he is.

Popoki grabs the top of the axe and presses the butt of the handle into the ground.

"This here, is a two-handed battleaxe."

Popoki runs his hand along its staff. "It's effective at dealing heavy damage, as it has an extremely wide swing arc. If you put your body weight into it, you can cleave anything off your opponent. It's why execution-er's use them for decapitations, so they only need one swing, it's the same with two-handed broadswords."

Images flash in Feilece's head of his father taking the axe to one of the chicken's necks. At the last second of his swing, the chicken head turns into a person's. He flinches.

"You okay there, boy?" asks Popoki.

"Yeah, I'm fine. Carry on, please."

"Okay, well, the metal part of the axe is called the head. The part where it connects to the staff is called the shoulder. Similar to our world, each region is named after a part of the human body, all except the blade. As you can see, the head fans out from the shoulder to the blade, which is called the bit. The pointed top of the bit is called the toe, and bottom is called the heel. You following so far?"

"What kind of person has a toe and heel connected to their head?" Niria appears. "This is stupid, who cares what all the shit's called."

While Feilece would accuse his sister of being impatient, he can't help but share in her sentiments.

"Now," Popoki continues, "because the staff of the battleaxe is so long, you have a lot of freedom over where you can put your hands, making the weapon versatile. I'll demonstrate a few strikes for you." Popoki picks up the axe and steps back. "Observe the stance, it's important you understand how your body moves, and what you can do to get the most out of your movement."

Feilece slows time down to a crawl as Popoki moves into position. He solidifies the exact image of his mentor in his mind, memorising exactly where his feet are placed and how he moves. He goes as far as to memorise how the man's muscles are contracting, where he's clenching, and where he's relaxing.

Popoki runs through different strikes with his hands in various positions to showcase the weapon's versatility. With time moving in slow motion, Feilece gathers everything he needs and as Popoki exits his stance, Feilece returns time to normal.

"Here, I don't wanna overload you with information before you have a chance to try it out," says Popoki, handing the axe to Feilece. "Now go through the movements I showed you, and I'll correct you wherever you go wrong."

Feilece slows time once again and turns his concentration inward. Applying the model demonstrated, he enters into an exact copy of Popoki's stance, taking his time to make sure he's perfectly poised. He delivers the strikes, immaculately. He doesn't have the same arm span as Popoki, so he has to improvise, but he's confident he's pulled it off adequately. Popoki is visibly impressed.

"Wo—," Feilece returns time to normal so he can hear Popoki speak, "—ow! I would say you were a natural but even that doesn't feel right. Did your father give you lessons?" Popoki asks.

"I used to watch him hack at firewood but he never let me wield the axe myself. Do you think I'll be a great warrior?"

"You're picking it up so quickly I'd say you'll probably even show your father up."

Feilece's face falls. "Do you hate him? For what he did to Sickle & Scythe?"

Popoki takes a deep breath before answering. "I did … for a long time." He looks over at Kasi. "It's why I joined the Reapers, it's why I came all the way out here. But …"

"You don't anymore?"

"I think I understand him a little bit better. He was

revered as such a great fighter, but he didn't care about that. He wanted to make the fighting stop. Because I loved fighting so much, it never really occurred to me that he might have hated being an executioner."

"What changed in you?"

Popoki doesn't take his eyes off Kasi.

"I watched him fight someone who is very dear to me. I was looking forward to it, it was supposed to be cathartic, seeing him in battle again. But then he almost killed her and I suddenly felt a pain I had never felt before. I realised I had been causing that same pain to others my entire life. Years spent fighting Demons … PanoApo turned into demons … now I kinda feel like I'm the biggest demon of them all."

Feilece turns to Kasi who has a concerned frown, then he looks back at Popoki.

"Do you worry about admitting something like that in a place like this? Where everyone is looking to you as their brother-in-arms?"

"Whether it's here, there, or anywhere, you must always speak your mind."

"It is sad to hear of your pain, Popoki." Kasi walks over and gives him a hug. "I'm sorry I pushed her to fight so much. I'm sorry I put so much faith in her. I shouldn't have left her alone in the end. We're building a family, I need to be more careful."

Popoki looks at Feilece, his eyes showing a growing anger.

"We're building a family that kills families, Kasi."

Popoki pushes Kasi away and grabs his things.

"You know what it's all for." Her voice takes on a more serious tone. "You know the importance, the ends will justify—"

"The Grothia," Popoki interrupts. He takes a deep breath. "Do you seriously think it's possible?"

"Have I ever shown a lack of faith?"

"No, but you've already proved how little power your faith has over reality."

Hearing the name Grothia stirs something inside of Feilece. It makes him think of his clock and the weird feeling he gets when he looks at it. The name never used to make him feel this way. He has to ask, "are the Grothia … real?"

They look at him.

"Your father never talked to you about the Grothia?" asks Popoki.

"Whenever I would ask about his past, he would always dismiss the subject. My sister, Epo, would read me books about old wars and kingdoms but I would never make much sense of them. I always thought they were fiction. If they're truly real, then who are they?"

Kasi kneels down and looks at Feilece. "I don't mean to cause you distress but I ask you this … what we Reapers have done to this Basin, to your family … do you think it's cruel?"

Feilece begins to sweat, his hands get clammy, his eyes haze. "Yes …"

"Well, the Grothia family have done all that and worse to this entire country."

"There are many kings in Koilia," Popoki says. "Each with their own territory and following. If the social hierarchy were a tree, the kings would be on the top branch and the Grothia …" Popoki looks up at the Mother. "They would be up there with Her."

Kasi stands. "The Grothia are just one family and yet every single person living upon this land sleeps, every night, terrified of their shining blue eyes. Your father saved you the fear by keeping them from you, but he only delayed their destined grapple over your psyche."

"But how?" Feilece asks. "How do they have such power?"

"It's ancient," Popoki says. "They've been revered for all of history as the strongest people to ever live. It was said that during the endless wars, every single battle the Grothia joined would instantly turn in their favour. With such fighting prowess, it's no wonder they get so much praise in this warmongering world. Some believe they're messengers from the Mother Herself; that She sees through their blue eyes."

"Grothia, huh." Niria sits atop the monolith. "Maybe they're the key to making you into the strong warrior you envision yourself to be."

Feilece thinks quietly. If he can figure out how they're so strong, maybe he can recreate it. But then what? More fighting? If the Grothia came to power by swinging swords, is the answer really to swing more swords?

"Why do you want to fight them?" Feilece asks Kasi.

"Why else? To end their tyranny," she says.

"But if they earned their throne through war, isn't bringing them more war just as tyrannical?"

Popoki crosses his arms and rubs his chin.

Kasi smiles. "It depends on what you're fighting for. This is more important than you know."

Feilece doesn't believe her.

"Look," Kasi says, her arms raised. "Both of you, it's going to be okay. Schizo has a plan."

"Schizo is a murderer," Feilece says.

"Schizo is a fighter," says Kasi. "He's willing to do whatever it takes for the wyll of the country. Ours is a virtuous cause. Through our effort, we will achieve the peace your father thought he was working towards."

Feilece feels she's out of line speaking about his father but he doesn't know enough to argue with her.

If Anema was trying to make peace, why did he do what he did? Why did he kill Schizo's and Kasi's fathers? How would more killing stop the killing?

"Maybe he was an idiot," Niria says, interrupting his thoughts. "Or maybe killing was all he knew. Maybe he had not yet learned what love was."

A rustle comes from the nearby bushes.

"Seemo!" calls Popoki, turning in a haste.

The three watch with disappointment as a pig emerges then rushes back into the woods.

XX

S HE'S NOT YET acclimated to the camp. She won't be seen as a Reaper. Seeing her abusers will remind her of her trauma. Them seeing her might spark some desire. They could hurt her. All of these are good reasons why Epo should not leave Rago's tent. But she wants to go out anyway.

It's been a week since Epo moved into Rago's tent. The old man has made the outside off-limits until he's done priming her as a Reaper. She's convinced him she will stay inside, for she does agree with the man's logic. She can't help but be fearful of the outside. Her trauma is still fresh in her memory; she wouldn't want to incite that horror upon herself.

All that is considered, but still, she has to see Dorean.

'Wyll and Identity', a psychology book by Cerebrum wyll scientist, Dr Logi, has become one of Epo's new favourites. Dr Logi states wyll and identity are diametrically opposed, as wyll is purely instinctual while identity is reasonable. While wyll and instinct can inform identity, 'who we are' is still largely a cerebral effort and when one is on the brink of death, the brain dumps the deeper intellectual functions to promote basic survival. Dr Logi argues that is what wyll truly is: unfiltered thought.

Epo likens what her sister is going through to that of analysis of soldiers during the endless war. Dr Logi called them 'the somnambulist', soldiers who would seemingly have no other thoughts in their heads other than to kill. No reports of somnambulist patients recovering exist; they would either die in battle or never get their minds back and wander the many forests of Genus until they collapsed. Dr Logi tried techniques on what few patients he could find but every time it seemed like a somnambulist was about to recover, they would soon after succumb to wyll-death.

In order for Epo to further understand her sister's condition, she has to do some analysis of her own.

Night-time; the Mother's eye is but a faint arc in the northern sky. Epo, making sure she's keeping as quiet as possible, leaves her bed and makes her way to the tent entrance. Rago sits at his desk, head resting upon a book, a small patch of drool wetting the page. Knowing he'll get angry if he sees that he's ruined another book, she grabs a small feathered pillow and gently moves his head to replace the book with it. As she dries the book and places it back on the shelf, she realises how easy it would've been for him to wake up. Is she trying to get caught?

She pauses at the entrance. A large part of her wants to go back to bed. She closes her eyes and pokes a hand outside, feeling the cold night air. She runs her hand down the fabric of the tent from the outside then examines the thick substance on her fingers. Epo admires the ingenuity. Each tent is made from fabric affixed to a brazier atop a wooden pole. Examining the fabric, it's made from a mixture of woven wool with tough leaves then treated with flame-retardant sap to extinguish any embers from the braziers. Though the design is impressive, Epo can't help but wonder why go to such lengths when a simple lantern in every tent would suffice. These tents are sturdy, sound-proofed and immune to burning. The Reapers have found a good balance between privacy and safety.

She realises she's distracting herself and tries to psych herself up. Using the somnambulist approach, she pushes her thoughts aside and wills herself to step outside.

It's dark and quiet and cold. She tries to stop herself, but her first instinct is to look over at the stables. She sees the shadowy silhouette of the structure and tears come to her eyes. She once liked the stables. The animals they kept there; the bustle of life. Now it's a miserable reminder of the pain she had to go through. Part of her wishes her wyll had broke so she wouldn't have to keep the memories.

She quickly corrects herself. She needs these memories. She needs her wyll; she will have the strength to make her trauma mean something. She turns away from the stables and begins her search.

She has no idea where Dorean's tent is located. She can only assume she's staying with Louma. Judging by the time it took Louma to get to Rago's tent the day she moved in, Epo estimates her tent must be close to the house. She will start her search there.

Looking down from a slope, she views an assortment of tents. Some are lit and some are dark. The braziers indicate who is awake and who is asleep. Out of a nearby lit tent, stumbles a tall, bald, male Reaper. They look at each other; Epo recognises him.

"Hey, I know you."

Epo freezes. Thoughts of the torture she went through under this man flow through her head. She should have stayed in Rago's tent.

"Boys," the man slurs to the people in his tent. "It's the little fuck-toy we used to play with."

One by one, three other men emerge. Epo knows them all. Their faces contort like demons in her vision.

"What's she doin' out here?"

"Maybe she misses us." A man with long hair steps out of the tent and approaches Epo.

Epo can't move; she's petrified.

"Maybe she wants to try out some group action."

Epo's heart pounds.

"Hey, come on," a second man from the tent says. "We were having fun drinking, why do we have to ruin it with work? Just let her be, yeah?"

The bald Reaper grabs the man's head and slams it into the ground. The man struggles but can't get free. The long-haired man laughs.

The bald man kneels in close to his captor. "Listen here, boy-lover, if you're looking to grow yourself a pussy then maybe we should give you your own cabin for a bit."

The man on the ground has a tattoo on his shoulder. That's the last man she was with when she was saved by Rago. He was so rough before, but now he's being chastised for showing the slightest inkling of kindness.

It dawns on Epo like the blinding first rays of Mother's light. These aren't men, they're children. They even referred to her as their toy. These people, they're no monsters or demons, they're small-minded creatures who are kept from maturing.

"Alright, stop it," says the third Reaper. "Let him go and let the girl be." He speaks with more authority than the others.

"Aw, why can't we make this night better?"

"Because, you idiot, Rago took her under his brazier. If you think it's a good idea to cross a general then by all means, get yourself cast out, just keep my name out of your mouth when Schizo is carving out your brand."

Reluctantly, the two aggressive Reapers retreat back into the tent. Before the tattooed man joins them, he turns and Epo sees a deep sadness in his eyes.

Since the first day of her torture, Epo wondered how such people could exist. In a world where every living person has a piece of the Child inside them, how can anyone treat another with such cruelty? But it's obvious to her now, people aren't made this way. This behaviour is learned.

Though these men are not absolved or forgiven, Epo feels a shift in her perception. Instead of fearing and hating them, she pities them. Though they stole her innocence, they don't have the freedom to even attempt to be better people, lest they be beaten down and made to conform. Though they may still talk and hold memories and make connections and decisions, they are still like the somnambulist; they're heartless.

"I'm sorry you had to go through that." A woman's

voice comes from behind Epo.

Epo turns and looks at her. She recognises her from the day her parents were killed. She also remembers her visiting Feilece in the stables. She is gorgeous; this is the visitor Feilece spoke of, the night before the invasion.

"Epo, isn't it?" The lady says as she approaches.

Epo nods, unable to relinquish a frown.

"Well it's nice to finally meet you. I'm Kasi. Feilece has spoken about you." She speaks softly, as if Epo is made of fragile ceramics and her words could cause cracks.

Epo tilts her head to get a look inside the tent Kasi came from. For a second, she sees a naked sleeping man before Kasi moves and obstructs her vision.

"Hey, are you okay." Kasi stoops to Epo's eye level.

Epo shifts away. "That man in the tent behind you, did you have sex with him?"

Kasi lets out a short laugh. "I'm not sure if that's any of your business."

"Do you spend every night with him?"

"It's still not your business."

"So that's a no. Do you sleep with someone different every night?"

"If you must know, it depends on who I've feelings for. Why are you asking me about my sex life?"

"I'm trying to understand how this village works."

Epo feels her eyes twitch, and her nose scrunches up. "My brother … he loves you."

"Is that so?"

"I know my brother. He can't hide an emotion to

save his life and when he feels something, he feels it completely."

Kasi chuckles. "Well, if that's true then it's great news."

"Great news for who?"

"For him. Love is a great thing to feel."

"And how would he feel if he knew how you spent your nights?"

Kasi doesn't reply, she just smiles and rises to her full height.

"You're manipulating him," Epo says. "You're making him part of this system. Turning him into one of them."

"I'm giving him something to live for. I'm giving him wyll."

"Tell me, how many men here do you have living by your wyll?"

Kasi looks over towards Rago's tent. "What is happening with you and Rago?"

Epo stalls. Since leaving Rago's tent, she's been subjected to a range of different emotions. First, she was anxious, then terrified by her old abusers, then she felt pity. Now, her anger flares. All of these emotions, Epo has had no control over. She hates this woman. She wants to slam her head into the ground. She wants to yell and chastise her for what she's doing to her brother. She has become part of the system. It's time she took control.

Cunningly, Epo changes her demeanour and gives Kasi a kind smile. "I'm sorry, I haven't exactly been acting pleasant. I'm Epo, it's nice to meet you too."

Kasi squints. "Interesting."

"I have a question, I don't suppose you can show me to Louma's tent?"

"You wish to see your sister?"

"I won't speak to her or anything … I just want to see her, I'll look from the outside."

Kasi thinks for a moment. "Okay."

XXI

A S EPO AND Kasi walk through the village, Epo looks up at the night sky. Three of the celestial siblings twinkle in the blackness.

"Do you think it's the same out there the way it is here?" Epo asks.

"Are you asking if I think there are people living on the other Children?" Kasi looks up. "It's possible. The Mother actually visits them though, we see it happen as the days go by. Perhaps those Kids were never lonely enough to bring about something like us."

"I wonder. If people do exist out there, would they be allowed to be as cruel to themselves as we are to each other."

Kasi stops and stares at the girl with a frown.

Epo continues walking and then looks back at her. "What's the matter?"

"You're the second child to talk to me like this."

"Like what?"

"Like you're wise beyond your years."

"After the things I've been through, is it really so wise to ponder on the nature of people?"

"When I was your age, all I was thinking about was

how to change my life," says Kasi.

"Maybe I'm doing the same thing."

Kasi gives a minor laugh. "I like you, little Epo."

Epo changes her tone, becoming serious. "Were you abused … like me?"

"Well, abuse comes in many different flavours. Growing up in Koilia with no family to protect me, I learned pretty fast that abusers are almost everywhere. If you don't mind me asking, how are things with Rago?"

"Rago's okay. He's not a bad man."

"Are you sure about that? If it weren't for Rago, you wouldn't have gone through everything you did."

Epo hangs on the lady's words. What she says is true.

Kasi sighs and gestures to a nearby tent. "We're here."

It's a big rectangular tent with the fabric pulled so taut it's close to tearing. Epo parts the fabric so she can peek inside without giving herself away. Epo sees Dorean and her eyes widen. She's right there, sitting on a chair, staring forward. She shivers nervously, Epo wonders what is wrong with her.

Epo examines her as best she can from her position, looking for signs of somnambulism.

"You aren't even a little bit broken, are you, Epo?" says Kasi.

"I think you would agree we're all at least a little bit broken, aren't we?" Epo jokes but Kasi's eyes are serious. Epo loses her smile.

"Did you hear something?" Louma's voice comes from inside. Dorean doesn't answer her.

Louma approaches Dorean; she's obviously drunk. Her voice sounds like her larynx has gone through decades of punishment. "I asked if you heard anything outside."

Dorean struggles as she answers, eyes shifting in and out of contact with Louma's. "I … I don't."

Louma smacks Dorean and she falls to the ground.

Epo rears back clamping her hand to her mouth.

"Is this what you came to see?" Kasi says.

"This place." Epo speaks through shivering lips. "You breed and teach nothing but hatred."

"That is simply not true. It may look like it from where you're sitting but there's more to being a member of the Reaper family than being cruel."

"I don't understand. Through all this, what are you hoping to build?"

"Strength."

Epo looks at Kasi and realises she isn't talking to any old Reaper. Kasi lives it; she believes in it.

Kasi squats next to Epo. "It may not seem like it upon first glance, but there is love here too. Go ahead, take another look."

Epo looks back inside the tent and sees Louma hugging Dorean tightly.

She's pleading. "I'm sorry I hit you. I love you so much, I'm so sorry."

Dorean is hugging her back, tears streaming from her eyes.

"You may not believe her," says Kasi. "But Louma truly does love your sister. We all love each other. And any new members that come along, we accept. We love them and they all eventually learn to love us back.

And at the same time, we teach them to be strong."

"Why?" Epo asks calmly, acting like she didn't just witness her sister being assaulted. "Why teach them to be strong?"

"Because they'll need it for what is to come."

"For your war?"

"Hmm, what has Rago told you?"

"Not much, but why would you need so many soldiers if you weren't planning a war?"

"Very astute …"

"So, what? You build up this 'family' of yours, then force them to die on some battlefield?"

"Not by force, but by wyll. It is their wyll to fight. They do not fight for me, I help them fight for themselves. We are a free people, and by our swords, the whole country will be free."

"You're missing something very important in your logic."

"And what is that?"

"It is their wyll to fight because you made it their wyll to fight."

They stare at each other. Kasi's eyes glare.

"These people are no freer than I was when I was in that stable. Your family is broken," says Epo.

"What do you know!" Kasi blurts out her words, then looks away and takes a slow breath. She closes her eyes and speaks calmly. "I know my family better than you do. These are my people." Kasi opens her eyes and looks at Epo's clothing. "This sign right here," she says pointing to the Reaper insignia on Epo's chest. "This tells us that you are part of us. This tells you that you will be loved and cherished. This tells you that you will be strong, and that you will be remembered in Genus history until the Mother takes her Child back. We are Reapers, it is our job to uproot the weeds and sow the seeds of the future."

Epo lets the woman finish her pitch, then looks at Dorean. Seeing her sister cry tells Epo she is no somnambulist. She has her answer, it's time to leave.

She looks back at Kasi. "I'm sorry … for insulting your family."

Then she gets up and walks back to Rago's tent.

XXII

"WHAT THE FUCK are you doing?" Louma slurs, slamming her cup down.

"Uh." Killer delays as she thinks hard about how best to respond. Any minor slip-up will turn this situation sour.

Louma doesn't give her time. "Uh, uh, what are you, one of the fucking sheep!" She stands and smacks Killer around the head.

Killer stumbles and drops the logs she was carrying.

"I … was getting firewood … like you asked me to."

"Oh, so it's my fucking fault now is it? What took you so long?"

"I was only gone five minutes."

"Yeah, whatever." Louma sits back down and takes another sip of her drink. "Well, hurry it up before the fire goes out."

Killer's arms shake as she picks up the logs. Before she left to fetch the wood, Louma was normal. She was drinking her wine joyfully, smiling and insulting Rago. Then suddenly, out of nowhere, she changed. It happens every time she drinks. All Killer wants to do is make her mother proud and happy but she keeps failing.

Killer puts a log on the end of a firestick and lifts it out of a hole in the top of the tent, dropping it into the brazier. As the log adds to the fire, the brazier overflows with ash and a trickle of soot falls to the ground.

"What the fuck is that?" says Louma in a dark voice.

"I …"

"Did you forget to clean the ash out today?"

"Y … you said … you would …"

"What's that!" Louma shrieks.

"You …"

Before Killer can reply, Louma picks up her cup and hurls it at Killer's head. Reflexively, Killer brings her arm up and deflects it. Louma then stands, shoves Killer to the floor then kicks her in the stomach.

"You're just like the fucking rest of them!"

Louma paces around the tent. "You're going to disappoint me. You don't love me, they didn't love me, he didn't love me. You're all here to fuck with me."

Louma slumps back in her chair. "Disappointment. Parents, Apo, Rago … Seemo."

Killer shifts back and hugs her elbows, trying to take up as little space as she can. Tears stream from her eyes.

"Are you fucking crying?" asks Louma.

Killer quickly wipes her face and forces the tears away.

Louma sighs. "Oh, fuck the Mother … Look."

Louma walks over and sits by Killer. "Look, I'm sorry, okay. I get all fucked up in the head. Can you forgive me?"

Killer tries to think of the correct reply.

"I asked you a fucking question."

"I forgive you, Mother," Killer says quickly.

The tent goes quiet for a moment. Killer feels she needs to apologise but she doesn't want to make her mother more angry so she keeps her words to herself. Then she wonders if her mother is waiting for an apology and will be even more angry if she says nothing.

"I'm sorry, Mother. I …" Killer then realises Louma isn't listening to her, she's staring at her cup on the ground.

"You spilled my fucking wine."

Killer's mouth shivers as she tries to speak. "I."

Before Killer can say anything, Louma grabs her by the hair and drags her to a stand. She pulls out a wooden chair, places it in the middle of the tent then slams Killer down on it.

"You don't talk, you don't cry, you don't even fucking move unless I tell you to. Do you understand?"

Killer doesn't reply, she keeps her eyes forward and body rigid.

"Good."

Louma picks up her cup, sits back down in her chair and pours a drink. Out of her peripheral vision, Killer can see Louma's spiteful eyes staring at her as she sculls backs her drink.

Though she feels like a failure, Killer is happy she at least has clear instructions now. Don't move, don't cry, don't talk. She can do that. She just has to stare. Keep staring; don't move.

She sees her mother's head tilt on its side and hears the windy breathing she does when she's fallen asleep. Killer continues to stare forward; she will not let her mother down again.

The tent parts and a figure appears in the recess. Though she cannot look directly, Killer recognises the figure as the little girl from Rago's tent.

Killer can't tell why, but she suddenly gets an unyielding urge to cry. She doesn't even know this girl and yet she wants to race outside, pick the girl up and hug her close. She wants to bawl her eyes out and tell the girl she loves her.

Why is her brain doing this to her. Why does it have to make everything so hard for her. She fights her urges, refusing to move or cry. Keep staring; don't move. She has to be strong … for her mother.

The girl is talking to someone outside. Killer can't hear what they're saying, only murmurs.

The voices wake Louma. "Did you hear something?" she asks.

Killer doesn't respond; she's not allowed to talk. Keep staring; don't move.

Louma gets up and stands in front of Killer, looking down her nose at her. Killer keeps staring; she can't disappoint her mother.

"I asked you if you heard anything outside?"

Killer doesn't know what to do. Does she answer or keep to her original orders? She can't decide; she's failing again.

Louma smacks her. Killer falls off her chair. She

once again chooses not to move, but this time, it's not because she was ordered to. She lies on the ground aching, eyes glazing over. Tears emerge and gather where her cheek meets the ground.

Why can't she figure out how to please her? Why must she keep failing? Louma makes it so difficult; it has to be for a reason. This all has to be worth something because if it isn't … if this is all for nothing, why bother going on?

As Killer questions the meaning of her efforts, she feels her body get lighter and more brittle. Her skin grows cold.

"Seemo?" Louma says in a shaky voice.

Killer looks up to see Louma's eyes gushing with tears.

Louma helps Killer to her feet then wraps her arms around her.

"Killer! I'm so sorry."

Killer, feeling warmth and weight return to her, hugs Louma back.

"I'm sorry I hit you. I love you so much, I'm so sorry,"

Louma pulls away then starts kissing Killer's face, talking in-between. "It's you and me, you got that? Nothing else matters. Not this town, not the past, not Koilia. Not the Reapers, not the Grothia, no one! You and me, that's all that matters. We'll beat the Grothia, then we'll beat the Reapers. We'll sit atop the Ab-dominals and everyone will be ours. Once we control them all, they will stop disappointing me. Seemo failed to live up to my expectations, but you won't. I built you … from scratch. There's not a single imperfection in you."

Louma stops and sits on her bed, swaying drunkenly. "Together, we'll rule Genus." Then she slumps down on her side and falls asleep.

Killer gazes at her mother, mind blank and heart empty of all emotion but a slight rhythmic hiccup. She covers her mother with a wool blanket and slides a feather pillow under her head. She crosses the tent to her own bed and sits down. She doesn't want to sleep; she wants to watch her mother sleep. She wonders if her mother will wake back up. Half of her wants her to wake back up and come and give her another hug. But the other half is scared she'll wake up and hit her again.

Killer lies down and curls up into a ball. What if she disappoints her mother in her sleep? She fears she'll never sleep again.

XXIII

—⌇—

"**A**LRIGHT, GIMME YOUR hand," Popoki says to Feilece as he pulls out a stool and takes a seat. Feilece places his hand on Popoki's.

"Let the Mother see it, we'll need Her light," says Popoki, pulling Feilece towards him.

Feilece angles his elbow and the Mother's evening light shines over an open gash on his outer forearm.

"This is gonna hurt," says Popoki as he readies a sewing needle with twine and presses it against Feilece's skin.

Feeling the sting of the needle as it pierces into his arm, Feilece lets his heart rate quicken. With time sped up, he can get this procedure over quickly. He watches Popoki's hand race as it sews the wound shut.

"You'rehandlingthisprettywellforakid."

Feilece can only just make out what the man is saying.

After a few seconds, Popoki is done and Feilece lets time go back to normal.

"We'll let that heal for a couple of days. No more training, just relax."

"It's okay, we don't have to stop our daily routine. I

won't make that mistake again."

"You're a tough boy, Feilece, but a warrior must know when to fight and when to rest. Though it may not seem like it, it is still training."

Feilece nods.

"Hey, don't worry about it," says Popoki. "You're progressing well. You'll catch up to me eventually."

Popoki stands, picks up his stool and goes inside his tent, calling, "come on, it's time to eat."

"Not just yet," says Feilece as he looks out over the paddock to the road leading to Tiris.

"You're gonna watch them again?"

"Yeah."

"What are you looking for? Do you think you'll recognise some of them?"

"I don't really know."

"Well, whatever. It's up to you if you want to eat cold food." Popoki walks into the tent, leaving Feilece to gaze.

Over the horizon, horses pulling big carriages come into view. The carriages are meant to carry horses so they're basically big empty cabins with gates at the back. Feilece counts ten of them; only half of those that left a few days prior.

The carriages halt at a hitching post. The riders dismount and unlock the carriage gates. People emerge slowly.

Often, people show up on foot. But the bulk of the new recruits come by carriage. Feilece counts around ten to twenty Tirians per carriage. On their faces, he reads anguish, stress, nervousness, awkwardness, but mostly, sadness.

Reapers wearing grey clothing approach the Tirians and lead them away to their respective living quarters. Feilece barely recognises any of them. They look like strangers from a distant time.

Feilece pokes his head inside the tent and looks at his clock. Shortly after moving into Popoki's tent, he snuck into his old house and stole it from the wall along with the pinhole camera. Popoki didn't seem to care, he let the boy make a hole in the roof to let in the Mother's light so he could project it.

He stares into the Mother's indifferent eye, immersed in that feeling he gets. It's like he's in an infinite void, screaming in the language of the celestials. Calling for help. A sound that nothing alive can hear.

"Eat your dinner, boy." Popoki's voice snaps Feilece out of reverie. He takes a seat next to Popoki as the man shovels boar meat and bread into his face.

"Popoki?"

"Mm?"

"What do the colours mean?"

"Mm …" Popoki finishes his mouthful. "I told you it doesn't matter to you. You're a general's apprentice, the colours don't apply."

"I still would like to know."

"Alright, if you're that curious."

Feilece gets to work on his dinner while Popoki talks.

"Every new recruit starts off as the colour grey like the colour of clay, it represents the Child. While grey, they take shifts in doing pretty much everything, they train, they hunt, they harvest, etc. During this phase, they're tested to see what colour best suits them between red and green. Green represents the grass and the leaves. Those that find themselves green are tasked with cultivation, harvesting, maintaining, cooking. All that kind of stuff. Red represents blood, they become hunters and are given more emphasis in their training."

"Who chooses what colour they get?"

"The grey-clothed director. He has a bunch of fellows that do the testing then he goes over the numbers and designates."

"What if someone is designated a colour that they don't want? Do they get to change it?"

"I'm not sure. I think they can make a case to do further testing but if they're not suited, they're not suited."

"I thought everyone was free here."

"Yeah, but just because you're free doesn't mean you know what's best. I don't hear of many people complaining about their positions so the process appears to work well."

Feilece disagrees. There a plenty of reasons why someone wouldn't speak out. Perhaps they're scared of alienating themselves or their peers, or they're scared of change. Maybe they've been convinced the process works so they assume their feelings must be wrong and go against their own interests for the sake of the system. With only one man in charge of who gets what colour, it's beginning to feel like to be a Reaper is to have your life decided for you.

Kasi talks about freedom constantly, so it surprises Feilece she would let a system like this run.

"What about the other colours," Feilece asks.

"Yellow and black? They both represent the Mother, one for the day and one for the night. The yellows make up the bulk of the army and they are our best fighters. Black Reapers are trained in espionage and assassination; they fight during the night when the enemy is most vulnerable. They're also our protectors. They maintain the perimeter, keeping a constant watch for possible threats."

"I've noticed the black and yellows have their own part of the village separate to the other colours."

"Yeah, it distinguishes the ranks. The red and greens are mixed in with the greys because they all came from being grey themselves."

"Do red and greens not grow to be yellow and black the way greys do?"

"Not exactly. Black and yellows are mostly made up of our older members, those from Sickle & Scythe or former Demons. In order for a red or green to earn a higher rank, a black or yellow must take them on as an apprentice then they're given their new clothes when their master grants it."

"I guess that explains why they set themselves up in the north where the terrain is higher. They get to look down on the lower colours and pick out possible apprentices."

"Yep. A lot of Reapers, though, like to take on apprentices so they have their own personal worker waiting on them day and night. They never actually let them earn their colours."

"Is that what I am, your waiter?" Feilece jokes.

Popoki smiles though his eyes betray he doesn't find it funny. "That's not the way I like to do things."

Popoki takes both of their empty plates and puts them outside to be collected by the night cleaner.

"It's a pretty efficient system you've set up here," says Feilece.

"Yep, everyone does their part. It was all Schizo's doing. He wanted everyone to feel like a part of something bigger and stronger than themselves."

"What about the generals? Where do you guys fit?"

"We generals are detached from the whole process, but we're still warriors and part of the whole family. We're trusted to find our own place among it all."

"Do generals ever take on apprentices?"

"No, it's not our duty to promote anyone."

"But you took me in."

"Yeah, Schizo wanted me to keep an eye on you. Figured I might as well make the most of it. As you say, 'efficient'."

"Is that what this is about, I'm an order from your boss?"

Popoki smiles and says casually, "nope."

Feilece chortles.

"You should watch yourself around the other Reapers though," says Popoki. "As no doubt, they'll be jealous of you becoming the first apprentice to a general. You get the good meals and don't have to do much work. I try to be as handy as I can to bridge the gap in our standing but even a lot of my old Sickle friends can't get over my position. Sometimes I wish I had been made a yellow or black instead of a general."

"How does one become a general?"

"Only Schizo can decide."

"What makes him choose?"

"There are a bunch of reasons. Rago he chose because he admired the old man's science. Louma and Seemo were somewhat political. The hunting brothers were guardians of Kasi so they came along with her."

"What about you?"

"We knew each other from Sickle & Scythe. He was just a kid at the time. He used to look up to me; I thought he was a little brat."

Popoki's eyes go sad. "His father and my brother were lovers. After your father …" Popoki looks like he's about to start crying but he stops himself. "Well, anyway. After Sickle broke up, I had nowhere to go so I became a street fighter. I was good, I was starting to build up a bit of a name for myself. I hit a streak of fifty nil." Popoki goes to his liquor cabinet and pours himself a mug of homebrew beer.

"What does that mean?"

Popoki winces from his first sip. "Fifty wins with no losses."

"Wow."

"But then, after one of my fights, I got a random challenger from the audience. To my surprise, it was my old fellow Schizo, all grown up."

"Did you fight him?"

"Of course."

"What happened?"

"He completely destroyed me. He didn't even break a sweat."

"He's that good?"

"I was just as surprised as you are. He then went on to tell some grandiose speech about his new group and ended up recruiting every spectator there."

"So that's when you joined?"

"No, I didn't join until later on. He asked me and I refused so he invited me around to their headquarters to reminisce on our old Sickle days. He brought me to the castle of our old employers, the PanoApo. The place had been abandoned after The Apo had been slaughtered by your father and other Sickle members."

"Why would my father do that?"

"The Apo were tyrannical … or something. I'm not so sure, I was too young at the time to take part in the massacre and Sickle didn't last long after that."

"I see."

"So I went and dined with Schizo and while I was there, I met the most beautiful woman I had ever seen with this amazing blonde hair that looked like the Mother's light."

"Seemo."

"Yeah … I didn't know it at the time, I thought I was feeling a wanting for true battle and the Reapers could provide, but I'm sure of it now, I joined because of Seemo."

Feilece nods.

When they train every morning in Monolith Meadow, Feilece can tell Popoki's mind is elsewhere. Although he is an attentive teacher, often he takes a moment to scan the trees for movement. Feilece has never met Seemo, so he doesn't know much about the connection she and Popoki share. But he does feel empathy for the man as he watches his heart break every day when she doesn't show up.

"What about Kasi?" Feilece says. "How did she become a general?"

"I'm not sure how they met, they were already married by the time I had joined. They certainly suit each other. It bothered me at first because when I met up with Schizo after not seeing him in years, he was a completely different person to the kid I remembered. It's natural for people to change over time but it was weird, as if the kid I knew and the new Schizo were not the same. But then he remembered everything from the old Sickle days …"

Feilece lets his mind wander, losing track of the conversation. 'They certainly suit each other'. Feilece chooses not to believe this. Kasi only belongs with him. Schizo must be removed from the situation. But if he's as good as Popoki says he is, how will Feilece ever have a chance?

"Feilece?"

Feilece blinks. "Huh, what?"

"I said it's getting dark; you should probably go to bed. Rest that arm of yours."

"Um, I'm not feeling tired, I might go for a walk first."

"Fine by me, just don't wake me when you get back."

Feilece slyly takes his axe when Popoki looks away and leaves the tent. He makes his way to the stables and goes to Djent's cabin. Djent quickly wakes up. Feilece puts his hand in the cabin and Djent rubs his head against it.

"How about some night training, huh boy?"

Djent huffs.

Feilece releases the latch and the ram makes his way into the open. Feilece climbs on his back and they ride out into the woods.

It's dark until Feilece's eyes adjust to the low light emitted by the sleeping Mother. Djent doesn't heed the darkness at all. He brings Feilece to the tree they usually visit. The bark of the trunk is crushed inwards, dented by horn butts.

Feilece climbs off and gets into stance with his axe in hand. "Let's see how well this works." He performs a downward slice. Pain shoots up his arm. He winces, drops his axe and grapples his elbow. Djent whines as if he felt the pain too. He stands behind Feilece to give the boy something to lean on.

The pain … he wants to ignore it and carry on but he can barely feel his arm.

Djent nuzzles him.

"It's okay, I'm fine. It's going to take longer than I thought." Feilece pats Djent then picks up the axe. He spends the rest of the night practising one-handed techniques while commanding attack patterns with Djent.

XXIV

E PO INVOLUNTARILY PRESSES her tongue against her upper lip as she meticulously tries to tie her ponytail into a braid. She parts her hair into three segments, folding one over the other, then the third over the first. Two over three, three over one, one over two. She finds the process therapeutic. Concentrating deeply on a simple task, to the point where the rest of the world disappears, sharpens her wits so she can better comprehend the concepts in Rago's books.

With not much else to keep her entertained, she turned to her hair. When stripped of all levels of engagement other than a groggy old man and his books, one finds entertainment in things once thought to be trivial. She's fallen in love with her hair, as it's become a great deterrent from boredom between her lessons.

Growing up, all she thought about was reading, and now she's submerged in a world of nothing but letters, words and paragraphs. She can't help but venture elsewhere for respite, lest her eyes become permanently crossed.

"What is this facile fascination you've developed

with your hair?" Rago enters into the tent with a wooden basket full of food.

"It makes me look pretty, I am a girl, you know."

"You are a girl, yes, but not a simpleton."

"I've also been locked up in a tent for over a month with nothing but books to satiate the tumour of tedium I can feel growing in my brain. Sometimes black print is not enough."

"Tumour of tedium, a clever word choice."

"I thought of it yesterday and have been waiting for a chance to use it."

She elicits a small chuckle from the old man. "By the way, you have a stalker. I spotted that Lixi acolyte watching the tent again. His appearance has been more frequent lately. Make sure you keep yourself wary when I'm not around. We can't have that brute defiling our progress here."

Epo holds her hair against her chest. She's not told Rago of her little trip out of the tent she took a few weeks ago. To her surprise, no one else has brought it up either. She suspects the men she bumped into are keeping it secret for self-preservation—Rago won't be happy with them threatening his star convert—but why hasn't Kasi spoken of it?

Epo returns to working on her braid. She finishes the final fold and ties a loop of red string at the end.

"What do you think?" Epo approaches Rago, shaking the braid up onto her shoulder and running her hands down it.

"I find it menial at best. Now eat your dinner."

Epo pouts and sits at Rago's table. She serves herself a plate of roasted vegetables garnished with flowers from Monolith Meadow.

"No meat today?" Rago asks, sounding flat.

"After you told me about how they've been treating the cattle, I've sworn off it."

"Are you growing a heart for the cows, now?"

"It's a funny expression, that: 'growing a heart'. Assuming one was once heartless." Epo throws a touch of sarcasm into her voice, enough to be mildly entertaining while maintaining her point.

"Whatever," Rago says. "After this, I would like to run a test on you to see how this whole experiment is coming along."

"How about a trade? You can run an experiment on me if I can run an experiment on you."

"At what point did you start thinking you were in any position to propose any trading?"

"Since I figured out your tests were completely reliant on how honest I decide to be."

Rago softly grunts.

"You give me all these books to learn from but you don't give me any way of practically applying the skills. You're the only one I'm allowed to speak to, so I might as well practice on you."

"What test are you hoping to run on me?"

"Just a simple test of motivation."

A smile twitches on Rago's face.

Epo recently found a book among his collection showing the wear of one that has been read many times. A book titled 'Motivation: Delving into the True Essence of Wyll'.

"Very well," he says. "After I'm done, you may ask whatever questions you like."

The two finish their meals and Rago clears the table. Epo sits patiently in her chair while Rago retrieves his journal and sets himself up on the opposite end of his desk.

"Alright, you know how this goes now. A series of questions, answer truthfully, blah, blah, blah. Are you ready?"

Epo nods, her braid flapping.

"We'll start off simple, what is your name?"

"Epo Anemelos."

"Have you, at any point, felt disconnection from that title at all?"

"Disconnected? No."

Rago scribbles in his journal.

"You felt the need to clarify, why is that? Is there a particular feeling you have felt towards that title that is out of the ordinary?" Rago and Epo lock eyes for a moment.

"It's not that I feel disconnected from my name, it's that my name doesn't seem as important as it once was."

Rago twitches another smile as he writes.

"Can you tell me the name of your father?"

"Anema Anemelos."

"Does hearing his name cause any distress or bring about any ill feeling at all?"

"I feel …" Epo struggles to think. Rago watches her intently. "Simply hearing his name doesn't invoke any harsh feelings, but if I chose to think about him deeper … I can't help but feel …" Epo can't find the right word to describe it.

After a few seconds of silence, Rago interjects. "It's

okay, I have one more question about your father then we can move on. Is that alright?"

Epo nods, her eyes well up with tears.

"I want to ask you to close your eyes and take yourself out of your role for a moment."

Epo closes her eyes and lets Rago's voice direct her.

"You are no longer Epo Anemelos, you are no longer your father's daughter. You are a nameless girl with no lineage. You are a figment in time."

Epo feels her consciousness leave her body. She looks down on herself, sitting in her chair. She feels empty, bereft of attachment.

"I want you to recall memories of Anema, filter through them and find ones that stick out to you, ones that define him."

She imagines herself floating above the farm, looking down upon Anema as he works in the fields. He's harvesting crops, rustling sheep, fixing equipment, chopping wood.

"Do you see him?" Rago says.

"Yes," the girl whispers.

"Good. Now, how would you describe him?"

She ponders for a while, watching the man work. Eventually, the perfect word appears in her mind, and she offers it up with a hush.

"He's small."

"That's good. You may open your eyes now, Epo."

Epo opens her eyes to the sight of Rago finishing up his analysis. The tears in her eyes have dried, and her skin feels numb. She struggles for a second inside of her body, and her mind.

"Thank you, that was very productive. You may go

back to reading now." Rago puts away his journal.

"Wait, wait, wait," says Epo, trying to blink away a growing migraine.

"Ah, yes. You wanted to run a test on me. Well, go right ahead. Unless you have forgotten what it was you wanted to ask me." Rago speaks with an air of confidence.

Epo stares at him for a moment. "Motivation!" The word comes blurting out of her face, as if it was pressurised in her throat. Rago frowns.

"Tell me," says Epo. "What motivates you, Rago?"

Rago leans back and crosses his arms. "What motivates me to do what?"

"To … live. To do what you do." Epo stumbles through her first question.

Rago smiles condescendingly at her. "Are you sure you don't want to prepare a bit before we start?"

Epo takes a deep breath and tries again. "What motivates you to break people's wyll and replace their old identities with a new ones?"

Rago looks impressed. "Well, I would say that I am motivated by science. I'm fascinated by what defines a person. Breaking one's wyll reverts them to their purest form, one without attachment."

"Science … I wonder about that."

Rago furrows his brow.

"Do you have any children, Rago?"

"I do not."

"Did you ever want children?"

"There was a time where I wanted a child, yes."

"Were you with someone at the time, did you have a wife or a girlfriend?"

"Yes."

"So why didn't you two have a child together?"

"There were … complications. Where are you going with this?"

Epo makes her voice clinical. "Through this line of questioning, I am hoping to extend to you the opportunity to perhaps consider the fact that maybe your motivation stems from a particular feeling of inadequacy. You were unable to impart your will onto a child, so you instead break people down into a form akin to a newborn and impart your will upon on them. Do you feel there is any validity in this statement?"

Rago stares at her, glaring. Epo stares back, expressionless.

"You are very perceptive, aren't you, girl."

Epo takes a breath. "Let's talk about something else. Tell me, Rago, what did your parents do for a living?"

A few seconds pass before Rago replies. "They ran a homeless shelter on the outskirts of Koilia. The hunters of Eftheia would provide them with food and they would feed people in need."

"That's a selfless way of living. What motivated them?"

"They always told me everyone deserves a meal. I suspect there was more to it than that."

"Explain."

"I assumed they were on a venture to clean up the streets. If they were to show through their efforts, they were able to make Koilia a more respectable place, it could've earned them favour in the eyes of one of the kings. They raise the collective status of the people of Koilia, then they themselves rise in class. It's quite smart, really."

"And what happened to them?"

"They died in a street brawl, killed by the very people they strove to help." The man's voice betrays no sadness or anger, he simply states it as fact.

"I see," says Epo. "I wonder about the whole 'rising in class' motivation you've bestowed upon them. In your memory, is there any instance of them coming across as politically engaged, or even relatively smart people?"

"I couldn't say, I was only a boy when they died."

"And you think your parents, living on the outskirts of the city, had some complex scheme of using the homeless to rise in class … are you sure they weren't just kind people?"

"I'm sure they were very kind people, but kindness is not a motivator. Read that book again."

"I found that I don't agree with everything in the book," Epo says, smiling.

"Is that so."

"I think kindness is a great motivator, I would even go far enough to say it's one of the purest motivations there is."

Rago says nothing.

"Here, I'll demonstrate." Epo steps up from her chair and goes to the tent's entrance.

"What are you doing?"

Epo pops her head out of the tent and looks around. Rago gets up from his chair.

"Where did you say you saw that stalker?"

"He was a couple tents down on the left, why are you—"

"Ah, there he is."

Epo walks out of the tent into the darkness of the night, in the direction of her old abuser.

"No! Stop!" Epo hears Rago scramble to catch up to her as she walks towards the large man. As she approaches him, she remembers all the pain he caused her. She knows the threat she faces.

Seeing his face, she remembers it being pushed into the dirt by his fellow. The man tried to be kind and it was beaten out of him. One instance of the man being kind does not mean she's safe. He could take her back to his tent and have his way with her. He could be crazed and kill her. This could undo all the work she has done. But she doesn't fear any of that. She has a hunch about him, so she walks right up to him, and stares into his eyes.

"Is there something you want to say to me?" She keeps her voice soft.

"I … uh." He stutters, and shifts nervously.

"It's okay, you can talk to me."

"I miss you." A tear creeps down the man's face.

In Epo's mind, she recoils. This man has no business missing her after how he treated her. He is a monster and deserves all the pain that he pushed onto her. But she knows this is the monster inside herself talking, the words of a great weakness grown from her pain. To battle this dark side of herself, she must be strong enough to deny it the nourishment of her anger. Kindness is the purest motivator.

"What is it you miss about me the most?"

The man sniffs. "I miss all of you: your touch, your warmth … but most of all, I miss your smell."

Epo smiles. She reaches into the man's belt and

pulls out a dagger. She takes her braided ponytail into her hand and pulls it taut. Raising the blade to the base of the ponytail, she swipes up, cleaving the braid from her head. Her hair becomes free and drapes around her ears as she holds her severed ponytail in her hand. She puts the dagger back into the man's belt. She takes him by the hand and places her braid into his palm.

"Now you may carry a piece of me with you wherever you go."

She looks up into his eyes.

"Are … are you the Mother?" the man asks.

"Even if I was, everything would be the same." She releases the man's hand then turns and walks away.

She returns to Rago.

His jaw is dropped. "Why did you do that? Your hair … after how he treated you."

"No good comes from causing more pain, but some good can be had from alleviating it." She walks into the tent followed by a demanding Rago.

"Tell me why you did that! Why take that risk for a person who was so horrible to you? Was it for my benefit? Are you just proving a point!"

"Proving a point was not the main motivation, but it just so happened to coincide. The motivation is much more simple."

"Then explain to me!"

"You know, I find it fascinating this gets to you so much. Are you so far gone you can't even recognise a simple act of kindness?"

"So you were just being nice … to a man that beat and raped you for months. That doesn't make any sense."

"I did it for the same reason your parents opened their shelter. Because everyone deserves a meal."

Rago sits down, rests his chin on his knuckles, and stares into nothingness.

"That man out there is as much a victim as I was," says Epo. "Only, instead of him being the abuser, it was you … and your 'science'."

Rago doesn't reply; he continues to stare.

"One last question, then the experiment is over. If your parents could see you today, what do you think they would say to you?"

Rago just grunts.

"That last question was for you to ponder on your own. The test is over. I'm going to bed."

Epo leaves the speechless man to his thoughts, and pulls the curtain on her room. She lies down on her stack of cushions.

She closes her eyes. A screaming rage echoes inside of her, chastising her for showing such a man, her rapist, kindness.

How could she do such a thing and hold any dignity? How can she harbour such weakness? That man deserves to die for what he's done. He should be dead!

She listens to the voice, respecting every word, but she can't help to perceive a specific subtext saying 'I am not in control'.

She takes the voice and imparts it into a reflection of herself in her minds eye. She looks down upon this version of herself as it rages and screams and cries. From this perspective, the voice is small.

If she were listening to anyone else, she would think they had all rights to be as angry as they could possibly be. She would be on her side, she would seek revenge on her behalf, she would go to war to make things right. But this isn't someone else she's listening to, these are her own deep-seated screams. And she's not going to let them steal her resolve.

They've already taken her innocence. She won't let them take her kindness as well.

XXV

"DEMONS!" LOUMA CALLS to the trees. "Want to go on a hunt?"

Killer looks around, curious about who her mother is addressing. They're deep enough in the forest that all she can see is brown and green, lit up by yellow cascading rays of the Mother's midday light.

"Shh." A soft sound comes from a nearby tree.

Killer looks up to find a man with long black hair crouched on a thick branch. Killer is amazed, the man was in such plain sight but she didn't see him.

"Get back," Louma says in a hushed tone as she pulls Killer behind the trunk of a nearby tree.

Peeking out, Killer sees a furry creature creeping on its two legs a few hundred metres away.

"It's a griffit cub," Louma whispers.

The animal stands almost as tall as Killer with short newly formed horns, an elongated neck and puny underdeveloped wings sticking out from the top of its shoulders.

"I've only ever seen them in drawings."

"Hush now, Killer," Louma says.

The griffit turns its head and Killer gets a look at its

face. It's not like the drawings; they usually depict something much more menacing. Their gruffer features must develop with age. Seeing this creature with its big alert eyes, face wet with tears and shaking drawn-in arms, all Killer sees is a terrified child. It must have been startled by Louma's call earlier. It has a strangely familiar face, akin to that of her own people.

Killer hears the pinging tension of a bowstring being pulled back above her. She looks up to see an archer with long white hair, perched on a branch with his bow drawn.

"Watch, Killer," Louma says with serious intonation.

The bowstring is let loose and the arrow flies right into the griffit's legs. The creature screams as it falls to the floor, prepubescent wings fluttering uselessly.

"Nice shot, Choris," Louma says.

The black-haired man jumps down from his tree. "About time. We've been tracking that thing all night."

"How have you been, Diakho?" Louma asks with a smile.

"Busy. What are you doing here?" He looks over at Killer. "Taking your pet out for a walk?"

"Her name is Killer, dickhead. Although, in saying that, it has taken me this long to realise I haven't actually made her kill anything. So, I figured it was time for another one of our hunts."

Choris jumps down from his tree, stares at Louma for a moment, then walks over to the griffit cub.

"He says it'll be a pleasure to have you two along," says Diakho.

"It doesn't feel like that's what he said."

"He's just annoyed that all we've had to kill since we got here are creatures of the forest, and you know what, so am I."

"You are bored?" asks Louma.

"We are thirsty. Schizo's war better come soon."

"Well you guys killed a griffit, that's pretty exciting. They're supposed to be rare in these parts, aren't they?"

"It's not unheard of. They just don't form big groups around here as they're known to do. This far north, they've only ever been seen in small family units."

Killer kneels down before the griffit. The poor thing is cowering, and curled up into a ball. Seeing it tremble, Killer can't help but feel a deep-seated attachment. A flash occurs in her mind and for a moment, she sees a naked young woman, not unlike herself, lying in place of the griffit.

Killer swallows. "It looks scared," she says.

"It is said griffits have the emotional intelligence of our close ancestors. Though it is not the same as killing a person, it's close enough," says Diakho as he stands over the griffit. "All animals feel fear when they know they're going to die."

Diakho throws a knife into the griffit's head.

Killer stumbles back.

"What the fuck are you doing?" Louma says, shoving Diakho.

"What!"

"We should of let my daughter kill it. She needs the experience."

Diakho squints. "Your daughter?"

"Uh, yes … it's part of the conversion process I've developed," Louma says.

"Right. Well, we earned the right to that griffit's life. Killing its mother last night wasn't enough."

They killed its mother too. Killer feels a tension in her chest. What if her mother died, would she be next? Would she find herself curled up into a ball as hunters finished her off? Will she feel fear when she knows she's about to die?

"What about Killer?" asks Louma.

"Don't worry, we'll find something for her. She should be going for smaller prey on her first hunt anyway."

"Very well. Daughter. Come to me."

Killer quickly pushes her thoughts out of her head and stands before her mother.

"My sweet Killer," Louma says framing Killer's face in her hands. "I've been training you every day to fight, to survive. Today you learn how to kill."

"We've got something," Diakho says as he directs everyone's attention towards a boar sniffing around in the forest. Choris primes his bow.

"Okay, here are your orders," Louma says to Killer. "Choris is going to wound that boar but not kill it. It is then up to you to go over to it with your sword and rid it of it's life."

"O … okay."

"I don't just want you to kill it either. I want to savour the feeling it gives you. Swoon over the dominance you feel knowing you are alive and it is dead because of you."

Killer hears a growing ringing in her ears.

"Oh, and you must kill it quickly, lest it succumbs to wyll-death. That way, it won't be your kill then, will it?"

"Yes, mother."

"Very good, now, get ready."

Killer stares at the boar. Her heart beats quicker with every passing second. Choris pulls back on his bowstring and the ringing in Killer's ears grows louder. She doesn't know if she can do this—she must do this.

Choris lets loose his arrow. The thing sticks into the boar's rump. The pig squeals and runs into the woods.

Without a thought, Killer races after the fleeing prey. She hears her mother yell from her behind but can't make out the words through the intense screeching inside her skull. She assumes they are words of encouragement as she dashes past tree after tree in pursuit of the injured boar. It is quick, keeping a solid distance from Killer. She loses track of time as she runs. Before long, she begins to feel fatigue growing in her limbs. The boar won't slow down. Killer's legs get tired, making them sluggish. She can't stop. She can't fail her mother. She was ordered to kill the boar, she must kill the boar, nothing else matters.

She trips on a root and smacks her head against the base of a tree as she falls to the dirt. The boar runs out of sight.

Killer pushes herself up and rubs her head. A migraine pulsates in her brain so she takes a deep breath and calms her heart to alleviate it. As her headache subsides, so too does the ringing in her ears. Suddenly, she finds herself in the silence of the forest.

"Mother." She calls but gets no reply.

"Mother!" She screams but the words dissipate quickly among the trees.

She hugs her shoulders and brings her knees in close as she sits with her back to the bark. The trees sway, drawing closer to each other. They feel like they're pulling themselves towards Killer, encroaching on her space.

She finds it harder and harder to breathe as the trees come closer and closer. In her head, she starts hearing the grunts of men. She feels cuts upon her skin, matching up with her scars.

"Stop!"

Terrified, she jumps up and runs through the forest aimlessly, crying and screaming for her mother.

She finds a break in the trees and the blinding Mother's light. She runs towards it until she finds herself in a meadow. A big slab of smooth rock sits at the centre.

She feels her legs give way and stumbles into the grass. Lying among the flowers, she feels safer. The trees aren't forcing themselves upon her anymore. The Mother is watching.

After a while, she sits up and presses her back to the rock. She takes a few deep breaths and tries to calm herself down but she's still terrified. She wants her mother … all she wants is her mother.

Looking around, she doesn't recognise this place but she still feels connected to it. Strange images appear in her mind, images and feelings associated with this meadow. Memories of a life that is not her own. She pushes it all out of her head.

Feeling control return to her legs, she brings them in and hugs her shins. She presses her forehead to her knees and starts crying.

"Where are you, Mother."

She hears a rustling in the grass on the opposite side of the rock. She startles and pulls away. Slowly, she creeps around the rock to take a look. She doesn't see any animals but, in the trees further away, she sees something moving. She only caught a glimpse, but whatever it was, it was massive. Its colour sparks a weird feeling in Killer's mind; something to do with that particular shade of purple.

She starts hallucinating. She sees a shadowy figment of a girl her own height running in from the woods. She's naked and holding a sword. Killer pulls her own sword from her belt and looks at it. It's the same sword.

A monster chases the shadowy girl. Killer feels an ominous déjà vu. The monster attacks and the girl stabs her sword through its chest then a man comes along and pulls the monster off her. Killer stands over her and looks down upon the shadowy girl. Killer doesn't recognise her, but she hates her with a flaming passion.

Her heart rate quickens, the ringing comes back, her vision shakes and rage bursts forth. Killer takes her sword and starts slicing at the shadow girl. The blade goes right through her and digs into the dirt. Killer doesn't stop, she hacks at the ground, over and over, as chunks of the Child fly in all directions.

She hears a sound behind her and turns around to the sight of a boar running through the meadow with an arrow sticking out of it.

Overcome by blood-lust, Killer dashes over to the boar. She knocks it onto its back and starts stabbing it. Blood squirts out; the boars screams. Killer's arm tires, but she doesn't stop. She can't stop. She keeps stabbing it until the beast no longer looks anything like it once was. It's a mound of entrails and yet, Killer can't stop stabbing.

"Killer! Stop!"

The voice of her mother reaches Killer's ears. Like an automaton, Killer sheaths her sword and stands.

Louma runs over. She looks down at the boar then at Killer, frowning.

"Why did you run off like that? I told you to stay."

"I ..." Killer can't find her words. She never heard such an order; she's failed once again.

"By the Mother's dangling tits, look at this fucking thing," Diakho says as he prods the boars remains with a knife. "Well, no one's going to be eating this. But at least you got what you came for, right?"

"Yeah ... I guess we did," Louma says incredulously.

"Mother!" Killer says in desperation. "I'm sorry, I didn't hear your order to stay. I don't know what happened—"

"It's okay, my daughter. You're okay."

Tears stream down Killer's face.

"No, no, it's okay," Louma wraps her arms around Killer and holds her close.

"Listen, we'll go back to camp and eat some food and have a nice calm night. This was only your first time, we'll ease you into it. I'm proud of you, my daughter."

Killer hugs her mother, squeezing tightly.

XXVI

R AGO STRIDES INTO the tent with two loaves of bread in his hand and a smile on his face.

"Look what I have here."

"Uh, bread," Epo says, raising her eyebrows.

"Upon first observation, it may look like mere bread, but I assure you, it represents something far more valuable."

Epo smiles, amused by the goofy old man, until she realises the bread is all he has. "Wait … is that our dinner?"

"It is," he says, proudly.

Epo squints at the man, inaudibly demanding an explanation. Every night since Epo moved into Rago's tent, his dinner table would be adorned with an assortment of food. Stews, meat, vegetables; bread was only ever a side dish.

Rago paces back and forth as he tells his story. "I was waiting at the serving desk for the chefs to prepare our normal general's meal, watching the greys in line getting their dinner. It got down to the last four. They were new recruits, Tirians, skinny little things, and they were exhausted. The server came out and put two loaves of bread on the bench, and said this is all we have left for the day."

Epo, reading ahead, can't help but smile.

"I thought to myself, two loaves of bread is nowhere near enough for these poor fellows. Then they brought out our dinner."

Epo cuts him off. "Everyone deserves a meal, right?"

Rago grins at her. "Precisely. You don't mind, do you?"

Epo, sitting atop her pile of pillows, extends a hand out. Rago tosses her a loaf and she bites into it. It's some of the most delicious bread she's ever had.

"I'm thinking," Rago mumbles with a mouth half full of bread. "The Reaper numbers are growing so fast that the demand for food is getting too much for the stores to handle. I notice most nights, we don't finish our food and it gets wasted. I'm sure it's similar for a lot of those in the higher colours too. I might talk to Schizo—no, wait, he's in Tiris still—I'll talk to Kasi about maybe setting up a redistribution service for the greys on days when food is scarce."

"Do you think she'll agree to it?"

"She should. Food is a right, especially when there is enough to go around. It's egregious to think people are going to sleep hungry when there is food going to waste. Maybe I'll speak to Popoki, he's pragmatic, I think he will agree with me. Perhaps he can help make a better case—"

As Epo listens to the man speak, her skin grows warm. Her efforts are working. If she can unlock compassion in this man, she can turn the whole of Genus.

"Your parents would be proud, Rago," she says.

Rago looks at her with a flash of surprise, then his brow furrows and eyes go distant. "I'm not sure about that. My mother, maybe. You remind me of her, actually. Similar smiles."

A grin creases across Epo's face, then she remembers that she has a test today. "Oh yeah, do you want me to get ready?"

"You know what," Rago says with uncharacteristic nervousness. "Maybe we should hold off on the tests for a little while."

"Oh?"

"Yeah, uh, we need to let the current, um, results settle. We can revisit the experiment at a later date and figure out where to go from there."

Staring at Rago, Epo sees a smile form on his face. She takes another bite of her bread.

"Well, I guess we'll be too busy anyway running our own food service," Epo says.

"Hah! Precisely."

The two are interrupted by Kasi pushing her way into the tent.

"Oh, Kasi, welcome. How unusual it is for you to visit," Rago says.

Kasi doesn't respond; she stares at Epo with sinister eyes. Epo frowns at her.

"It's good of you to come by actually, I have a proposition," says Rago.

Kasi looks at the bread in Rago's hand. "Is that all you're having for dinner?"

"Uh, yes. That actually has to do with what I want to propose."

"Rago, leave us," she says.

"Excuse me?"

"I said leave."

"You're kicking me out of my own—"

"Do I have to say it a third time?"

"No, no."

Rago fidgets with his bread as he makes his way to the exit. Before he leaves, he shares a concerned look with Epo. Epo silently signals with her eyes that she will be okay. Her heart starts to beat quickly. She lied, she doesn't know if she'll be okay.

Kasi leans against Rago's desk and stares at Epo. The two lock eyes. Kasi looks at her the same way Plios used to look at Niria when she had broken something. Epo is scared. Some unspoken fight is happening as they stare at each other, and she is losing.

"Do you know a man named Lagne, Epo?"

Epo doesn't respond. She reaches deep into her memory but finds nothing attached to this name.

"Lagne was a boy who grew up in Koilia. When he was young, his parents sold him off to the church of Lixi," Kasi stands and paces, running a finger over the books of Rago's library. "Do any of these books have anything about what they do to little boys in the church of Lixi?"

Epo remains silent. She has read up on the church. They believe sex is a sacred ritual that brings one closer to understanding the nature of the Child by binding the emotional states of two individuals. They also believe the Child to be a male, so male children are seen as sexual conduits to their deity.

"I'm sure you can relate to the pain Lagne went

through," says Kasi. "When we found him, he was near dead in the street, exiled. Abandoned by those that made him, he was left to waste away. Part of his body had already succumbed to wyll-death but he was still hanging on for some reason. There was still some strength to him. We saw the worth in him and we brought him back, we gave him wyll. Through our training, he earned his colour and he became mighty. No doubt, you met him a few times at least."

The man with the Lixi tattoo—her stalker—was big and muscular. It couldn't possibly be the same person.

"Today, Lagne didn't make his hunting regimen."

Epo shifts nervously.

"When his brothers went to check on him, all they found was a pile of bones and this." Kasi takes a clump of hair from her pouch. "I didn't recognise the colour at first, but then I remembered you."

She tosses it at Epo. Staring at the hair, Epo's heart sinks in her chest. It's her braid.

"I've been thinking a lot about what you said," Kasi continues. "That we are not free; that we are broken. I won't lie, I thought for a moment you might be right. That maybe my whole ideology is wrong. But that didn't last long. Are we completely free? No, no one is. We are in a constant prison of psyche. At any moment, we could be turned to dust on a whim. A simple fault of mood and we're gone. Freedom is not inherent. Freedom is afforded through a driving wyll, a goal to strive towards. Only by working for something are you truly free to live."

"You're trading one prison for another," Epo says

keeping her eyes on the braid.

"A lesser prison!" Kasi yells, stealing Epo's attention.

"Do you think what you went through was unique?" Kasi asks. "There are countless families all over Genus, right now, going through the exact same treatment yours went through. And it's not going to stop."

"That doesn't mean you have to march everyone to war."

"We live upon Genus, a Child of war and hatred. A celestial consciousness spread out among our small valueless lives. We fight and kill each other because we are built to. It is the process of the Child putting Its mind back together. Pain is the language of the Child."

Epo feels an outburst bubbling. "It's only like this because people like you perpetuate it! I've read the history books, the endless war was over centuries ago. We can work towards change now."

"There is no peace. Peace leads to boredom, then depression then wyll-death. War gives us meaning, it keeps us strong and I'm not going to let you and your stupid ideas of compassion infect my soldiers."

Kasi steps closer to Epo and stands over her. Looking up, Epo feels claustrophobic. This lady who portrays herself so calm and soft, Epo never knew she could be so intimidating.

"You have two options: become a Reaper, adopt the mentality, fight in my war … or die."

"That is not a choice."

"Sure it is. No matter what prison you are in, freedom will always exist in some form or another. You should be happy I'm giving you a choice. Remember your father, Anema. Your mother, Plios."

Epo feels smaller and smaller with every mention of her loved ones.

"Your brother, Semnos. Your sister, Niria. They all died because of me. With my word, your sister, Dorean, and brother, Feilece, can be added to the list. Don't force me to take their lives too. I don't like being forced to do things." Kasi leaves.

Epo shivers. Rago enters and rushes over to the girl. "Oh dear, are you okay?"

Epo doesn't respond; she stares blankly.

"Oh Mother. What did she say to you? Here, lay down."

Rago helps her into her bed of pillows and throws a wool blanket over her.

"Rago …" Epo says, quietly.

"Yes, do you need anything?"

"Don't bring bread anymore. Your idea … it's not going to work."

XXVII

FEILECE, AXE IN hand, makes his way through the village towards the stables. The wound on his arm has almost healed so he won't have to train in the cover of darkness after tonight. He wonders how far his secret training has taken him, and if Popoki will be surprised.

Walking past the last stretch of tents, Feilece is blessed with the sight of Kasi emerging from a tent nearby.

"Kasi … Hi," he says, nervously.

"Oh, hey Feilece. What are you doing out here this late?"

"Just out to do some sneaky training. Popoki says I should be resting my arm but I need to get stronger."

Kasi laughs softly. "It's good to see you're driven but you should probably listen to your teacher." She takes Feilece's hand and examines his wound. Feeling her touch sends a jolt of excitement through Feilece.

"I do respect Popoki but I don't want to waste any time," says Feilece. "I want to become the soldier you need me to be."

They look at each other. She's so beautiful, Feilece

doesn't want to take his eyes off her.

"Take your time, Feilece. Greatness isn't achieved by rushing."

Feilece doesn't want to disagree with her so he changes the subject. "What about you, what were you doing?"

"Uh, there was a minor infection about to start so I put a stop to it before it got out of hand."

"Wow, the beauty of the Mother, a heart big enough for a family this large, and now you're curing illness. Is there anything you cannot do?"

She chortles. "That's very flattering."

"No, I mean it." Feilece adopts a more serious tone. "You are the strongest most amazing person I have ever met."

Kasi smiles, cheeks blushing. "Well, thank you. You're not so bad yourself. After everything, seeing how hard you work: it's inspiring."

"Well it all starts with you, Kasi. The thought of you fills me with enough energy to last to the end of time itself."

"Feilece."

"You make me strong enough to move the Child Itself. I truly believe you are Mother-sent, your presence on this land makes the Child smile, I can feel it."

"Okay, stop now."

Feilece quickly kills his momentum. "I'm sorry. I don't mean to make you uncomfortable."

"It's okay, I'm not uncomfortable. It's just … I like you, Feilece, but as I said, greatness shouldn't be rushed."

"It's not rushing if it's meant to be. If something is great then it was always great, and if that thing happens to pass by without my input, I wouldn't forgive myself. You said so yourself, the strong fight for what they want."

Kasi doesn't reply. Feilece knows she wants him, he just has to make it easy for her. "You don't have to say anything. With me, you are free to be and feel however you want. And I already know how you feel about me."

Kasi still says nothing. Feilece takes a chance. "Can I … stay in your tent tonight?"

Kasi smiles, bites her bottom lip and looks around at the black sky before finally resting her eyes on Feilece. "Time … Feilece."

Feilece's heart sinks.

"Time is on your side. Use it well. Grow, become strong, learn to be a man and a warrior. We'll have our time together, just not right now."

Kasi places a hand on Feilece's shoulder as she walks by him.

Feilece's mind toils. This can't end like this.

"I love you, Kasi!" he says turning to her.

She stops. Feilece drops his axe, runs in front of her and takes her by the hand. "And I know you love me too. I swear to you, with all of my heart, no one will ever love you as much as I do."

"What do you know of love?"

"It may sound strange but I have been through an entire lifetime with you, Kasi. I know we work together, I know we are meant to be. Love is the coming together of two people that are made for each other. When two become one. We are the one." Feilece loses track of what he is saying. His old mind is telling him to stop talking but his body and mouth move on their own. "Schizo isn't meant for you, I am. They are not your family, I am. You and me, we are all that's necessary in this world." Tears stream from Feilece's eyes.

Kasi kneels down and places her hands on Feilece's face, rubbing his tears away. "Oh, Feilece, you are not listening to me. We will have our time together; you have to wait. Don't worry, I'm not going anywhere. You will not see this great thing pass you by."

They both look into each other's eyes for a moment before Kasi presses her lips to Feilece's. Sparks ignite in Feilece's mind. The hairs on the back of his neck stand up, electrified. Every cell inside of him becomes ecstatic.

Kasi pulls away, licks her lips, then stands and leaves Feilece alone.

Time is on his side. All he has to do is wait.

"Haven't you waited enough?" Niria appears from one of the tents. "Didn't you just go through a lifetime waiting for this 'greatness' to come by?"

It doesn't count; he wasn't waiting when he was trapped in time because he was with Kasi the whole time.

"No, but you weren't though. Are my words not getting through to you at all?" she says, annoyed. "That wasn't real, Feilece. That was a fucking fantasy!"

And what's wrong with that. The feelings were still real.

"But they weren't her feelings, you idiot. They

were just a bunch of shit to make you the centre of attention."

Feilece can't stop crying. Why is Niria saying this?

"Because Kasi doesn't love you, Feilece. She's fucking using you, you know this. It's not even being hidden. Your 'love' that you cherish so much is being used to dig ropes into your skin and move you like a puppet."

No, that's not all it is. There's true love there, there has to be. Kasi is the future.

"Kasi is the past now, Feilece. You've already lived that life. This is a different one. Let her go."

If Niria never thought Kasi was worth it, then why hasn't she said anything until now?

"I was waiting for you to come to the conclusion on your own but I should've seen it earlier, she's dug herself too deep into your head. You need to get her the fuck out of here!"

What the fuck does Niria know about it! She's only here to torture him for not having the strength to grab her hand when she reached for him.

Niria is rendered speechless.

She speaks so much about what's real and what's fake, when she's just a figment of his imagination. She not real, she's dead.

Feilece looks at Niria directly. Niria looks back, scared.

"Feilece …"

Niria, "fuck off!"

Niria looks disappointed as she turns into a puff of yellow smoke and dissipates.

Feilece falls to his knees. He stares at his axe laying

in the grass. The bit stares back at him, reflecting the shimmer of a nearby brazier fire. It feels like it is judging him harshly.

XXVIII

"**M**OTHER?" KILLER WHISPERS as she walks by sets of yellow and black tents in the darkness of night, the waving light of her lamp splashing against the tent fabric.

Louma started drinking earlier than normal today. Most of the evening was spent screaming about Rago. Apparently, she saw the man give his dinner to some new recruits. She cursed him, frustrated as to why he never treated her with such kindness.

Before long, her anger turned to Killer. Louma beat and swore at Killer, then she told her to spend the night alone as she left in fury. Hours have passed since she left and Killer can't sleep. Her mother ordered her to spend the night alone but whenever she closes her eyes to sleep, she sees horrible visions. A woman getting her head chopped off, a young man being stabbed through his chest, an older man crumbling into dust.

Haunted by her visions, Killer can't help but seek out her mother. She knows she's going against her mother's orders but every second she spends alone, she feels a growing murderous urge inside of her. It terrifies her.

After searching around their tent to no avail, Killer climbed up the hill to the tents of higher colours. She's never visited this part of the camp before, and it feels different to the camp at the bottom of the hill. The tents are well-kept and made with better material.

Killer hears the sounds of people talking, laughing, and drinking. She follows the sound to a tent with its brazier still lit. She hears grunting and slapping from inside, and the sounds of a woman in distress.

"I'll be back, you two. And I got your arse next"

"Yeah, hurry back."

Killer watches a naked man walk out of the tent sculling back on a bottle. Oblivious to her standing there, the man wanders around the back of the tent.

Killer parts the opening flaps of the tent and peers inside. Her eyes catch the sight of a naked woman on her elbows and knees, with a man behind her thrusting his pelvis into hers.

Killer can't take her eyes off them. She feels a deep connection to the act. Killer can't see the woman's face, but her hair is the same colour as Louma's. Killer instinctively goes to call out to her but the man beats her to it.

"Oh Mother!"

"Yeah, call me Mother as you cum in me," the woman says, turning her head.

Seeing her face, Killer doesn't recognise her. Watching the two move causes something to stale in Killer's mind, making her lose her focus. A vision plays in her mind of a man thrusting against her not unlike what she's seeing. Grunting and swaying and blood, strain and pain. Fury ignites in Killer's chest, burning her insides.

Where is Mother? She needs her mother.

"Oh Mother, Mother, I'm cumming!"

Killer steps inside the tent.

"Mmm, that was great," says the woman as she turns to face the man. Then she sees Killer standing there. "What the fuck."

"Hey! Who … What are you doing?" the man says as he gets up and grabs his sword.

Killer doesn't respond, she stares at the ground.

The man points his sword at her. "Hey, talk. What are you doing here, you creepy bitch?"

Killer slowly brings her eyes up and meets the woman's.

"Oh, fuck, look, look! She's got murderous eyes. Get her; knock her out!" says the woman.

The man goes to swing the butt of his sword at Killer's head. Without taking her eyes off of the woman, Killer catches the man by his wrist. He struggles but can't break free from Killer's grasp.

"My mother …" says Killer. "My father … you killed them."

"What are you talking about, girl. I don't even know who—"

In one swift motion, Killer steals the sword from the man's hand and cleaves his head off.

The woman screams as his head hits the floor.

"What's going on in there!" calls the second man from outside.

Killer, sword in hand, slowly approaches the woman.

"Alright, bitch, you wanna fuck with me?"

The woman grabs her own sword and swings it at

Killer. Her strike is better than her lover's but still nothing compared to the training Louma put her through. Killer dodges then stabs her sword through the woman's stomach.

"Heh, nice one, you fucking bitch," says the woman before falling flat on her face, dead.

Looking down, all Killer can see is the back of her head.

"Mother?" Killer throws her sword to the side and scurries to the back of the tent, hugging her knees closely. "No, no, no. Mother. What have I done?"

Flashes of Louma abusing her snap in her mind. She sees a crumbling man, a beheaded woman, a man with a sword in his chest. She grabs her head with one hand and starts bashing it with the other, trying to force the visions out. She hears Louma's voice coming from the corpse of the woman.

"Is this what you want! You want your mother dead?"

"Mother, I'm sorry! I'm so sorry!"

"You're gonna die for this, daughter!"

"No, I didn't know what I was doing! I don't know what's wrong with me!"

The man from outside bursts through the entrance. "What is going on," he asks, his voice shaking.

Killer stares at him, eyes as wide as they can get.

"You did this?"

"No … I … I don't know."

The man pulls the woman's sword from her dead hand and approaches Killer. Killer tries to move her arms or legs but she's petrified. The man swings his sword down at her. In the last split second before the sword cleaves a chasm in her skull, her mind goes blank and feeling returns to her body.

Quickly, she flips out of the way and grabs her sword.

The two warriors stare each other down.

"I'm sorry," says Killer. "I don't know what happened."

"Well, it looks like you killed my fucking lovers. And for that, I'm gonna fucking kill you."

The man attacks with a barrage of trained hacks. Killer is able to dodge and deflect them, but she's struggling to keep up. The man knocks the blade from her hand and kicks her to the ground.

"Fucking die!" He straddles Killer and with an underhand grip, and rears up to stab his sword through her head.

In the most minor of moments, everything gets flushed from Killer's mind. All cares disappear. Even her mother vanishes from her thoughts. All that fills the void is the need to kill.

Killer turns her torso and flips the man onto his back. She grabs him by the neck and holds herself over him. She makes her fist and thrusts it into the man's face with bone breaking strength over and over. The man's head mangles in a mash of blood, flesh and bone. Finally, she stops. She slumps down on top of the man's body. Thoughts struggle to catch in her brain. She looks around the tent. Everything is coated in blood. Her energy depletes and she falls onto her side. She's so tired.

She closes her eyes and the visions play once again. The crumbling man, the beheaded woman, the stabbed man. Only this time, they don't frighten her.

She wraps an arm around the man whose head she pounded into mulch. She holds him close, feeling an overwhelming comfort emanate from his body.

Tears stream from her eyes as she drifts off to sleep.

SHE WAKES TO the sound of screaming. It's daylight and a group of people have gathered outside.

"What?" she says as she wipes rheum from her eyes.

"You," says a man in black clothes, speaking with a weary voice. "You're Louma's convert, aren't you?"

"Mother?"

Killer looks around and sees the blood. She sees the body with the mashed head. She looks at her hands, they're stained red and two of her fingers are snapped.

Panicked, all she can say is, "I need my mother."

XXIX

EILECE WAKES AND does a big stretch. His eyes catch with the clock and his mind is stolen for a moment as it ticks forward. The weird feeling has become more intense as time has gone on. As if whatever is causing the feeling is getting closer. At some point, it changed from a scream to a pulse, beating at the core of his very essence. It's ominous. It never used to scare him before but now it does. Tick. Tick. Tick.

He checks the wound on his arm. It has healed and doesn't hurt when he moves anymore. Excited, he jumps up out of bed.

"Hey, it's all healed up, we can get back to training," he calls out to Popoki, but Popoki's sheets have been strewn aside and the man is nowhere to be seen.

"Popoki?"

Feilece goes outside and looks around. He sees Reapers going about their day. He tries to get someone's attention but is mostly met with ignoring sighs until one finally responds.

"What do you want?"

"I'm just wondering if you know where Popoki has gone?"

"The general? Yeah, I saw a few yellows come fetch him not long ago. They went up the hill."

"Okay, thank you."

"Yeah, whatever."

Feilece makes his way up into the territory of the higher colours and sees a small crowd of people gathered around a large tent. He pushes his way through them until he sees Popoki inside.

"Popoki!" Feilece says as he hurries into the tent.

"Wait, Feilece, don't—"

"Dorean?" His oldest sister sits in the corner of a large wooden cage, shivering and hugging her knees. She's stained from head-to-toe in dried blood.

"Feilece," Popoki says coming to the boy's side.

"No, don't ..." Feilece stops him. "Don't send me away."

He moves in closer to the cage and stares at Dorean, eyes beginning to water. Dorean was always so strong. Nothing ever got to her. She always had a solution to any problem. She would argue vehemently, and she would always be right. Now she cowers, trembling like a timid sheep.

Dorean looks up and Feilece catches her eye. Slowly, she moves. She unfurls from her ball and creeps as close to Feilece as the cage will allow, eyes streaming with tears.

"Feilece," Popoki says.

Feilece ignores him.

Dorean reaches a hand through the bars of her cage, extending it out towards Feilece.

It's the second time one of his distressed sisters has asked to hold his hand. This time, he does not hesitate.

He clasps her hand firmly.

Dorean's eyes strain as she freaks out and pulls her hand back in. She scurries back to her corner and rocks back and forth in a ball, whimpering.

Feilece's empty hand shakes. "What is happening?"

"Killer, here, was found in this state in a tent littered with dead bodies," Popoki says, carefully.

"Killer?"

"That is her name."

Feilece's heart sinks. "Is that so …"

"What is the meaning of this!" Louma comes stomping into the tent. "What have you done to my daughter!"

"Mother!" Dorean calls as she presses herself up against the bars.

"Oh, daughter." Louma tries to hug Dorean through the wooden bars.

Watching the two embrace, Feilece feels tears brim behind his eyes. Quickly, he forces them away. This is what they've turned his sister into; he knows he must learn to accept it. He can't show weakness; he must be a warrior. He must be strong, for Kasi.

"What have they done to you, my daughter?" Louma asks, stroking Dorean's hair.

"She killed three yellows," Popoki says.

"What?"

"This morning, she was found in a tent with their bodies. It was a massacre."

Louma pulls away from Dorean. "Is this true, my daughter?" Though her words sound dark, Feilece spots the corner of her mouth betraying a slight smirk.

Dorean's eyes widen in shock.

"Killer?" says Louma.

Dorean responds to her mother with a scream and a scamper, curling back up into a ball and digging her head into her knees.

"Look, she's in distress," says Louma. "You must give her to me. I'll get her back to normal."

"I'm not sure I can put my trust in that, Louma," says Popoki.

"Excuse me?"

"She is your convert …"

"Yes! She is my convert so you must return her to me at once!"

"And it is clear to me you have obviously failed in your task."

Louma gets up into Popoki's face. "I am not a failure."

In this moment, Louma is terrifying but Popoki does not cower in the slightest.

"The girl needs help, Louma."

"I agree, so let me help her."

"You are not good for her."

Louma scoffs and snarls.

Popoki continues, "she needs the help of an expert."

"No … you don't mean …"

"I've sent for Rago to come analyse—"

Louma grabs a sword rack and slams it into the ground. The rack shatters and its contents scatter.

Louma pants short breaths. She approaches Dorean. "Daughter …" She reaches her hand into the cage. "Come to me, daughter. We have to go now. Come with me."

Popoki and Feilece remain silent, watching the general plead.

"Killer! Come to me now!"

Dorean doesn't move. She stays in a ball, whimpering at the back of her cage.

"Fine then. You damaged little bitch. A daughter follows her mother orders! You are no daughter of mine!"

Louma stomps out. The tent becomes eerily silent but for the sounds of Dorean's whimpers.

Popoki takes a deep breath and shares a weary look with Feilece.

"That woman is not okay," says Feilece.

"Yeah, and she's supposed to be a psychological genius," Popoki says with a short laugh.

"You called for me?" asks an old man standing at the entrance.

"Ah, yes, Rago. Thank you for coming …"

The voices of the two men drift over Feilece as he focuses on Epo.

The two youngest Anemelos siblings stare into each other's eyes. Desperation clouds Feilece's heart. He's lost Niria, and now he's lost Dorean. Epo is all that's left. He frowns, hoping to see something in Epo, anything that will make him believe she still exists. Compassionate Epo, always with an unrelenting smile. The happy little girl who would read to Feilece whenever he felt down. The one whose ears were open to anyone's troubles, at any time, no matter the situation.

Feilece pleads internally. Please, Epo, show a sign you're still there.

Epo breaks eye contact, looking down with a sullen expression.

That's it. The Anemelos family is finally dead.

Feilece trades out all other thoughts for those of strength and stoicism.

He marches up to Epo, "sister," he says in an emotionless tone as he extends a rigid hand out to her.

Slowly, she brings her hand up and clasps it around Feilece's, "brother."

They're siblings, the last remaining members of their tortured family. It's been so long since they've seen each other; they've both been through so much. And they're greeting each other like their father used to greet strangers on the streets of Tiris.

"Popoki," Feilece says, turning away from his sister.

"Yes?"

"My arm has healed. Can we get back to training?"

"We're a little busy here, Feilece."

"Actually," says the old man. "Would you mind leaving me and my assistant alone for this procedure?"

"Oh, sure. Then I guess we're free," Popoki says turning back to Feilece.

Feilece gives Epo one last disappointed look then leaves with Popoki.

"Alright, everyone!" Popoki addresses the crowd outside. "Everything is being dealt with. You can get back to your lives."

The crowd disperses. Feilece marches back to their tent and Popoki has to jog to keep up to him.

"Hey," says Popoki as he puts a hand on Feilece's shoulder. "Are you okay?"

Feilece says nothing. He keeps marching.

"Didn't you want to spend more time with your sister?"

Feilece's stops walking and stares at the ground. All of his muscles suddenly feel sapped of energy. He can't force them back anymore, tears flow from his eyes.

"I don't have any sisters anymore."

Popoki kneels down and hugs him.

XXX

“HOLD UP,” RAGO says as he pulls Epo with him to hide behind the corner of a tent.

Epo frowns. “What are we doing?”

“Just … give it a second.”

Epo pokes her head around the corner and sees a small crowd of people gathered around a tent.

“That’s where we’re going, right?”

“Yes, just don’t be seen.”

“Fuck off!” comes from a woman in the crowd. Epo watches Louma push past the people in a fury and disappear between the tents.

“Wow,” says Epo.

“Yep.”

“How did you know she was there?”

“The messenger summoned us for some issue with Louma’s convert. Sorry, your sister.” Rago corrects himself. “If they’re summoning me, it means it must be something she cannot handle. I knew she wouldn’t enjoy that. And if she knew I was coming, there would be no way she would stick around.”

“I get all that, but how did you know she was there at this exact moment?”

Rago ponders for a moment. "I don't know. Call it a hunch, I guess."

"Hey," Rago says. "Are you sure you want to be here for this? I'm not sure what condition your sister is in, it might be a bit disturbing."

"Yeah, I need to learn to …" Epo doesn't want to finish that particular sentence, so she says something else. "I want to see her."

"Okay."

The two make their way through the crowd and enter the prison tent.

"You called for me?" says Rago.

Epo's mind almost completely switches off as she sees Feilece. He's dressed in Reaper attire. His muscles are bigger; he is bigger. He looks strong, he looks smart, he looks content … and he looks like a Reaper.

Feilece's eyes meet hers. Epo's heart starts to race. She wants to run over to him and hug him. She wants to hold him like she did when he was a baby. But this man in a boy's body that used to represent her little brother, she doesn't recognise anymore.

She wants to cry but her body doesn't let her. Inside, she's too dry.

Feilece frowns at her. It makes him look like the others: her depraved abusers. She can't stand to look at him anymore.

In a tough stride, her brother approaches her and put his hand out.

"Sister." The word is spoken as if he feels nothing for her at all.

Rago told her that Kasi was in charge of his conversion. Of all the methods that were used, hers was by far the most effective.

Epo doesn't want to settle with a mere handshake, but this is all he's offering her so of course she'll take it.

She grabs his hand, "brother," the word stings her tongue as it leaves her mouth.

"Popoki," Feilece says. He takes his eyes off her and Epo feels a rush of relief. It's as if the boy's gaze causes her whole body to stress.

"Yes?" says Popoki.

"My arm has healed, can we get back to training?"

Training … He's just another soldier. He truly has become one of them.

She can't take this anymore. Being around Feilece is causing her to panic so much that she feels she's about to collapse. She gives Rago a look of distress and the old man quickly picks up on it.

"We're a little busy here, Feilece," says Popoki.

"Actually," Rago says in haste. "Would you mind leaving me and my assistant alone for this procedure?"

Popoki and Feilece leave the tent. As soon as Feilece is outside, Epo falls to her knees. Panting and sweating profusely.

"Are you okay?" Rago rushes to her side.

"Feilece … he's one of them." Anger builds inside of Epo. "One of these heartless wretches."

"Hey, hey." Rago rubs her back.

"Why!" Epo starts punching the grass. "Why are you like this! Why do you make us like this!"

Epo bursts into tears.

Rago sits next to her. "Perhaps …" he says in a guilty tone. "Instead of aiming those fists down, you might want to aim them up."

Slumped, Epo looks at Rago with tired eyes.

"The Mother watches," Rago continues, "all the time, as all this happens. The Child doesn't know any better—It's just reacting to being, to existing—but She knows." He points up at the yellow light shining through the roof. "And all She does is observe." A tear runs down Rago's cheek. "I wonder what type of ink She uses to write down Her analyses."

Epo doesn't reply. She moves closer, and leans on him.

Dorean screams. "Fuck off!"

Remembering why they came, Rago and Epo approach Dorean's cage. The delirious woman is swiping her hand at an unknown entity, terror plastered across her face.

Seeing her sister covered in blood scares Epo but she tries to not let it get to her. They're there to help Dorean. Epo must engage her analytical brain.

"What is she doing?" asks Epo.

"I'm not sure."

"Have you not seen this behaviour before?"

"On rare occasions, converts will succumb to a kind of existential fear and fall into catatonia. When I first looked at her, that's what I thought had happened but I've not seen this before. She seems to be fighting something."

"Could it be Dorean? Could my sister be fighting to return to herself?"

"I wouldn't hope for it."

Dread creeps into Epo's mind. "Why?"

"Conversion disconnects one's wyll from their body. The wyll stays as it was but the body keeps changing, growing. If the original wyll were to be reconnected, it wouldn't be psychologically synchronised. It would be like waking up one day as a completely different person. She would believe she wasn't herself and immediately succumb to wyll-death."

Epo leans against the bars of the cage. All of her effort was for nothing. Her whole family is gone.

Rago places a hand on her head. "I'm sorry, Epo."

"How much more of this do I have to take?"

Dorean swipes her hand again but it stops midway, as if someone is holding it.

"Now that's odd." Rago returns to scientist mode, removing his hand from Epo's head and pulling a journal from his pocket. "Subject is undergoing partial paralysis. It's as if her perceived threat is retaliating."

"How can that be? There's nothing there."

"Our brains direct our wyll. If we believe in something enough, our wyll makes it so."

"Are you talking about wyll-manipulation?"

"She's not bending reality like the Bloomer wyll-users did during the wars. No, I think this is something else. If she's not controlling her arm, maybe someone else is."

Dorean regains control of her arm and she scurries back into her corner.

"What are you saying, Rago?"

"I'm thinking there are two wylls inside of your sister."

"Two wylls?"

"Maybe you were right. Maybe Louma failed to completely disconnect Dorean's wyll when she converted her. Maybe Dorean is still in there."

"Does that mean … she's going to die?"

"It means we might as well make ourselves comfortable. It might take a while."

XXXI

T HE WOODEN DOORS to Killer's cage creak shut and the latch locks. Killer sits on her knees staring at the backs of her hands. The blood has dried and settled into blotches upon her skin. She can't tell where the blood stops and her skin starts.

"You know," says the Reaper who shoved her into her cell. "If it were up to me, I'd thrust my spear right through your fucking head. Murderer."

Killer doesn't acknowledge the lady. She was trained to kill and now that she has, she's being punished for it. She needs her mother … her mother will fix everything.

The Reaper leaves; Killer sits alone. Her mind can't help but drift back to memories of the tent. The blood; the bodies. She recalls the feeling she had as she snuggled up to the corpse of her victim before falling asleep. Anxiety builds in her mind.

A faint whisper wafts through her ears. "Dorean."

"Who …" Killer's throat is stricken before she can finish speaking, as if a hand has pulled her larynx taut. She can breathe fine but she can't make a word come out. She grapples at her throat, trying to get it to free her voice. Her hand feels foreign as it touches her neck. She feels as if her head is somehow disconnected from her body.

There's a thud on the ground next to her, as if someone dropped a sack of dirt from the ceiling. Killer tries not to look at it, something is telling her to steer her gaze elsewhere but her eyes move on their own.

It's a head. A severed lady's head. Killer's hearing mutes; all she can hear is her own heart pounding.

Slowly, the head's eyes open and look up at Killer. Her mouth starts moving and Killer hears a desynchronised choked rasp of a voice in the back of her head.

"Dorean … reach deep … remember."

Killer screams out nothing but a hacking breath, then covers her face with her hands.

In the dark, she hears the wispy voice of a man. "Dorean."

Why do they keep calling her that?

"We love you … Dorean."

She feels the embrace of a man with large arms wrap around her from the back.

Killer makes a gap in her fingers and looks out. She sees burly arms materialising in front of her. She feels the embrace lighten as she is coated in dust.

Regaining control of her voice, she shrieks, feverishly patting away the dust. She pushes herself to the back of her cage. She pulls her legs in, digs her eyes into her knees, holds her hands to her ears and rolls onto her side.

Mother … she wants her mother.

She feels the morning light shining on her as the

tent flaps part and a person enters. She looks up, hoping to see her mother. She's disappointed as her eyes lay upon the bald and bearded general.

"Hello, Killer. How are you feeling this morning?"

He speaks calmly. Killer can tell he's trying to make her comfortable with his presence but it's not going to work. She doesn't know if he's real or another phantom. She huddles back into a ball. She will only talk to her mother.

"I would like to ask you a few questions about last night, is that okay?"

She gives him no response.

"I've heard some pretty serious accusations against you. I need to know if you remember anything. Why were you there in the middle of the night? Did you know the people in the tent? Did they attack you first?"

Killer remains silent.

"Okay, that is fine, we don't have to talk about last night. I have one other question for you. Do you remember the time we met in the woods?"

Killer tries to keep quiet but she feels an over-whelming compulsion to speak. She tries to stop herself but she can't. She looks into the man's eyes and says, "the meadow."

"As I thought." Popoki stands and gets the atten-tion of someone outside. A man in black clothes enters.

"Director," Popoki says to the man.

"General."

"This woman is under my protection. No matter what anyone else says, she is not to be executed. Post guards, make sure nobody tries anything during the night. If anyone wants to contend this rule, send them to me."

"What if I want to contend this rule?"

"Then speak your mind."

"She killed our people. Our siblings. Should she not be punished for this?"

"Believe me, she's being punished." Popoki puts a hand on the man's shoulder. "I'm asking you to trust me. There's more to this than it seems. I'm doing what I know Schizo would want."

"Well, you know him better than I do. Fine, you have my word no harm will come to her."

"Thank you."

The black-clothed director goes to leave but before he does, Popoki asks one more favour. "Can you send someone to get Rago. Tell him it's urgent. He must be here at once. Tell him Louma's convert is having issues."

The black-clothed director nods and leaves.

Popoki sits upon a chair. He rests his elbows on his knees and massages his knuckles. He looks over at Killer and whispers, "you better be worth it, Dorean."

Another person enters the tent. Killer is blinded by yellow light and a loud screech envelopes her hearing. She curls up, closes her eyes and covers her ears. She tries to scream to counteract the cacophony in her head but all she can muster is a whimper. Then, suddenly, the sound is gone. The light warms her skin. She opens her eyes and looks up at the figure. The warmth invites her towards it. It's the Mother. The Mother is here to save her.

She creeps towards the figure and extends her hand. The figure grabs her hand firmly and the light disappears. Instead of the Mother, she sees a man. He stands over her, gripping her hand. A pain shoots down her arm.

Before she can truly register what is happening, a sword protrudes through the man's abdomen. His blood spatters against her face. She screams, pulls her hand free and scurries backwards.

Why is all this happening to her? Why is she being haunted by these demons? Where is her mother? She should be here.

"What is the meaning of this!"

It's her voice!

Killer opens her eyes and goes to the cage's bars. "Mother!"

"Oh, daughter." The two embrace each other. Killer feels everything fall away, the bars, the tent, the people. She's there alone with her mother. Everything is going to be okay.

Killer feels her mother's heartbeat. She feels her lungs expand and contract. Her mother and the bearded man talk with each other but Killer doesn't bother to listen; she's just enjoying this moment of reprieve.

Louma pulls away. Killer looks into her eyes, silently pleading for them to continue their embrace.

Her mother speaks in a dark voice. "Is this true, daughter?"

"She's not your mother, you know." The voice of a little girl sounds in Killer's head.

No ... no, no, not another demon.

"Your real mother is dead."

A naked girl with skin beaming yellow like the Mother walks through the wall of the tent and up to

Louma. "Don't you remember?" The girl places a hand on the back of Louma's neck. "I remember. I remember the blade hitting her right here."

A flash of her mother being beheaded plays in Killer's mind and she curls into a ball.

She loses all hearing but for the sound of the little girl's steps approaching her in the grass.

"What are you doing, Dorean?"

Killer wants to talk; she wants to scream and say that her name isn't Dorean, but she's been rendered mute once again.

"If you aren't Dorean, then what are you doing in my sister's body?" says the girl.

This is Killer's body. She is daughter to Louma. She is an apprentice and a Reaper soldier. There is no Dorean!

"Killer, huh?" The girl takes a seat next to her. "Not the most fitting name. Your mother has horrible taste." The girl makes herself comfortable. "Our father once made Dorean chop the head off one of the chooks. She cried about it all night. She was no killer."

Killer is getting sick of hearing about this Dorean person.

"She was soft," the girl continues, "but still firm where she needed to be. She got it from our mother. She was the first born daughter so she had a lot of time to absorb a lot of Mother's eccentricities. It's been decades since I've seen them. I was trapped for so long. But I never stopped thinking about them. I never stopped missing them. There was no better family in all of Genus. And I know you know what I mean … Dorean."

The sound of a rack smashing interrupts them. Louma reaches into the cage. "Come to me daughter. We have to go now. Come with me."

"This," the girl says as she points at Louma. "Is not your mother."

Shut up.

"She is a monster; a beast who has dug her claws into your mind and torn it to shreds."

"Killer! Come to me now!" Louma orders.

"Don't do it, Dorean."

Killer wants to move but she's stuck in her ball.

Louma scowls. In this moment, she truly looks like a monster.

"You are no daughter of mine!"

Tears run down Killer's face as she watches her mother storm out.

Everything goes dark in Killer's vision. She's left alone with the luminous girl.

"This is not you. You know I'm right."

Who is this girl? What is she? Why is she here? Why won't she go away?

"I'm not an apparition, Dorean. I'm you sister, and I love you."

Sister … what sister. Killer has no sisters. Killer only has Mother.

"She is not your mother, Dorean!"

All Killer needs is her mother, and now, because of this stupid little girl, this fake person, this figment of her mind, this demon … because of her, Mother has left.

"Dorean …"

Her name isn't fucking Dorean!

Killer gets her voice back. "Fuck off!"

The girl sighs. "Why do my siblings keep telling me to fuck off."

Killer swipes at the girl. Her hand passes through her, streaking puffs of yellow smoke in the air with every attack.

"Alright, I'm getting sick of this."

The girl catches Killer's wrist in her hand and Killer's whole arm goes numb and stiff.

The girl brings her face close to Killer's. "Give me back my fucking sister, you demented slave."

Killer stays strong.

The little girl hangs her head. She releases Killer's arm—feeling returns instantly along with a dose of pins and needles—and she stands.

"I can see you aren't ready yet. It's okay, I'll try again tomorrow."

The girl disappears and the darkness dissipates; the tent goes back to normal. Killer is lying in the corner of her cage being watched over by Rago and the little girl her mother ordered her to kill. Another order she has failed at.

All she can do is lay, whimpering and begging for her mother's return.

XXXII

<hr>

I N THE BLACK of night, a minor light from the closed
eye in the sky comes through the hole they made for
the clock in the ceiling. Feilece can't sleep. He stares
into the sky watching one of the celestial siblings
twinkle blue and white.

He can't stop thinking about his sisters and how
much this place has changed them. What they must
have gone through to become as they are. It's unfor-
givable. Feilece doesn't have to forgive, though. He has
to let go of them.

Kasi is his family, his future. His old family is long
gone … the sooner he accepts that, the sooner he can
get on with his real life.

A tear rolls down his cheek. He catches the tear on
his finger and looks at it. He doesn't feel particularly
sad, so why is he crying?

He feels a nagging on his mind. A slight itch; a
craving to see Niria. He quickly pushes it away. She
doesn't approve of his love; he has no use for her. He
has to forget about her too.

A light beam shines through the crack at the entrance to the tent. He recognises the colour: the distinct

yellow Niria's body emanates. He tries to ignore it but his eyes keep darting back to the light. Eventually, he caves. He gets up and goes outside.

He expects to greet his luminescent sister but she isn't there. He stands alone in the sleeping village. Another yellow light shines further along. Feilece follows it until he is guided by yet another light. Niria must be leading him somewhere.

He tells himself to give up and go back to his tent but his body won't listen. He keeps following the lights but Niria is nowhere to be found.

He eventually arrives on the hill, in the territory of the Koilian Reapers. He follows Niria's light around a bend and then it disappears. The lane is dark but for one tent with its brazier lit. Feilece creeps towards the tent, not to keep quiet, but because of a crippling sense of foreboding. Something tells him he doesn't want to see what's happening inside this tent, but he can't stop himself.

As he gets closer, he hears the sounds of people moaning. He hears male grunts and a woman ... a woman with a familiar timbre to her moans.

Feilece's hand shakes as he peers inside. He sees a group of naked people, five men and one woman. The woman is in the middle and she is surrounded: one below her, one behind her and one in front. Two men are at her sides with their wrists tied to woodblocks; she services them with her hands. Her face is obstructed but Feilece recognises the men. They're the five directors, the overseers of the Reaper village.

Their naked bodies all move in rhythm with each other. Muscles contracting, accentuated by sweat and ecstasy.

Feilece can't find a thought. He watches this grandiose sex act occur, dreading what his eyes are about to behold.

"Mother!" The man in front finishes then falls onto his back, giving Feilece a full view of the woman's face.

Time stops completely as Feilece's eyes behold the sight of the smiling euphoric face of his future.

Kasi … with all of these men. Stuck in time, Feilece is forced to stare at this image. After everything, nothing is as torturous as this.

He wants to barge into the tent and kick the men off her. He wants to take an axe and drive it into their heads. He wants to coat the tent in their blood then go to her. He wants to hold her. He wants to pull her away from this. He wants to save her. But he can't move.

"That's amazing."

Feilece sees the shining body of Niria walk through him and approach the mass of bodies. "Even after seeing this, you're still willing to fool yourself."

Kasi is being abused.

"Take another look, little brother." Niria frames Kasi's face in her hands. "Does this look like the face of someone who isn't enjoying herself?"

Feilece can't deny this is the happiest he's ever seen Kasi. But it can't be; she wouldn't do this.

"What do you think she's been doing this whole time? This village is hers, she can do whatever she wants with these men."

No. She is being taken advantage of.

"These men are tied up, Feilece. She's not the slave here; she's the dominating force."

Feilece refuses to accept it. These men are monsters, he must kill them for what they've done to his love.

"Why?" Niria gets in close to Feilece, obstructing his vision. "Why are they monsters? Why must they be punished? They're all having fun. They all want this. None of them are doing anything wrong. They're just having sex."

Niria grabs Feilece's hair. He feels her fingers electrify the skin on his head.

"Admit it, little brother. You're only angry right now because you are jealous. You want all these men gone because you want her all to yourself. Your 'future', your 'love' … it's all based on basic desire."

That's not true. They loved each other; they had a life together. They meant the world to each other.

"And yet, when you were stuck in time, you were completely okay with sleeping with other women."

That was different.

"Why? Because it wasn't real? Because it was your fantasy? Well then, now you're going against your own logic. You don't love her, Feilece, you just want her to touch your little thing again."

It can't be … it can't all be for nothing. She's all he thinks about, she's everything he's working towards. Without her, he has nothing.

"And that's exactly how she wants it to be. Why do you think she gratified you that one time then never again? She's obviously not against sex. She wanted to distract you from what's important and inject herself into your head. And she has. You saw Dorean. You saw what they turned her into. Everything that was once her has been replaced. And now, you're the same."

Niria disappears and time slowly goes back to normal. Met with the sight of Kasi once again, Feilece feels the urge to vomit. He stumbles away and heaves his dinner into the grass.

He's just another convert. She stole his heart and attached strings to it. She would've kept him dangling on them until every vein flowed blood poisoned with her influence. His wyll is hers. But it was not just her. He was willing to throw everything away—his wyll … his life … his family—all because she was pretty. How could he be so weak?

He has nothing left now. He kneels in the grass and sits on his heels. His mind empties and he feels his muscles lose their weight. He looks down at his hands resting on his knees. Lit by the light of Kasi's tent brazier, he watches the colour leave his skin and loses feeling in his fingers. He hears Kasi moan in pleasure. A flake peels from his knuckle and flies off in the breeze. He doesn't fight it. With nothing left to live for, he closes his eyes and lets the nothingness consume him.

Before his wyll depletes, he feels arms wrap around him. He feels a warm breath upon the back of his neck. At first, he thinks it's Niria giving him one last embrace before he withers away, but these arms feel bigger. He feels arm hairs tickle the skin of his chest and shoulders. He feels a course beard prick the back of his head.

"Dad?"

The presence disappears with a waft of the wind.

Feeling returns to Feilece's fingers. His muscles regain their weight, in fact, they feel bigger. A warmth emanates inside of him, heating every follicle of his being. There is still something he can live for. Something he must do before he dies. His eyes open.

He picks himself up and makes his way back to his tent. Popoki lays in his bed, breathing steadily in a deep sleep. Feilece grabs his axe and goes to Popoki's side. He holds the axe by its shoulder and presses his forehead to the cheek of the blade.

He closes his eyes and whispers, "thank you, Popoki. For everything."

He makes his way out of the tent and over to one of the carriages they use to transport Tirians. It's packed with supplies. They must be planning to take it to Tiris in the morning. He contemplates walking there but it's a long trip and he's going to need as much energy as possible.

He climbs into the carriage and builds a fort among the supplies to hide in. Now he has to wait and try to get some sleep.

Tomorrow, he will kill Schizo.

XXXIII

D OREAN LAYS ON her back, snoring at the back of the cage. Epo and Rago sit with their backs against the bars, bored.

"She has a completely different person sleeping within her skin, but she still snores like my older sister," Epo says.

"Snoring is caused by mouth anatomy. You can't convert an elongated uvula," says Rago.

"This sound used to keep me up for days. I would hear it all the way down the hall, it would annoy me to death. Now … it's oddly soothing."

"Speak for yourself."

"Louma is … well, terrifying. It doesn't seem like something she would put up with," says Epo.

"She snores too. Although, in her case it's because she's an alcoholic."

Epo smirks. Rago never speaks about their relationship so she was able to put her suspicions to sleep with that one sentence.

"Earlier," Epo says. "Dorean was crying and whispering that she wanted her mother. She was talking about Louma, wasn't she?"

Rago takes a deep breath. "I suspect so."

"But Dorean is already converted. Why would she create a parental relationship with her?"

"Because, even though you'll never hear her say it, she's lonely. She can't conceive, you see. And she's the kind of woman who always wants things she cannot have. I suspect that's why she became interested in my work. Dorean is the closest she will ever get."

"Seeing how Dorean is turning out, it seems like Louma isn't the greatest of mothers."

"I don't know if I would completely blame her," Rago says.

"What happened between you two? Why does she hate you so much?"

"Oh, she always hated me. When I first met her, I thought to myself 'this woman will be the one to kill me' and I still believe that to be the case today."

"But then you got together?"

"I wasn't good to her. I treated her like ... another subject to one of my experiments. I taught her about conversion therapy. I made her into what she is. There was once a time when I looked at her and felt giddy, like a boy with a new toy. Now, I look at her and I only see hate."

Rago looks into Epo's eyes. "I have to confess something."

Epo clenches her jaw.

"The books, the lessons, the tests," Rago continues, "they were all attempts to mould your wyll into one akin to mine. You are my convert, Epo."

"I know that, Rago. It wasn't exactly hard to figure out."

"That's not all. The method I was using is unlike anything I've ever used before. Instead of using dominance or manipulation to create a master and slave dynamic, I used a symbiotic method."

Epo realises what the man is saying. "You aren't confessing to me … you're confessing to yourself."

"When I first saw you try to fake having broken wyll, I was so impressed. I wanted to be as strong as you. Since I've been with these people, I've lost a lot of who I was. I wasn't trying to convert you … I was trying to convert myself."

Through her time in his tent, Epo has learned Rago is no Reaper. Reapers are products for war. Killers, torturers, mindless followers, fodder. They adopt the mantle of wickedness in an attempt to absolve their weaknesses and attain a feeling of power. But they're just scared and estranged. They're given a sword and pointed at a target. Epo recognises their faces, their behaviours. She's grown up with them her whole life. She looks at the Reapers and sees the sheep that used to occupy the fields. Sheep's Basin was an apt location for their base of operations.

Rago is no man of war; he's just a desensitised behavioural scientist.

A tear runs down Rago's face. "I killed your sister."

"W … what?"

"Niria. Through my methods, she was taken by wyll-death. She's dead because of me."

Epo already knew Niria was gone, she felt it the moment her life ceased to be. She never thought about it before, but it was Niria's passing that gave her the strength to go through with her plan to escape the stables. Even though she always knew, hearing the truth still shocks her into tears.

"I am sorry, Epo … but don't forgive me. I don't deserve it. I deserve everything Louma has planned for me."

Rago stands then kneels before Epo. "Listen, I may be responsible for Niria's death but I won't let you come to the same fate. Tomorrow afternoon, we'll make a pack and I'll take you into the woods. I saw your sister trying to escape with you there on the day we arrived, I assume you have a boat, or raft. Take it to Koilia. Ask for a group known as Nomia, they're essentially the Koilian police. They're not incredibly effective—I've been on their wanted list for decades— but they have ties to the Grothia. Tell them about us. Grothia are arrogant, if they hear of a force in the north plotting against them, they'll certainly come to meet us and you'll be rewarded. You're smart, you'll figure out what to do. You'll live."

"What about Dorean?"

"I'll stay and keep her safe. Maybe I can come up with a deconversion process that won't kill her. I don't know."

"What about you? If they find out you've lost one of Animia's children, you'll be put to death."

"They won't kill me. Looking at how Louma's convert is going, I'm still the best wyll breaker they've got. I'll make up an excuse for your escape."

Epo ponders for a moment then the memory of Kasi tossing her braid at her plays in her mind.

"No."

"No? No what?"

"Don't bother."

"Epo, you can escape this place."

"I am this place, Rago." She looks over at Dorean. "It's taken a hold of me the same way it's taken the rest of my family."

"What are you talking about?"

"Lagne."

"The Lixi man?"

"They found the braid I gave him with his remains. Wyll-death … just like Niria. I wanted him dead and he died." Tears stream down her face.

Rago sits next to her, puts an arm around her and holds her close.

"You didn't kill Lagne, Epo. You freed him. You showed him kindness. You showed him that kindness can exist in this place. The weight of everything he has done—everything he did to you—it's no wonder he lost the will to live. I won't pretend to know his thoughts as he left this plane, but I can say that since meeting you, I have felt that maybe Genus is better off without me here."

Epo nestles into Rago's chest. Though she feels robbed of her kindness, she was at least able to pass it off to someone else.

XXXIV

FEILECE WAKES TO the shaking of the carriage as its wheels roll over cobblestone. They've arrived in Tiris.

Feilece rubs his eyes and prepares himself. He didn't plan beyond this. From their voices, it sounds like there are three men driving the carriage. If he slows time, he thinks he can take them out. Feilece remembers his father telling him that because of how narrow the streets are in Tiris, carriages are only allowed at the entrance. This at least means the carriage won't be surrounded by Reapers, but it's possible more Reapers will be awaiting the arrival of the carriage. Feilece hopes he has what it takes.

The carriage comes to a stop and Feilece feels the weight change as the drivers get out. Looking through a small crack he made in the carriage with his axe the night before, Feilece watches two men walk by. One of them is a yellow; it will be harder than he thought.

"We'll go get more hands," says the yellow Reaper. "Little Dick, start unpacking and wait for us."

"Y, yes, sir."

Feilece sighs in relief. He got lucky this time.

The carriage doors open up and Feilece sees the crates ahead illuminate in the Mother's light.

"Little Dick … let's see how big your fucking dick is," the Reaper murmurs to himself as he unloads crates onto the ground.

Feilece, axe in his hand, waits for the perfect moment. After a few crates have been unloaded, Feilece gets a good view. It's Paldi, the man who killed Niria. As hate grows inside of Feilece, he feels his heart about to speed up but he stops and instead slows it down. Time slows to a creeping pace; Feilece is afforded more freedom to plan.

Paldi curses in a deep tone as he drops one of the crates, spilling its contents.

As Paldi gets to work picking everything up, Feilece moves from his hiding space. Slowly, he extends his axe out of the carriage to the disgruntled Reaper. Paldi expects nothing. This is Feilece's moment to exact revenge.

Feilece wraps the beard of his axe about Paldi's neck and pulls him choking into the carriage. He embeds the axe bit into the wall of the carriage, pinning him.

"What the fuck!"

Feilece puts his hand over Paldi's mouth and pulls his sword from his sheath. He puts the sword to Paldi's throat. "Yell and I will slice this through your skin."

The fear in Paldi's eyes tells Feilece he acknowledges his words. Feilece pulls his hand away.

"F, uh, Feilece? What are you …"

"Where is Schizo?"

"The lord? I … Why are you …"

Feilece runs the blade across Paldi's neck, drawing blood.

"Okay! I'm sorry. He … I don't know, he's probably at the town centre. He's giving a speech today."

Feilece thinks back to his memories of Tiris. His father brought him here a few times but they only went to the trading district and to Semnos' school. He played around with those memories so much when he was stuck in time that everything is jumbled up with fantasy. He needs a guide.

He can't leave Paldi here, he'll go back to his Reaper buddies and warn them. He can't kill him either. They'll find his body and it'll amount to the same.

Feilece pulls his axe free but keeps the sword at Paldi's throat.

"Take me there."

"Yeah, okay."

Paldi and Feilece exit the carriage. Feilece holsters his axe but he keeps Paldi's sword in hand and aimed at Paldi's side. He stays close to Paldi to keep the sword hidden but after walking deeper into Tiris, he notices that he doesn't have to try so hard. No one's paying any attention.

Feilece follows Paldi through the cobblestone streets. He walks by multiple storey houses made of wood, all much bigger than the house he grew up in. He feels no envy for these living conditions. All the houses are clumped together, sharing views of nothing but other houses. Feilece had fields of grass and the Mother's light in abundance. This town would be lucky to have a single cobblestone touched by the day's shine without the filter of a building's shadow. It's the middle of the day and yet the light is scarce, thinly spread throughout the streets. It's confusing. Feilece distinctly remembers this place being a lot lighter. There were bulbs of clear water that would redistribute the Mother's light through the town. Maybe he was fantasising.

Nevertheless, Feilece can feel overwhelming anguish smothering every alleyway. He watches a crying woman, her skin slowly turning dark and grey. The woman's face goes blank and her body turns into dust and bone. The ground is littered with bones like these.

Feilece swears it used to be an exciting and joyous place. The people smiled and wore brave expressions instead of dreary sunken faces. It's no wonder his father stopped bringing him here after the incident.

There is one addition to the town he knows for certain wasn't there when he was a kid. On every corner, the Reaper insignia has been painted.

As they walk through an alley, a faint tone drifts on the breeze. It's soft and pretty in timbre but the music is dark.

"Why are you doing this, Feilece?" Paldi says.

"Don't talk to me, Paldi."

"I don't get it. If you want to see Schizo, you could've asked. Why are you being so aggressive?"

"I said don't talk."

"You're wearing the clothes, you're one of us aren't you?"

Feilece knocks Paldi's ankle with the side of his sword, tripping him to the ground. Feilece stands over Paldi and puts the sword to his throat. He wants to scream in Paldi's face, telling him he is not one of them … but he stops himself; Paldi is crying.

"Is it because of what I did to Niria?"

Feilece's hand shakes uncontrollably.

"Because I'm sorry, I'm so sorry. I didn't mean to …"

"Shut up."

"I didn't know that would happen! They told me I was saving her!"

"Shut up!"

Feilece slices the sword across Paldi's neck. Blood gushes out and floods Feilece. It torrents and submerges Feilece until he feels trapped under water. He chokes and fights but before long, his body starts to go limp.

He has no idea what is happening but he refuses to give up. He is on a mission; he cannot fail before he has tried. He thrashes against the blood. He sees the Mother's light above him and he swims towards it.

Feilece stands alone in the alley again. The dark music still plays. Paldi is nowhere to be seen.

What just happened? He decides to follow the music. He sees a flickering of a candle on the side of a nearby building where the music emanates from. He turns the corner to find a small crowd of people gathered around a man playing a string instrument with a long neck. He plucks the strings with the fingers on one hand while using the other hand to play different notes. His hands are red as if painted with blood. The man wears all black clothes, complete with blood-red ropes wrapped around his forearms and a big black cloak. His large conical black hat is tilted so Feilece can't see his face. At first, he thinks it's Schizo, but somehow, he knows it isn't.

The music … Feilece has never heard anything like it before. It feels as if the music is speaking to him directly. He looks around at the other people. They're all sick and weak. They're entranced by the music, propped up on it like tired kids leaning upon a post. They all sway in unison and have no expression on their faces.

Feilece's eyes fall upon Paldi. He looks deep into his eyes. He's stuck in the same trance as everyone else.

The music stays the same volume, but somehow Feilece feels it getting louder in his head, as if it's resonating in his skull. Feilece looks over at the musician. The man lifts his head. Feilece watches as the man's face slowly comes into view.

Their eyes meet. The black at the centre of the musician's pupils turn to red then to hazel as it reaches to the edges of his corneas. Through the man's presence alone, Feilece feels an incredible intensity overcome him. He feels the ground shaking beneath his feet, as if the Child Itself is responding to their visual communication.

SUDDENLY, FEILECE IS standing at the gate to Semnos' school. He feels younger, Genus Itself feels younger. The town is lit well and gone is the feeling of dread that strangles Tiris.

Feilece looks to his side. He wants to cry but the tears refuse him. Anema stands with his arm around Plios. They look well with big smiles upon their faces.

"Semmy!"

Feilece hears Niria's voice and quickly turns his head to see his three sisters standing close by. Niria is waving frantically.

This must be fantasy. No … Feilece is certain of it, this is a true memory.

Feilece looks back through the gate and sees his brother. He feels a sense of joy before he realises who is walking next to Semnos.

It's Paldi. Without his Reaper uniform, he looks like any old student. A deep rage builds inside of Feilece as he looks into Paldi's eyes. On Paldi's face is a smug kind of lust … and he's looking at Niria.

"YOU'RE IN A unique position, little brother."

Feilece is sitting with Semnos by the side of a pool of water at the base of a large waterfall.

Feilece feels himself speak and he has no control over it. "What do you mean?"

"You're the youngest of us; you get to watch all of our mistakes and learn from them."

Looking out at the water, Dorean is teaching Niria and Epo how to row their father's boat. Niria is struggling to keep the thing from swaying.

Feilece turns back to Semnos. "But you don't make mistakes."

"Oh, I make a lot of mistakes," he says with a laugh. "And they'll become a lot more apparent with time."

Semnos' voice becomes serious. "As I get older, it

feels like time keeps getting faster and faster. Sometimes I get scared, wondering if I'll wake up tomorrow and I'll be Dad's age. And I worry I would've made as little impact on this world as he has."

"I don't understand."

Semnos smiles. "That's okay, Feilece," he says as he scruffs up his hair. "Don't you worry. Whatever the Child has in store for our lives, I know you will be the one to carry our family name. Just keep an eye on the clock. Don't let time pass you by."

FEILECE SEES NIRIA'S hand. Her body turns to dust.

FEILECE GRIPS THE sword in his hand tightly then plunges it into Paldi's stomach. Paldi wretches forward and falls onto his hands and knees. Broken out of his trance, he tries to scream but instead coughs up blood.

Slowly, Feilece removes the axe from its holster. He hovers the blade over the back of Paldi's neck. With a heave, he raises the axe and brings it down. Paldi's head drops onto the stones.

The musician's hand stops plucking and the final notes ring out. Feilece looks at him, making eye contact with his red-hazel eyes. No one in the crowd is reacting to what Feilece did. The musician places his red palm on the strings and the sustained notes come to an end. As the music stops, the entranced Tirians crumble into piles of dust and bones.

XXXV

FEILECE STANDS ALONE, staring at the musician. The musician moves his instrument and stands. As he stands, the ropes on his arms move on their own. They wrap around his fingers and palm, creating a tight knot from his knuckles to his elbows.

He approaches Feilece. Feilece stays strong. All logic is telling him to fear this man, but he refuses to. He feels some kind of kinship with him, as if they share something on a deeper level of existence.

The man stands in front of Feilece. They both stare at each other until he lifts one of his roped arms. He presses a thumb to Feilece's head. Feilece feels something moving in-between the connection, something flooding into his pores. Feilece's eyes roll back and he sees red.

He feels energy surge inside of him, flowing through every vein.

The musician removes his hand. Feilece starts panting as his vision returns to normal.

The musician's hand slowly moves as he points down an alley next to them. The alley is empty, and riddled with shadow like everywhere else.

"Thank you," Feilece says to the man as he leaves.

He wonders for a moment if he should have tried to understand everything that just happened. Who was the man, and what power did he hold? But Feilece knows deep down he is not ready to understand it. Looking into that man's red-hazel eyes, it felt like he was staring at the clock. He knows he will see him again.

Before he makes it to the end of the alleyway, he hears a voice.

"People of Tiris!"

He remembers this voice, he heard it on the day his life was destroyed. He turns the corner into the city centre and he sees him, the red-haired man, Schizo.

Feilece moves his eyes over the quad. It's an open area with the Mother's light illuminating it. He sees poorly maintained houses, abandoned trade stalls, and depressed people without direction. They lay in the court, or meander aimlessly looking malnourished. The only people showing any kind of vigour are those standing around a stage at the centre of the quad. The stage is elaborate and strongly built. Feilece remembers a fountain once stood there, but now it's masked by this structure decorated in Reaper insignia. And on top, stands Schizo.

"Though our efforts have done much for your poor town in the recent months, I still look around and see the same decay I saw when we first arrived. I see broken people. I see broken wyll. We've helped clean and build and foster strength as much as we can, but we can only go so far under such constraints."

Slowly, more people gather around the stage. People emerge from their homes with a glimmer in their eyes.

"Is this all you have to offer? A town reduced to a wayward pointless wyll, bereft of passion, excitement, intrigue, and direction? Is this all you are? I, for one, believe this not to be the case!"

Upon hearing the man's heated words, Feilece sees hope rising in the Tirians.

"I believe we are all soldiers of Genus! And we soldiers of Genus are not meant to squander our wyll away to the addictive dark recesses of depression! We soldiers of Genus are not meant to be piles of dust and bone! We are meant for glory! We are meant for greatness!"

More Tirians gather. Their numbers are now reaching hundreds.

"We are meant to carve out our names in history, and leave our corpses among the grass as a reminder we were here! We exist! Do not let yourselves be forgotten!"

"And what glory are you offering us today?" a cynical voice calls from the crowd.

Schizo smirks.

"I'm not offering anything today, for you have not earned anything yet. What I am willing to offer, though, is a promise. A promise to make you all into better people. Capable people!"

"Will you save Tiris from this depression?" A desperate voice from the crowd.

"I am sorry for your town, such a great loss would weigh heavy on any city, or nation, or people. What I offer is a way for one to better themselves. For the one ... not for the all. The first step to saving your people, is to first save yourself. It may sound harsh, but this town has become a source of sadness and dread. You must toss aside this den of anguish and venture out. A new start; a new setting. I can help you; I can bring you into a new world, and make you shine."

The crowd begins to murmur among themselves until their attention is stolen by the man standing above them.

"Follow me, and be afforded the opportunity to become the best you can be! I will train you to fight, I will teach you to be strong, you will be given the chance to prove yourself in battle! A chance for glory!"

"But we are a humble people, we aren't soldiers," a cowardly voice calls from the crowd.

Schizo signals to one of his Reaper recruits.

"Fear not, my fellow Tirians!" The young man steps onto the stage. "You all remember me, correct? In fact, you may all remember me as quite the ruffian. A common thief without a future. Struggling to maintain the pathetic life I had. Well not anymore! They took me in, they trained me, they showed me the importance of discipline. And for the first time since before the night of death, I felt a sense of hope. I now look forward to the future, instead of ruing the thought of it!"

He gestures at Schizo. "This man is a kind and intelligent lord. He has great ambitions and will serve us well. He will give you a reason to live again, as he ushers us into a new land full of opportunity!"

Schizo takes over. "Don't think I don't know how hard change can be. I too lost everything over the course of a single day. As a kid, I lost my father, and with him, everything else. I thought the Child was forcing me to die alone on the gritty streets of Koilia. But then I realised I wasn't being condemned, I was being tested. I built up my strength and I am now a lord of my own army and my own kingdom. Join me and I can teach you to be strong. I can teach you to take back your wyll and your lives. Our castle awaits us in Koilia!"

A few Tirians cannot contain themselves, they begin cheering and a cacophony grows.

"Join me! And be among the first of the new order that will sow its name into the Child and reap ourselves true glory! Follow me, and become a Reaper!"

Enthusiasm spreads like an infection among the crowd and, before long, the entire city centre is overcome with noise.

Feilece watches Schizo leave the platform and mingle among the people. With nothing but a few energetic words, Schizo was able to turn these people from lifeless ghouls into impassioned followers.

Feilece slows his heart and watches all the desperate people celebrate in slow motion. He can't help but feel a familiarity with them. Tossed into a world of disarray, they let their wyll fall into a deep black. It's no wonder Schizo's message is so potent, his words have sparked their hearts. A simple spark can illuminate an entire world if there's enough darkness.

Feilece's hand shakes as it clutches the axe. These people ... they're more slaves. More converts to throw to their death fighting his war. Schizo didn't even blink as he uses their tragedy against them. Taking their weakness and using it to mould them into puppets.

Feilece can't let him get away with this.

Now's the time. He'll use the cover of the crowd to get in close and embed his axe in the back of the man's head. Feilece can't risk losing a real fight. This man's life must end and it must end now.

"Hey, kid."

A sharp tingle runs from Feilece's heels to the top of his head. Slowly, he turns and finds the two Reapers from the carriage who left him with Paldi. One red; one yellow.

The yellow tosses Paldi's head at Feilece's feet. "You do this?"

Feilece doesn't say anything.

"Hey, I know this kid," says the red Reaper. "I seen him around the camp, he's Popoki's apprentice."

"Ah, the Animia spawn. This family, they really do love to kill us, don't they."

Feilece enters a stance.

"Hah! This should be interesting." The yellow nods to the red. "Get him."

The red pulls a spear from his back and enters a stance. Feilece hasn't practised much against polearms but he's confident in his abilities. He takes a deep breath and slows his heart.

The red goes to attack but Feilece can read his movements easily. He's able to dodge and deflect at ease. He's even able to slice the man's arm.

The man curses, then goes in for another attack. Concentrating on the spear, Feilece goes to deflect it but then he finds his axe stops moving. He looks up at his weapon to find the red Reaper has his hand gripped around the shoulder of the axe.

Feilece tries to pull the axe free but his arms aren't

strong enough to overpower him. Terrified, Feilece feels his heart quicken. Time goes back to normal.

The Reaper scoffs. "Cut by a fucking prepubescent. I'm never gonna live that down."

Feilece goes to run but he can't stop his heart from racing, making time speed up. The red Reaper cuts him off and slams him against the wall. The man holds Feilece by his neck. Unable to breathe, Feilece chokes until his heart slows to a normal rate.

"Stop," says the yellow Reaper.

Feilece is released and he falls onto the cobblestones.

"We can't kill him, he's a general's apprentice."

"But he killed our man."

"Little Dick isn't much of a loss anyway. We'll have Schizo decide what will become of the boy."

Hearing Schizo's name ignites a fire in Feilece's heart. He quickly jumps up, grabs his axe and runs into the crowd.

Tirians move out of his way as Feilece rages past them, creating a gap in his path.

"Get back here, you little fuck!"

Feilece feels the red Reaper's hand around his neck again. Feilece stabs the toe of his axe into the man's foot. The red screams and releases Feilece. Feilece then spins around and embeds the axe in the man's neck. The red Reaper falls to the ground, dead.

Feilece turns back to Schizo and continues on his hunt. Schizo notices the boy. They lock eyes as Feilece runs at him. Feilece expects to see fear on the man's face, but he's not showing any. Instead, Schizo smiles.

Feilece gets in close and screams out a battlecry as he swings the axe down upon Schizo's head. A loud thud resonates through the vicinity as Feilece's axe chops into the wood of the stage.

Feilece can't believe it, his target was right in front of him.

"Is that all? Cousin?" Schizo asks, his voice smug.

No, Feilece can't stop now. He pulls the axe from the wood and faces Schizo. He throws a barrage of trained swings at the man, incorporating everything Popoki has taught him, and Schizo dodges every single attack with ease. He doesn't even bother unsheathing his sword. There's nothing Feilece can do.

Feilece doesn't give up. He keeps swinging until his axe collides with the yellow Reaper's sword. The yellow pushes against Feilece's axe, making Feilece trip onto his back.

"I'm sorry, my lord," the yellow says. "He got away from us."

"That's alright. Just get him into one of the carriages. It looks like I'll be returning home today after all."

Schizo gestures to a few of his guards then walks off. Feilece tries to not let him leave but he is stopped by the yellow Reaper.

"Just give up, kid."

Feilece taps into his training and delivers a bunch of attacks to the yellow. Easily, the man deflects them all. Feilece is completely outmatched.

"Enough of this." The yellow dashes in close and smacks Feilece around the head with the butt of his sword.

Feilece stares up at the Mother as his consciousness slowly fades.

XXXVI

FEILECE OPENS HIS eyes to a blurry sight of red and black. He tries to rub his eyes but he can't move his arms. He looks over at them and sees they're splayed out at his sides, suspended in the air. He can't feel the ground at his feet either, it's as if he's floating. His eyes adjust on their own and he quickly realises he is not in the real world.

An infinite horizon spreads out in all directions. Dark, empty, blood-red skies meet matte-black still water. He looks up at the Mother but She has been replaced with a black hole surrounded by a ring of hazel luminescence.

Feilece hovers there in this grand empty space. He doesn't feel scared; he doesn't feel uncomfortable in any way. All he feels is curiosity.

He failed in his task to kill Schizo. He was stupid to think he could defeat him. Not even his father could survive against the Reaper lord, and Animia was apparently unbeatable. Feilece is just a boy. A naive little kid with nothing but fantasies as the foundation for his strength. He thought the decades of stillness would give him an edge, but there's no substitute for real world experience.

Schizo would not go easy on him for an attempt upon his life, of this, Feilece has no doubt. Perhaps Schizo has already killed him, and this is where one is taken upon their death. Is he to spend the rest of eternity floating in this empty world? If so, Feilece doesn't mind. He's used to this by now. He's just sad that he couldn't do anything for his sisters. He's sad he couldn't avenge his father.

Music begins to play behind Feilece. It's a similar sound to the music the black-garbed man was playing in Tiris but it feels different, distorted. He can't turn his head to look, he's stuck staring forward. Ripples appear in the water below, emanating from something in the distance, footsteps. Slowly, a figure begins to appear, going from translucent to tangible. A great warmth overtakes Feilece.

"Dad."

Anema stands before Feilece, looking as real as life.

"Hello, Son."

Tears form in Feilece's eyes. "So ... I am dead then."

Anema smiles. "No ... this is another one of your fantasies."

"This doesn't feel like fantasy."

"Well, to be honest, I don't actually know what this is," Anema says with a chortle.

"Why did you do it?" Feilece says through his tears. "Why did you kill Schizo's father? Why do we have to suffer?"

"I ..." Anema takes a deep breath and his face turns surly. "It was my job to kill. It was all I ever knew, even as a little boy. But, somehow, I never got used to it. Every time I would watch the life leave someone's face, I would always feel like mine was being taken with it. I hated it … but everyone was doing it." A tear escapes Anema's eye. "Schisma, he was the only man I ever met who I thought shared in those feelings. Him and his group of farmers turned soldier, I believed in them. But once we had achieved our goal. Once we had killed the Demons and PanoApo, I thought we were done. The Apo would no longer have their grip over the land and the Demons would no longer be organised enough to sow dissent. I thought we would work on building the people up but then I found out that Schisma wanted to go back to war." Anema wipes the tears from his eyes. "Once I was done with him, there was only one other person left to kill."

Feilece speaks softly. "Yourself."

"I didn't want to give Koilia another fucking corpse so I travelled north. I always liked sheep. Why not lay down my dust upon the grass that shares their name. Then I met your mother. Her parents had died and she was trying to tend the farm all on her own."

Anema gives Feilece a guilty look. "I never intended to have Semnos. I never intended to start a family. I didn't think I could. Why would the Child gift me with something so precious after all the pain I had caused It."

He falls to his knees and sobs into his hands. "I'm so sorry, my boy. I'm sorry I brought you to this place. I'm sorry you have to pay for my mistakes. You don't deserve this." Anema looks up at Feilece. "No one deserves this. I wish I could fix this for you. I wish I had answers for you. But I'm weak."

Seeing his father's confession, Feilece is not sad. It

doesn't hurt his hope, it bolsters it. This is what weakness looks like. Feilece knows he can do better than this.

Feilece smiles at his father. "It's okay, Dad. I'll figure it out."

Anema smiles back then he closes his eyes, and his skin starts to flake. Anema's withered remains fall and sink below the surface of the black water.

"Hey," Feilece calls out. "Mr. Musician."

The music stops and the black-garbed man appears, strolling into Feilece's peripheral vision.

"Thank you for showing me this."

The man doesn't respond, he just stands in front of Feilece with his face obstructed by his large hat.

"Now tell me … how do I kill Schizo."

"COUSIN."

THE MUSICIAN STARTS walking towards Feilece, raising his hat to get a look at the boy. Feilece sees that the man's mouth doesn't move and yet, Feilece can hear the man's voice in the back of his skull. It's a deep and booming voice.

"Trust not in your skill. Trust not in your axe."

"COUSIN."

"TRUST NOT IN your training. Your experience is your inexperience." The man places a hand on Feilece's chest. "Your wyll is in your blood. Trust in your wyll."

"COUSIN!"

Feilece's eyes open to the sight of Schizo yelling in his face. His arms are splayed out at his sides and bound to a piece of wood. Four thick metal bracelets are embedded into the wood, strapped to his wrists and biceps. His legs dangle high above the floor. There are blood covered torture instruments all around him. He's not in a tent. These walls, this roof, this floor. Though nothing is as it was, Feilece can still recognise this room. It's his parents'.

"Ah, it's about time you woke up. I was beginning to worry that the butt of a sword may have stolen you from me," says Schizo.

"You kept me alive."

"Do you know how many recruits that stunt of yours cost me? You can't shove your axe into some-one's neck before they've signed up, it makes everyone skittish. You have to ease them into the brutality slowly through hunting and training, then ... you show them war."

"You should not have kept me alive."

Schizo cracks up laughing. "And why is that? You want to have another crack? Let's go. I'll get you down from there and we can do this thing. I'll give you as many tries as you like. It'll be my pleasure."

Feilece frowns at the man.

"I didn't think so."

"Schizo!" Louma bursts into the room. She looks dishevelled and haggard. It's as if she hasn't slept all night and she sways and smells of alcohol.

"Please, sir, you have to help my daughter," Louma says. She grabs him by his shirt and he shoves her off.

"Please!" she says from her knees.

"Your daughter? What are you talking about?"

"They think I failed to break her. They want to kill her. You must stop them. She won't do it again!"

"Ah." Schizo's eyes shift to the side of their sockets, looking smugly at Feilece. "You're talking about Animia's eldest daughter. I heard she was having issues. I've also heard the other one has been secretly influencing Rago in a particularly unfavourable way."

"Rago!" Louma stands in haste, fuming. "That man needs to die. I overheard him talking to his little friend last night. He plots against us. Schizo, give me permission to kill him. Give me the order, I'll destroy him. Just please save my daughter."

"Shut up." Schizo smacks Louma to the ground.

She looks up at him with quivering eyes. "But … I heard him …"

"I trust Rago much more than I trust you, you failed Apo guard."

Louma's hands begin to shake.

"I brought you on to help sway any remaining Apo supporters. Without Seemo, you're nothing but another soldier. And now I see you can't even break some farmer girl. What a disappointment you are."

Schizo turns his back on Louma and gives all of his attention to Feilece, slowly stepping towards him.

"And as for your 'daughter', I will give no order to save her. In fact, I'll give the opposite. The other one too." He stares deep into Feilece's eyes. "The Animia blood is proving too troublesome. Best to be done with them."

Feilece maintains eye contact, showing no fear.

"Fuck you!" Louma grabs a nearby sickle and swings it at Schizo's head. Without looking, Schizo grabs her arm and redirects her strike into the wood of Feilece's harness.

The blade nicks Feilece's cheek and a dribble of blood flows out. Feilece doesn't flinch.

Schizo elbows Louma in the face then boots her out the door. She scurries off, shoving a Reaper in green clothes to the ground as she exits.

The green-clothed Reaper quickly corrects himself then addresses Schizo. "My lord, I've been sent to retrieve you."

"Have you now?"

"A dire situation is unfolding on top of the hill."

"What?"

"They didn't tell me, they just said you're needed urgently."

"Fine." Schizo looks back at Feilece. "Before you leave, tell Popoki to bring the two remaining Animia daughters to this tent."

"Yes, my lord."

Schizo closes in on Feilece. "I'm going to kill your

sisters in front of you. Then you would have watched me send every single person you love back to the Child. And it doesn't end there. I will leave you alive. I will torture you, the same way I tortured your sisters. I can see you're strong; you won't succumb to wylldeath. But with enough time, and enough pain, you will break. Then I will march you into war. And I will finally let you die, not by my hand, but by that of my enemies. Then—and only then—will Animia have truly paid for what he did to me."

Schizo's red hair wafts as he turns to leave.

"Schizo." Feilece grabs his attention once more. "I will kill you. I will avenge my family."

Schizo smirks. "And when exactly will you exact your revenge upon me?"

Feilece smirks back. "I don't know. Could be this week, this decade, this lifetime. It could be while you're awake. Could be while you're asleep. But before I decide when you will die, I first must ask you to consider one thing."

"And what's that?"

"Do you not deserve to die?"

Schizo smiles and nods. Then he leaves.

Feilece is left to hang and wait for his sisters to be brought before him and executed. The very thought of it makes the beating in his chest race. He was able to keep his heart under control while Schizo was in the room but it was through a simple refusal to show fear. And now the man is gone, Feilece can't help but be overrun with hatred.

Schizo was right, by the end the day, everyone he ever loved will be dead. Even Kasi has been reduced to a corpse in the back of his mind. He was unable to save his sisters. Maybe if he had spent less time thinking about Kasi, he could've come up with a way to keep them alive. Schizo is retaliating to Feilece's attack … it's Feilece's fault his remaining family is going to die.

Though he's lost hope for his family, Feilece is not without a sense of confidence. A confidence built upon spite and rage. Before Feilece draws his final breath, Schizo will die. He just has to trust his wyll.

XXXVII

<hr>

EPO WATCHES RAGO pack clothes and food into a pack. She doesn't bother to help him.

Rago looks over at her. "Would you like to pick out a book or two. Small ones so they'll fit. You can read them on the journey."

"I've already read them all."

"Well, you can read them again."

"Why?"

"Epo."

"Why are we doing this? I already told you. I don't belong out there," she says.

"You don't belong here either." Rago kneels before Epo and grabs her hand. "Please, Epo, find your strength. I know it's there. You are not a Reaper."

"Neither are you!"

Epo stands and begins pacing. "I can't make it on my own." She looks into Rago's eyes. "Will you come with me?"

"What about Dorean?"

"There's nothing we can do for her. She's not Dorean anymore. Feilece as well. They're Reapers now. I have to accept that."

Epo hears a familiar voice outside. "I don't like that." Epo turns in a snap.

Rago gets up. "Okay, then at least help me—"

"Shh, stop." Epo slowly creeps towards the tent's entrance. The afternoon dim light of the Mother shines through the crack. Epo notices an extra light beam shining at a different angle. There's another light source on the other side of the tent.

Epo exits the tent. Her eyes tear up. "It can't be."

"Oh, but it is, dear sister."

Rago comes to Epo's side. "There's no one here … who are you talking to?"

"Niria!" Epo leaps forth and hugs her shining sister.

"Niria's wyll lives …" Rago whispers. "I didn't kill her."

Epo grasps Niria's hands. "How is this possible?"

"I'm not really sure. I remember dying, kind of. I lost all feeling in my body except for my hand. Then, I was stuck in Feilece's mind for a long time. Then I felt him grab my hand and suddenly, I was here, like this."

"It sounds like you somehow passed your wyll onto Feilece at the moment of your death. Or maybe, he pulled it out of you. He saved you."

"I guess he did, but now, he's the one that needs saving."

"What do you mean?"

"He's gotten himself into a bind. You have to break him out."

"Uh, I don't know."

"Epo, they are not Reapers. They are still your family."

"They are?"

"Feilece was caught trying to kill Schizo. He was trying to avenge our father."

"Feilece." Epo smiles.

Niria grabs Epo's shoulders and presses their foreheads together. "I know you're scared, my sister. I know you think this place has corrupted you. But frankly, that's fucking stupid."

Niria pulls away and they both lock eyes. "That bitch, Kasi, is a demon and she can fuck right off. You—my lovely sister—compared to these wretches, you're the Mother. And we Anemelos are unbeatable."

Niria stares off into the distance. "It's ironic. It took dying for me to realise how much I wanted to live." She looks back at Epo. "Don't waste your life, and don't let them have it either. Don't let them have Feilece or Dorean's also. Those two belong to us."

Epo closes her eyes and takes a deep breath.

"Rago," she says, opening her eyes and looking at him.

"Yes?" he says.

"Feilece has been caught for trying to kill Schizo. Would you mind helping me save him?"

Rago smiles. "Of course I'll help."

Epo leads Rago, by Niria's direction, to their old house.

Rago steps ahead. "I'll go in first and see if it's clear. Does your sister know what room he is in?"

Epo relays the information from Niria, and Rago enters the house. Epo hides in the bushes. Peeking around the corner, she sees hordes of Reapers gathering for dinner. She sidles in under a window and waits.

"Our parent's room." Niria says, staring at the window covered in thick hemp to keep the Mother's light out. "Do you remember barging in there when we couldn't get to sleep."

"We would stay up and I would read to you all, considering how bad Dad was at it." They both chuckle. "Then I would lay down and just … be. Savouring the moment."

Niria's eyes go sad. "You're not going to like what they've turned the room into."

Epo inhales slowly. "It can't be any worse than what they've turned us into."

"When you go in there," says Niria, "Feilece may seem … different. Like there's a bigger force working inside of him. But don't worry; he's still there. He's still our little brother."

"What do you mean? Aren't you coming in with me?"

"No, I … he doesn't need my help anymore."

Though Epo doesn't understand, she doesn't argue. Instead, she closes her eyes and gives Niria another hug.

"Don't forget, Epo, they can never break us."

The blade of a sickle pierces through the hemp on the window and traces a jagged hole.

Rago appears. "Hey, come on."

Epo looks at Rago. "She's gone."

"I'm sure she's not gone far. At least we now know what Dorean was swiping her arm at. Anyway, get in here," he says as he leans out of the window and lifts Epo through it.

Epo climbs down from the windowsill. Her eyes

blink as they look around the room. She silently thanks Niria for preparing her.

Her eyes settle upon a block of wood with her brother bound to it. He doesn't acknowledge them; his eyes stare straight as if he's in a trance.

"Oh, Feilece."

"Yeah, I found this was digging into his cheek." Rago tosses the sickle to the ground. "You try and get him out, I'll keep watch."

Feilece is too high for Epo to reach so she pulls over a wooden frame and climbs on top of it. She puts her hand on Feilece's face.

"Oh Feilece, my poor brother. I was hoping they wouldn't do this to you. I was hoping we girls could take all the hurt so you didn't have to."

"You did, for the most part," says Rago. "The tortures he's been through are nothing compared to the torture you were put through."

"You're wrong. We may have gone through more physical pain, but he had to listen to us, knowing he couldn't help us. Feilece is a sweet boy, his mind couldn't handle that kind of stress."

"You may be right. This trance he's in, it looks a lot like a broken wyll. I'm so sorry, Epo."

"It can't be."

Epo rests her forehead on Feilece's and closes her eyes. Through the veins on Feilece's head, Epo can feel his blood pumping fast. She presses her hand against his chest and feels his heartbeat raging, then its tempo slows down.

"Epo!" Feilece awakes from his trance suddenly. Epo almost falls from the frame.

Feilece pants harshly, keeping eye contact. "Oh thank fuck, I didn't miss you."

"Feilece?"

"Yeah, it's me."

Tears burst from Epo's eyes as she wraps her arms around him.

"Epo … is it really you? I thought I had lost you. I thought they'd broken your wyll."

"I thought they'd broken yours."

"They did. Actually, I think I broke myself." Feilece jokes. "Listen, sis, Schizo is planning to kill you and Dorean."

"What?" says Rago from across the room.

"So you have to leave as soon as you can and make sure nobody sees you, he's already sent guards to look for you."

"Isn't that a coincidence, we were already on our way out," says Epo.

"Well, don't wait. Go as quickly as you can."

"Not without you."

Epo picks up the sickle from the ground and starts sawing at Feilece's binds but it's no good.

"Sis …"

"I need a bit more strength. Rago, give me a hand."

"Epo …" Rago says, frowning. "There are Reapers approaching from the kitchen."

"No! First we have to get these braces off then."

"Sis …"

The two siblings stare at each other.

"Epo." Rago places his hand on her shoulder. "We must go."

"No. We're not leaving him here. Niria sent me here to save him."

"Sis!"

Epo turns back to her brother.

"You have saved me. You've saved me the pain of watching you die. Now go."

"How can you ask me to leave my little brother in this state, with these demons?"

"Don't worry about me. They can't hurt me, not anymore. Go, get to safety. I will meet up with you eventually."

"What about Dorean? We can't leave her either."

Feilece smiles. "You said Niria brought you here?"

"Yeah."

"She's showing me you two can be saved. It's okay, I'll get Dorean. You concentrate on escaping."

Rago interrupts them, "we must go now."

"Why are you helping my sister? What is your agenda?" Feilece glares at him.

"There's no way I can make up for what I've done to your family … but I'll do what I can."

Feilece nods.

Epo hugs Feilece one last time.

"Don't worry, sis. Once I'm done here, I'll come meet you. Whether it be in a few hours, a few days, or a few years. We will meet again"

"Somehow, I believe you. Farewell, little brother."

Epo and Rago leap out the window. Peering around the side of the house, Epo sees something has all the Reapers riled up. They're all scurrying around with fraught expressions on their faces.

"They seem distracted," she says.

"Good, we can use that our advantage."

They run towards the forest. Epo smiles, her heart filled with a new sense of hope.

XXXVIII

THE WOODEN BAR of the cage scratches at Killer's back. Her wrists are tired and legs are numb from being huddled together for so long, but she doesn't want to change position. She tries to take up as little space as possible, scared that if she moves, she'll awaken the apparitions that have been haunting her. She's been at peace since she woke up, so she must be doing something right. Only an order from her mother would be enough to make her move.

"You seem less stressed today," says Popoki in-between mouthfuls of nuts. "How are you feeling?"

Killer doesn't reply, she mustn't, though she can't help her eyes from flicking looks at his food.

"Do you want some?" Popoki prepares to throw a nut. "Here, open your mouth."

Killer diverts her eyes, trying to ignore him.

"Okay," Popoki says with a long breath. He puts the sack away and takes a seat close to the cage.

"Do you enjoy being a Reaper, Killer?"

Killer furrows her brow. She doesn't understand the question.

"How about your mother?"

She glares at him. Her heart begins to pound.

"How do you feel about the way she treats you?"

"My mother treats me just fine!" she blurts out quickly and without thought.

"Ah, so you can speak."

Killer holds herself tighter, forcing her mouth closed.

"You probably don't remember, but we actually met a couple of times before you were … uh, born? I guess? That sounds weird to say. Let's just say, before you met your mother."

There was no time before she met her mother. This man is speaking nonsense.

"The woman you were, she reminded me of someone I held very dear. She was smart and cunning and strong … and she was caring. I had an older brother like that once. He was really the only family I had. I followed him everywhere, copied everything he did. I wouldn't move unless he told me where to go."

Killer wonders why he's telling her this. What does he want from her?

"My brother was … so full of life. But when his boyfriend died, he became like you, the way you are now. Broken."

Killer feels her heart start to pound once again.

"And where he went, I couldn't follow him anymore. I had to live for myself for once. And when the Reapers came along, I could see I was being pulled back into the same role I used to fill: that of a follower. I thought nothing could bring me back into that life, not without someone like my brother there to guide me. But I found another, and before I knew it, I was back following. Love, it grabs us by the chest and drags us through life, with no way of stopping it."

Killer watches tears run down his cheek, confused. Following is everything; there's no other reason to life but to follow orders. It's nothing to cry about.

"I used to think people were different to animals," Popoki continues, "I thought it was our ability to make decisions that separated us. But we're all still animals."

Popoki stands and looks down at Killer. "Tell me, do you love your mother?"

"I love my mother with every fibre of my being!"

"Yeah," he says smiling. "You look like an animal."

"Daughter … I love you too. I love you so much."

Popoki spins around and Killer's eyes meet with a sight that makes her launch from her seat.

"Mother!"

With hair splayed in all directions, sunken black eyes, blood dripping from her nose, and clothes stained with dirt, Louma stands at the entrance holding a leaf-blade in her hand.

Popoki steps towards her. "Louma, what are you doing?"

Louma stabs her sword into Popoki's gut. She grabs him by the throat and pushes him against the cage.

Popoki growls. "You fucking psychotic—"

Louma pulls the sword free and tosses him to the ground.

"Stand back, daughter!" she says as she rears up and cuts the latch loose on the cage door.

"Mother."

"Daughter."

The feeling of her mother's arms around her as they embrace fills Killer with such vigour that she feels like she could stick a knife in the celestial Mother and drag the Child home.

"Now, daughter, I have an important order I need you to fulfil. This will be the most important order you will ever get," Louma says as she filters through the scattered swords on the ground she threw down yesterday.

"Yes, Mother. I promise I will not fail this time. I will do everything you ask me to without hesitation."

"Good." Louma picks up a second leaf-blade and puts the handle in Killer's hand. "I recently saw the old fuck! Run into the woods with your little sister."

'Little sister' Killer thinks to herself with a flash of confusion.

"What I need you to do, is chase them down and kill them."

Killer takes a second to respond.

"You said no hesitation. Can you do this for me!"

"Uh, yes, of course, Mother."

"Okay, and don't worry, I'll be there with you." She slurs her words, "this is a mission for both of us."

Killer sees the corpse of a Reaper waiting for them outside the tent. He lays face-down; he must not have seen Louma coming.

"Fuck, it's almost dark," says Louma. "We'll need help. Come with me, Killer."

The two make their way over to where the village meets with the maize fields and the forest.

"Diiiiakhoooo!" Louma screams loud enough for half of the village to hear her.

"Fuck the Mother." Diakho emerges from a nearby tent. "What the fuck … What do you want, Louma?"

"I thought you would be in the woods."

"We taking a night off. Go hunt on your own."

"Wait, wait, wait, wait, wait," Louma runs in front of him. "This prey … you don't want to pass up this opportunity."

Choris comes out of the tent and gives Louma an intrigued eye.

A sinister, murderous smile curls onto Diakho's face. "You mean …"

"I do mean …"

Choris grabs his bow and Diakho pulls a knife from his waist.

"Let's hunt."

XXXIX

<hr>

MAKING HIS WAY up the slope into upper Reaper territory, Schizo perceives a tension among his followers. Sweaty brows, frantic eyes, people rushing forward, people running away. Fear, anxiety, confusion, dread.

Schizo grabs a Reaper by the scruff of his neck. "Speak. What is happening?"

"I'm not sure, my lord. Yellows have been running around telling everyone to grab arms and rally at the northern field. Apparently, a few have already succumbed to wyll-death."

"What!"

"Through fear alone. It's looking like war, sir. It's come to us. I need to get my spear."

Schizo watches the man run off, letting his mind wander.

War ... from the north? That doesn't make any sense. There's nothing to the north but fields and mountains. Any farther and they're in a different country. Also, the town is surrounded by Schizo's best men, keeping eyes on any incoming forces from all directions. There's no way an army could slip past them. He's only been back in the village for a few hours, what could've possibly happened in that time?

He continues up the hill. Walking through a series of black and yellow tents, Schizo sees most of them are empty. His forces must be ready.

He makes his way to the northern end of the village where Reapers are gathering in formation. Moving through legions of yellow and black clothed Reapers, he sees fear rising among his soldiers.

Pushing himself to the front of his army, Schizo stands looking out over a small quarry. At its centre, stands a man. Behind him is a giant black amorphous mass. A mound or pile of some sort, he can't make out what it is in the evening light.

Examining the man from atop his hill, all Schizo can see is a long black cloak and wide conical hat.

"Who goes there?" he calls; his voice echoes over the quarry. Upon finishing his question, his eyes adjust to the dark and he finally sees what he could not before.

His jaw drops. His eyes strain. His shoulders loosen and his legs go weak. It's a mountain of bodies … in black clothes.

"What … How …." Schizo loses all control over his vocal folds.

"Sir?" a timid soldier says. "What … do we do?"

Schizo coughs and blinks profusely. "This is some trick. It has to be."

"They're all dead!" says another soldier.

"No! They can't be! They have to be sleeping. He must be an illusionist. He's put them under a spell," says Schizo.

He can tell his men don't believe him. He has to inject them with some morale.

Schizo turns to his people. "Reapers! Do not trust your eyes! This is a farce, and that is just a man! He's trying to intimidate us with tricks! But are we intimidated?"

"N … no," the murmurs of a few indecisive Reapers.

"What you mean to say is 'we are not'!"

The Reapers all puff out their chests. "We are not!"

"Are we scared?"

"We are not!"

"Are we weak?"

"We are not!"

"Are we strong?"

"We are strong!"

Sheep's Basin shakes with a cacophony of cheers.

Schizo raises a closed fist and they all turn silent. "The Mother's eye is almost closed. She closes it because She does not want to see what we are about to do to this man! I don't know who this man is but he made a grave mistake on this day. Now show me what you've been training for, get down there and collect this man's head!"

Cheers break out once again as hundreds of Reapers, adorned in yellow and black, race down the hill. It's just steep enough that they don't trip when they run.

Schizo watches, curious. Though his words are strong, he doesn't feel them. He doesn't know what he feels.

A particularly fast Reaper makes his way ahead of

the pack and dashes towards the intruder. Schizo watches intently as the Reaper goes to take his sword to the intruder's neck.

In a blink, the Reaper is suddenly flung up into the air at great speed. Two of his limbs tear off from the sudden shift in movement, and his guts spill out as he rises higher He gets as high as the lowest clouds before coming back down and splatting, body mangled upon the quarry grass.

The other Reapers start to hesitate in their advance. The black-cloaked man strides towards the shaking army. Schizo watches, unable to form a single thought.

A Reaper tries to run but the man cuts them off, covering the distance of at least a hundred metres within a second. He delivers a punch into the Reaper's chest and their insides explode out of their back.

The black-cloaked man dashes between distressed soldiers. One more second, there are ten more exploded Reapers.

A group of yellows try to attack, all swinging their weapons in synchronised patterns. It amounts to nothing. The man catches their weapons upon his red roped arms and they shatter into pieces.

Those that try to attack are beaten. Those that try to run are destroyed. Those that can't do either turn into dust in the grass.

To Schizo's eye, the man looks like a lightning bolt, moving through his forces, turning all of the warriors he's spent his life collecting into lifeless mounds of flesh and blood.

Within a few minutes, the entire army, hundreds of

well-trained soldiers, are decimated. The man stops and walks slowly up the hill towards Schizo. The man can move at such great speed, that seeing him choose to walk slowly is far more terrifying. The remaining members of Schizo's army scatter in all directions, their faces stricken.

Schizo gazes into his beaming eyes as the black-cloaked man approaches.

"The red-hazel fighter," Schizo says. "I thought you were a myth."

The man raises his hand. Schizo doesn't move; he can't move. The man presses a thumb to Schizo's forehead. Schizo feels something moving, like microscopic worms wriggling on the man's finger.

The man smiles and pulls his finger away.

"Why …" Schizo can't stop his voice from quivering. "Why are you here?"

The man speaks with a low grizzle. "The same reason you are. To build strength."

"Who are you?"

The man doesn't reply but instead opens his eyes wide. Like water mixing with dye, the colour of the man's eyes shift and change.

"No," Schizo says. "It can't be."

Eyes that once showed hues reminiscent of a forest aflame are traded for a glowing mechanical blue. A colour unlike anything found in nature.

"The Grothia blue … you are Grothia."

Schizo's legs move on their own. He turns and stumbles. He doesn't register anything. He doesn't think at all. He just runs.

XL

⸏⸏⸏

FEILECE TRIES TO move his arms, testing the strength of the binds. It's no use. The strongest man alive couldn't pull his arms free from these metal braces. There's no lock or opening mechanism at all, they're hammered directly into the frame. Schizo intends to have Feilece hang there until the end of his days.

Feilece is not discouraged. Somehow, he will find a way. Schizo will die ... and he will get Dorean to safety. There is no question of 'will' it happen; all that matters is *how* it happens.

The door swings open and the words, "general's apprentice," are spoken in a confident cadence.

Three Reapers in red clothing enter the room, each with their weapon of choice. By their demeanour alone, Feilece can tell he's supposed to be intimidated. It isn't working.

"The village is in a bit of an uproar right now so we figured we would pay you a visit."

One of the Reapers approaches, the man's breath stings Feilece's nostrils. "You killed our mate ..."

Feilece doesn't apologise; he doesn't gloat. He

310

stares into the man's eyes, acknowledging the man's feelings. It hurts when someone close to you is suddenly gone. Knowing you'll never see them—speak to them, laugh with them, be with them—ever again.

What comes next … Feilece has earned.

The man pulls a knife from his belt and slowly runs the blade up the middle of Feilece's torso, just deep enough to draw blood. Every muscle in Feilece's body contracts and spasms but he refuses to scream.

"Remember, we can't kill him," says another red.

"I know … I don't want him dead anyway. He can't pay if he's dead."

Feilece's heart wants to speed up—let the hours rush by so he doesn't have to feel it—but Feilece stops it. Instead, he opts to do the opposite.

Feilece takes a breath and slows his heart right down to a crawl. The man's hand takes over an hour to get the blade all the way to the boy's clavicle.

In this state, Feilece is forced to feel the steel of the knife inside of him for so long it becomes a part of him. It doesn't ease the pain, but it makes it easier to grow familiar with. On top of pain-management, Feilece must use all of his strength to keep his heart slow. This is his training. If wyll is dictated by how well one is willing to survive, then this is the true test of what he is willing to live through. He will trust his wyll.

The men torture him. They cut patches of flesh from his skin, they press red-hot iron against his body, they pry out his fingernails, push needles into his muscles and twist them. They spend a good hour extracting enough pain from Feilece to avenge their friend. To Feilece, though, it is much longer. He experiences at least a week of solid torture.

He learns a lot from his efforts. He learns how to control the rhythm of his heart to the proficiency of a trained musician. He learns that all forms of pain are an illusion set by the mind. That pain itself is not something one can bestow upon you, but rather something cultivated from within oneself.

Feilece wonders how far this idea of illusion goes. If pain is dictated by the victim, how much of the real world is under that same canopy. While under the same constraints of slow moving time, Feilece has always accepted that his body is no different to anyone else's. That even though he can perceive time differently, his body is still trapped within it. Now, he wonders how much of that is true.

He pushes his arms against his binds, concentrating not on trying to move them, but rather, trying to move through time itself. Nothing happens so he slows time down further. The torturers pose, frozen. Feilece concentrates, more deeply than he ever has, on a single muscle in his arm. After a day, he feels a twitch.

Decades spent trapped in time, and Feilece never thought of trying this. Was he too weak? Was he too content with his fantasies? Or did he just never believe that he could?

A month passes. Everyday, he strains to the point of nearly breaking his brain, trying to move in even the slightest way possible. But nothing works. Every twitch he feels is instantly snapped back into place. He would need the relative strength to lift a mountain for the simple act of moving a finger.

He lets time speed up a little. The torturers move

like prowling beasts, creeping through the air. Feilece experiments, attempting to move one of his wrists. He can feel the press of time against his skin, trying to keep him slow. Fighting against it feels like trying to move his hand through soil, the weight of time crushing against him.

He speeds it up further and the weight of time lessens. At what he estimates to be about ninety percent of normal speed, moving his hand at a regular pace feels like moving it through water. He can work with this.

He pushes his wrists against the binds; the metal rings move through the wood as if it's made of goat butter. Feilece's eyes widen … he cannot believe how easy it is.

The deep clang of metal on hardwood floor permeates through the room.

"The fuck?" One of the Reapers drops his burning rod and pulls his sword from its sheath. The other two follow suit.

Feilece grabs his bicep binds with opposing hands and pulls them free. His legs buckle as they hit the ground and he falls onto his face. His body twitches and spasms as he's reminded of every cut and burn.

"How's that possible?" says one of the Reapers.

"It shouldn't be, no man could perform such an escape."

"Did we weaken the wood somehow?"

"What does it matter? We need to get him back in the restraints before Schizo gets back."

"Yeah, you first, mate."

Feilece hears footsteps enter the room from the

hall. These steps have a strange—conscious—rhythm to them.

"Hey, who are ... Glak!"

Unable to move his head, Feilece is treated to the sounds of his torturers being silenced. Voices replaced with gargled and muffled screams, and the squelching and breaking of innards and bones.

Feilece wants to lift himself up but his whole body is numb. He feels a waft of air on his naked body and then the feeling of soft fur against his skin. The pain dissipates as Feilece feels life return to him.

Feilece sits up. He's been adorned with a black cape. Feverishly, he wraps the cape around him and lets out a deep sigh, eyes fluttering.

He sees the man in black holding one of the squirming Reapers up by the neck in one hand.

"Who are you?" Feilece makes sure to keep his voice sounding tough.

"My name is Fasma." As he finishes his introduction, the Reaper in his hand succumbs to wyll-death. Fasma is left holding an empty skull.

"You've been watching me ... this whole time. I could feel you. You were in my clock."

"I was not. I was simply following a signal."

"I don't understand. A signal from who? Why?"

"I would never assume to know as to why I was sent here, but keep your eyes open for the blue lady."

Fasma turns to leave but Feilece stops him.

"Wait. None of this makes sense. How was I able to escape? How are you able to do the things you do? What were those visions you showed me? What are you?"

Fasma kneels before him. "I am just a man; as you are. This too, was a man." Fasma places the skull of the Reaper in Feilece's hands. The skull is bone dry and brittle. This man went from stabbing and burning Feilece to a mere skull in his hands.

Feilece doesn't want to squander this opportunity. "What is it? What is wyll? What does it mean to have wyll? What are we?"

"We are the clay upon which our wyll sculpts what we become. And our wyll is whatever we decide it needs to be."

"I was told wyll is our willingness to stay alive," says Feilece.

"Whoever told you that has a very small mind."

He puts a hand on Feilece's shoulder. Somehow, this simple contact makes every follicle spark with energy.

"I cannot tell you what wyll is," says Fasma. "Neither can anyone else. Such would only stagger one's understanding, and stifle their potential. Think less about what wyll is and more about who you are. Who do you want to be? Whatever you decide, make sure it is strong."

Fasma turns and goes to leave once again but Feilece demands more.

"Wait. My sister is in danger; can you help her?"

"I am sorry, but that is not my fight." Fasma leaves.

Feilece ruminates on his words. He's free now, he has to decide what to do next. He has to avenge his family. He has to kill Schizo, it's his mission, and he might not get another chance again. But should revenge take precedence over his family? He has to choose who he wants to be, an avenger or a saviour.

Closing his eyes, he sees his sisters. He feels their hearts beating alongside his own. He knows what he must do.

Exiting the house, a shiver runs up Feilece's spine. Though it is the darkness of night, he can still see dead Reaper bodies and wyll dead bones are scattered on the ground.

Looking upon all this death and decay, Feilece doesn't feel fazed or afraid but rather, content. He looks for the body of the smallest Reaper he can find and strips it down. The armour is still a little big for him, but it'll do. He throws on the leather brigandines then straps on the bracers, gauntlets, and greaves. He ties Fasma's cloak around his neck. Picking up an axe left on the grass, he sees his father in his reflection upon the bit.

A recruit watches him, eyes stretched as far open as they can go. The skin on his hand is a different colour from the rest of his body, a dead dark ashy hue. Feilece approaches and grabs the man's hand. Slowly, he watches the tension in the man's eyes relax. Colour returns to the recruit's hand.

Making his way up the hill, the upper-territory is eerily silent and bereft of life. Feilece makes his way over to Dorean's prison tent. A puddle of blood leads from the ground to a chair with an injured man sitting upon it, arms wrapped around his stomach.

"Popoki!" Feilece rushes to his side. "What happened?"

Popoki coughs. "That bitch, Louma ... she finally went crazy."

Feilece moves Popoki's arms to get a look at his wound. All he can see is blood.

"I stitched it closed as best I can but it won't stop bleeding."

"We have to find you help."

"There are more important things going on. Louma took your sister in to the woods, they're going after Rago."

"But—"

"When she saw you," says Popoki, "she reached for you. Your sister is still there, Feilece. You can save her."

"What about you?"

"Don't worry about me, I still got some fight left in me. I'll be fine."

Popoki stands, showing an impressive resilience. "There's something I have to do before I die." Popoki pats Feilece on the shoulder. "Go, get your family back."

Feilece watches Popoki limp out of sight.

He feels warm fur rub up against his hand and hears the soft grunt of a ram. "Djent … you knew I needed you."

Djent trots on the spot and puffs up his chest. He looks taller than he ever has. A piece of splintered wood from a gate is stuck to the end of one of Djent's horns. Feilece pulls it off and tosses it to the ground as he climbs aboard the furry stead.

Looking over Djent's head, Feilece catches eyes with Kasi. He slows time to get a good read of her. She pleads, silently asking him to go to her. She wants her convert back.

Feilece rears Djent up and rides past her, not bothering to look back. They ride west, paying no mind to obstructions. The ram tears through the village, smashing through tents like they weren't even there. Lit braziers fall upon their homes, causing fires to break out.

They ride into the darkness of the trees; half of the village lays demolished in their wake.

XLI

E PO AND RAGO reach the river. The water rages. They feel a cold spray in the air from waves crashing up against the river bank.

"Didn't you say there was a boat here?" asks Rago.

"Yeah, sorry, I got lost a while back. Everything looks the same in the dark. Dorean was always more of a hunter than I was."

"It's okay. We found the river at least, now, we just need to follow it."

"Do you think Louma is still tracking us?"

"We haven't heard anything since that call she made last night. If Louma had found us at any point, she would've made herself known."

"I guess the darkness helped us," says Epo, pondering.

"Those hunters are a worry," says Rago. "But they shouldn't know about your boat so we should be in the clear. In any case, we better hurry just to be safe."

The two follow the river bank south until they come to a place where the terrain drops sharply, tossing the river into a waterfall.

"I know this waterfall." Epo rushes ahead.

Standing on the cliff edge, Epo can see over the top of the canopy, and where the river meets the horizon. Epo wonders why she never climbed up here before; this is one of the greatest sights she's ever seen. She closes her eyes and breathes in the free air.

At the bottom of the waterfall is a large pool of slow moving water.

"Ah, there's our boat," Rago says as he points down the cliff. "It's more of a canoe than anything. What was I really expecting, though?"

Rago creeps towards the edge. "I don't know how we're going to get down there. The cliff face looks rather slippery, we'll die if—"

Before Rago can finish his sentence, Epo steps forward and leaps from the cliff, hearing Rago scream, "are you crazy!" behind her.

Feeling nothing but air all around her, Epo feels unbound even by the Child Itself. She feels weightless, empty. She crashes feet first into the water, piercing deeply, where the Mother's light can't follow.

She floats for a moment in the darkness, her mind feeling a strange sense of serenity. Gone are thoughts of her family, of the farm, of the Reapers, of the pain. Just blank, black, nothing.

The emptiness is so enticing that, in this moment, she could so easily let her wyll go and dissolve her ashes into the dark waters.

"Epo?"

Epo opens her eyes and she's laying on her back in

a lush field. The Mother shines not from the north but in the centre of the sky, and Her light is not yellow but a pure white. The sky is a light blue instead of its usual warm hue. She's only seen sights like this in illustrations. Art books from the north.

"Epo."

The sound of this voice brings a tear to Epo's eye. She whispers to herself, "Mum."

Epo props herself up on her elbows. Plios stands ahead of her with a furrowed brow and sunken expression.

"Mum!" Quickly, Epo gets up and runs to her. She jumps at Plios, and they both rest into each other's arms.

"You're here, you're real, I can feel you. How is this possible?" Epo says.

Plios chuckles. "Oh, Epo … always so full of questions."

Concerned with the tone of her mother's voice, Epo pulls back and looks into her eyes. "Mum … why are you crying?"

"I'm so sorry, my dear."

"Why? What are you sorry for?"

"I didn't ask enough questions. If I had your smarts, none of this would've happened."

Epo presses her forehead to her mother's. "What do you mean?"

"Your father tried to tell me about his past. He tried to warn me about all of this … but I ignored him. I didn't want to know about it. I wanted him; I didn't want his baggage. So we pushed it aside. We had you guys and I got everything that I wanted. I just wanted love."

"It's not your fault, Mum."

"But it is my fault. If I had died alongside my parents, you would've never gone through all you did. All of you have had to endure such pain because of my selfishness. If you had been born to anyone else, you would be happy and safe. You didn't deserve us, and we didn't deserve you."

"No, Mother." Epo stands. "That's bad logic. A series of events does not prove causation, it merely implies it. It is not you who put us through what we went through, but it was you who gave me the strength to get through it."

Epo holds her mother's face in her hands. "I question things because you taught me the value of information and gave me the freedom to think for myself. I would not be happier with another mother. No matter what I must go through, it was worth every second we had together. No matter what happens, we will always be connected."

"Oh, Epo … you've become so much smarter than I ever imagined."

Epo smiles. "Thanks, Mum."

AN EPIPHANY AWAKENS in her brain. Epo's eyes force open to the sight of darkness. Feeling a tightness in her chest and throat, Epo coughs up the last of her air and inhales water. She thrashes to no avail. She thinks she's going to die until she feels something wrap around her chest and pull her upwards.

As she's dragged through the water, her brain gets

to work. She is her family, she is their wyll, she is their strength. They didn't die, they passed their wyll onto her and Feilece and Dorean, it's how they've been able to survive this whole time. She will live for as long as she can, for them.

She bursts through the surface of the water, Rago's arms are wrapped around her.

"Epo!" he yells as he pulls her to the bank. "Are you okay?"

Epo vomits up a torrent as she nods.

"I'm an old man, are you trying to fucking kill me!" Rago asks, drawing ragged breaths.

"I've figured out how to save my sister."

"What are you talking about?"

"Her wyll isn't broken, nobody's is, because our wyll is not just our own."

"You mean it's the Child's?"

"No, it belongs to one's family. It just came to me; my family never died. They passed their wyll onto us."

"Do you have evidence of this?"

"Think of it, both Feilece and I are wyll anomalies. How likely is that to happen in the same family at the same time?"

Rago ponders. "Schizo argues it's your father's wyll."

Epo shakes her head. "It's not just his wyll, it's because our family was so big. Wyll is shared through the blood, we keep a part of each other inside of us. Look at the Grothia family. The books tell of their incredible feats. Well they're the biggest family in Genus, imagine that collective wyll permeating through them all."

"That … is a fascinating theory. But what of the Child? If wyll is passed on to family members, what does the Child get?"

Epo shrugs. "Maybe there is no Child."

Rago lets out a hearty laugh. "That brain of yours … it never ceases to amaze me."

"So I can save my sister, I just need to reintroduce our family's wyll somehow. She won't perish if we're all there to help her. I know it."

"I'm very happy for you," Rago says as he stands. "Perhaps you can come up with a method on our trip to Koilia. You'll have time in the future to save your sister but for now, we're still in danger." He extends a hand and helps Epo to her feet. "Let's get to the boat."

"Okay."

She slowly regain strength in her legs as they walk towards Anema's boat.

"Getting the canoe passed the rocky part might be an issue. How much training have you—"

As Rago speaks, a dagger flies through the air, cutting through the rope keeping the canoe tied to the bank. The boat slowly drifts into the current of the stream.

"No, no, no!" Rago wades into the water to stop it before it drifts out of reach. As he approaches the boat, an arrow with a flaming tip hits the boat right where Rago is reaching.

Shocked, Rago falls backwards into the water, getting caught in the current. Epo quickly grabs a vine and tosses it out to him. He grabs it and she pulls him to safety. They watch as the boat slowly engulfs in flames as it drifts down the river.

"There goes that little plan, I guess." A voice comes from the woods.

Epo and Rago both share a look of terror as Louma emerges from the trees. Rago pushes Epo behind him.

"How'd you find us?" asks Rago. "You have those Demon hunters track us?"

"Part of the way, but they lost your trail in the night. If it weren't for my daughter, you two would both be sailing safely to Koilia right now." Dorean appears from behind Louma.

"Dorean," Epo whispers to herself.

"What do you mean?" says Rago.

Louma grabs Dorean by her cheeks. "I asked her what she would do if she was looking to escape. She told me of this place."

"What did she say exactly?"

"She told me of a boat near a waterfall."

"You asked her a personal question and she recalled something from her past to answer it?"

Louma squints at the man. Rago bursts out into a fit of laughter.

"What is so funny?" Louma says.

After calming down, Rago responds. "Mechanical memories: how to churn butter, weave hemp, tend to the crops ... these are the only memories that should remain in one with broken wyll. But a memory of the location of her dear dead dad's boat? That's leaning onto the sentimental side."

Louma fumbles for words.

Rago continues. "You're a second rate wyll breaker, and you'll never replace me."

"Second rate? Here's your second rate! Killer, stab your sword through this man's chest!"

"Yes, Mother," Dorean's voice is staggered, as if she's exhausted most of her energy.

Dorean strides towards Rago, pulling her sword from its sheath. Epo looks up at Rago. He's smiling.

Dorean thrusts her sword into Rago's chest so far it comes out his back.

"Rago!" Epo catches the man as he slumps to the ground.

Dorean falls to her knees, panting.

Tears well up in Epo's eyes as she looks at Rago.

"Don't cry for me, girl. I'm only finally receiving the judgement for my long years of treating people like test subjects."

"Why are you okay with this? You had changed, you could've spent the rest of your life helping people."

"Looking upon your sister, she is not as broken as I once thought. I doubt Louma could break anyone. No … that's my skill, my legacy. The act of breaking wyll through means of torture dies with me. Nothing makes me happier than this fact."

Dorean, callous to the emotions being shared between the old scholar and her sister, pulls her sword from the man's chest.

"Epo … she looks tired. Her implanted persona will be weak … don't squander …"

Epo holds Rago's head as the life leaves his eyes, the final remnants of his wyll, trapped inside his dead body.

Dorean points her sword at Epo. Epo stares up at her drone of a sister.

"What would you like me to do to the girl, Mother?" asks Dorean.

Louma offers no response. Epo sees an emotion she didn't expect on her face. Staring down at Rago, grief glistens in her eyes.

"Mother?" says Dorean.

Louma's eyes drift from Rago to Dorean. A tear leaves her eye and she catches it on her finger. She stares at the tear and her hand begins to shake. Her eyes change from a morose gaze to furious stress and her face scrunches up into an expression of painful hate.

"Kill her," she whispers quietly.

"What?"

"Kill her. Kill your sister. Kill her!"

For a second, Epo notices a flash of confusion come over Dorean's face. Dorean looks down at Epo. With sword in hand, the killer slowly approaches her.

XLII

～

EPO CRAWLS BACKWARDS as Dorean holds her sword at her, following the girl with the tip.

"What did I just say? Kill her!" Louma yells.

The two hunters jump down from their trees and join the screaming general.

"Having trouble controlling your pet, Louma?"

"Shut up! Killer, what are you doing! Follow my orders!"

Diakho smirks. "She's not listening, Apo wanna-be."

"Listen here, you dirty fucking demons." Louma gets up in Diakho's face. "If it weren't for my house, your people would've never moved from your shit-filled huts in the fucking woods. Now shut the fuck up!"

She screeches so loudly that both hunters have to rub their ears.

Epo adopts a compassionate expression and stares deeply into Dorean's eyes.

"Dorean … you are not alone inside your head. We are all with you."

Dorean's face barely changes as she points her sword at Epo, but her sword hand begins to shake.

"Semnos. Niria. Plios. Anema. They are with you, as am I. Listen to us!" Epo shouts.

"Kill her!" Louma screams louder.

Dorean shakes her head, then swipes the blade at Epo's throat. Epo closes her eyes and waits.

She hears the sound of clashing steel, then opens her eyes to the sight of a black cloak flowing in front of her. Her vision adjusts and she sees her brother, blocking Dorean's sword with an axe.

"Feilece! You made it."

"Looks like all three of us made it. I'm sorry about your friend."

Dorean breaks from Feilece's block and goes to slice at his throat but he dodges back and pulls Epo away.

"I think we can save her, Feilece. Her wyll is tied to ours."

"Okay, how?"

"I'm still trying to figure that out."

"Choris, deal with this boy!" Louma screams.

"Don't kill him," Diakho adds, "maim him and take him back to Schizo."

Choris lines up his body with the shot, rests an arrow upon his finger and pulls it back against the bow string. The instant before he can loose the arrow, his body lunges forward. The arrow flies off into nowhere as the sound of ribs cracking fills the air. In his place, a tough looking ram steps forward.

"Shit!" comes bursting out of Louma's mouth.

"Brother …"

Diakho throws daggers at Djent, making the ram bolt. Diakho runs over to his brother, and kneels before him, touching his lifeless body. His arms begin to shake, his eyes strain, his teeth clench. In an ascending crescendo, he lets out a blood-curdling scream.

"Get over it, Diakho!" Louma says, but the hunter doesn't respond. He runs off into the woods after Djent.

"Don't go! Fuck!" yells Louma, beginning to sweat.

Dorean, eyes stuck in contact with Feilece's, begins twitching. Her face spasms, as if there's an internal conflict raging in her mind. Without warning, Dorean begins viciously attacking Feilece.

Epo observes that no commands were given. Dorean is following her own direction … or no direction at all.

"Killer! You aren't using the techniques I taught you, calm down." Louma yells but Dorean doesn't listen, she continues to attack like a dog turned rabid.

Feilece dodges and deflects every attack. He moves as if his body doesn't follow Epo's understanding of momentum.

Epo screams messages of family and wyll at Dorean in an attempt to snap her out of her Killer state, but nothing gets through to her. Dorean shows no sign of slowing or fatigue. Her face is restful, staring blindly without expression. Somnambulist.

"You're words aren't working, sis," says Feilece, panting in exhaustion.

"She's not following Louma's orders anymore. I think our presence has disrupted the mentality of the 'Killer' personality. She's running on pure instinct."

"So what do we do?" says Feilece.

"We have to break her."

"What!"

"Break the new wyll, Killer's wyll. Then we can put Dorean back in."

"You want me to torture her? Torture Dorean?"

"To save her … yes."

Distracted, Feilece takes a slice to his arm, staining Dorean's sword with his blood.

"Feilece!" Epo calls out.

"No!" Feilece says. "I will not torture her. I will not use their methods. I refuse to break anyone's wyll, especially Dorean's."

"Then what can we do?"

"Dorean doesn't deserve more pain … I know someone who does."

Feilece smacks the back of his axe against the handle of Dorean's sword. Her arm flings back and the sword goes flying into the air. Lining himself up with the arc of the airborne sword, Feilece catches the sword by the handle in an underhand grip.

He rears up and tackles Dorean to the ground. Holding her sword high above her head, he looks down at her.

"What are you doing!" Epo shouts.

The blank expression that was once upon Dorean's face shifts to fear as Feilece brings the sword down hard.

The steel cuts her cheek as it stabs into the soil next to her face. A small dribble of blood rolls down her cheek and connects with the blood of Feilece, stained upon the blade.

As Epo sees the blood mixing together, a thought creeps into her head.

"Killer, right?" Feilece says. "You are lucky you are inside my sister, because there's no way I could hurt her. But, thankfully, I've been paying attention to the lessons these invaders have forced upon me."

Dorean stares into Feilece's eyes, unresponsive, pupils dilating.

"You who have taken over my sister's body and mind … you, like the rest of us, were raised." Feilece stands, steps over Dorean's body, extends his axe out, and directs his weapon at Louma. "By someone you call mother."

"Hah! Really? You want to try your luck with me?" Louma takes her sword from its sheath. "Be warned, boy, I don't play like your sister there. Never teach your pets to swipe harder than you can."

As the two engage in a fight, Epo runs over to Dorean who is suffering major spasms in the grass next to her sword. Epo holds her head and tries to keep her still. Dorean chants the word 'Mother' over and over as her body jerks and twitches.

"She's not your mother, Dorean. She doesn't care about you."

Dorean's face contorts and tears flow from her eyes.

"She would've let you die. She did not raise you, we did. Me, Feilece, Semnos."

Dorean's spasms get worse with every name Epo lists. Epo runs her hand down the edge of the sword, drawing blood onto her palm.

"Niria, Plios, Anema. Remember who you are. We are you, and you are us."

Epo touches her bloody hand to the wound on

Dorean's face. Dorean's muscles cramp up, causing her to arch her back and froth at the mouth. Then she slumps down and goes completely still, a blank emptiness in her eyes once again.

"Dorean?" says Epo. There's no response.

"Killer! 'Get up and finish off that girl!" Louma yells. Still, there's no response.

"Oh, enough of this!" says Louma. "I'm sick of this whole damn family!"

Louma kicks Feilece onto his back and saunters over to Dorean's still body in the grass. She swipes her sword at Epo, making her stumble back. Louma wags her sword at Dorean's face.

"Daughter, remember who you are. Remember who made you." Her words seethe through her teeth. Tears start falling from her eyes and her voice becomes a whine. "Are you going to disappoint me too?" She snaps back into rage. "What good is a daughter that doesn't follow orders!" She plunges her sword towards Dorean's chest.

"No!" screams Epo.

The blade halts. A cough. Blood splats on Dorean's face. Awareness slowly manifests in her eyes.

"You awake yet, sis?" Feilece holds himself over Dorean, Louma's sword sticking out of his back.

Without saying anything, Dorean retrieves her sword and plunges it into Louma's stomach.

"Fuck!" Louma catches the blade with her hand, sacrificing it to stop the stab from being fatal. Feilece falls into Dorean's arms and she holds him close.

Tears drop from her eyes onto the boy's shoulders. "I'm sorry … I'm so sorry, Feilece. I was too late."

Epo rushes over and examines Feilece's wound. She touches the spot where the sword stabbed him and finds no blood.

"Feilece, I think the cape stopped the blade."

Dorean's eyes widen. She sits up, holding Feilece in her lap. He coughs up more blood.

"Are you okay?" asks Dorean.

"That fucking hurt. It's hard to breathe … but I think it's getting better. Is it really you Dorean?"

Dorean laughs and wipes her tears away.

"You used to hate it when we swore."

"I think we're all a bit different, sister." Epo joins the conversation. "Welcome back." Tears well up in her eyes.

The three final members of the Anemelos family embrace each other.

XLIII

⸗

"How touching," Louma says with a voice betraying a little too much jealousy.

She coughs and a squirt of blood shoots from her abdomen. "You killed my daughter … don't think for a second I'm going to let you get away with that."

Dorean rises and pulls Feilece up with her. He coughs up another spittle of blood, making him feel nauseas.

"I'm sorry, brother, but we're not safe yet. I remember training with her, even if she is injured, I can't beat her alone."

"I'll be fine. Let's kill this bitch."

Dorean and Feilece go on the attack.

"What can I do?" asks Epo.

"You've done enough, Epo. Let us handle this now," Dorean says.

Louma, holding her stomach with one arm and her sword outstretched in the other, scowls at the two as they approach.

"I don't care if I'm bleeding, or how many of you there are. I'll fucking kill you all. Pathetic fucking farmers."

Her words are fierce but her voice breaks as she speaks.

Feilece tries to slow time but it makes his nausea worse, causing his heart to speed up. He struggles to keep time running at normal speed. Without his ability to slow his perception of time, he doesn't know how well he'll do in this fight. He looks up at Dorean and feels a boost of morale. With both of them working together, this fight will be easier.

Suddenly, Feilece feels a sharp pain in his back and falls to the grass.

"Feilece!" Dorean kneels down and holds him.

"Something hit me!" He looks at the ground and sees a small throwing knife.

"Diakho! Thank the fucking Mother!" Louma shouts.

The black-haired hunter walks out from among the trees, dragging Djent behind him by the horns. The poor ram is riddled with knives.

"Djent!" Feilece screams.

"The ram lives," Diakho says in a low grizzle. "So that you may see him die."

"Fuck you!" Feilece screams then charges at him.

Dorean calls out but he isn't listening. He won't let Djent die. He runs at Diakho, holding his cape over his head for protection. Diakho throws his knives at him, but they deflect and fall to the ground. Feilece hacks at the man with his axe, but he's too quick. Diakho dodges Feilece's swings, while Feilece protects himself against Diakho's knives. The two are at a standstill.

Feilece tries his best but Diakho is too fast for him. It's frustrating, considering the power he usually has over time. Diakho is toying with him, stretching his revenge for his brother out as far as it will go.

"You have no idea what you took from me," Diakho says with a crackle to his voice.

Rage builds in Feilece. "I don't? What about my brother! My mother! My Father!"

"Those connections are nothing compared to what we shared. He wasn't just my brother, he was me."

Diakho squats and embeds two knives into Feilece's legs. Feilece stumbles forward. He tries to move but his legs won't work.

Diakho circles Feilece, kicking and cutting him.

"Everything we went through. Everything we achieved. Everything we became."

Feilece can't think, he tries to slow time but he feels sick and coughs up more blood.

Diakho grabs Feilece's chin and looks into his eyes. Feilece sees a dark empty void in the hunter's pupils.

"Do you have any idea what it's like to share your wyll with another person?"

Diakho puts a knife to the boy's throat then pulls his hand away from his chin so Feilece has to hold himself up on his injured knees, or be cut. Diakho holds another knife up to his own throat, cutting his own skin slightly.

"Choris was everything. I've nothing left but revenge and death. Let us both visit the Child together, shall we?"

Feilece can't talk; he can barely move.

"Who knows, maybe the Child will be gracious. Maybe I'll get to see him once again. We were supposed to die on a battlefield together, surrounded by our victims." Tears form in Diakho's eyes. "Maybe the Child will let me apologise to him."

Feilece feels this is the end of his life; he can't contain the beating of his heart. He lets his heartbeat speed up for a moment, but it's still enough for time to speed by. In a split second, he watches Diakho disappear in front of him, dragged off into the woods faster than he can comprehend. Time normalises and Feilece is alone, wondering what just happened.

XLIV

L OUMA SCREAMS A battle-cry and charges at Dorean, striking with her sword. Dorean quickly deflects the strike with her own blade. Dorean, knowing she can't win in a straight fight, quickly resorts to fighting dirty. She feigns a sword strike but instead leans in and delivers a hard punch to Louma's stomach, forcing the general to scream in pain and fall to her knees. Dorean throws an overhead strike at Louma to slice her head open but the general catches the blade with her own.

"You shit-kicking fucking farmer bitch!"

"How does the pain feel, you horrid cunt? Does it make your muscles twitch and cramp? Do your bones feel like they're growing and shrinking? Does your brain feel like it's pressing against your skull! Does your psyche feel like it's raging inside your mind?" Dorean, remembering all the pain Louma put her through, presses harder and harder against the general's defences with every question she raises.

Her sword creeps closer and closer to Louma's head. She wants to split this bitch's skull and see her brain. She wants to be covered in her blood. She wants to hear her scream in agony as the bitch feels all the pain her family has suffered all at once.

"Dorean," calls Epo with a lilt to her breath.

Dorean glances at her little sister's. What is Dorean doing? This isn't her. She's not a killer. The word 'killer' spirals in her mind as she remembers every second she spent as this woman's puppet. A numbing sensation spreads throughout her body. She feels as if her skin doesn't belong to her, like her body and mind are slowly separating.

She looks down at Louma. This poor excuse for a mother, she did this to her.

"Tell me, Mother," she says. "Does it feel like you're about to break?"

Fury steals the muscles in Louma's face. Louma pushes against Dorean's blade, rising to her feet.

"I will never break." Louma talks through her teeth, spitting up sputum. She kicks out Dorean's leg and pushes her to the ground. She hacks at her in a crazed frenzy, screaming as she slashes. "I am not some weakling! I did nothing wrong. I did all I could. I watched them die! I will not be like them. I will never break again. I will not disappoint!"

Dorean deflects as much as she can, but she's only able to stop half of Louma's onslaught. Cuts open bloody wounds all over Dorean's body, as flesh flies. Dorean stops the fatal blows, but she knows she can't keep it up forever.

Finally, she sees an opening to retaliate and kicks Louma's stomach, right in the wound, pushing the insane woman into a backward roll that draws her far enough away that Dorean can find space to move.

Dorean struggles, holding herself up on her hands and knees, blood dripping on the grass.

Epo calls out. Dorean clambers to her feet, every movement coupled with crippling pain. Looking at the cuts on her arms, she's reminded of the torture she endured as Louma's subject. Her mind teeters on the edge of breaking once again.

A voice inside her head says, "you can't kill her. You aren't supposed to."

Dorean knows the voice well. "I'm not meant to kill her, you are."

"But she's my mother."

"She's your captor. You can see inside my mind, you can see what a mother is supposed to be. Don't be her slave anymore. Set yourself free."

"Dorean! Remember who you are!" screams Epo.

"I." Killer turns to Louma. "Am a killer!"

"No!" Epo calls out but it's not enough to stop Killer as she rushes at Louma and plunges her sword into the general's chest.

Silence fills Dorean's ears for a moment as she stares into the eyes of her torturer, seeing a reflection of herself. The first thing that enters Dorean's hearing is the sound of her siblings both calling out her name in unison, as she looks down to find Louma's sword pierced through her chest.

Dorean slumps down onto her side, feeling the dissonance between her mind and body once again.

"Fuck!" Louma tries to stand but stumbles for a few steps before falling.

Epo rushes over to Dorean, followed by a staggering Feilece. They sit by her, holding her, eyes welling up with tears. A warm feeling comes over Dorean.

She smiles. "Killer … she got what she needed. She's gone."

Louma's breathing wheezes as she stares into the woods. "I couldn't save them … I watched them die. I'm sorry. I failed you."

The Anemelos siblings listen, curious. They see a face of a woman in the dark of the forest … a woman with blonde hair.

"There you are, my darling," Louma says, tears drifting from her eyes.

"Oh fuck … oh fuck, oh fuck!" Dorean draws ragged breaths.

"Don't speak, it'll cause you pain," says Epo.

"Leave … leave now, quickly."

"We're not going anywhere, sis," says Feilece.

"You don't understand—"

Dorean breaks into a coughing fit. She feels as if she's about to lose the hold she has on her body, but she can't let go without ensuring their safety.

"Don't you look beautiful, darling." Louma extends her arms out. "Come and give Louma a hug."

The siblings watch Louma, until their eyes are diverted and they stare blankly, trying to comprehend the sight before them.

"What is it?" Feilece whispers.

A woman's head attached to a giant mass of pulsating purple skin slides through the forest like a demonic slug. Gangly appendages poke in all directions, forming deformed arms and hands. Spindly spikes swirl out, tickling the air. A human leg can be seen among the mess, sticking out at an unnatural angle.

Dorean expends what little energy she has shaking her siblings, trying to snap them out of their fear and get them to escape. But they aren't responding. It's impossible.

The thing creeps towards Louma. They watch as its jaw detaches, revealing razor sharp teeth, then its jaw closes around Louma's head. Louma's screams echo from inside the beast, as its bulbous limbs grapple Louma's torso from different directions and tear it to pieces.

"Get out of here!" Dorean screams, grasping. Feilece stands but his legs give way. Epo catches him and holds him up. The creature devours Louma, then turns its attention towards the three siblings.

"Run!" Dorean calls.

Feilece and Epo look down at Dorean. "We can't leave you," says Epo.

The mysterious being approaches, limbs swinging.

Feilece and Epo hug Dorean. One final family hug.

"It's weird." A deep voice rumbles behind them. "Even in this state, I'm still in love with that face."

Popoki stands above them. His face shows no fear; instead it's a mix of sorrow, disappointment, and shame. Wasting no time, he walks towards the beast, pulling a serrated sickle from a sheath on his waist. He doesn't appear to notice the gaping hole in his stomach.

A hand extends from the purple mass. Popoki catches it, stretches it before him and cuts it off. The appendage flaps, purple blood spilling from the wound, before the bleeding stops and a new growth emerges from the wound.

What once resembled a malformed arm and hand turns into a big inert mass of pulsating flesh. Hands and spikes try to reach for Popoki, but he's too quick, and skilled with his sickle. He cuts each appendage off, leaving them all to grow into gross masses. Eventually, Seemo becomes a pile of immovable skin.

With a serious expression, Popoki climbs up the girl's mound of a torso until he's up behind her head. Reaching around and holding her chin up with his free hand, Popoki puts the serrated edge of his sickle to his love's throat and begins sawing into the purple flesh.

The sounds of her muffled whimpers bring tears to the man's eyes. With every carve through her neck, Popoki's skin becomes increasingly grey.

As the sickle saws through the back of her neck, Popoki drops the tool. The mound deflates below him and turns to blood and ash in the grass.

He stands in the wake of Seemo's remains, holding her head in his hand, staring into her eyes.

"The last demon … is dead."

The skin and muscles of Popoki's hands and legs lose all colour and begin to flake. His big chest sinks and his broad shoulders shrink.

With his final ounce of wyll, he presses his lips to the mouth of Seemo's severed head.

Dorean, Epo and Feilece watch as his body flakes, becoming a pile of dust and bone on the ground. His remains mix with Seemo's.

XLV

——

FEILECE AND EPO prop up Dorean as she coughs blood into her hand. The relief of knowing her siblings will be okay calms any stress in Dorean's mind, and with it, her energy drops to zero. The monster is dead, Feilece can protect Epo. They're smart kids, they'll be fine.

Tears stream down the faces of Feilece and Epo.

"Are those tears for me?" Dorean asks gently.

"I couldn't save you," Epo says.

"But you did. You got me my body back. It's not your fault I couldn't … hold onto it."

Dorean looks up, the Mother's morning gaze shines through the canopy.

"I gave up. I let them break me. I just … wasn't strong enough. And when I lost the connection to my body, I lost my connection to all of you. I couldn't feel Mum or Dad, or Semnos or Niria. I couldn't feel you two. I was alone, in a void of darkness, trapped and separated from the world."

"But you were still there; you were still alive," says Epo.

"Not in any way that really mattered. I could feel

myself falling away, disappearing. It was actually Killer that saved me. Her love for Louma reminded me of my love for you all. It gave me strength."

"Your feelings must have bled into her consciousness," Epo whispers.

Dorean coughs again. Blood fills her mouth and Epo comforts her.

"Don't talk anymore, Dorean, you'll just cause yourself more pain."

"So you fought," says Feilece. "You fought to get back to us. If you could fight then …"

A tear forms in Dorean's eye. "No. I didn't fight at all. I didn't see a point. Everything I was willing to fight for was already gone."

Feilece hangs his head.

"I thought fighting would only bring me more pain." Dorean smiles. "Until I saw Niria."

Feilece and Epo look at each other.

"She visited me yesterday," says Dorean. "A big shining light in the darkness. I thought she was the Mother at first. That girl always had so much energy." Dorean laughs herself into another cough.

Feilece and Epo both smile.

"She told me about you two," Dorean continues, "she told me you needed me. And that if I chose to fight, if I choose to help … I would die."

"So you knew this was coming …" says Epo.

"Of course … and nothing has ever made me happier. So don't make tears over me. I got to use my death to save my little brother and sister." Dorean pats their heads. "And now … I can feel you all again."

Dorean lays flat. The grass feels like a cushion on the back of her head. The rest of her body barely feels like it's there. She's never been more relaxed in her life. "I … I was really looking forward to going to school. Bloody Semnos." She smiles. "You two have done such a good job … but remember what Dad would say. Don't waste time rejoicing small victories."

She looks over at her brother. Feilece holds her hand and stares intently into her eyes. "Don't let that bastard win," she says.

"I won't."

The leaves slowly dance in the wind. Puppets attached by strings to their branches, manipulated by surrounding forces. A leaf breaks from its branch and floats towards Dorean. It drifts through the air as it falls—one final moment of life—before it touches down on Dorean's stomach.

DOREAN SEES NIRIA standing over her. The yellow-skinned girl extends a hand. "I'm glad you made your way back, sister."

Dorean reaches up and takes Niria's hand. As she's being pulled up, she feels arms reach under her armpits and lift her to her feet.

She looks over her shoulder and her eyes twitch. "Semnos."

"Hey, Dorean." He smiles. "You were amazing out there. I'm so proud of you, my sister."

"Dorean."

In the distance, Dorean sees the silhouettes of two old farmers. She runs to them, tears releasing into the wind, and wraps her arms around them.

THE LEAF SINKS into Dorean's skin as the area around it turns dark and dead. The wind picks up speed. A breeze swirls through the trees. The wind carries particles from Dorean's body as she dematerialises. Dorean's bones make her final gentle impact upon the ground.

XLVI

✦

FEILECE AND EPO sit in silence for an indistinct period of time. It's the first time Feilece has felt time stop without actually stopping it. They stare into the empty space that once harboured their older sister.

Feilece looks at the leaf-blade resting among Dorean's bones. A flash of the same sword stabbing through Semnos' back plays in his head. The same sword stabbed through his father. The same sword slicing through his mother's neck. The same sword shaking in the hip sheath of Paldi as Niria turned to ash. The same sword piercing Dorean's chest.

He grabs the sword, turns, and tosses it as hard as he can into the river behind him.

Pain from the wounds in his legs move like tremors through his body, causing Feilece to drop to his knees.

"Hey," Epo says, rushing to catch him. "Don't exert yourself."

"They're all gone, Epo. All taken from us."

A sensitive smile appears on Epo's face. She pulls her brother in close and holds his head to her chest. She strokes his shoulder. Feilece stares forward, unseeing.

"You know, when Niria used to annoy me when I was reading my books—do you remember? With her incessant need to constantly be playing," says Epo.

Feilece doesn't respond. Laying in her arms, he remembers how Niria used to feel. How Dorean used to feel, how they all used to feel together as a family. Old feelings he'll never feel again.

"I used to listen to her repeat 'come play with me' over and over, all while thinking to myself 'by the Child, won't this bitch die'."

Though he finds her words harsh, Feilece chuckles.

"Now," Epo continues, "I would tear all my books to shreds just to hear her annoy me one last time. It may feel off, but I think there's a point to the anguish. The loss, the grief, it … brings us closer."

"So what are you saying? I should be happy they're gone? I should relish in this feeling?"

There would be anger in Feilece's words if he could muster up the energy. There's no way he can let himself feel anything negative towards the only family he has left.

"They took their bodies, their voices, their smells, their words, their thoughts, their futures … but their wyll? No, we get that. And with their wyll inside us, they can never truly die. Relish not the feelings of grief, but relish in your own life, your own body, your own voice, your own thoughts … your future. For it is also theirs, and it's all they have now."

With words alone, Epo is able to lift the darkness looming in Feilece's heart. Feilece grabs Epo's hand and squeezes it. He sits up and looks into her eyes. He can't stop the smile from forming on his face, and he doesn't want to. He's never been more proud of anyone in his life.

They both look out at the lake. A ray of light from the Mother shines down into the water. It illuminates the yellow skin of Niria as she stands atop the surface. She's back, but this time, she's not alone.

They all stand together. Niria in the front, Semnos behind her with hands on her shoulders, Plios and Dorean by his sides, Anema at the back, towering over them.

"You see them don't you?" Epo says through tears. "They'll always be there; they always have been there. The Anemelos wyll is timeless."

Seeing their proud faces, Feilece feels a burst of energy. He moves from Epo's embrace and struggles to his feet. He hears a grunt behind him, and he turns to see Djent also struggling to his feet.

"Djent," Feilece calls out, hobbling over to his old friend. Feilece hugs him fiercely as Epo pulls the knives from his body.

"You okay, boy? I knew that long-haired bastard couldn't kill you," Feilece says, patting his neck.

Djent licks his face.

"I got all the knives," says Epo. "He didn't flinch as I pulled them out. Does this ram feel pain?"

"Physical pain is easy. Ain't that right, boy?"

Djent lets out a low rumble of agreement.

Epo runs her hand along the ram's war torn spine. "This guy used to scare the shit out of me."

"Really? How? He's adorable."

"I was a scared little girl; he was a big beast that could trample me at any moment."

"You know he wouldn't do that. He's a good boy."

"He's a strong boy, and I'm not a scared little girl anymore." Epo picks up one of the knives from the ground and slices the Reaper insignia from their clothes, then gets to work on the material. "There," she says, pulling away from her piece. She's carved curved lines over the Demon eyes and connected the Sickle & Scythe to make them resemble Djent's horns.

"Why horns?" asks Feilece.

"The horns of a ram are stronger than any weapon made by man. What better way to represent our family?"

Feilece nods. The symbol injects him with confidence. Knowing it exists makes him feel more free.

Epo points at the river. "They destroyed Dad's boat. I guess we won't be escaping to Koilia."

"No … we're not done here." Feilece climbs on top of Djent, patting and whispering to him to make sure the animal wasn't in pain from the added weight.

"What's the plan, brother?"

"I still have a mission, Dad's mission."

"Do you really think you can kill Schizo?"

"Not alone. But, as you've made perfectly clear, Dad is still with me."

Epo chortles. "And that's why it's your burden."

"Let's go, sis."

Epo climbs aboard, wrapping her arms around Feilece's waist. The ram rears up and gallops towards Sheep's Basin.

XLVII

✦

S LOW-PACED, MEANDERING STEPS traipse over countless tiny blades protruding from the ground. A one-armed man with red hair wanders aimlessly. He's surrounded by shapes without detail. Pyramid after pyramid, some black, some yellow, all smooth with missing texture. Some lay flat with a strange light dancing on top of them. Puffy blobs float in the sky, doused in yellow from a hovering glowing crescent.

"Schizo, my lord!"

The noise is shrill and distorted. It comes from an oval sitting atop an assortment of red squares and circles.

"What's happened, my lord? Where are all the upper colours?"

The one-armed man ignores the strange creature and continues to drag his feet forward. He sees a structure at the bottom of a slope. The structure is made of rectangles and it looks robust. He moves towards it.

Getting close to the house, he hears voices. "Whatever it was, it took out both of our yellow and black units. All we have left are fucking greens and greys!"

"We still have a few reds left."

"My point is we don't have a fucking army! We're done."

Looking inside the rectangular structure, the one-armed man sees five polygonal creatures sitting around a circle. Grey, green, red, black and yellow.

"The Reapers are never done! Like Schizo said, we are the bringers of the new world."

"We have to talk to Schizo. He'll know what to do."

"His body wasn't among the dead."

"Half of those bodies were indecipherable."

"Do not speak ill of our family!"

"Do not accuse me of things I am not doing!"

"Stop! Our enemy is not here at this table; our enemy is somewhere out there."

"Where? We found nothing, no signs of an opposing army. The only dead we found were our own."

"We should have been there."

"If we were there, we would've just added to the pile."

The black creature, the only one yet to make a sound, stands and directs its oval at the one-armed man.

"Perhaps we should speak to one who was actually there."

In sequence, all the other creatures turn their ovals at the man then stand stiffly.

"My lord!" They all make the same noise in unison.

The one-armed man stares, swaying from side to side.

"Uh, my lord?"

A new creature appears. This creature is thinner than the others and comes with far more detail. The one-armed man sees she has eyes, a nose and a mouth. She has long flowing hair.

"Schizo …" Her voice isn't as hurtful to the ears. "Directors, leave now!"

"What!"

"Gather anyone who still wears the Reaper insignia before the house. Don't waste time."

"Let's go." The black creature herds the rest of them out of sight.

The woman approaches the one-armed man. She brings her hands up and brushes her fingers across his face. Then runs them down his neck, his shoulders, his arms, his palms. She curls her fingers into the recesses between his own and squeezes. She raises both of their arms up and moves their hands behind his head. His peripheral vision is obstructed by arms and her face is so close to his that he can't see anything else.

"Look at me, my love. Remember me."

He stares into her eyes. They feel like they reach into his skull. He feels movement in his throat.

"Who are you?"

Fluid appears in her eyes. "Please … come back to me."

The man begins to feel something, though he has no idea what.

"Remember who you are, Schizo."

"I don't know that name."

"Yes, you do. You're broken right now. But it's okay, I can fix you."

The fluid flows down the lady's face. He recognises the emotion.

"Yes, follow it. Come back," she says.

It's love. His love is crying.

"You're almost there, come on."

"Kasi?" he says.

Kasi sighs, then presses her lips to his. A shock electrifies through his system and detail starts to return to everything. She pulls away and stares into his eyes once again.

"Schizo … am I Schizo?"

Kasi presses her forehead against his.

"You are Schizo," she whispers.

"I am Schizo." His eyes flutter as his mind is flooded with recollection.

"Fuck!" He pulls his hands free of her grasp and clutches them to his head. "I thought I was over this!"

Kasi touches his arm. "Don't bring more pain to yourself."

Schizo embraces his wife. "Thank you."

"It's been a long time since your wyll broke, my love. We must be in a bind."

Schizo pulls back from her and looks around the room. He wipes tears from his eyes before they have time to escape past his eyelids.

"How long was it this time?" he says.

"I'm not sure, I haven't been able to find you all night."

"Hopefully I didn't do too much damage in that time. You're getting good at bringing me back."

"I'm the one that made you, you can always trust me. You were going so well, though, I was worried I may be out of practice."

Schizo looks at his wife. "I'm sorry, I'm so sorry, Kasi."

"What for?"

"I don't think I can build you the family I promised you."

"Oh, but you can. I know you can. Look what you've achieved thus far? How many people you've turned to our movement? You even avenged our fathers. You're doing a fine job."

"Our village is in shambles, most of our members are dead. This vision is dead."

"It's okay, a threat has emerged, we can't tackle it right now, so we pack up and move somewhere else. We carry on, we grow stronger. This is just like back home."

"Kasi—"

"If we could do it here, we could do it anywhere—"

"Kasi, it's Grothia."

Kasi swallows and takes a moment before she replies. "So?" She shift nervously. "We're doing this to fight them, right? Well if they're attacking us, it means we're scaring them. They came all the way up here; it means we're getting through to them. We're breaking them already."

"It was only one of them, Kasi."

"One Grothia?"

"One man took out our entire army."

Kasi's lips tremble. "Whatever. It doesn't matter. We leave. We gain allies."

"All the other Abdominal nations fly Grothia banners."

"So we go north. We'll go as far as fucking Cerebrum!"

"The other countries will not go to war for us."

"I don't care!" Kasi snaps at him. Schizo looks into her eyes and sees something he's never seen before. Fear.

"What's wrong? What has you so afraid?" Schizo asks.

Kasi is uncharacteristically quiet. "The Grothia are here, why wouldn't I be afraid?"

"When the combined forces of the houses of Koilia were at our doors, you were stoic and unflinching. You are the strongest person I know, nothing fazes you."

"I am still human, love. Now let's get to it before we lose even more family."

She turns and goes to leave the room, but Schizo will not let it go. "You once told me that the future is where chaos reigns, to never be attached to anything without first imagining it gone within a second. You taught me that if you can absolve your fear of chaos, nothing will ever affect you again. You aren't scared of the Grothia. If you're afraid, it means you came into contact with your past."

Kasi frowns and stares at the ground. "I saw Feilece … right before he took his pet and destroyed half of what we built. He looked into my eyes."

Kasi goes silent.

Schizo puts a hand on her shoulder. "Are you upset you didn't break him?"

"No. We all fail sometimes. He looked into my eyes and I saw his father."

"You met with Animia when we first arrived and it

didn't affect you then."

"I didn't see Animia in that old farmer … but I saw him in that boy's eyes. I saw the man I watched kill my family."

Tears brim in Kasi's eyes.

Schizo puts his arms around her. "Okay, we'll leave. Let's go gather what remains of our people."

The Reaper lords exit the house and climb a ladder to the roof. They look out to the sight of only a few hundred Reapers, all gathered and awaiting direction.

"Is this really all that's left?" Schizo recognises a couple of dozen old members; the rest are all recruits from Tiris. The recruits look at each other, collectively confused as to why they are now the majority.

"Reapers!" Schizo casts his voice out among his people. "I know you all must have questions."

The Basin becomes an uproar.

"Where is everybody!"

"I saw the farmer boy tearing up the village with his ram, what's going on?"

"Where are the generals?"

"What are we going to do?"

"Calm yourselves!" Schizo yells.

The Reapers all go quiet.

"What we are going to do is migrate. We'll travel … north."

Confused murmurs sweep across the crowd.

"Tell us what happened to the other Reapers!" someone calls.

Schizo frowns at Kasi. She nods.

Schizo turns back to his people. "All of the upper colours are dead."

There's a collective gasp.

"What happened?"

"I don't know. I didn't see it. What I do know is that it is attached to this land. A lot of you may recall an event that left Tiris in disarray recently, I'm thinking this is the same demon."

The recruits collectively shudder.

"That is a lie!"

Heads turn towards a boy on the back of a galloping ram approaching from the west.

XLVIII

"GET THEM! KILL them!" The pitch of Schizo's voice is high. It almost mimics a child's screech.

Feilece runs his eyes over the remaining Reaper crowd. Greys and greens tend to cower away while a resolute formation of reds and few yellows line up to stop him.

"Epo, keep a tight grip. You may want to close your eyes."

"No. It's okay. I don't want to shield myself anymore."

"Very well. Djent, you know what to do."

Djent huffs.

A group of spearmen create a spiked blockade ahead of the charging ram. All sound goes mute in Feilece's head but for the beating gallop of Djent's hooves, and the drum of his own heart. The rhythm of his heart slows while the galloping remains constant, creating a polyrhythm.

Feilece ducks behind Djent's horns as they come in contact with the blockade. The staves snap and splinter. The Reaper bodies are cut through like dolls made of soft clay. Djent and Feilece are coated in blood. Any Reapers not in direct contact are knocked aside by shockwaves.

Djent comes to a stop and shakes intestines from his horns.

The remaining Reaper attackers shake, and look up at Schizo for direction.

"I said kill him!" Schizo's voice is higher.

Feilece sees a frown on Kasi's face as she stares at her husband. She turns her gaze towards Feilece and her eyes shift, widening ever so slightly.

The Reapers refrain from movement, hands grasping shaking weapons.

"You heard our lord." The yellow-clothed director steps forward. "What have we been training you all for? To cower to some kid on a goat? Get the fuck in there!"

The Reapers edge forward, still keeping their distance.

"You too," Schizo says with dark eyes pointed at the directors.

Feilece watches the yellow-clothed director look up at their lord with a concerned expression.

"Alright," the red-clothed director says smugly as he steps forward, a bloodthirsty grin upon his face.

Feilece dismounts and Epo scoots up, grasping Djent's horns.

Feilece runs his hand along Djent's neck. "Make sure I'm not blindsided, and keep her safe."

Djent's stomps a foot down and runs his gaze over the petrified crowd.

Feilece pulls his axe out and approaches the red-clothed director. He doesn't rush or creep, he doesn't embellish his steps in any way.

The red-clothed director unsheathes a two-handed longsword from his back.

Holding it in one hand, he points it at Feilece. "I'm gonna have fun kill.i.n..g...y...o...u,...b......o......y."

With time slowed down, Feilece can feel the tension of time straining the wood in his axe. This must be why Fasma doesn't carry a weapon. He'll have to make sure not to move too fast, lest he breaks his own equipment.

In an instant, Feilece closes the gap between them and shatters the man's kneecap with a prod from the top of his axe.

He waits as the red-clothed director slowly lurches forward through the air. Staring into his spread eyes, Feilece brings his axe down on the back of the director's neck. His head floats to he ground like an over-sized leaf.

The grey, green and yellow-clothed directors surround Feilece. They all pull out swords and try to stab them into the boy but he jumps into the air, leaving a dent upon the dirt as he kicks off the ground.

Rising through the air, Feilece looks into their faces. In his mind, he sees their naked bodies moving. He sees Kasi.

Feilece's knuckles go white as he swings his axe in an arc, through the heads of the grey and green-clothed director. Driving his axe through their skulls and brains feels like cutting through twigs and dew. He uses the momentum of his swing to turn in the air and face the yellow-clothed director. Before the man has time to react, Feilece delivers a downward strike, cleaving through the director's shoulder to his opposing armpit.

Feilece lands to the sound of clapping.

"Impressive work," the black-clothed director calls.

"Elekri!" Schizo yells. "Why aren't you killing this boy!"

"I signed up to fight with you, Schizo, not die with you. Plus." The director tears off his Reaper badge, and in doing so, rips off the whole sleeve. "I don't work for liars."

"What lie do you speak of?"

"You know very well what happened to our people. I saw it on your face when you returned this morning. Eyes empty, in horror from what you had seen."

"That's not ..." Schizo doesn't finish his sentence. His arms shake and fists clench.

"The boy knows; why don't we ask him." Elekri looks at Feilece. "Tell us, Feilece, who is responsible for the deaths of our people?"

Feilece lifts his axe up and points it at Schizo. "That man right there."

Schizo clenches his teeth so hard they look like they're about to shatter.

"Nonsense!" Schizo leaps from the house towards Feilece, pulling his sword from its sheath while in the air.

Quickly, Feilece slows time and jumps back to avoid the attack. Djent rears back, forcing Epo to fall off him, then he charges at Schizo. Watching the ram pass under his legs, Feilece aligns himself and lands on Djent's back. With Schizo in sight, the battering duo aim to turn the Reaper lord into smithereens.

Schizo rolls to his side and holds his sword out. Because Djent is moving so fast, the blade cuts through his leg with ease. Djent's bleats loudly.

They tumble over each other as they roll across the field. Coming to a stop, Feilece, pinned by Djent, tries to move but the ram isn't responsive.

Without giving Feilece any time to recover, Schizo sheaths his blade, picks up a nearby spear and javelins it at Feilece's head. His aim is true. Feilece's face sinks as the spear flies towards him, unable to do anything to stop it.

In the nick of time, Djent jerks his head up and the spear deflects off one of his horns, missing Feilece's head but embedding itself in his shoulder. Feilece cries out in pain.

"That damn fucking ram destroyed my town." Schizo pulls out his sword and approaches the Djent. "You will watch, boy, as I stick this blade through your stead's heart."

Feilece pulls the spear from his shoulder and aims it at Schizo, holding it over Djent's body.

Schizo laughs maniacally. "You think you can really stop me? I'm gonna kill the beast, and then you, and then I'm gonna kill that Grothia piece of shit! I don't care how strong he is!"

The man is obviously crazed but his words still cause Feilece to wonder. What Grothia?

"I'll kill him, you'll see. Then I'll go down to Koilia and kill every other Grothia there is. I'll lay waste to all of Koilia!"

Feilece makes out a distinct purple glow around the

edges of Schizo's pupils.

"Give your wyll to the black." A strange rasp can be heard in the man's voice, as if he suddenly grew a couple of new folds in his larynx.

Schizo raises his arm to plunge his sword into Djent but Feilece knocks the blade away with his spear. Djent rises onto three legs and butts Schizo with his horns before falling back to the dirt. Feilece, now free, picks up his axe. He faces Schizo and gets into a stance.

Schizo bursts into a frenzy of manic sword swings. Even with time slowed, Feilece finds it difficult to manoeuvre around his attacks. Schizo, getting progressively more frustrated, spits out words with every swing. "Why. Can't. I. Hit. You."

Feilece looks for an opening but Schizo's strikes are too fierce and constant. Feilece steps to give himself space but comes in contact with the exterior wall of his old house.

Schizo grins. Though Feilece has power over time, Schizo is still the better tactician.

Schizo raises his sword, ready to strike Feilece's head. Feilece tries to block it with his axe but he moves it too fast and the strain of time snaps it in half. Without thinking, Feilece covers his face with his arm. He tries to slow his heart as much as possible but the organ is being difficult.

The sword slowly comes into contact with his fore-arm. It slices through his skin. Feilece winces. He's sure he's dead until the blade comes to a complete halt when it hits the bone.

"What!" Schizo yells.

Without wasting his moment, Feilece attacks. Schizo dodges back then delivers a hard knee into the boy's sternum. Winded, Feilece falls to the ground.

Schizo stabs his sword towards Feilece's head. The sword slices Feilece's cheek as he jerks his head out of the way. He feels the wall vibrate as the blade is embedded in the wood.

Feilece, holding a pommel in one hand and an axe head in the other, smacks the pommel against Schizo's shin and swings the axe towards his head. Schizo blocks with what's left of his amputated arm, letting the axe cut into his stumped elbow. He doesn't respond to the pain at all; he stares at Feilece with wide bloodshot eyes.

Schizo takes his hand away from his sword and grapples Feilece by the throat. With the axe head sticking out of his elbow stump, he brings it to Feilece's face and slowly stabs the toe of the bit into Feilece's eye. Feilece screams.

"You were supposed to love her," Schizo says. "You were supposed to fall for her, fight for her, die for her."

"I did love her."

Feilece smacks the pommel against the side of Schizo's head, sending the Reaper rolling across the grass. Feilece stands, pulls Schizo's sword from his house and aims it at him.

Schizo rages. "I don't care if I have to become Chaos Itself. I'll kill every fucking thing that moves. A million lives for every Reaper you fucks took from me!"

"No!" Feilece's voice echoes across the basin. "It was you who took them. You took them from their homes, from their lives. You made them Reapers. They would still be alive if it weren't for you!"

"And if it weren't for your father, I wouldn't be here."

Silence befalls the basin. Schizo, panting and sitting on his knees, looks up at Kasi.

"We met on opposing sides. Your father had just killed her parents. She was our captive. There was no tolerance between the Demons and Scythes back then. They tortured her every day for a year, trying to break her wyll, but never did. And it seemed like she was only getting stronger."

Feilece looks up at Kasi. She stares down at Schizo, moisture building in her eyes.

"I would watch her through the bars. I was a kid too. I wanted to be like her … but I was weak. When your father betrayed us, I broke almost instantly."

Feilece looks back at Schizo. The man's gaze burns with hatred.

"She found me, lost with no identity. She built me up, gave me purpose, turned me into what I am."

Feilece lowers the sword slowly, staring at the ground. This whole time, the true object of his revenge was the woman he fell in love with.

"I was her first convert," Schizo says. "Her first follower, the first member of her new family. That's all she wanted … a family. You could've been part of that family."

"I already had a family, until you came and tore them from this land. I had a home. A mother. A father." Tears start streaming down Feilece's face.

"And now you're just like us." Schizo smirks.

"I'm nothing like you!"

"Look around, farmer boy. These bodies you've painted the grass with, do you not think we loved them like we do our own blood?"

"I really don't think you do." The black-clothed director steals everyone's attention.

"Elekri," says Schizo. "How could you say that? You've been with us from the start."

"I have, but we actually knew each other a lot longer than that. I, too, was one of the Demon kids captured by Sickle & Scythe. All of us Demons were pretty strong back then … Kasi's father made sure of that." Elekri shares a dark look with Kasi. "I remember you would visit me." Elekri turns back towards Schizo. "You would spit at me and call me names. You were a little shit. When I met up with you after everything happened, you were completely different. I thought Kasi had done a Mother fucking good job. But you didn't recognise me. Whenever you would speak about the past, it would sound hollow. How can you claim to love anyone like family, if you don't remember what that feels like?"

Schizo's fist clenches so hard that blood flows from his palm and drips from his knuckles.

"I followed you," Elekri continues, "because I thought you could teach people how to be strong. But look at you … defeated by a little boy."

Schizo screams. He pulls the axe head from his stumpy arm and throws it at Feilece. Feilece deflects it with the sword. Schizo launches towards Feilece, bloody fist swaying in the air.

Feilece slows time and lets the man get close. In the last moment before Schizo can attack, Feilece sidesteps and pushes the leaf-blade through Schizo's back.

XLIX

"SCHIZO!" KASI CRIES out from on top of the house.

Feilece steps away from the skewered man. Schizo takes a step forward then stumbles. He coughs, blood gushes from his mouth, then he falls into a kneel. He breathes in quick staggered breaths. His hand shakes as he leans an elbow upon his knee. He looks up at Kasi. On his face, Epo still sees strength.

Though she has not yet grown accustomed to the sight of wanton brutality, it still brings catharsis to see the man who murdered so much of her family with a sword in his back. She's not proud of this feeling. She doesn't think that she could've ever forgiven him … but she still would've tried.

"Kasi …" Schizo coughs, trying to speak. "Don't worry … my love. I won't die … just yet. We will still make our family."

A single tear runs down Kasi's cheek. "I put so much effort into you. I put my trust—my faith!—into you. I made you … If only I had made you better."

"Kasi …"

"I loved you." Kasi throws her voice outwards. "I

loved every one of you! Why was that not enough? Family are supposed to stay together. We're supposed to be strong."

"I won't … leave you … Kasi. We are still … a family," says Schizo.

"No, Schizo … how can I love you in that state. You're of no use to me anymore."

Tears stream from Schizo's blinking eyes.

"No!" Epo cannot let this injustice carry on. "Everything you just said is wrong."

"Keep your thoughts to yourself, Animia spawn." Kasi spits her words at Epo.

"Family are not supposed to be anything. We don't choose our families and we don't choose to love them. Love is built in from the start. You don't have to be strong in a family … love is the strength. And Family don't have to stay together either because they'll always be together, regardless. Through time, through space, through death. You don't understand, Kasi … in a true family, there is no such thing as separation."

"Oh, I understand just fine. Why do you think I built this place? Why do you think I brought all of these people together? We were going to be inseparable but you started fucking everything up! You don't understand what it takes to care for so many people."

"I do know that when Lagne died, the first thing you did was try to use him to bring me down. Instead of grieving for one you claimed to love, you tried to break someone else in to take his place."

"I wanted to make you part of my family."

"You cannot make family, Kasi. You can only accept when family comes along. People are not yours to make into anything. To love is to accept one for who they are, and let them be who they want to be, and who they need to be. Family are supposed to help each other … not *make* each other."

Kasi sneers. "Your father … made me who I am. How can you say we don't make each other?"

"My father didn't make you, he didn't have the authority to. He didn't teach you how to love. He didn't teach you about family. No, that was someone else. And they were wrong too."

Kasi falls to her knees. Her brows crease together and eyes depress. "Have I been wrong my whole life?"

Her skin starts to go grey.

She stares down at Schizo. The Reaper lord looks up at her, face wet with tears.

"Did you truly love me?" she says.

Schizo smiles. "With every follicle of my body, and every charge of my wyll."

A smile quivers on Kasi's lips as her face becomes awash with tears. Particles of skin flake from Kasi's body and blow away in the wind. Before long, Kasi is gone.

L

"FEILECE," SCHIZO CALLS out to him in his final moments of decay.

Feilece stares at him.

"Come to me … cousin."

With a long and hard breath, Feilece goes to the Reaper's side.

Schizo puts his hand on Feilece's shoulder and looks him in the eyes. "You are … strong. Whether or not … you accept it, you … are a Reaper."

The top layers of skin and muscle flake away.

"Don't trust … your Grothia friend."

Schizo's bones topple into a pile at Feilece's feet.

Feilece furrows his brow. What Grothia friend?

"Well," Elekri says in a playful tone. "Think I've had enough of this cult shit for one lifetime. I'm going home. If you ever find yourself in Koilia, come find me. We'll have a drink together."

Feilece frowns. "When we first spoke to each other, you tried to have me kill Djent."

"I wanted to see if this place had actually gotten to you. But to my surprise, you had gotten to Popoki instead. I'm glad you didn't kill him; that ram is entertaining.”

Djent hoists himself up on his three rickety legs. He stumbles for a moment then corrects himself. He lets out a bleat.

“Amazing.” Elekri shakes his head. “Just became a tri-ped and he’s already mastered it. With wyll like that, the ram’s gonna outlive us all.”

“Feilece!” Epo runs over and Feilece catches her in a hug.

“Are you alright, sis?”

“Yeah, I’m fine.”

“Are you sure? Your words … Kasi.”

“My words didn’t kill her. She was being kept alive on bad ideals. I don’t think there’s anything I could’ve said to help her.”

Feilece pulls her head close to his chest. “Yeah … you’re probably right.”

“Hey.” Epo pushes herself away. “Do you hear that?”

“Is someone playing guitar?” Elekri says from across the field.

Looking around, Feilece watches all of the remaining Reapers’ expressions go blank and they all begin to sway in place. Finally, the soft tones of plucked strings reach Feilece’s hearing.

“Oh no.”

“This sound … it’s mesmerising,” Epo says in a vacant tone.

“No … no. Fuck.”

Feilece walks out among the Reapers and pushes himself through the crowd, keeping his eyes alert.

He looks back at the house and sees a large cone

hat atop the roof. Feilece slows time. He kicks against the ground with enough force to leave a crater. He launches into the air above the house. His ankles buckle as he lands and he falls on his face at Fasma's feet. He pushes himself up onto his elbows.

"Fasma." Feilece looks into the man's red-hazel eyes. "Stop this."

"You have done well, Feilece. Keep living. Keep strong. And keep your eye out for the blue lady."

"Fuck the blue lady! What are you doing?"

Fasma's hand stops plucking; the notes ring, somehow vibrating for longer than they should. He reaches down and grabs Feilece by the throat. He lifts him up to his level and stares deeply into his one remaining eye.

"What did you just say?"

Feilece struggles to speak. "You're ... going to kill them all."

Fasma drops him into a coughing slump and goes back to playing. "They are weak. They are already dead."

"No." Feilece rubs his chest as he rises to a stand. "They're not dead yet. They don't have to die."

"It is my job to relinquish all weakness. Their wyll is better off back with the Child."

"If it's weakness you're trying to eradicate, then you might as well send me off with them. For I was once as weak as them."

Fasma stares at him.

"This wyll you hold," Feilece continues, "this great strength. You could not have attained it without first knowing great weakness, am I correct?"

Fasma slows his fingers, reducing the amount of plucks.

Feilece takes a deep breath. "Surely, you've known what it feels like to be that weak. But you turned it around, you turned your weakness into strength."

"What are you trying to say?"

"What I'm saying is." Feilece ponders for a moment. "If it is your mission to eradicate weakness, is it not better to help them become stronger, rather than killing them?"

Fasma slows his fingers further.

"If you kill them all now, then you're sending the Child a bunch of weak wyll. Teach them to be strong, like you taught me. Will the Child not grow stronger with them?"

"I came to you because the blue lady directed me to you."

"Did you ask her why?"

"The blue lady does not speak for she has no mouth. She is but a flickering light on the horizon."

"Well maybe she didn't send you to me, maybe she sent you to this town. Tiris suffers greatly from weakness. Maybe the blue lady brought you to me so I could convince you to save them."

Fasma walks to the edge of the roof and looks out. He takes his hand off the fretboard and lets the final notes ring out. One by one, all of the Reapers fall into a deep slumber. Epo nearly succumbs too but stops herself, wide eyes blinking. Elekri's snores can be heard from a nearby hay bale.

Fasma lets out a long breath through his nose. "It will take some time."

Feilece smiles. "Time … That's easy for us, right?"

In an instant, Fasma disappears.

Feilece climbs down from the roof and walks over to Epo.

"What just happened?" Epo says, looking out at all the sleeping Reapers.

"I think I." Feilece can't believe his own words. "Stopped a messenger of the Mother from committing genocide."

"Messenger of the Mother? … huh."

"What?"

"Well that's what devotees call the Grothia."

"Grothia … did I just speak to a Grothia?"

"Did they have blue eyes?"

"No."

"Then they weren't Grothia."

Is that right? Maybe some Grothia don't have blue eyes. Schizo told him not to trust Grothia. But who gives a fuck what Schizo says.

"Hey." Epo makes Feilece look at her. "Please don't stress. Look." She waves her hand out at the basin. "We got our farm back."

Feilece frowns, looking at all of the Reaper tents. "Do we really want it back?"

"I don't think we can go back to being simple farmers." Epo laughs.

"Then what are we?" Feilece looks down at a bloodstain on the ground. "Are we soldiers?"

"No, we're family."

Feilece puts an arm around her. "Yeah. I guess, we're all we have left."

"No, that's not what I mean."

Epo steps forward. The midday gaze of the Mother watches over the field of sleeping soldiers.

"What I said to Kasi, it doesn't just apply to those you love. Family aren't just those that raise and care for you. We're all connected. Everyone is worthy."

"Worthy of what?"

"Compassion." Epo turns to Feilece with a wide smile.

"So, what do you want to do?" asks Feilece.

"I don't really know. I haven't thought that far ahead yet."

"Well, we can at least stay a bit … that would be nice."

"Yeah."

They sit down together in the grass, both with an arm wrapped around each other. Djent limps over and lays down behind them. With Djent's fur against his back, Feilece's muscles begin to ease and relax.

A part of him wants to slow time, milk this moment for as long as he can, but he decides against it. He just lets it be. He rests his head on Epo's shoulder, and she rests her head upon his. The last carriers of the Anemelos wyll.

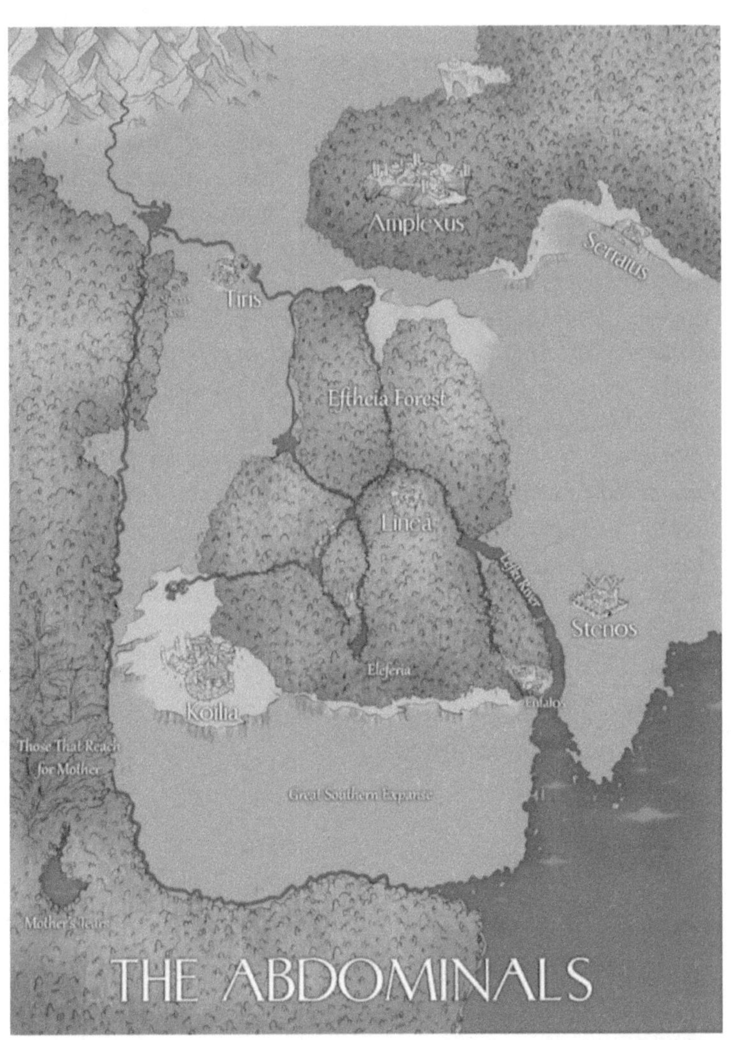

Amplexus
Serratus
Tiris
Eftheia Forest
Linea
Light River
Stenos
Eleferia
Koilia
Entalos
Those That Reach
for Mother
Great Southern Expanse
Mother's Tears
THE ABDOMINALS

SICKLE & SCYTHE

Sickle & Scythe started as a small group of simple Koilian farmers and tradesmen. They were justice seekers, applying vigilante support for innocent people living under regimes that they saw as corrupt. If people were in danger, and the higher ups were doing nothing to help them, they would step in. For their morals, Sickle & Scythe were loved by all the peoples of Koilia, but hated by the Lesser Kings. Though they tried many times, Sickle & Scythe were able to avoid the Lesser Kings' attempts at destroying them. Within a few years, Sickle & Scythe grew into a full on brotherhood. They grew big enough to rival even the forces of the Demon tribe as they were moving from the western forest and into Koilian territory. For over a decade, Sickle & Scythe fought the Demons: their sworn nemesis.

Schisma

Founder of Sickle & Scythe.

Schizo

Son of Schisma.

Animia

The great executioner. A famous Koilian fighter and soldier.

Apoko

Former tactician. Schisma's advisor and lover.

Popoki

Little brother of Apoko.

DEMON

Named after the demons of old: an ancestor of the griffit, who's brutal nature lead to their own extinction. The Demon tribe was a small group of woodsmen living in the forests west of Koilia. The children were trained in battle from young ages, and killed they were deemed weak. They were ravagers, pillaging other tribes and Koilian settlements. The PanoApo, fearing their followers were losing respect in the hierarchy, hired the Demon tribe to threaten their own people so they would become more dependant on the PanoApo's protection. The Demons ended up being too much for the PanoApo to handle, so they hired Sickle & Scythe, facilitating aggression between the two groups. The Demons turned on the PanoApo, and upon realising what the Apo turn into when under intense pain, the Demons made it their mission to hunt down all the PanoApo and turn them into the monsters that they believed was their true nature.

Aresi

Leader of the Demons.

Kasi

Daughter to Aresi. Demon princess.

Travma

Demon general and prime hunter.

Diakho

Son of Travma. Twin brother to Choris.

Choris

Son of Travma. Twin brother to Diakho.

Elekri

Bastard son of Aresi.

PANOAPO

One of the oldest families in Koilia. The PanoApo bloodline came to power a century into Grothia's rule. The Grothia were impressed by the Apo's abilities of healing and their unnaturally long lifespans, so they gave them a portion of Koilia to rule over.

Seech

> *Oldest father of the PanoApo family, and king of the estate.*

Seemo

> *Daughter to Seech and final Apo.*

Louma

> *Seech's personal guard.*

About the Author

I'm Theo. I was born in New Zealand and have been here for the last thirty-something years. I have been working on the world of Genus for around four years now. This book is the first in what I intend to be a long series. A Timeless Wyll wasn't intended to be as long as it became. I went for a short story and I got a novel. I guess I loved the characters too much. I play music, I play video games, but most of my time is spent stuck inside my own head. I tend to prefer fantasy over reality. Nothing makes me happier than writing. It's funny, being an author always felt like a fantasy. A decade ago, I was trying to become an astrophysicist.